STATE OF SUSPENSE

FIRST FAMILY SERIES, BOOK 7

MARIE FORCE

State of Suspense
First Family Series, Book 7
By: Marie Force

Published by HTJB, Inc.
Copyright 2024. HTJB, Inc.
Cover design by Kristina Brinton and Ashley Lopez
Cover photography by Regina Wamba
Models: Robert John and Ellie Dulac
Print Layout: E-book Formatting Fairies
ISBN: 978-1958035559

The First Family Series

More new books are always in the works. For the most up-to-date list of what's available from the First Family Series, go to *marieforce.com/firstfamily*

CHAPTER ONE

The ride home to Washington from Dewey Beach bore no resemblance whatsoever to the first couple's sexy trip to the beach in the presidential limo known as The Beast. Sam had been called back to work a day earlier than planned after the murder of U.S. Attorney Tom Forrester. She and Nick were being transported to the White House on *Marine One* with their kids, Scotty, Alden, Aubrey and Eli as well as Eli's wife, Candace, and Skippy, the first dog, on board as they lifted off from Delaware.

Nick reached over to take Sam's hand, knowing how much she hated to fly, even short distances on the chopper. "What's the latest?"

Sam checked her phone. "Freddie said Forrester was shot in the head in his car on Constitution Avenue. They're on the scene, and that's all they know so far."

"How're you feeling?"

"I'm in shock. I've worked closely with Tom and his team for years. Like all jobs in law enforcement, there're inherent risks to being a prosecutor, but the murder of a U.S. Attorney is rare. Tom was one of the good guys. He always did the right thing. Until recently, that is."

During a recent investigation, Forrester had asked Metro Police Chief Joe Farnsworth to release Randy Bryant, a man tied to a murder-for-hire plot. Later, it was learned that Randy's father, U.S. Congressman Damien Bryant, had taken Forrester's family hostage and instructed Forrester to get his son released from custody. MPD Homicide detectives had been stunned by the order, which was way out of character for the by-the-book prosecutor.

"Are you thinking Bryant had something to do with Tom's murder?" Nick asked.

"That's the obvious conclusion, but we've learned not to assume anything. We'll have to dig in to figure out what really happened." She looked over at him. "I'm sorry our vacation is ending this way."

"Don't be. We had a wonderful time, despite reality interrupting far too often." He leaned in to whisper in her ear. "As long as I get to sleep with you every night, it's like I'm always on vacation."

Sam laughed. "Sure it is."

"If I have that to look forward to at the end of the day, I can get through anything that comes my way."

"Now you're speaking in rhymes?"

His face lifted into a big grin. "I didn't mean to."

"Okay, Dr. Seuss. I hear what you're saying, and I agree that the end of the day is often the best part. But there's a lot of crap to deal with in the middle that'd make a sane person crazy."

"Are we still sane?"

"For the most part." She gave him a side-eyed glance. "We'll see if that lasts for seven more years."

"Less than three."

"I'm seeing seven."

"*Three.*"

Scotty looked up from a book he was "suffering through" for school. "What are you guys fighting about?"

"How many more years Dad will be president."

"Seven," Scotty said emphatically.

Nick scowled at him. "I thought you were on my side."

"I am, and I believe you'll cruise to reelection. Won't even be close."

Sam pointed at their handsome, dark-haired fourteen-year-old son. "What he said."

"I hate everyone right now."

Sam and Scotty laughed at the face he made.

Aubrey released her seat belt and went to sit with Nick. "You don't hate us."

He brought her onto his lap. "I was just kidding, sweetie. I love you guys the bestest."

"That's not a word."

"How do you know?" Nick asked. "You're in first grade. You haven't learned all the words yet."

"Lijah said it's not a word, so it isn't."

"Because my word is law around here," Eli said with a laugh.

"Well, is it a word?" Aubrey asked.

"No, it isn't," Nick said, "but it's fun to pretend like it is."

"I told you."

"You were right." He kissed the top of her blonde head. "You're a very smart first grader."

"Wait till they have to read stuff like this." Scotty held up his copy of *Beowulf*. "Who decided eighth graders need to read something from like a thousand years ago? It's Old English. I can barely handle *new* English."

Sam bit her lip so she wouldn't laugh out loud. "Aren't there CliffsNotes for that?"

"Sam!"

She looked at her husband. "What?"

"Don't tell him about that. He needs to *read* the book."

"What are these CliffsNotes of which you speak?" Scotty asked, intrigued.

"I can't remember," Sam said.

Scotty held up his phone. "Shall I go to the Google?"

Recognizing defeat when she saw it, Sam said, "When I was in school, they were study guides to help students understand things like *Beowulf*."

"And you're *just now* telling me such a thing exists? I thought you loved me."

"I do love you! That's why you need to read the book."

"Honestly, Samantha."

It was all she could do not to giggle helplessly at the disapproval in Nick's tone. "If you read the whole book, I'll get you the study guide to help you understand it. Deal?"

"Fine," Scotty said. "It's a deal."

"Nice save," Nick muttered.

"I don't know if you've noticed, but I'm very good at this parenting thing."

That made Scotty laugh, which earned him a glare from his mother. "That's not funny."

"It's all funny. As always, you guys are a disaster. Keep an eye on them, Eli, so they don't ruin the twins the way they've ruined me."

"I'll be watching. Don't worry."

"I feel judged," Sam said.

"As well you should," Nick said. "If it were up to you, we'd be raising a feral bunch of uneducated savages."

"Is that an option?" Scotty asked.

"*No*," his parents said together.

"For once, they agree," Scotty said to laughter from the others.

As the chopper set down on the South Lawn of the White House, Sam soaked up the final moments of family togetherness before work intruded once again. "I'm sorry I have to go right to work, guys. I'll be home as soon as I can."

"It's okay," Alden said. "Eli's gonna take us to the pool."

"That sounds like fun." She wished she could join them. Nick had been teaching the twins how to swim recently, and they were making great progress.

"We'll take video for you, Mom," Scotty said.

"I'd love that."

"Before you leave," Nick said, "don't forget the Canadian visit on Tuesday. You're needed here at three o'clock for tea with the prime minister's wife, and then the state dinner is that night. With Shelby suddenly on maternity leave, Lilia has all the info you'll need."

The thought of those obligations, on top of a high-pressure new murder investigation, was enough to make her head explode. But for his sake, she smiled and nodded. "I'll be there. Don't worry."

"What? Me worry?"

She'd given him plenty of reason to worry about whether she'd be there when he needed her, but their first state visit was a huge deal, and she'd be there to support him no matter what she had to walk away from at work. Thankfully, she had an amazing team backing her up there, especially lately, as both Freddie and Gonzo had taken the lead on cases and handled them masterfully.

The first family walked across the lawn in a now-familiar ritual of kids running, dog barking and parents waving to the gaggle of reporters recording their arrival at the White House. They were slowly getting used to everything they did being news around the world.

"I never imagined something like that would start to feel routine," Sam said to Nick.

"I know, right? Whose life are we living?"

"Let me know when you figure that out."

He glanced over at her, looking as relaxed as he ever was these days. "Thanks for a great week. I needed it so badly."

"Me, too. Let's do it again soon, huh?"

"Yes, please."

As she hugged the kids at the stairs to the residence, Scotty whispered in her ear, "Get me those CliffsNotes thingies."

"Will do."

"You're the best."

"I know."

His snort of laughter rang out as he chased the twins and Skippy up the stairs.

Sam hugged Eli and Candace. "Thanks for coming to the beach." She was still wrapping her head around the fact that he'd gotten married, but anyone could see they were ridiculously happy to be back together after spending years apart.

"It was a blast," he said. "Thanks for having us."

"Are you guys heading back to Princeton tonight?"

"Probably in the morning. I don't have class until one."

"Hopefully, I'll see you before you go."

Nick gave her one last hug and kiss. "Be safe out there."

"Always am."

"Right." He rolled his eyes. "Love you."

"Love you, too."

As he followed the kids upstairs, Sam crossed the main foyer to where her lead Secret Service agent, Vernon, stood waiting for her. She'd kept the messenger bag containing her service weapon, cuffs, notebook and other work items with her while the staff would manage the rest of their luggage.

Vernon greeted her with a smile. "No rest for the wicked, huh?"

"Never."

Vernon held the door and gestured for her to go out ahead of him.

Her other primary agent, Jimmy, opened the door to the SUV for her.

"Thank you, Jimmy."

"No problem, Sam." She'd insisted they call her by her first name when they were alone.

"Where to?" Vernon asked.

"Let me check." She called Freddie. "Where am I meeting you?"

"Come to HQ. We're heading back from the scene now to figure out a plan."

"I'll be there in a few."

"Welcome back."

"I'd say thanks, but..."

"Yeah, it's a tough one."

"How's his team holding up?"

"Not great from what I've heard. People are shocked and devastated. And as you might expect, the Feds want in on this. We've got them at arm's length for now, but we're not sure how long we'll be able to hold them off."

"That's just great." Jurisdictional battles were the last thing she needed with a U.S. Attorney headed to her morgue.

"To be expected with something like this, I suppose."

"I guess so. What's the latest from Stahl's house?" Sam had succeeded in mostly punching out of that nightmare for the weekend.

"Eleven bodies found so far. They're only about halfway done with processing the scene."

She wondered how it was possible to still be shocked by the disgraced former lieutenant who'd twice tried to kill her. "What about the storage unit?"

"There's been a hang-up there. The company has changed owners, and the new guy isn't returning calls to give us access. We've got O'Brien and Charles working on finding him."

"Part of me hopes that takes a while."

"Right? We're all terrified of what's in that unit."

"Makes me shudder. I'm almost at HQ. See you in a few."

They followed the medical examiner's van into the lot and parked outside the morgue entrance.

Vernon held the car door for her.

"We'll be here for a while before we head out," Sam told him.

"Got it. Let us know if you're going outside to brief the press."

"Yes, dear."

He chuckled at her solicitous tone.

Sam waited for Dr. Lindsey McNamara. "Nice to see you, Doc."

"You as well. Hope you had a nice vacation."

"It was... eventful."

"So I heard."

Sam shifted her gaze toward the body bag on the gurney that Lindsey's team unloaded from the back of the van. "I can't believe this."

"You and me both."

"I'll let you get to it."

"Are the Feds wanting in on this?" Lindsey asked.

"Yep, but it's ours for now."

"I'll have my report to you ASAP."

"Thanks, Doc. By the way, Terry said something to Nick about you not feeling well last week. How're you doing?"

"Still a little off, but better than I was. Thanks for asking."

Sam thought she looked paler than usual, but hopefully, she was on the upswing. They parted company at the door to the morgue. As she traveled the winding hallway to the pit where her detectives worked, Sam was relieved there was no chance she might run into suspended Detective Ramsey. He was awaiting trial on assault charges for ramming his car into Sam's Secret Service SUV.

Thankfully, no one had been hurt in the incident. Since assaulting federal agents and officials with a deadly weapon had resulted in felony charges, she hoped they'd seen the last of Ramsey at HQ. She was still amused to be considered a "federal official" as first lady.

Sam followed voices to the conference room, where Gonzo was updating a fresh murder board with photos from the Forrester scene. Though she'd already heard how Forrester was killed, she recoiled from the sight of her murdered colleague. She owed him for many things, most particularly for taking her case to a grand jury after she pushed Ramsey down the stairs, leaving him with a broken wrist and a concussion.

Forrester could've taken the matter straight to trial, as it was a clear-cut case of assault, but he'd gone the grand jury route to hopefully cut her a break, which she'd gotten when the grand jury declined to indict. He'd saved her career, even if her problems with Ramsey got much worse after that.

"Sam?" Freddie approached her. "Are you okay?"

She'd been staring at the image of Forrester, bloody and dead. "I was thinking about how he saved my ass once upon a time."

"Yes, he did."

"Tom was one of the good guys." She glanced at her partner, the fire in her belly for justice flaming the way it did any time murder struck too close to home. "We're going to find whoever did this to him, and we'll make them pay."

"We sure as hell will."

CHAPTER TWO

S am tried to shake off the grief for her colleague and friend as she sat next to Freddie, facing the board. "Bring me up to speed."

"We got the call from Dispatch at zero eight twelve," Gonzo said. "A woman walking by the car noticed broken glass and blood. From what other witnesses said, she put on quite a show, screaming and yelling for help. A guy who heard her screaming called it in."

"Did either of them see it happen?"

"No, they both came upon it after it had already gone down."

"Where was Forrester's wife when he was killed?" Though she had no reason to suspect his wife, in a homicide investigation, they always looked at the people closest to the victim.

"At home and still under the protection of the FBI after she and her girls were rescued from the kidnapping."

That ruled her out.

"Do we have Archie pulling video from the area?"

"He and IT are on that as well as tracking the pings from Forrester's cell phones as soon as the warrants come through. We've requested access to his personal and work phones. The responding officers didn't know who he was, but we recognized him when we arrived on the scene. I immediately called Captain

Malone, who alerted the chief. Out of courtesy, the chief contacted the Attorney General's Office."

"Which is why we're already fending off Feds," Sam said.

"That's to be expected. They know the case is ours, but we can tap into their resources as needed."

"I was just coming by to say that very thing," FBI Special Agent-in-Charge Avery Hill said as he stepped into the room. "Whatever we can do."

"Thank you, Avery." Sam smiled at him. "I'm sure you've got a lot going on with a new baby at home. We wouldn't want to keep you from your family. How are Shelby and the baby anyway? I can't wait to meet Miss Maisie."

"They're doing great. Noah is absolutely smitten with his new baby sister."

"I'll make sure to stop in to see them when I get home." Avery, Shelby and their kids were staying with Sam and Nick at the White House while they secured a safer home after theirs was invaded by people Avery had arrested years earlier. "In the meantime, we've got a lot to do here."

"We're very upset about Tom's murder," Avery said.

"As are we."

"The murder of a U.S. Attorney is a big deal."

"We're aware of that, Avery, and you can rest assured that we'll give it our undivided attention until we bring his killer to justice."

"You're telling me to get lost, right?"

Sam smiled. "I never said those words."

"Fine, I'll go, but please let me know what we can do to help. Tom was a friend."

"To all of us."

Avery gave a curt nod and turned to leave.

Sam exhaled with relief. "That was a close one. We need to jump on it, so we don't get squeezed out. What's our plan?"

"I'd like to talk to his team first," Gonzo said, "and then his family. I want to know the details of the time they spent with Bryant's people and what they said to threaten Tom."

"Are we thinking this'll lead straight to Congressman Bryant?" Freddie asked.

"We can't make that conclusion right out of the gate," Sam said. "Tell me more about Forrester's connection to Bryant."

"The AG personally asked Forrester to look into Bryant's campaign finance issues," Gonzo said, "and where there's smoke, there's usually fire. The theory is that when Bryant caught wind that Forrester was closing in on his nefarious network of drugs, guns, gambling, hookers, etc., he panicked and ordered his goons to kidnap Forrester's family. Then he used the leverage to get Forrester to back off or lose his loved ones."

"How was that related to the arrest of Bryant's son?"

"It wasn't," Gonzo said. "But when the congressman heard we had his son in custody, he used the safety of his wife and daughters against Forrester to get the USA to order the release of Randy Bryant."

"And the reason he did that was because Bryant still had his family."

"Right," Gonzo said.

"Bryant must be in it pretty deep if he'd go so far as to kidnap the family of a U.S. Attorney," Sam said.

"That's the thinking," Gonzo said.

"How can this *not* be related to Bryant?" Freddie asked.

"It probably is, but we still have to fully investigate," Sam said. "Where's Bryant now?"

"He was released on bond, as was Kent Sanders, who agreed to cooperate for immunity. The rest of his guys are still in custody."

"The same thugs he would've sent to do Forrester?"

"Yeah."

Sam processed that information. "Would Bryant have done it himself?"

"I just can't picture that," Gonzo said. "He's a weasel who sends others to do his dirty work. I don't think he'd have the stones."

Which meant the most obvious suspect was looking less so already.

"Let's start at Forrester's office and then go see his family," Sam said.

With O'Brien and Charles working on finding the new owner of Stahl's storage unit facility and Green away for the weekend, Sam, Freddie and Gonzo left for the U.S. Attorney's Office.

Sam waited until they were in the back of her Secret Service SUV before she said, "I want to thank you both for taking the lead on the last two cases. I didn't realize how badly I needed a break until you gave me the chance to take one, and I appreciate knowing I can leave things in your capable hands. That means everything to me."

"We'd say it was no problem, but..."

Sam and Freddie laughed at Gonzo's comment.

"I know it was a load of trouble."

"We handled it," Gonzo said. "I gotta say, though... That Fortier case was one of the crazier ones I've been involved in. Forrester orders us to release Randy Bryant even though we've got him dead to rights on the murder-for-hire of Rachel Fortier. Then Randy's dead, but wait, it's not him. It's another of his father's stooges dressed to make us think it's Randy—even carrying Randy's student ID—but his face is bashed in so we can't ID him by sight. When the mother told me Randy was sleeping in his bed in Milwaukee, I thought I'd lost my mind."

"The reports made my head spin trying to keep up with the narrative," Sam said. "Where are we with getting the real Randy back here to face the charges?"

"His mother promised to bring him here by tomorrow," Gonzo said.

"You believe she will?"

"She's been straight with me through the whole thing. I have no reason to believe otherwise. She knows we'll send the marshals after him if he doesn't turn himself in."

"I'll feel better once he's back in custody. What's to stop her from taking him and leaving the country?"

"We tagged both their passports, just in case," Freddie said.

"Good thinking."

They arrived at the U.S. Attorney's D Street Northwest office, surrendered their weapons at security and walked through the metal detector.

Sam led the way to Forrester's third-floor suite. Once there, they followed voices to the conference room, where the staff gathered.

Assistant U.S. Attorney Faith Miller stood to greet them with hugs.

"We're so sorry, Faith," Sam said.

"Thank you. Needless to say, we're in shock."

"We can't imagine." Gonzo hugged her. "Tom was a good guy."

"He was the best. We loved him."

Her sisters, Hope and Charity, came over to them, and they exchanged hugs and condolences.

Sam rarely saw the identical Miller triplets together and was amazed once again by their striking resemblance, even if they sported different hair and clothing styles. One of them had told her years ago how rare identical triplets were. As someone who'd endured fertility struggles, Sam couldn't believe such things were even possible.

"May we speak in private?" Sam asked.

The other staffers were huddled in subdued groups, comforting one another.

"Sure," Faith said.

They followed the sisters to a smaller conference room.

Sam closed the door. "Again, please accept our heartfelt sympathy. We hate to intrude at a time like this, but you know how critical the early hours are in a homicide investigation."

"We do." Hope wore her hair longer than the other two. All three were dressed more casually than Sam had ever seen them, as they'd been home for the weekend when they received the news about their boss's murder. "We'll do anything we can to help find the person who did this to Tom."

"First, we'd like to know everything there is to know about his dealings with Congressman Bryant."

"I wondered if you'd look in that direction first," Faith said.

"Are there other directions we should be taking?" Gonzo asked.

"As always, this office is involved in a number of complex prosecutions," Charity said, "but the situation with Bryant had occupied much of Tom's time recently." She was the curviest of the three. Sam had watched more than a few men go stupid in the head at the sight of her.

"How can we find out what was happening with the Bryant investigation?" Sam asked.

"Other than the basic info I already gave to Gonzo, I haven't found anything more in his office or on his computer," Faith said, "even though we knew he was working on it. When he and his family first went missing, we looked through everything. There was nothing about Bryant."

"Did that strike you as odd?"

"To have no paper trail at all?" Hope asked. "Definitely."

"Is it possible he was asked to do the investigation without leaving a trail?" Gonzo asked.

"It's possible, yes," Faith said, "but not really feasible. Tom was brilliant, but even he couldn't keep track of something that complicated in his head."

"So you think there's a record somewhere?" Sam asked.

"If there is, we can't find it here," Charity said. "We want to look at his house for it."

"That's our next stop. Would one of you mind coming with us?"

"I'll go," Faith said. "I pulled a warrant because I figured you'd want to start there, too."

Sam appreciated working with people who knew what they were doing. "That saves some time."

"Hope and I will continue to sift through other cases for leads," Charity said.

"That'd be helpful," Sam said.

"Whatever we can do to find his killer," Hope said tearfully.

"Thank you." Sam hugged Hope. "Hang in there."

"We're trying."

They walked out of the building with Faith a few minutes later.

Vernon and Jimmy waited at the curb and jumped out to open doors for them. They'd allowed Sam to go into the U.S. Attorney's Office unescorted since it was a secure facility.

"This doesn't suck," Faith said when they were settled in cozy warmth in back seats that faced each other.

"Not at all," Sam said. "Do we have Forrester's address?"

Faith recited the Gaithersburg address for Vernon.

Sam settled in for the forty-five-minute ride to the Maryland suburb. "Why didn't Tom have a driver and security?"

"He had both, but he'd chosen to go out on his own the last few days."

"I did a search for information about murdered prosecutors." Freddie looked up from his phone. "Even though police officer killings are on the rise, prosecutor murders are extremely rare. There's an association for District Attorneys that reported thirteen prosecutor deaths in one hundred years, but that stat is from ten years ago. Most of them are state and local DAs. There's one unsolved U.S. Attorney murder in Seattle."

Faith nodded. "We receive regular briefings on that case. Happened twenty years ago. The department uses that cold case as a reminder to stay vigilant. The Seattle police and FBI continue to investigate."

"Had you heard of any threats to Tom or experienced an uptick in threats at your office?" Gonzo asked.

"We receive threats every day from people who feel they're being unfairly prosecuted or railroaded or fill in the blank on how we're abusing our power. Most of them are idle threats. Some we report to the FBI for further investigation."

Sam sent a text to Avery. *I found a way you can help us. Faith Miller said some threats received by their office are sent to you guys for investigation. Can you look into that and let me know if anything stands out?*

I'll get right on that.

Thanks. How are Shelby and the baby?

Wonderful. Coming home (to your place, that is) this afternoon.

Can't wait to see them.

"Avery is taking a look at that angle," Sam said.

"What's our plan with Forrester's family?" Faith asked. "Word is they're in rough shape from their own ordeal, and that was before they found out he'd been murdered."

"Have we gotten a statement from them since the kidnapping?" Sam asked Gonzo.

He shook his head. "They were too upset to talk. They were taken to GW's ER after being rescued from the hotel where they were held. They spent last night there for observation and were sent home this morning only to learn Tom had been killed."

"Who told them the news?" Sam asked.

"Tom's top deputy, Conlon Young."

"Why don't I know that name?"

"He doesn't work on cases. He's the head administrative officer. He assigns cases, tracks every development, makes sure filing deadlines are met, in addition to many other things critical to efficiency and effectiveness."

"I never gave much thought to how that happened."

"It's a critical role that keeps us from screwing things up. When Gonzo called me to tell me the news about Tom, I immediately called Conlon. He went to the Forresters' house to notify the family. As far as I know, he's still there. He and his wife, Nikki, are close with Tom and Leslie." Faith glanced out the window as the city whizzed by in a blur of people, buildings and vehicles. "I still can't believe he's dead."

Sam empathized with her after having lost Detective Arnold, her dad and then her brother-in-law. She was still processing Spencer's death, weeks later. "It'll take a while for it to seem real."

"I suppose you're right."

"Tell me about his arrangement with the AG on the Bryant case," Sam said.

"I don't know much about that."

"Would Young know?"

"If anyone in the office has the lowdown on that, it would be him. It was highly unusual for Tom to take on anything without at least some staff support."

Sam made a note to herself. *Find out why the AG wanted Forrester to handle the Bryant case personally.* As she wrote that, she experienced a twinge of anxiety over possibly having to speak to the Attorney General, a member of Nick's cabinet, about a case. That struck far too close for comfort, not that anything would stop her from talking to him if it came to that.

She hoped it didn't.

The Forresters lived in a gated community with stately brick homes. "Where were the wife and kids when they were taken hostage?" Sam asked.

"At home."

"How's that possible in a gated neighborhood?"

"While you're talking with the family, I'll double back on the security people," Freddie said.

Vernon used his Secret Service credentials and Sam's badge to gain access to the neighborhood. He stopped the SUV at the curb of one of the larger brick homes on the street. It had third-floor dormers, black shutters and an elegant look to it.

As they got out of the vehicle, Sam noted a driveway full of cars, which meant the word was out among Tom's family and friends.

Sam glanced at Faith. "We'll need to speak privately to his wife—and daughters if their mother agrees."

"I'll do what I can to make that happen."

Freddie took off at a jog toward the security facility at the entrance to the neighborhood.

Sam, Faith and Gonzo were met at the door by a middle-aged man who looked like he'd been crying.

Faith took the lead. "Conlon Young, meet Lieutenant Holland and Sergeant Gonzales."

"Come in." Young led them to a formal living room. "How can we help you, Detectives?"

"We'd like to speak with Mrs. Forrester," Sam said.

Young was shaking his head before she finished saying the word *Mrs.* "She's not available for that right now."

Sam bit back the urge to snap at him. "Mr. Young, as I'm sure you're aware, the initial hours in a homicide investigation are the most critical. Since Mrs. Forrester and her daughters were caught up in something involving her husband's work, it would be extremely helpful if we could talk to them."

"They're distraught. We all are."

"I understand."

"Do you?"

Taken aback by his tone, Sam said, "As a matter of fact, I do." She stared at him without blinking. "Believe it or not, family members and close friends are always distraught after the murder of a loved one. We still need to talk to the people closest to the victim as soon as possible."

Young obviously didn't care for her comment, but thankfully, he didn't argue the point. "Give me a minute." He left the room.

Faith grimaced. "I'm sorry. He's upset."

"I understand." The guy had immediately rubbed Sam the wrong way, and not just because he'd objected to her request. As someone who worked for the U.S. Attorney's Office, he'd know better than most how these things worked.

They waited a long time, long enough that Freddie returned from checking in with the neighborhood security personnel. "They said they aren't allowed to talk to us directly. He gave me a card for the main office."

"Let's request a warrant for last week's logs and any footage they have," Sam said.

"I thought you might say that, so I called Malone to get that moving."

"You're the best."

"I know, right?"

"While you're basking in the glow of your own glory, see what they have here at the house for security and request a warrant for any info we can get from there, too."

"I, uh, already did that, too. There's a sign out front with the name of the security company."

"Damn, he's good," Gonzo said.

"Learned from the best."

"His sucking up is also exceptional." Sam glanced at Faith. "Sorry for the banter. It keeps us sane."

"I understand. No apologies needed."

"What's taking so long?"

"I'll find out," Faith said as she rose to leave the room.

"I already hate this case," Sam said.

"That took longer than usual," Gonzo said.

"Don't make me laugh. It's disrespectful."

She hoped they came back soon, because this day was getting away from them, and they had miles yet to go.

CHAPTER THREE

Another fifteen minutes passed in uneasy silence before Faith returned with Mr. Young and a woman Sam assumed was Mrs. Forrester. As they approached the open French doors to the living room, Conlon and Faith each had an arm around the woman. They guided her to the sofa and sat next to her. The woman had reddish-brown, shoulder-length hair and a trim figure. Deep, dark circles under her brown eyes made her look as if she'd been awake for days.

"This is Leslie Forrester," Faith said. "Leslie, this is Lieutenant Holland, Sergeant Gonzales and Detective Cruz."

"We're so sorry for your loss," Sam said. "We had a tremendous amount of respect and affection for Tom."

She dabbed at her eyes with a tissue Faith handed her. "Thank you. He spoke of you all so fondly."

"We apologize for intruding at such a difficult time."

"I understand you have a job to do, and I... I want to know who did this to my Tom." Her voice broke on a sob. "I just can't believe he's gone."

Faith rested a hand on Leslie's knee. "While you talk to Lieutenant Holland, would you mind if I took a look in Tom's home office for some things we need at work?"

"Not at all. You know where it is."

"And you're okay with me taking anything we might need?"

"Of course. I want to know who did this to him and us."

"Thank you."

After Faith had gotten up to leave the room, Sam said, "I know it's such a terrible shock, but we're trying to understand what occurred in the days before Tom was killed."

Again, Leslie wiped tears from her eyes. "Three days ago, he called to say he was sending someone to pick up the girls and me, that I was to pack a few things and go with them. He said he'd join us shortly."

"Did he say why he was asking you to go with these people?"

"He didn't."

"When they arrived to pick you up, did you authorize the neighborhood's security personnel to admit them?" Sam asked.

"I did."

That answered one pressing question.

"Who came to pick you up?"

"A man named Kent Sanders."

Sam recognized his name from the reports on the Fortier case. He was one of Congressman Bryant's bodyguards and had taken an immunity deal to testify against his boss. "Where did he take you?" Sam already knew the answer but wanted to hear the details from Leslie.

"To a suite at the Washington Hilton. They told us to make ourselves at home and to order whatever we wanted from room service."

"Did you ask why you were there?"

"Many times, but they just said Tom had asked them to keep us safe, so that's what they were doing."

"And Tom never told you why he'd asked that of them or what was going on?"

She shook her head.

"Had anything like this ever happened before?"

"No, never. I know he worried at times about how his work might endanger us, but he said we'd done everything we could to make our family safe, and we had to live our lives."

"Did Tom come to the hotel at any point?"

"No, we never saw him again after he left for work that last morning when we were all here at home."

"The people you were with at the hotel... Did you hear them talking about anything that might shed light on why you were there?"

"They were hardly ever in the room with us. The only time we saw them was when food was delivered."

"Did you ask to leave?"

"A number of times. They said it wasn't safe yet."

"And they provided no details about the alleged threat?"

"None."

"Did they take your phones?"

"They did. They said it was so we couldn't be tracked and that it was for our own safety. I was allowed to speak to Tom once a day, which usually happened at night. Being without our phones was almost as difficult as being away from Tom. We felt very cut off from our lives."

"Did you feel like you were in danger while you were in the custody of these people?"

"No, but I worried about Tom. If we were in danger, why wasn't he there with us?"

"We're looking into that. Did Tom mention anything special about his work in the days and weeks leading up to when you were taken into custody?"

"Nothing out of the ordinary. His work was always busy and intense, but he tried to leave it at the office when he was home with us."

"Why were you taken to the ER after the FBI rescued you?"

"After our rescuers barged into the room, we were upset, so the agents thought it would be a good idea to have us checked out at the hospital."

"Did they arrest the men who'd held you?"

"I think so. They were in an adjoining room, so I didn't see that part."

A teenage girl with long dark hair and her mother's brown eyes appeared at the door. She wore a long-sleeved T-shirt with plaid pajama pants.

Her mother held out a hand to her. "Come sit with me, honey. This is my younger daughter, Aurora."

"We're very sorry for your loss," Sam said to the girl.

"Thank you. I recognize you from TV. My dad thought it was cool that he worked with the first lady." She leaned her head on her mother's shoulder. "Are you going to find out who did this?"

"We're working on that right now," Sam said, "and thank you for telling me that about your dad. I liked working with him, too. We all did."

Freddie and Gonzo nodded in agreement.

"I was asking your mom if there was anything different about your dad in relation to work or anything else in the last few weeks."

"He was super stressed," Aurora said. "When he drove me to my softball game last Saturday, he was on the phone the whole time. He never does that when he's with us." She stopped herself when she seemed to realize she was speaking of him in the present tense. "Or at least he never did that before. Naomi said he was distracted when he drove her somewhere the week before last, too."

"The girls would notice that," Leslie said, "because Tom made a point of giving us his full attention when he was at home. I'd been taking care of my mother, who had hip replacement surgery three weeks ago, so I'd been distracted, too."

"You've been very helpful." Sam put her card on the coffee table. "If you think of anything else he said or did, or any other odd things, please call me. My cell number is on there."

"You can just give people your cell number like that?" Aurora asked.

"I can give it to you." Sam gave her a playful look. "You aren't going to put it on Instagram or anything, are you?"

"Oh, no. I'd never do that."

"I know. I was kidding."

Faith returned to the room, carrying a laptop. When her gaze met Sam's, she shook her head.

Damn it. Sam had hoped there'd be a paper trail on the

Bryant investigation in Tom's home office. Where else would it be if it wasn't at home or at work?

"I was wondering," Leslie said tentatively, "if you might be willing to say a few words at Tom's service."

"I'd be honored," Sam said, moved by the request. "Tell me when and where."

"I should know more in the next couple of days."

Sam handed her a different card. "That's for my chief of staff at the White House. Lilia will work with you to get me where I need to be." Then she placed her notebook and pen on the table. "Will you please give me your cell phone numbers and Naomi's in case we have more questions?"

Aurora wrote down the numbers and gave the notebook to Sam.

"I'll keep you posted on the investigation, and again, you have our deepest sympathies."

"Thank you," Leslie said as she hugged Faith.

Conlon Young showed them out.

"I'd like to speak with you one-on-one," Sam said to him. "Your place or ours?"

"Twelve thirty at my office on Tuesday? I need tomorrow to help plan a funeral."

"I'll see you then."

They made their way to the SUV.

"Back to HQ, please, Vernon."

"Right away, ma'am. There's an accident on the GW Parkway, so we may experience some delays."

"Awesome." Sam looked forward to the day when she could zip around the city like George Jetson had, although that would entail flying, one of her least favorite things. Until that day, DC-area traffic was a cross to be borne. "Thoughts?"

"It's interesting that Leslie and the girls had no clue they were being held hostage until they were rescued," Gonzo said.

"That stood out to me, too," Sam said. "They were obviously well cared for and bought the story that Tom needed them in a safe place while he took care of business." She glanced at Gonzo. "Where's Congressman Bryant?"

"Released on bond this morning pending trial."

"With or without monitoring?"

"Without."

"Well, that's unfortunate." People on bail awaiting felony charges should always be monitored, in her opinion, especially if they had the resources to run and had ordered a murder, among other crimes. "Let's go see him."

Gonzo gave Vernon the address for Bryant's local home in Adams Morgan. When they arrived after almost an hour in traffic, the place looked deserted.

"Big change from when we were here before," Freddie said.

"How so?" Sam asked.

"It was surrounded by security and popping with activity."

"Huh. I wonder if the congressman has been humbled by his arrest."

"Nah," Gonzo said. "He's not the type for humility."

"I'll wait for you here," Faith said. "Four of us might be too much."

"We'll try to be quick," Sam said.

"I'll check in with my sisters to see if there's anything new."

They went up the stone stairs to the three-story townhouse.

Freddie rang the bell.

"I wasn't expecting a nice, normal doorbell at this place," Sam said.

"It's about the only thing about this guy that's nice or normal," Gonzo said.

When a short, middle-aged, bald man with dirty clothes, an unhealthy red complexion and the start of a beard came to the door, Sam glanced at Gonzo for confirmation that he was their guy.

Gonzo gave a subtle nod.

Sam showed him her badge. "Lieutenant Holland, Metro PD. I think you know my partners, Detective Cruz and Sergeant Gonzales."

"I like how you introduce yourself, as if you're just another cop."

"I'm just another cop when I'm on the job."

"Whatever you say. What do you want?"

"A few minutes of your time."

He hesitated before he took a step back to admit them.

A stale, musty smell was her first impression.

Bryant led them past a kitchen that had dishes stacked in the sink and takeout boxes scattered about the countertop.

Sam made a face at Freddie, who nodded in agreement.

"What's this about? I've already answered a million questions."

"We have a few more." Sam nudged a pile of clothes out of the way so she could sit on the sofa.

"Where're all your people?" Gonzo asked.

"Gone."

"Gone where?"

"Wherever people go when the party's over. The Feds froze my assets, so I can't pay them. People don't stick around when the money's gone, and team members are being arrested."

"You must've been relieved that your son wasn't murdered," Freddie said.

"Of course I was."

"If you ask me, you knew all along it wasn't him who was dead," Gonzo said.

"I don't recall asking you."

"Who gave the order to Aaron to murder Zach and make it look like it was Randy, right down to the red Vans sneakers?"

"I don't know anything about that."

Sam hoped he could tell they didn't believe him. "What was your relationship with U.S. Attorney Tom Forrester?"

Bryant's face twisted into a scowl. "I had no relationship with him. Not anymore."

"Yet he was investigating you for campaign finance irregularities?"

"He was talking to my team about that. I wasn't involved."

"The U.S. Attorney himself was investigating you, and you had no involvement?"

"That's what I said."

"Did you ever meet him?"

"We were friendly. In the past."

"Friendly how?"

"We played cards together a few times, rubbed elbows the way people do in this town."

"As you know," Sam said, "your electronic devices have been seized as part of the investigation into the death of Zachery Calder, as well as your business dealings here in the District."

"So?"

"Do you want to think about your relationship with Forrester before you answer again?"

"No, I don't," he said with a hard stare. "I knew him. I thought he was a friend until he wasn't."

"It must've made you angry that he was investigating you and your campaign."

"I didn't care about him or his investigation. I knew he wouldn't find anything."

Gonzo gave an ironic chuckle. "It's amusing you should say that, because Kent Sanders told us you were the one who ordered Forrester's family detained, which is another word for 'kidnapped' in this case."

"That's a lie! I heard Kent got full immunity in exchange for a bullshit story full of lies."

Gonzo eyed him skeptically. "Why in the world would bodyguards who worked for you kidnap Forrester's family unless you told them to?"

"How should I know? They had their own shit going on. You should ask Kent and Aaron about that."

"Don't worry," Gonzo said. "We will."

"How did you feel when your son was arrested on murder-for-hire charges?" Sam asked.

"How do you think I felt? You have kids. How would you like to hear that one of them had been arrested for such a thing?"

"I understand you were estranged from Randy and his sister."

"So? That doesn't mean it didn't upset me to hear he'd been charged."

"Did you tell Tom Forrester to release him or else?"

"Or else what? I didn't tell him to do anything."

"And yet, men who worked for you had his family stashed at the Washington Hilton," Sam said. "Interesting coincidence."

"Whatever they did with his family was on their own. I had nothing to do with that."

Sam snorted, which the congressman didn't appreciate.

"What's so funny?"

"You are. You expect us to believe your son was arrested, Tom Forrester's family was kidnapped by men who work for you, and Forrester ordered us to release your son—and you had *nothing* to do with any of that? Or the murder of the prosecutor who was about to turn your life upside down while you're facing a primary challenger? Don't you see how funny that is?"

"I don't find the humor in any of this."

"What goes on at Capital Retrofitters?" Gonzo asked.

"What's that?" Bryant asked with a blank expression.

"The place where your pal Zach was found murdered. We were told you run a business out of there."

"I don't know what you're talking about."

"Did you have someone kill Tom Forrester?" Sam asked.

Bryant's expression lost all color before it turned thunderous. "Get out of my house, and don't come back here."

"Is that a no?"

"*Get out!*"

As they got up and walked to the front door, Sam kept one eye over her shoulder. She wouldn't put it past Bryant to shoot at them from behind. When people were cornered, they could be unpredictable.

She took a deep breath of the cool, fresh air that was a welcome relief from the stench inside Bryant's house.

"I don't know about you guys, but I can't wait to see what the dumps of Bryant's and Forrester's phones show."

"I can't either," Gonzo said. "The guy is so full of shit, his eyes are brown."

"Do we like him for Forrester's murder?" Freddie asked.

"Not sure yet," Sam said as they got into the SUV. "He was locked up when it happened, as were his henchmen. You know how I feel about things being too obvious. What would he have to gain by killing the U.S. Attorney when the gig was already up for him?"

"Maybe to keep it from getting worse?" Gonzo asked.

"He's already looking at multiple felony charges," Sam said. "What would one more do to change the equation?"

"What if that one more was the worst one yet?" Freddie asked.

"I suppose that's possible, but what's worse than ordering a murder to take the heat off your own son?"

"We don't have him on that," Gonzo reminded her. "We've only got his goons nailed on that."

"I want to see the one who was given immunity," Sam said.

Freddie found Sanders's address in Arlington and gave it to Vernon, who did a U-turn to head toward Northern Virginia.

"Can you do me a favor in the meantime?" Sam asked Freddie.

"What favor?"

"Will you find the study guide for *Beowulf,* and have it sent to Scotty as soon as possible?"

"Ugh, are they still teaching that book?" Gonzo asked.

"Unfortunately, yes, and he's struggling." She pulled her credit card out of her wallet and handed it to him. "He needs our help."

"I'm on it."

"Thank you."

"No need to thank me. This is like community service."

Sam laughed. "No shit, right?"

Why was there traffic even on a Sunday? As they crested the Memorial Bridge, she glanced up the hill at Arlington National Cemetery, where the perpetual flame lit in honor of President Kennedy burned brightly.

It occurred to her, right at that moment, that someday her own husband could be honored with burial at Arlington.

The very thought of such a thing made her go cold all over with dread.

"What's wrong?" Freddie asked from his spot across from her.

"The view of Arlington had me thinking about presidential burial places."

"Don't do that."

"Why does my brain go there? It's not like I *want* to think about such things." Since they were stopped dead in traffic, she was able to fixate on the flame. "President Kennedy was forty-six when he was killed. That's eight years older than Nick is now."

"Don't forget what you're always telling me," Freddie said.

"What's that?"

"That when you spend as much time as we do mired in murder and mayhem, it's too easy to imagine it happening to people close to you—that's especially true when it happens to be someone you work closely with, like Tom."

"I'm pretty wise, aren't I?"

The other three laughed, as she'd hoped they would. "Again... sorry to be irreverent at a time like this, Faith."

"It's okay. It helps to be with friends." She looked up from her phone. "They haven't found anything in Tom's office about the Bryant case. Archie and his team came to pick up the computer."

Sam was glad to hear someone on her team was making progress. "If there's something on that computer or the laptop from his home, Archie will find it."

"Hope said there's pushback from Main Justice about the computer being out of the hands of the federal government."

"Tell her to assure them it'll be handled with the utmost sensitivity."

Sam texted Archie to make him aware of the security concerns coming from the Justice Department.

On it, he replied. *Not my first rodeo with them.*

I have every confidence in you and your team.

We'll get you what we can shortly. I understand we're to focus first on his correspondence with Congressman Bryant.

Yes, please.

You like him for this?

I don't know yet. Early days. And he was locked up when Tom was killed.

Got it. Will be back to you ASAP.

Thanks.

Sam's next text was on the secure BlackBerry she used to

communicate with Nick. *I can't believe I'm even saying this, but I need an audience with your AG. What's the best way to make that happen without it going through you?*

Best question ever from my cop. Let me check with Terry and get back with you.

This conversation never happened.

Gotcha, babe. Miss you. Is it gonna be a late one?

I'm giving it a couple more hours, and then we'll pick it up in the AM. What are my kiddos doing?

Playing Boggle with Eli and Candace.

Sam could picture them gathered in the third-floor conservatory and wished she were there with them. *How are things with the Littles and Candace?*

Seems a little better. Hard to tell. But the newlyweds have toned down the PDA.

We're all thankful for that.

HAHA. Were we ever like that?

I think maybe we still are, but I can't be sure...

I'll ask Scotty.

NO!

His row of laughing emojis made her grin like the loon in love she was with him. She'd never had *that* with any other man. What would've seemed ridiculous to her before him was anything but now. Only he could make her forget, even if just for a few minutes, the grim reality she dealt with every day at work.

CHAPTER FOUR

S am's flip phone rang with a call from Darren Tabor, her reporter "friend" from the *Washington Star*.

"Yes?"

"I'm calling about Forrester. What do we know?"

"Not much yet."

"I'm hearing it might be tied to Bryant and that you and your team met with him. Any truth in that?"

"Early days, Darren. Early days."

"You got *anything* for me? The murder of a U.S. Attorney is big news."

"I'm aware."

"So that's a no?"

"That's a 'nothing yet.' We're working the case and doing what we do. As soon as I have more, I'll let you know."

"Like, you'll let me know and no one else?"

"Maybe."

"Don't tease me, Sam. It hurts me too much later when you disappoint me."

Damn if he didn't make her laugh. "I'll try not to disappoint you."

"What are you hearing from Stahl's house?"

"I'm sure you've received the latest update."

"Is it true there's a storage unit?"

"Yes."

"What's happening there?"

"We're working on tracking down the new owner."

"Is that on the record?"

"Not officially. Everything on that one is coming from the chief. Don't get me in trouble."

"Would I do that to you?"

"Gotta run, Darren."

"I'll check in later."

Sam slapped the phone closed just as the BlackBerry buzzed with a text from Nick. *Here's a number to call.*

Thank you. Nice to have friends in high places.

You can thank me properly later.

I'll look forward to that.

Back at HQ, she went into her office, closed the door and made the call.

"Reginald Cox."

Wow, Sam thought. *That's impressive.*

"This is Lieutenant Holland with the Metro PD. I wondered if you might be available for a brief interview."

"I assume this is in reference to U.S. Attorney Forrester?"

"You assume correctly."

"I've asked the FBI to work on that investigation."

"That's not how this goes. He was murdered in the District, which means we have jurisdiction."

"I'm sure you understand that we prefer to investigate the murder of one of our own."

"And I'm sure you understand that's not going to happen." She held her breath, waiting for him to reply while praying this wouldn't get ugly. "General Cox, I have a job to do. I'm asking for your assistance. I assume we have the same goal here—to quickly determine who killed U.S. Attorney Forrester."

"You assume correctly."

"Are you available today?"

"I'm at home." He gave her the address of his Georgetown condo. "You'll encounter my security in the lobby. I'll let them know you're coming."

"Thank you very much. We'll be there shortly."

A knock on the door preceded Freddie poking his head in. "Archie is looking for you."

"Tell him to come in. We're heading out in five minutes."

"Where to?"

"To interview the AG."

"As in *the* AG?"

"As in the one and only."

"Wow."

Sam understood his amazement. An interview with the country's top law enforcement officer certainly wasn't an everyday occurrence. She wondered if she ever would have gotten access to Cox without being married to his boss. Probably not, but whatever. She wasn't about to look a proverbial gift horse in the mouth.

Freddie left and returned with Archie.

"Got some film to show you. Can you come to the conference room?"

"Yep."

She took a seat at the table as Archie pressed play to start a video on a wall-mounted screen.

"This is from one of our cameras on Constitution Ave." Archie stepped closer to the screen to point. "Watch this jogger as they approach the parked car." Sam kept her gaze fixed on the figure dressed in dark clothing as they ran along the sidewalk. She held her breath as the person got closer to the car.

"He—I'm assuming it's a man—barely pauses as he goes by the car, but I was able to zoom in to where he shot Tom." Archie played that part of the film next.

She could clearly see the window shatter and the person inside the car slump forward.

How often did they catch a homicide on film, let alone one as high-profile as this?

Of course the film was of little use to them without a face to go with the body. But they now had a description of a compact but muscular person, who was most likely male.

"Tell me we got this from multiple other angles," Sam said.

"I wish I could." Archie sighed as he sat across from her. "We have one camera that's out for repair on that block and another that's been giving us fits for a while now."

She glanced at Gonzo and Freddie. "Did our witness report anything that would help?"

"He didn't see the actual shooting," Gonzo said. "Only the aftermath."

"Of course he didn't see it."

"We'll be looking for pings in the area to figure out who was nearby, but if this was a professional hit, the person wouldn't have been stupid enough to carry a phone. I've got the text chains printing now if you want to come up and grab them in a few minutes." Archie stood and headed for the door. "We're looking at numerous other cameras in the area, hoping to get a look at our shooter from a different angle. I'll keep you posted."

"Why can't we ever get lucky enough to catch a killer red-handed, arrest them and call it a day?" Freddie asked.

"Because what fun would that be if they made it too easy for us?"

Her partner gave her a sour look.

Gonzo grunted out a laugh. "What's our next move, boss?"

"Freddie and I are going to see the AG. Can you work on the text traffic?" Sam checked her watch and saw it was getting close to five thirty. "Let's give it two more hours, and then we'll pick it up in the AM."

"Should we have someone work overnight to keep the Feds from taking over?" Gonzo asked.

Sam sighed as she decided he was probably right. "Good point. Call in Dani and Gigi to take over from where we leave off."

"Cam and Gigi were away for the weekend," Gonzo said, "but they should be back by now. I'll get Gigi and Dani up to speed."

"Thanks." She gestured for Freddie to come with her.

"I can't believe we get to interview the actual AG," he said after they'd grabbed their coats to head for the morgue entrance.

"He puts his pants on one leg at a time, just like you do."

"Okay, then. So we're not allowed to be impressed by the AG."

Sam shrugged. "Whatever. He's just another witness to me."
She gave Vernon the address for Cox's Georgetown building.

"I'm sure you're not just another cop to him."

"I really hope that's how he treats me."

"Do you think it could become a thing if the media catches
wind of you interviewing him as part of a case?"

"So what if it does? I'm just doing my job."

"Uh, okay."

"What is it you want to say, my grasshopper?"

"There's nothing at all routine about the first lady, in her
capacity as a homicide detective, interviewing the U.S. Attorney
General as a potential witness in the murder of a U.S.
Attorney."

Vernon let out a low whistle. "What he said."

"You're supposed to be on my side at all times."

Vernon glanced at her in the rearview mirror. "I am, except
for when I'm on his."

Freddie chuckled.

Sam glared at him. "That's not funny."

"Yes, it is."

"I also agree with him that once the media catches wind of
this interview, there'll be intense interest," Vernon said. "Jimmy is
calling in some reinforcements to meet us in Georgetown."

Sam couldn't believe he thought that was necessary.
"Seriously?"

Vernon met her gaze in the mirror. "Dead seriously."

THE NEED for extra security annoyed her. She knew they were just
doing their jobs, but she wished she could simply do hers, the
way she used to. As soon as she had that thought, she felt guilty
because the reason she couldn't do her job the way she used to
was because her beloved husband had become president under
the craziest of circumstances. Even months later, surrounded by a
Secret Service detail, Sam had to constantly remind herself that
she was putting up with the inconvenience because he'd asked
her to.

Sam was incredibly proud of Nick, but his "promotion" had also changed everything for her, and not always in a good way.

As they approached Georgetown, traffic slowed nearly to a stop, which only added to her frustration. She leaned forward to see what was causing the delay and was shocked to see media trucks lining the street. "Mother*fucker.*"

"They probably figured you'd get here eventually," Vernon said.

"Is there a way to get me in there without it turning into a complete spectacle?"

"Let me see what we can do." Vernon took a right turn and pulled onto a side street off M, the main drag through Georgetown.

While he made a call and explained the situation, she forced herself to be patient, to allow the agents to do their jobs so she could do hers.

Remember how much you love Nick, how you'd do anything for him, even when his job interferes with yours.

While she waited, she put her head back against the seat and closed her eyes so she could revisit some of the better parts of their recent vacation, such as when they'd exchanged the perfect gifts. He'd given her a gorgeous platinum watch, engraved with his thanks for the best two years of his life. She'd given him a T-shirt that said I LOVE YOU MORE. THE END. I WIN.

As she ran her fingers over the watch, she smiled, recalling that day and the others they'd spent alone at the beach. Being with him made her happier than anything ever had, and it had gotten even better when their kids joined them for the final weekend. After years of painful infertility struggles, she now had three kids to call her own, as well as a bonus son in Eli and now his wife, too. They had the family of their dreams, even if none of it had happened the conventional way.

What did convention matter when their White House was full of love?

And what did she care about a few delays on the job when she had him and their children to go home to at the end of every hard day on the job? So what if "home" these days was the freaking White House? Her dad used to tell Sam and her sisters to enjoy the moment, because all things, even the best of things, were temporary.

She hated to acknowledge that was true, which was why she tried to live every day to the fullest, to make sure the people she loved knew she loved them and to do her best in all things.

Her ringing phone interrupted the philosophical direction her thoughts had taken. She sat up a little straighter when she saw Chief Farnsworth's name on her caller ID.

"Hello, sir."

"What's the latest on the Forrester investigation, Lieutenant?"

"I'm about to interview the AG at his home in Georgetown."

"As in the actual Attorney General of the United States?"

"Yes, sir."

"I'm under tremendous pressure to bring the Feds into this investigation."

"As am I, sir."

"I'm assigning several other detectives to your team for the time being. Please use them to move this along as quickly as possible."

Sam wanted to plead with him not to do that, but she knew better than to question him. "Who's coming to Homicide?"

"Detectives Lucas and Harper from SVU and Coheeny from Explosives. I've asked them to report to your pit at zero seven hundred. Deputy Chief McBride has also made herself available as needed to assist."

"We appreciate the help. I've got O'Brien and Charles chasing down the new owner of Stahl's storage unit. I'm planning to let them see that through since they're close."

"That's fine. We've got a matter of days, Lieutenant, if that, before the Feds take over. Let's make them count."

"Yes, sir. If I could ask... How are you?" He'd been under enormous stress since the latest news about Stahl had come to light, and Sam was worried about her beloved uncle.

"Having the time of my life."

Sam smiled at the expected reply. "I hope you're taking care of yourself."

"Marti is seeing to that. She's hovering over me like a mother hen."

"Good."

"Hope you got to relax a little on the vacation."

"We did, despite everything."

"I was so sorry to hear about the shooting at Fort Liberty. What a tragedy that was."

"Indeed."

"Will you be traveling there this week?"

"Not right away. There was some pushback to a visit at this moment."

"Sorry to hear that."

"We understand the rationale." The shooter had reportedly objected to being offered a dishonorable discharge for his refusal to serve under an unelected president. As such, the brass at Fort Liberty had thought this might not be the time for the unelected president and first lady to make a condolence visit.

"I'll let you get to interviewing the AG, of all people. Let me know how that goes."

"Will do."

"Have a good evening."

"You do the same."

"How is he?" Freddie asked after she'd slapped the phone closed.

"He said he's having the time of his life."

"I'll bet. Stahl is a nightmare for the entire department. Everywhere I go, people ask me if I knew him and if I had any idea what he was really doing, as if I wouldn't have done something about it had I known."

"No kidding. I hate when the shit that other people do bounces back on the rest of us. In other news, the chief is assigning three more detectives to our squad for this case and making Jeannie available to us as well."

"How do you feel about that?"

"I have mixed feelings. More people makes for more complications."

Vernon turned to her. "We've found another way into the building, but we're going on foot. Is that all right?"

"Whatever it takes." Sam wanted to get this done and go home. "How far is it?"

"Just a couple of blocks, and it's clear."

"Then let's do it."

They emerged from the SUV and headed toward the corner, with Vernon leading the way and Jimmy bringing up the rear. At times like this, Sam found the constraints of having a detail almost comical. Here they were, highly trained police officers, being escorted through Georgetown by federal agents as if they couldn't get themselves to their destination safely.

Nick had offered to resign the presidency if she couldn't bear to have a detail. Since she couldn't let him do that, she'd agreed to the added security. It had turned out to be not so bad, thanks to Vernon and Jimmy. They were great about rolling with her and were fun to be with. It was only at times like this, being escorted by them as if she couldn't take care of herself, that the new realities rankled.

"I hope no one else on the job sees us," Sam muttered to Freddie.

"I knew you were thinking that very thing."

"If you laugh, I'll smack you."

"I'm not laughing."

"But you want to."

"You said that, not me."

Sam hoped the scowl she directed his way would shut down the conversation.

His lips quivered with amusement that made her want to punch him.

"Don't punch me. I'll file charges."

When had he started reading her mind on top of everything else? "Whatever."

Thankfully, the walk was a short one, and as Vernon held open the back door to Cox's building, he scanned their surroundings with a sharp-eyed gaze attuned to trouble. "All clear."

"Thank you, Vernon."

It certainly wasn't his fault—or Jimmy's—that Sam felt confined by the security they provided. It was a fact of her life now, she knew, as she learned to live with it. But as much as she liked Vernon and Jimmy, she yearned for the days when she could run around the city more or less under the radar to do her job.

But every time she chafed, she also tried to remember that the only reason she had security was because Nick Cappuano was her husband. The security was a small price to pay for everything else that came with him.

An FBI agent met them inside the back door. He was tall and fit with close-cropped dark hair. He wore a suit, an earpiece and a serious don't-fuck-with-me expression. "Right this way."

He led them to an elevator that required a keycard and pressed the only button inside the car. "On the way up," he said into a radio.

Sam had so many questions about how they ran the AG's security, but she'd decided she was better off not knowing the details. She'd probably be terrified of the many extreme situations federal agents were trained to handle when it came to her family and other high-ranking officials like Cox.

The elevator opened into an elegant foyer. An arrangement of fresh flowers sat on a circular table.

"Right this way." The agent led them into a wide-open living space. To her left, she could see the Potomac River through massive windows.

They were taken to an office that was as distinguished as the man with graying blond hair who sat behind the large desk. He stood to greet them, revealing the muscular build of a former football player. "Reggie Cox." He extended a hand across the desk to Sam and Freddie.

Sam didn't bother to introduce herself. "This is my partner, Detective Cruz."

"Nice to meet you." A smile lit up his blue eyes. "I've heard such great things about you both."

"Thank you," Freddie said.

Sam could tell her partner was a bit starstruck to be meeting the AG. This was a first for both of them.

"Have a seat." He gestured to two upholstered chairs in front of his desk. "May I offer you anything?"

"We're fine, thank you," Sam said. "We appreciate you taking the time to see us on a Sunday."

"I'm devastated by Tom Forrester's murder. I'll do whatever I can to assist your investigation. I've offered the full resources of the FBI and the Justice Department to your chief."

"We appreciate that, and we'll call on them as needed. As part of a previous investigation, we learned that you'd asked U.S. Attorney Forrester to personally investigate Congressman Bryant's campaign finance irregularities."

"Yes, I did."

"Can you tell us why you took that unusual step?"

"As you might imagine, investigating a sitting congressman can make for a sticky situation, especially when you aren't sure the potential accusation has merit. After the matter was brought to my attention, I wanted it handled quietly by someone I had complete faith in, thus I asked Tom to look into it."

"How did the irregularities come to your attention in the first place?"

"We received an anonymous tip through our online portal."

"And that tip made it all the way to you?"

"Bryant is a sitting congressman. Yes, it came to me."

"Can you tell us what Tom uncovered?"

"I'm afraid I can't discuss an active investigation. I'm sure you understand."

Since she had a dead U.S. Attorney in her morgue, Sam decided to press him. "I understand the delicate balance needed for such an investigation. However, I'm sure you agree that the murder of a U.S. Attorney requires us to step outside the usual confines in our quest for justice on his behalf."

"I want justice for Tom Forrester as much as or more than anyone. However, Tom wouldn't want me to compromise a complex investigation, especially one he devoted countless hours to personally."

"According to his team, there's no paper trail for that investigation."

"He reported directly to me verbally."

"That seems highly unusual."

"It was, but so is an investigation of a ten-term congressman with powerful committee assignments."

Sam wanted to scream with frustration as she realized this meeting was pointless. He would stonewall her, no matter what she asked. "During your tenure as AG, how many times have you instigated investigations in which a U.S. Attorney reported directly to you verbally?"

Cox gave her a steely look that probably made other people wilt. It had no effect on her. "This was the first time."

"You've been in this business a long time," Sam said. "Like me, you've seen it all, right?"

"I guess you could say that."

"Then you'll forgive me when I tell you that all my Spidey senses are on alert to a much bigger story here than what I'm being told."

Was it her imagination, or did the Attorney General of the United States squirm ever so slightly? No, not her imagination. That was definitely a squirm.

"I'm afraid I've told you everything I can without jeopardizing a very important investigation." He stood. "Now, if there's nothing else, I have a lot of work to finish today."

Sam put her business card on his desk. "If you think of anything relevant to the murder of one of your U.S. Attorneys, please give me a call."

He held her gaze. "I'll do that."

Sam didn't say a word to Freddie, Vernon or Jimmy as they left Cox's place and walked back to the SUV, where other agents were dealing with the media.

"Wait here," Vernon said as he went ahead to help remove the swarm of reporters while she and Freddie stayed with Jimmy.

Sam seethed with outrage at the way the AG had treated her. He'd done that on purpose, probably because he wanted the FBI, which was under his command, on the case and not her. Too bad.

She had jurisdiction, and he could kiss her ass with his bullshit. So much for the brother- and sisterhood of law enforcement having one another's backs and working together for the common good.

Something stank to high heaven with this case, and she would figure out what it was, to hell with the almighty AG.

It took ten minutes to clear the way for Sam and Freddie to get back in the car as reporters shouted questions at them about Tom Forrester, the AG and whether she'd needed her husband's permission to meet with Cox.

This case was pissing her off, and it had only just begun.

CHAPTER FIVE

S am held her tongue until they were in their conference room at HQ with the door closed. Not that she didn't fully trust Vernon and Jimmy to be discreet, but she wasn't about to go off on the AG in front of them. "Was that the biggest sack of bullshit we've ever been fed or what?"

"The biggest sack for sure," Freddie said. "Not to mention he was smug and patronizing."

"All of that. This makes me more determined than ever to keep the Feds far away from this investigation. He's hiding something, and I want to know what."

"I hate to point out that could get sticky in light of your domestic situation."

"My domestic situation." Sam snorted out a laugh. "Do you mean because my husband, the president, is his boss?"

"Something like that."

"You'd think the AG would be extra helpful in light of that detail."

"You'd be wrong about that. Will you tell Nick how he treated us?"

Sam pondered the question for a second. "Probably not. He'd want to do something about it, which he absolutely shouldn't do."

"That's true. So what now?"

"I need to think about that."

She took a call from Archie. "Hey, what's up?"

"Are you in the building?"

"In our conference room."

"Be right down."

She closed her phone. "Archie's coming down. Let's hope he's found us a thread to pull."

Archie came in a few minutes later. "I have good news and bad news. What do you want first?"

"Give me the bad," Sam said.

"Forrester's work phone is encrypted. I can't get anything off it."

"*Fuck.*"

"Had a feeling you might say that." He placed an evidence bag containing the phone on the table. "The Feds might be able to get in."

"What's the good news?"

"On the personal phone, I found an ongoing dispute between Forrester and his neighbor that'd escalated in recent months."

"What kind of dispute?"

"The neighbor raises Dobermans. Apparently, they've escaped at times and ended up in Forrester's yard. One of them tangled with Forrester's Cavapoo. The dog required surgery that cost thousands of dollars. Forrester was suing the neighbor and had complained about the guy to Animal Control numerous times. The neighbor recently countersued." Archie placed a stack of pages on the table. "I printed the two suits for you."

"What the hell is a Cavapoo?" Sam asked.

"I knew you'd ask that." Archie put a photo of a white fluffy dog on the table. "A cross between a poodle and a Cavalier King Charles spaniel."

Sam winced. "Poor little thing wouldn't stand a chance against a Doberman."

"Exactly. The vet bill to save the dog was more than five grand."

"Holy shit," Freddie said.

"I wonder why Leslie Forrester didn't mention this when we spoke to her," Sam said.

"Probably because that's the least of her concerns at the moment," Freddie replied.

"I suppose so. Thanks, Archie. This gives us a thread anyway."

"You got it. We're still working on texts and emails, as well as film in the area where Tom's body was found. More to come."

After Archie left, Freddie stood to stretch. "Do you really think the neighbor would be stupid enough to off a U.S. Attorney over a dog dispute?"

"We've seen dumber things, but I'm not getting a buzz over this angle. How could his murder *not* be related to his work and Bryant holding his family hostage?"

"It has to be related to that," Freddie said.

"I want to look into the history between Cox and Forrester. Something about the way Cox acted earlier was off. I want to know why."

"I'll take a dive into that from home tonight."

Sam glanced at the clock on the wall. Almost seven thirty. "Go ahead home. Let's pick this up at zero seven hundred."

"I'll be here."

"Put out a note to our squad, as well as Lucas, Harper and Coheeny, to be here by seven."

"Will do."

"Thanks for working on Sunday."

"No problem."

"Sure it was, but I appreciate it anyway."

"It's good to have you back. Not as much fun without you."

"Aw, thanks, grasshopper. I missed you, too."

Carlucci and Dominguez were arriving as she prepared to leave. Sam took the detectives into the conference room to bring them up to speed.

"Archie is working the digital footprint, and here are the texts from Forrester's personal phone that you can wade through. I want financials on all the key players, including Cox."

"The AG?" Dominguez asked.

"Yep, as well as Forrester and Bryant."

"We have Bryant's financials already," Carlucci said. "I'll go through them again."

"Thanks for coming in."

"No problem."

Before she left HQ, Sam texted Avery. *Are you guys still up? I could use a couple of min when I get home and would love to see Shelby & baby if this is a good time.*

We're up. Will be for a while. Our little girl is a night owl.

Haha. See you soon.

Sam took the evidence bag containing Forrester's work phone with her when she headed to her office to get her coat. She would deliver the phone to Avery at home.

Asking the Feds for help was always a last resort, but in situations like this, it was foolish to pretend the FBI didn't have capabilities that were simply not available to her and her team.

She texted Vernon that she was on her way out and headed for the morgue exit.

Chief Medical Examiner Dr. Lindsey McNamara was coming out as Sam approached the automatic doors for the morgue. "I sent the autopsy report to your email a few minutes ago. It was a pretty straightforward case of a nine-millimeter bullet to the head. I've sent the bullet to the lab for further analysis. The tox screen will take a while longer, but there were no other significant findings."

"Thanks for the quick work. How're you feeling?"

"After an earlier burst of energy, I'm dragging. Whatever it is, I can't seem to shake it."

"Hate to hear that. Anything I can do?"

"Nah, I'll be fine.

Sam couldn't help but notice that her friend was much paler than usual. "Let me know if you need anything."

"I will, thanks. It's good to have you back."

"I wish I could say it's good to be back..."

Lindsey offered a small smile. "Believe me. I get it."

"And I'm always so thankful for that."

"Are you still borrowing my morgue for a dress fitting tomorrow?"

Sam cringed when she recalled asking Lindsey to use her office. "That's the plan."

"That'll be a first," Lindsey said with a smile.

"Appreciate the help at keeping it on the DL."

"My morgue is your morgue."

"See you in the morning."

"I'll be here."

When Sam stepped out into the late winter chill, Vernon opened the door and waited for her to get settled.

"Thank you, Vernon."

"My pleasure."

The interior of the SUV was warm and toasty as Sam settled in for the ride home.

"How's it going?"

Sam met Vernon's gaze in the mirror. "Slow."

"Are you thinking it's tied to Bryant?"

"How can it not be?"

"That's what we were saying, too."

"While that seems the most obvious, I've learned to look beyond the obvious." After a pause, she added, "The case that brought the twins into our lives is a good example. Their billionaire father was embroiled in a dispute with his former business partner, which had sent him and his family into exile with new identities. After the parents were killed in a home invasion and fire, we looked hard at the partner, but we couldn't make a case. Turned out a traffic altercation involving the wife led to murder."

"I remember that case. Jameson and Cleo Armstrong, right?"

"That's the one. At the beginning of that investigation, if you'd asked me to bet my life the partner wasn't involved, I'd be dead."

"We're all glad you're not dead, ma'am," Jimmy said.

"Haha, thanks. My point is we have to look at everything, not just the most obvious things."

"Agreed," Vernon said. "Especially in a situation like this one where you'll be under enormous pressure to get answers quickly."

"Yes, exactly. Thankfully, Captain Malone took care of updating the media earlier, so I didn't have to do that today. I'll be in the hot seat before long, though."

"What time are we leaving in the morning?" Vernon asked as they drove through the White House gates.

"Six thirty."

"We'll be ready."

"Thank you for working late on a Sunday."

"No problem."

When she entered the White House, Harold, one of her favorite ushers, greeted her with a warm smile. "Evening, Mrs. Cappuano."

"Evening, Harold. Is the president upstairs?"

"He is, ma'am."

"Thank you. Have a nice night."

"You do the same, ma'am."

Sam trudged up the red-carpeted stairs, feeling far more exhausted than she should have been after a week-long vacation. But the so-called vacation had been filled with far more drama than they'd anticipated, making it much less restful than it could've been.

She looked in on the sleeping twins and then on Scotty, who was watching a Caps game. "Who's winning?"

"Caps are up by two in the third."

"How's the book?"

He gave her a withering look. "It's horrible. Worst thing I've ever been forced to read."

Sam sat on the edge of his bed and scratched behind Skippy's ears, making the puppy sigh in her sleep. "I remember having to read stuff that just didn't interest me and how painful it was." Especially with undiagnosed dyslexia. Those were some seriously unfun years.

"'Painful' is a good word for it."

"I'll get that study guide for you right away."

"You're the best. Thank you."

"Anything for you, kid." She leaned in to kiss his forehead. "Don't stay up too late."

"This book will put me to sleep in no time."

Smiling, she said, "Love you."

"Love you, too."

She went into the suite she shared with Nick to find him tucked away in the small office attached to their bedroom. Each night, he drafted handwritten responses to ten letters from citizens in addition to reviewing the massive briefing books he brought "home" from the office.

Sam cleared her throat so she wouldn't startle him.

Prior to him becoming vice president, she would've snuck up on him and taken great pleasure in scaring him. That wasn't as much fun now that he lived with endless threats to his life.

He turned to her, smiling. "There's my favorite wife. I was just about to check on you."

"Here I am."

"How'd it go?"

"A lot of wheel-spinning so far."

"I heard you might've interviewed my AG."

"You heard correctly."

"How'd that go?"

Sam thought about how she should answer that question. "I think it's best if we don't talk about that."

"How come?"

"Because he works for you, and he's part of my investigation. If we're ever asked, it'd be better to say we never discussed it."

"Are you becoming a political wife right before my very eyes?"

Sam scoffed. "Hardly."

He stood and came to her, putting his hands on her hips. "It's kinda hot when you anticipate political concerns."

"You think everything I do is hot."

"That's very true." He nuzzled her neck, which had her leaning into him. "Today was a long day without you after spending most of a week together."

"For me, too. As much as I love my job—most of the time, anyway—I find myself thinking more often lately about what it will be like to be, um, retired someday."

His head whipped up, eyes gone wide with shock.

She laughed at his reaction. "Oh, shut up. I'm not saying any time soon. Just someday. In the far-off future when we don't have a million things competing for our attention all the time."

"I can't wait for that day."

"I would say me either, but I don't want you thinking I mean soon."

"Gotcha. But it's something to look forward to."

"For sure."

"Until that far-off state of nirvana, we have the Canadian state visit to contend with this week, as well as the meeting with my mother on Friday."

Sam frowned when she thought about meeting with his mother—voluntarily. Nicoletta had requested the opportunity to speak with them, hoping to make things right. In Sam's mind, that wasn't possible, but it wasn't up to her. Nick was curious about what she had to say, so they would take the meeting at their home on Ninth Street. Sam drew the line at having the woman to the White House, which she suspected was Nicoletta's ultimate goal.

"I'll be ready for all of it. I have a fitting with Marcus tomorrow afternoon. He's coming to HQ, and Lindsey is loaning me the morgue so no one will see it."

"Not sure how I feel about my first lady having a dress fitting in the morgue."

Sam laughed. "It does sound funny when you put it that way." She rested in the comfort of his embrace for another minute. "I need to run up to talk to Avery and see Shelby for a few minutes. Are you almost done?"

"I need another half hour."

"Meet you back here in thirty?"

He kissed her. "It's a date."

She went upstairs to the third floor to knock softly on Shelby and Avery's door.

Avery answered, looking tired but happy. "Come in."

"How goes it in baby central?"

"Busy and exhausting, but great, too."

Sam held up the evidence bag. "This is Forrester's encrypted work phone. Anything you can do with it?"

"I'll deliver it to our lab."

Sam handed it to him. "Obviously, time is of the essence."

"I understand. I'll put a rush on it."

"Thank you."

"Heard you interviewed the AG."

"Was it on the news or something?"

He huffed out a laugh. "Is that a rhetorical question? When the first lady, in her capacity as a homicide detective, interviews the U.S. AG after the murder of a USA, that tends to make the news."

"*Why* does that have to be news?"

Avery laughed a little harder this time. "Is that a rhetorical question?"

"I'm just doing my job. Why does everything I do have to make the goddamned news?"

"As we stand in your residence at the White House, you can ask that?"

"Shut up. You're supposed to be my friend."

"I am." He wiped away laughter tears that irritated her.

"Where's your wife? I like her better than you."

Chuckling, Avery gestured for Sam to lead the way into their suite.

CHAPTER SIX

Shelby, who was on the sofa with the baby asleep on her chest, smiled when she saw Sam. "Hey there. Come meet our Maisie Rae."

Sam sat on the footstool in front of them and leaned in for a closer look at the sleeping angel. She tried to ignore the too-familiar pang of longing. Why was it so easy for some people to have babies, but impossible for her? "She's *gorgeous*."

"We're pretty smitten, even if she has her days and nights mixed up."

"That's happened with all my nieces and nephews. Fortunately, they eventually figure it out."

"Noah did, so I'm hopeful for her, too."

"Where is my little pal?"

"Sleeping over with my sister Ginger to give us a minute with Miss Maisie. He was so excited to meet her earlier that we feared he'd be up all night if he was here."

Avery handed Sam his phone. "Pictures."

Sam scrolled through the photos of Noah holding his baby sister and then one of the four of them together. "Beautiful." She was deeply moved by the pure love on Noah's little face as he gazed at his new sister.

She handed the phone back to Avery. "How're you feeling, Shelby?"

"Like I got hit by a bus, but glad it's over and that she's finally here."

"We're so happy she's here."

"Imagine that she'll be able to tell everyone for the rest of her life that she came home to the White House after she was born."

"I love that," Sam said, smiling.

"Would you like to hold her?"

"Oh, um, if you're sure it's okay. She's so little."

"It's okay."

Shelby carefully transferred the sleeping baby to Sam's arms. "Don't worry if she wakes up. It's almost time for a feeding."

Sam held the tiny bundle close to her chest, gazing down at her perfect little face. "Good Lord, she's beautiful."

"We think so, too," Shelby said with a giggle.

Avery went to the sofa to sit next to his wife and held her hand while Sam gazed at the baby in awe.

"What an angel."

"You should hear the lungs on her," Avery said.

"She's a steel magnolia, like her mama," Sam said.

Avery smiled at Shelby. "God help me."

Shelby rested her head on his shoulder, seeming almost back to her old self after the horrifying home invasion she and Noah had endured.

As Sam studied the newborn, her eyes filled with tears of happiness tinged with the usual sadness. "Welcome to the family, Miss Maisie Rae Hill. We love you already." She kissed the baby's soft cheek and returned her to her mother. "I'll let you guys get some rest. I just wanted to check on you and see our new little love."

Shelby glanced at Avery. "We'd like you and Nick to be her godparents, if you're willing."

"Of course we're willing and honored to be asked."

"Home to the White House with the president and first lady as her godparents," Shelby said, sounding awestruck. "What a way to start a life."

"We do what we can for our people." Sam stood and leaned

over to kiss Shelby's cheek. "I'll check in tomorrow, Tinker Bell. Congratulations again. You make the prettiest babies."

"Thank you for everything. Being able to hide out here after what happened has been such a blessing to us."

"Our home is your home. Always."

Avery walked Sam to the door. "I'll check in tomorrow."

"Sounds good, and congrats, Dad."

"Thanks for everything. I'm working on getting us out of here."

"Don't stress about it. We're not." Sam gave him a kiss on the cheek and left him to head back downstairs, stopping halfway down when a wave of emotion overwhelmed her. She sat on one of the red-carpeted steps to give herself a minute to get it together before she rejoined Nick.

With her head in her hands, she let the emotion take over.

Just for a minute.

The baby fever didn't strike as often since Scotty and the twins had come into her life. However, as strong as she was the rest of the time, any time a newborn was placed into her arms, she was reminded of what she would never have. She'd made peace with that fact of her life, but it still hurt sometimes. Along with the joy of a new little person to love came the pain of her previous losses and the reality that she would never carry a baby she and Nick created together.

When his arm encircled her shoulders and his familiar scent filled her senses, she leaned into him. "I'm okay."

"I know."

She had no idea how long they sat there before he helped her up and kept his arm around her as they made their way down the rest of the stairs and into their suite.

After he closed the door, she turned to him. "How'd you know?"

"You weren't back for our date, so I went looking for you."

"I'm glad you did." She wiped the last of the tears off her face. "I'm really fine. I swear."

"I know you are, but that doesn't mean you don't feel a little sad every time we welcome another baby into our lives."

"I have nothing at all to be sad about."

"Sure you do."

She shook her head. "I'm so, *so* satisfied with our amazing family. We can't take a vacation without nonstop chaos. Can you think of any other two people who have less business bringing a baby into their lives than we do?"

"We'd find a way to make it work, but like you, I'm more than satisfied with the family we have."

"I'm so incredibly blessed, which is why I get so mad with myself any time this happens."

Nick hugged her. "Don't be mad with my favorite person. She's the best mom ever."

Sam laughed even as she dealt with more tears. "No, she isn't."

"Our kids think you're the coolest person on earth."

"They do not. You're the president. That makes you the coolest."

"No, Sam, they think *you* are. Scotty even said so after we got home earlier. 'How cool is Mom with the lowdown on study guides?'"

"He said that?"

"He did, and he's right. You're the mom he knows he can count on to help him with anything, even things he should be doing on his own."

Sam shuddered. "No one should have to do *Beowulf* on their own."

She loved his laugh and how his mountain of worries seemed to fall away for a while when they were alone together. Sometimes she felt guilty for being a somewhat crappy first lady —okay, she felt guilty about that all the time. But the one area where she truly shined was in giving him respite from the never-ending storm that came with being president.

That was her superpower.

"Take me to bed, Mr. President. I've got an early wakeup."

"There's nowhere I'd rather take you, my love."

They changed their clothes, brushed their teeth and crawled into bed a few minutes later, meeting in the middle as they always did, arms and legs intertwined, her head on his chest.

"Ah," he said on a sigh. "That's what I've needed all damned day."

"It was a long, damned day from vacation ending abruptly to now."

"Sure was, even if I had a nice day with the kids."

"I'm sorry I missed it. I hate missing stuff with them."

"They know that."

Sam's phone chimed with a text. She groaned. "I'm afraid to look."

Nick reached for the phone on her bedside table. "It's Lilia asking for a minute tomorrow to go over the schedule for Tuesday."

Sam took the phone from him and texted her back. *The only minute I have tomorrow is first thing. Can you do 6?*

I'll be there.

So sorry for the early hour.

No worries at all. See you then.

Sam adjusted her alarm to five fifteen and put the phone back on the table. "Just lost forty-five minutes of sleep."

"Thanks for taking one for the team."

"Anything for you."

He ran his fingers through her hair in a soothing motion that helped to relax her into sleep. Tomorrow would be there soon enough, and the craziness would begin anew. For now, though, they were just a husband and a wife, settling in for the night, not the most powerful couple in the world.

SAM ENTERED her office in the East Wing at one minute before six the next morning, still half asleep and groggy. She carried the to-go cup of coffee that Nick had made for her while she was in the shower. Ten cups wouldn't be enough to jumpstart this Monday morning. Of course Lilia was there waiting for her, looking fresh, pretty and put together, as always. Today, she wore a black suit with a teal silk blouse.

"How do you do that at the butt crack of dawn?"

Lilia knit her brows. "Do what?"

Sam flopped into one of the chairs in front of Lilia's desk. "Look so freaking perfect with every pearl in place at this ungodly hour."

Lilia laughed. "I took a shower and got dressed."

"I did the same thing, and you'll note there's a big difference between how you look and how I look." Sam wore jeans, a sweatshirt and running shoes in anticipation of a long day. "Elegance meets roadkill. I still say we need to have you play me for the next three years—except in the bedroom, of course."

Her adorable chief of staff turned bright red. "Stop it. No one in this world could play you better than you."

"Oh, please. Anyone could, and we all know it."

"What would Mr. President say?"

"He's biased."

"Yes, he is, and his opinion is the only one that matters in this debate." Lilia handed over a printed sheet. "That's the schedule for tomorrow, beginning with your tea with Courtney Hutchinson, the prime minister's wife."

"Do I have to drink tea? I hate it."

Lilia's lips quivered with amusement. "We can have some coffee brought in for you."

"Make it decaf, or I'll be awake all night."

Lilia made a note. "You got it."

"What am I supposed to talk to her about?"

"I made a list of potential topics, including family, children, your favorite causes and hers."

"How do you do that?"

"Do what?"

"Anticipate what I'm going to ask you and be ready with an answer."

"That's my job. We've worked together for a while now, and I'd like to think I understand what you need. Most of the time, anyway."

"All the time. You get me. It makes a huge difference, and I'm not sure I tell you often enough how much it means to me to have you and Roni and the others making me look good when I'm barely ever here."

"We enjoy making you look good. Speaking of that, Roni would like to schedule some time on an upcoming weekend for a photo shoot to use for upcoming social media needs." Lilia handed over another sheet of paper with a long list of pending dates, holidays, religious occasions and other important things that would need commentary from the first lady. "Our thought is to take maybe half a day, six to ten different outfits, with hair and makeup on standby to change things up here and there. That'll cover us for the next couple of months. And before you can balk, we'd do all the work. You'd just have to show up and smile."

"God, that feels so fake."

"It's not fake. It's you doing your best to manage two very demanding jobs."

"What if they found out I phoned it in ahead of time and wasn't here for any of those events?"

"That'll remain between us and the presidential photographer. We're all under ironclad NDAs, Sam. What goes on here stays here."

"In a perfect world, that's true. In the world I live in, I'm antsy about it."

"If I didn't believe this was a good idea, I'd never ask you to do it."

"I know. I guess I'm still a bit raw after having people throw tomatoes at me in Dewey."

Lilia's normally pleasant demeanor instantly hardened. "*That* was an outrage."

"Yes, it was, but it's also proof that a lot of people don't approve of us, and I'm constantly afraid of doing anything to make things more difficult for Nick."

"I'd never presume to speak for him, but if I had to guess, I think he'd probably tell you to do whatever works for you and not to worry about how it affects him."

"You're right. He would say that. Okay, let's set up the Saturday photo shoot."

"How would you feel about including the children?"

"That'd be up to them. I'll ask if they'd like to be part of it."

"Let me know what they say. Now, back to the state visit..."

They went over the rest of the details for the next day, which would unfold with military-like precision. Everything was planned down to the minute.

"It's impressive," Sam said when they were done.

"What is?"

"How you all put these things together like it's no big deal."

"We find it impressive that you know how to capture murderers."

"That's easy compared to this."

"We'll have to agree to disagree on that. I'll be right there with you tomorrow to keep things running smoothly, so just relax and try to enjoy an excuse to get dressed up and dance with your handsome husband."

"I'll be able to do that thanks to your amazing work—and Shelby's. Thank you again for filling in for her."

"It is entirely my pleasure."

"Nick proposed to me at the first Canadian state dinner we attended." Sam smiled at the memory of his Rose Garden proposal. "He said, 'At least you can't say I never promised you a rose garden.'"

"I love that, and look at you now, proprietor of the most famous rose garden in the world."

"Life is funny that way." She glanced at the gorgeous watch Nick had given her as an anniversary gift and saw it was after six thirty. "I need to get to work. Thank you for everything, and I'll make sure I'm back in plenty of time to be presentable for tea tomorrow."

"I'll see you then. If you have any questions beforehand, just give me a call."

"Thanks for coming in early—and do not say it was your pleasure, because that's a lie."

Lilia laughed again. "Okay, I won't say it, even though it was. Have a wonderful day."

"You do the same."

Sam left the East Wing and walked to the foyer to meet up with Vernon and Jimmy for the ride to work.

LeRoy, one of the butlers, was waiting with the coat she'd given him before she went to meet with Lilia. He held it for her.

"Thank you, LeRoy."

"My pleasure, ma'am. You have a nice day now."

"You, too."

As she stepped into the chilly morning, where the sun was just starting to make its appearance, she was thankful for the warm, cozy SUV that awaited her. "Morning, fellas."

"Good morning." Vernon's morning-person peppiness would've irritated her if she didn't like him so much. "How are you on this fine day?"

"Just ducky after a six o'clock meeting with my chief of staff."

"Ouch." Vernon and Jimmy knew of her disdain for mornings.

"You said it. Big doings around here this week. Apparently, I'm expected to be the first lady for a few hours."

Jimmy coughed to cover a laugh.

If they ever wrote a memoir about her, she'd be so screwed.

On the way to HQ, she perused the headlines in the copy of the *Washington Star* that Vernon always had waiting for her. Most days, she didn't bother looking at news that stressed her out, especially when it was critical of Nick. Today, she wanted to know what was being said about the Forrester murder.

The banner headline read U.S. ATTORNEY FORRESTER REMEMBERED FOR ETHICAL APPROACH TO JOB. She read Darren's story about Forrester's tenure as the local and federal prosecutor for the nation's capital. He'd interviewed more than twenty people who'd worked closely with him, including Faith Miller, several other Assistant USAs and Chief Farnsworth.

"Tom was an outstanding prosecutor who was able to see things from every point of view," the chief had said. "He was a tremendous supporter of law enforcement and of my department. We'll miss him tremendously."

A second story discussed how rare the murder of a U.S. Attorney was. "Federal prosecutors risk tremendous exposure in their roles," AG Cox said. "We've been fortunate as a nation to lose only a few of them to violence. The loss of Tom Forrester is heartbreaking on so many levels, as he was a longtime friend and close colleague. I've made the full resources of the Justice Department available to our partners at the Metro PD to ensure his killer is quickly brought to justice. In addition, we've ramped up security for all the hardworking U.S. Attorneys who help to keep our country safe by putting criminals in jail where they belong."

Tough talk from the AG, Sam thought, and his comments put added pressure on her and her team to quickly identify a suspect. She was also intrigued to learn that Cox called Forrester a longtime friend. Why hadn't he told her that?

She sent a text to Darren. *Nice job on the Forrester story. He was one of the good guys.*

Glad you liked it. Any scoops for me?

Haven't even had coffee yet. Stand down.

Hope springs eternal.

Amused by Darren, she took a call from Freddie. "Morning."

"Hey, how's it going?"

"As well as it ever does at this hour. I'll be there in a few."

"I wanted to let you know I did the deep dive on Forrester's relationship with Cox and discovered they go way back. Like, all the way to Yale Law School. They worked together as young prosecutors in New York for six years after graduation and then in corporate law before they moved back to the public sector around the same time. Cox was the managing partner at a corporate law firm before he was tapped by Nelson to be his AG. Forrester was a partner at the same firm when he left to become U.S. Attorney."

"Very interesting."

"I thought so, too. I wondered why he didn't mention to us that he's been close to Forrester for twenty-five years."

"That's a very good question. Also, it seems unusual to have an AG taken from the corporate ranks with only six years' experience in the trenches. Aren't they usually career prosecutors?"

"I think, like many things in this town, the political implications often take precedence over experience."

"True. Good work, Freddie."

"Thanks. See you soon."

Sam closed her phone and sat back to pick over the facts of the case thus far. Whenever she suspected there was more to a story, there usually was. Cox had held back with them yesterday, despite vowing to do whatever he could to find Forrester's killer. She would find out why he'd done that, even if it meant tangling with her husband's AG.

CHAPTER SEVEN

"I want to see Aaron," Sam said to Freddie and Gonzo when she arrived in the pit. Aaron Peterson was one of Congressman Bryant's security guards who'd been charged in the murder of Zachery Calder, another of Bryant's guys. They'd made it look like Zachery was Bryant's son Randy. The scheme—and their stupidity—boggled the mind. "Is he still downstairs?"

"Let me check." Gonzo went to his computer. "He couldn't make bail, so he's due to be moved to Laurel later today to await trial."

"Bring him up."

"I'll go," Freddie said.

"What're you thinking?" Gonzo asked Sam.

"That someone charged in a murder plot might be willing to deal on what he knows about the congressman, the U.S. Attorney and possibly the AG."

"True. Should we include Faith as the USA assigned to Aaron's case?"

"Yes, let's get her over here."

"On it. What else can I do today?"

"Get the three detectives they assigned to us up to speed and give them assignments?"

"Will do. We've got tons of data from the phones and computers to review. I'll put them on that."

When Faith arrived twenty minutes later, they briefed her on their plan to speak to Aaron.

"He may want something in return for info," Sam said. "How do you feel about dealing with him?"

"If the information he gives us leads to an arrest in Tom's case, I'd be inclined to give him something in exchange. But only if the info is good."

"Let's see what he has to say."

"He's in interview one," Freddie said.

"You want to come in with me?" Sam asked Faith.

"I think I should observe for now. I'm walking a fine line between personal and professional with this case."

"I get it." Tom had been a friend as well as her boss, and his case presented a variety of complicated concerns for her and others on their team. Sam left her at the door to observation and went with Freddie into the room where Aaron awaited them.

He had the muscular build of an ex-linebacker, or some other football position that required a lot of bulk. His blond hair was cut short, and he registered no reaction when they entered the room.

"I'm Lieutenant Holland. I believe you've met my partner, Detective Cruz."

"I have." He looked from her to Freddie and then back to her. "I thought I was getting transferred today."

"You are, but we wanted to talk to you first."

"What about?"

"Tom Forrester."

"I already told Cruz and the other cop, Gonzales, that I didn't know him. I babysat the family at the hotel, but I didn't have anything to do with him."

"Did you ever hear Congressman Bryant talk about him?"

"I heard Bryant railing about the campaign finance investigation a few times. Why do you care about him anyway? He got his family back, right?"

"Yes, but he was murdered."

That seemed to surprise Aaron, who sat up straighter. "What? When?"

"Early yesterday morning."

"I was in here then."

"I'm aware."

His gaze darted between her and Freddie. "Are you looking at Bryant for that?"

"Among others."

"Bryant doesn't have the balls to kill anyone, especially someone like Forrester. Besides, wasn't he locked up, too?"

"Would he order it done?"

"Possibly, but that wouldn't stop the investigation. Cox would just assign someone else to it."

Sam's antenna perked at the casual mention of Cox. "Do you know the AG?"

"I met him a couple of times. The congressman was friendly with him."

Isn't that interesting? "Friendly in what way?"

"The AG came to his weekly poker game, and they caught a few Feds games over the summer. That kind of thing."

A tingle attacked Sam's backbone, which happened any time she started to feel like she was on to something major in an investigation. "Did Tom Forrester ever come to the poker nights or baseball games?"

"A few times, here and there. Not as often as Cox, though. He and Bryant are tight."

Sam was outraged that Cox hadn't mentioned any of this to her and anxious over what she might have to do about it. How was it possible that her husband's AG might figure prominently in a murder investigation? What a freaking nightmare that could turn out to be.

"If Cox was so tight with Bryant, why do you suppose he asked Forrester to investigate Bryant's campaign finance irregularities?"

"I have no idea."

"How long had Bryant and Cox been tight?"

"As long as I worked for Bryant, so for more than five years."

"Had they become closer recently?"

Aaron thought about that for a second. "Yeah, I guess they

had. Cox was definitely around more. I remember thinking that for someone with such a big job, he sure had a lot of free time to chill with Bryant."

Sam was detecting something rotten. "Is there anything else you can tell us about Bryant, Cox and Forrester?"

"Just that there was a big argument among the three of them right before shit got real with Forrester's family and all that."

"Did you overhear the argument?"

"Not the specifics. Just the raised voices. Forrester and Cox left together and were visibly pissed."

"Did you see them together again after that?"

"No. The next day, Bryant told us to pick up Forrester's family and make them comfortable in a hotel. We were told to make it look like the order had come from Forrester because he was concerned for their safety."

Son of a bitch, Sam thought. *Cox is in this up to his eyeballs and totally obstructed their investigation.* "This has been enormously helpful, Aaron."

"I can't help but wonder what might be in it for me."

"I'll confer with the AUSA, who's observing, and see what we can do."

"I'd appreciate that. I'm resigned to doing some time for Zach's murder, but less is more."

"I get it. Detective Cruz, please take Mr. Peterson downstairs."

Freddie cuffed Aaron and escorted him out of the room.

Faith came out of observation.

"So," Sam said. "What do I do about my husband's AG being knee-deep in this?"

"That was going to be my first question."

"This is way above my pay grade. I'm taking it to the chief."

"Good call. Let me know what he has to say."

"How're you holding up, Faith?"

"I'm just... I'm in shock. You know what it's like to lose a close colleague suddenly."

"It's a gut punch." Sam recalled how the shocking loss of Detective Arnold had rocked her squad to its core, especially his partner, Gonzo.

"Yes, that's it exactly."

"What are you thinking for Peterson?"

"I'll put in a word for him at sentencing, but that's all I can really do since he's facing first-degree murder charges."

"Any word on who they're bringing in?" Sam didn't want to use the word *replace* in reference to Tom, and she hoped it wasn't too soon to ask such a thing.

"Haven't heard. I'll let you know when I do."

Sam gave her friend a spontaneous hug. "I'm here for you guys as a friend if there's anything I can do."

Faith returned the embrace. "Thank you. I'm glad you're speaking at the funeral. Tom would love that."

"You think so? I always suspected he thought of me as a headache more than anything."

"That was only when you pushed one of your fellow officers down the stairs and Tom had to deal with it."

"Ramsey totally deserved it." The disgusting SVU detective had said Sam had gotten what she deserved after Stahl wrapped her in razor wire and threatened to set her on fire. She had zero regrets about pushing him down the stairs, even if she'd come perilously close to losing her career over it.

Faith pulled back, smiling. "Yes, he did, and Tom thought the world of you. We all do. We think it's amazing you're still pounding the pavement when you could be doing anything you wanted."

"I'm doing what I want right here and trying to keep the other gig going at the same time." She wrinkled her nose. "I have to host a tea for the Canadian prime minister's wife tomorrow."

Faith made a visible effort not to laugh.

"If you laugh, I'll throat-punch you, grief or no grief."

Despite Sam's empty threat, Faith's lips quivered from her effort to hold back. "Do you drink tea?"

"No! I have no clue what even goes on at a tea."

"You're about to find out."

"Don't remind me."

"Will there be pictures from the tea? Asking for a friend."

"Have your fun. I'm off to talk to the chief about murder. That,

I know. Tea? Not so much." Sam left Faith laughing, which was a relief. These cases were tough enough when they didn't involve devastated colleagues who were trying to do their jobs amid terrible grief.

Outside the chief's office, Sam stopped to speak to his admin, Helen. "May I have a minute with him?"

"He's got a meeting in ten, but he's free right now."

"Thanks, Helen."

"You're welcome."

Sam knocked on the door to Chief Farnsworth's office and went in to find him stretching behind his desk.

"One meeting after another today."

"Not sure how you stand that."

He huffed out a laugh. "I can't stand it. I miss doing what you do."

"And you wonder why I never want to be promoted?"

"I don't wonder why. What can I do for you, Lieutenant?"

"I'm in a bit of a pickle."

"What now?"

"You say that like I'm always in a pickle."

His amused expression said it all. "What's the pickle *this* time?"

Sam took a seat in one of the chairs by his desk. "I'm picking up the scent of the Attorney General being part of the Forrester case."

"As in the Attorney General of the United States?"

"The one and only."

"Damn. When you do a pickle, you do it up big."

Sam smiled at her beloved, honorary uncle. "You know my motto. Go big or go home. I'm honestly not sure how to proceed with this. There's an obvious conflict of interest with me being involved with the investigation of my husband's AG."

"The pickle of all pickles."

"Indeed."

Farnsworth picked up his desk extension. "Would you please ask Jake to come in? Thank you, Helen."

"What's your thought?" Sam asked.

"To let Jake take the lead on paper while you continue to work the case."

"I like how you think."

"I figured you would."

Malone came in, seeming annoyed.

"What's wrong?" Farnsworth asked his friend.

"If people would just *do their freaking jobs*, nothing would be wrong."

"Who's pissing you off?"

"Most of them," Malone said.

"Yikes," Sam said.

"Not you or your team. You guys could teach the masterclass on how not to piss off the captain on a daily basis."

"Thank you. I think."

"By the way, I wanted to tell you that the Javier Lopez hearing has been pushed back a couple of weeks, so that's one less thing this week." He was charged in the fifteen-year-old murder of teenager Calvin Worthington. That'd been one of the cases Stahl had barely bothered to investigate, which Sam had solved in one afternoon.

"I'll take one less thing. Has his mother been notified of the delay?" Sam hated that for Lenore, who'd already waited far too long for justice in her son's case.

"Yes, I called her myself."

"Thank you."

"Anyway, what's going on?" Malone asked. "Helen said you wanted to see me?"

Farnsworth gestured for Sam to brief the captain on the situation with Cox.

Malone stared at her. "Holy..."

"Our thoughts exactly," Farnsworth said. "I'd like to make you the lead—on paper, anyway—and let Sam's team continue to pursue the investigation wherever it may lead."

"Do you think he was involved with Forrester's murder?" Malone asked.

"I don't know yet. Bryant's guy Aaron Peterson told us Cox was far more involved with Bryant on a personal level than he indicated to me when I talked to him. He held back on that, which is a huge red flag. Her was also quoted in the paper this morning as being a longtime friend of Forrester's, which he also never mention. Another red flag."

"For sure," Malone said.

"I have a thought... Tomorrow night is the state dinner at the White House. The cabinet usually attends. If I get a minute, I'll approach Cox in the social setting and let on that I know all about how he was buddies with Forrester and how they argued the last time they were together, after which Forrester's family was kidnapped. I'll see how he reacts to that."

"I don't know, Sam." The chief rubbed his chin as he considered that. "What if he gets angry?"

"What's he going to do to the first lady in the middle of a state dinner?"

"That's true, Joe. I think it's a good idea. Bring it up in a social situation to get a read on him."

"Proceed with caution, Lieutenant," Farnsworth said. "We're already under tremendous pressure to turn this case over to the FBI."

"Which would be a huge mistake if Cox is somehow involved," Sam said, since the FBI fell under the Attorney General's jurisdiction.

Farnsworth massaged his temples. "I can't wait until this shit is no longer my problem."

His words struck fear in Sam's heart. She didn't want to think about the day when he'd no longer be the chief. "Please don't leave me here by myself." Her gaze took in both men.

"You wouldn't be alone," Malone said. "Jeannie is deputy chief now."

"I can't imagine doing this job without either of you."

"We're getting old, pal," Farnsworth said with a small smile. "And running out of gas to deal with the nonstop bullshit."

To her great dismay, Sam's eyes suddenly flooded with tears. Was there anything worse than crying on the job, especially as a woman in a largely male profession? She took a deep breath and tried to get her emotions under control. "I'm sorry. Of course you should do whatever you feel is best. I just hope you know that despite all the bullshit, you're both loved and respected by the people who work for you, and you'd be deeply missed."

"That's very nice to hear, Sam," Farnsworth said. "Your loyalty doesn't go unnoticed. You should also know that we've more or less decided to stick it out for the three years that your husband is president, so we can be here to protect you to the best of our ability."

For a hot second, she was too flabbergasted to respond. "Seriously?"

"Very seriously," Malone said. "Skip would want us here as you endeavor to do something no first lady in history has ever done."

"You guys..." Tears spilled down her cheeks as she tried fruitlessly to manage them. "I don't know what to say."

"You don't have to say anything," Farnsworth said. "He'd do the same for us, and you know it."

"Stop." She laughed as she wiped away tears that wouldn't quit. "You're wrecking me."

The chief smiled. "We don't want you to worry about us leaving on top of everything else. We're sticking it out for you, kid."

"Please don't do anything stupid like die before you can enjoy a long retirement, do you hear me?"

They laughed.

"We'll do our best to stay healthy," Malone said.

"Thank you," she said softly. "You'll never know what this means to me."

"We know," Farnsworth said. "Family takes care of family."

As her chin quivered, she nodded. "God, I'm such an idiot, bawling like a baby over here."

"We won't tell anyone," Malone said. "We wouldn't want to ruin your reputation as a badass."

She laughed again as she wiped away more tears. "Gee, thanks."

"Don't eff up this situation with Cox, or we'll all be out on our asses," Malone said.

"I'll try not to." She took a couple of deep breaths to recover her composure after they'd flattened her with their news. "What are we hearing from Stahl's?"

Malone shook his head and released a deep sigh. "Thirteen bodies at his house, and we're getting closer to finding the owner of the storage unit. Charles and O'Brien are making progress, so I told them to stay on it."

"That's fine. Gonzo is working with the three detectives you assigned to get them up to speed and give them assignments."

"Let's keep up the pressure on Forrester," Farnsworth said. "I'll authorize whatever overtime is needed."

"That'll help, thank you. Although, I should mention I'm leaving at two tomorrow to meet with the Canadian prime minister's wife and to prepare for the state dinner."

"We're looking forward to that," Farnsworth said, smiling. "Marti and I can't believe we're invited to the White House."

"Same with me and Val. Unbelievable."

"Believe it. I'll see you there." She'd also invited every member of her squad and their partners, as well as Jeannie and Michael, her sisters, mother and stepmother. Lindsey would be there as Terry's date, which meant all her closest friends would be in attendance, except for Shelby and Avery.

For the first time, she started to look forward to an event that had loomed as yet another challenge to be endured rather than enjoyed. She needed to change her attitude and do a better job of appreciating the perks that came along with the many headaches. "I'll get back to it and keep you posted on all things Cox." She paused as she realized what she'd said. "And that's not a sentence I ever imagined saying to the two of you."

She left them laughing as she went back to the pit, overwhelmed by what they were doing for her and filled with love for two men who'd been part of her life from the beginning. They were right. Her dad would want them there for her during this unprecedented time, and their support meant everything.

"Everything all right?" Freddie asked when she returned to the pit, wearing obvious signs that she'd been crying.

"All good in the hood. What's up here?"

He gave her a curious look that told her he wasn't satisfied with her answer. "We met with Lucas, Harper and Coheeny to get them up to speed. They've gone to interview the rest of Forrester's staff, and then they'll be back to comb through the phone data. Gonzo asked them to submit a written report by four thirty."

"Excellent."

"I've gone through everything I could find about Forrester and Cox from the time they were at Yale Law, and I've pieced together an interesting narrative."

"Oh," Sam said, "do tell."

CHAPTER EIGHT

Freddie led her into the conference room, where he'd put together a timeline on one of the big dry-erase boards.

"First, tell me what's wrong."

Sam closed the door. "You have to keep it between us."

"Okay."

"The chief and captain told me they're planning to postpone retirement for the three years Nick is in office so they can have my back here."

"Oh wow. That's amazing."

"I know, right? They wrecked me when they said that's what family does for family."

"I love it. I'm so glad they're doing that."

"Me, too. It means the world to me, but it caught me by surprise, thus the tears that pissed me off. Now, tell me about this interesting narrative."

"Cox and Forrester met at UPenn as undergrads and pledged Lambda Chi Alpha together. Cox was later president to Forrester's vice president."

Sam became more furious with every new detail added to the puzzle. "Did he honestly think we wouldn't find out that they go way back?"

"He probably thought we'd take his word for it as the AG."

"That was a miscalculation on his part. What else have you got?"

"After college and law school at Yale, they were spent six years working in the New York City DA's office before being hired by the same New York City corporate law firm, where they spent the next fifteen years making small fortunes. Forrester was appointed U.S. Attorney twelve years ago, and Nelson tapped Cox to be his AG as part of his original cabinet. He left the firm as the managing partner."

Freddie added news articles to the board that had banner headlines about the untested attorney who'd been given the role of top law enforcement officer. "There was a huge uproar over Cox's appointment as he'd spent far more time in corporate law than criminal."

"I remember this vaguely now that you mention it." Before she'd gotten back together with Nick, she hadn't paid much attention to politics.

"Despite the controversy, Cox settled into the job, hired a team of well-regarded prosecutors and has earned mostly high marks during his tenure."

"Something about this whole thing stinks, and I can't figure out what or why."

"Agree."

"Let's go see Bryant again and see what he can tell us about this unholy alliance."

As they were headed for the morgue exit, paramedics came rushing in.

"What the hell?" Sam watched as they sped into the morgue and then took off running in that direction herself, nearly slamming into Dr. Byron Tomlinson as he came out through the morgue's automatic doors. "What's going on?"

"Lindsey collapsed."

"Is she okay?"

Byron seemed rattled, which did nothing to calm Sam's nerves. He was a doctor, for crying out loud. "I called for EMS when she didn't come to."

"Should I call Terry?"

"I would."

"Find out where they're taking her."

Byron nodded to show he'd heard her.

Sam did not want to call Terry with this news. Her hands were less than steady as she found his number in her contacts.

"Hey, Sam. What's up?"

"Terry... Ah, Lindsey collapsed at work, and they're taking her to..."

"GW," Byron said.

"GW ER."

"Oh my God."

"I don't know anything more than EMS is here preparing to transport her."

"Thanks for calling. I'll get right over there. Let me know if you hear anything else."

"I will." She closed her phone. "He'll meet her there."

When the paramedics rolled Lindsey out of the morgue, Sam was struck by how incredibly pale she was. The urgency with which the EMS team moved only added to her anxiety.

"I'll go with her," Byron said. "And keep you informed."

"Thank you." Sam called Captain Malone. "Lindsey collapsed in the morgue. EMS just transported her to the hospital."

"Oh no."

"Byron is going with her and will keep us in the loop. I also called Terry."

"Let me know what you hear."

"Will do. I was on my way to speak to Bryant again, but now I'm not sure what I should do."

"Go deal with Bryant. There's nothing you can do for Lindsey. She's in the best possible hands."

"You're right. It's just..."

"I know, Sam. It's upsetting, but I'm sure she'll be fine."

Sam hoped to hell he was right.

FOR A FULL MINUTE after ending the call with Sam, Terry stared at the far wall of his office, filled with dread. He'd known something was off and had encouraged Lindsey to call out of work so she could rest. The Stahl investigation had tapped her and her team to their utmost limits as they worked in concert with the FBI lab to identify victims.

He'd nearly had her convinced to take a break when Forrester was murdered, and all thoughts of rest and relaxation were forgotten.

She liked to say, "Murder waits for no one, except the medical examiner."

He understood that making light of the job helped her get through the grim tasks required of her.

He forced himself to get up, to move toward the door, to notify his lead agent that he needed a ride to GW and to walk to the Oval to tell Nick he was leaving. The admin outside the office waved him in.

Terry knocked and entered the room.

Nick was seated behind the Resolute Desk and looked up when Terry came in. "Hey, I was just going to buzz you about—"

"Nick."

"What's wrong?" He stood. "Did something happen to Sam?"

"No, to Lindsey. She collapsed at work. They're taking her to GW."

"Go," Nick said. "I'd come with you if it wouldn't cause a circus."

Terry heard what Nick said but couldn't make himself move due to intense fear. "I knew something was wrong, but she said she was fine. She wasn't. What'll I do if..."

Nick came around the desk and put his hands on Terry's shoulders. "She's young and healthy and probably caught a virus that's going around. You need to go to her. She'll be looking for you."

Terry nodded. "She's my reason, you know?"

"I do know. I get it. She needs you to be strong for her. Why don't we see if Harry can go with you?" Nick went back to the desk, picked up the extension and asked for Dr. Flynn. "Hey, Lindsey collapsed at work, and Terry is heading to GW. Do you think you could..." Nick nodded. "Thank you." He hung up. "He'll meet you in the lobby."

"Thank you."

"Don't let your mind run away with you. Get over there and figure out what she needs."

"I'm going."

"Terry..."

He turned back.

"If you feel the need to drink, please call your sponsor."

"I will."

"Promise me."

"I promise."

As he left the Oval and walked toward the lobby to meet Harry, Terry told himself this wasn't about him. It was about Lindsey. But there was no him without her, so he took Nick's warning to heart. It'd been two years since he'd been tempted to drink. He was so far removed from that life now it seemed like his spiral into alcoholism had happened to someone else. He tended faithfully to his sobriety with daily meetings. He never missed a day. He could only hope that all the work he'd put in would hold him up during whatever crisis might be awaiting him at the hospital.

Harry was in the lobby when Terry got there and came over to hug him. "Whatever it is, we'll deal with it and get her back on her feet, okay?"

"Yeah. Okay. Thanks for coming."

"Of course."

Terry's Secret Service detail used lights and sirens to convey them quickly to the hospital. While Terry was thankful for the expediency, it only added to the anxiety bubbling up inside him. He needed to notify Lindsey's mother and his parents, but he decided to wait to make those calls until he knew more.

"What can I do?" Harry asked after a long silence.

"Tell me she's fine and whatever happened is nothing to worry about."

"I hope I can tell you that very soon."

What if it was bad? What would he do?

"Try not to spin yourself into worst-case, Terry. It won't help."

"Trying."

How the hell long did it take to get to GW with the Secret Service blazing a trail? Too long. By the time they arrived, he was nearly paralyzed with fear.

"Come on." Harry gave him a push to get him moving. "Let's go see how she is."

One of Terry's agents escorted them inside, where they met up with Byron Tomlinson.

"Anything?"

"Not yet."

That Byron looked rattled did nothing to assuage Terry's nerves.

His agents asked for a private room where Terry could wait for news.

"Right this way," one of the nurses said.

Terry could tell that they wondered who he was to warrant such measures, but as Harry and Byron followed him into the room, he didn't have the energy to tell the nurses he was chief of staff to the president.

"I'll send Dr. Anderson in to speak with you."

"Thank you."

"Anderson is the best," Harry said. "He's a great friend of Sam's from all her many trips to the ER."

"That's good to know."

Terry appreciated Harry trying to keep his spirits up, but the panic intensified with every minute that passed in that small, airless room.

A quick knock on the door was the only warning they got that the doctor had arrived. "I'm Dr. Anderson, an ER attending physician."

"Terry O'Connor. I'm..." He could barely speak around the gigantic lump of fear in his throat. "Lindsey's fiancé."

Anderson shook hands with Terry, Byron and Harry. "Good to see you, Dr. Flynn."

"How is she?" Harry asked.

"We're rerunning her blood work, as it came back a little off. As soon as we have more info, I'll be back to update you."

He wanted to ask what *off* meant but was afraid he wouldn't want to know. "Is she awake? Could I be with her?"

"She's resting right now, but I'll get you in to see her soon."

Harry followed the doctor out of the room and closed the door.

Terry stared at that door until it opened again. "What did he say?"

"Nothing." Harry's furrowed brows put Terry on alert.

"Please tell me."

"They don't know anything for certain yet. It's better to wait for the test results to come back."

"Tell me, Harry. What do they think it is?"

"It could be anything from anemia to leukemia."

Byron gasped.

Terry felt as if a trapdoor had opened under him and sucked him into a deep, dark abyss. "That's n-not possible. She's perfectly healthy." Or she had been, until lately.

Harry put a hand on Terry's shoulder. "Let's wait and see what they find out."

The fact that Harry looked worried only added to the tsunami of anxiety and dread building in Terry.

"I need to see her."

"He said he'd be back for you as soon as he could," Harry said.

Terry sat and dropped his head into his hands, wanting to wail at the thought of her being seriously ill. They were due to be married in a few short months. There couldn't be anything wrong with her.

There just couldn't be.

ON THE WAY to Bryant's home, Sam watched her phone, hoping for an update on Lindsey.

"You don't think it's anything bad, do you?" Freddie asked.

"I have no idea, but she has been feeling off lately."

"She was so pale when they wheeled her out. Even her lips were pale."

"I saw that, too."

The BlackBerry she used to communicate with Nick buzzed in her pocket. She retrieved it to find a text from Nick asking if she'd heard anything about Lindsey.

Nothing yet, but she was scary pale when they took her out of HQ. Is Terry with her?

Hate to hear that, and yes, he left about twenty minutes ago. Harry is with him.

That's good. That'll help.

Let me know if you hear anything.

I will. You too.

"Terry and Harry are at the hospital." Sam put the BlackBerry back in her pocket. "I've completely forgotten where we're going or why." She hadn't been this rattled since the morning they found her brother-in-law Spencer unresponsive at Camp David.

"To see Bryant about the connection between Cox and Forrester and anything else he can tell us."

"Right."

Sam checked her watch. "I have to be back to HQ at three thirty for a dress fitting for the state dinner, which has never felt less important than it does now."

"You have to do what you have to do."

"It feels wrong to be thinking about something so stupid as a dress fitting when Tom is in the morgue and Lindsey's in the hospital."

"You know how she is. No muss, no fuss. She'd want you to do your thing and not worry about her."

"That's impossible." Over the last few years of working closely together, Lindsey McNamara had become one of Sam's closest and dearest friends.

They arrived at Bryant's Adams Morgan home and rang the bell. After a few minutes passed with no sign of him, Freddie rang the bell again and then pounded on the door.

"Police, open up."

"Do we have a number for him?"

"I think so."

"Find it and call it."

Freddie got busy on his phone. "Gonzo is texting it to me." After he made the call, he put the phone on speaker. It rang several times before Bryant answered with a grunt.

"Police at your door. Open up."

"I'm not saying another word to you without my lawyer present. I know what you're trying to do."

"That's too bad, because we might've been able to offer you some help later if you were to return the favor now."

"What kind of help?"

"That depends on the quality of the info you provide."

"I'll be down in a minute."

"Make it a quick minute. We're in a hurry."

Four minutes later, Sam's head was about to blow off her neck. "Where the hell is he?"

Freddie pounded on the door again as he looked through the glass on the right side of the door. "He's going out the back!"

They took off running, going in opposite directions toward the back of the block-long building.

Sam was aware of one of her Secret Service agents running after her, but she didn't take the time to figure out which one. Her chest and legs burned from the effort, proving she'd fallen badly out of shape while dining on White House cuisine. She rounded the corner and slammed head-on into Bryant, who was running even faster than she was. The impact sent both of them flying.

She managed to grab his shirt before she landed hard on her right hand, crying out from the pain that radiated from wrist to shoulder. Part of him had connected with her left cheek, which hurt like the devil as she forced herself to keep her wits about her, to grab her cuffs, to get them on him and then to try to catch her breath while managing a hand that didn't want to work the way it was supposed to.

And then a sharp pain from the vicinity of her hip registered, overtaking every other concern. If she'd rebroken her recently healed hip, she would kill Bryant with her bare hands.

CHAPTER NINE

S he wasn't sure how long she sat on top of Bryant, struggling to breathe, before Freddie appeared. When he saw her sitting on top of the congressman, he stepped up his pace.

"Look at you. I called for backup. Should be here any second."

Sam glanced up at him.

He gasped. "You're hurt."

"Nah, I'm fine."

"Your face is bleeding."

She reached up to see what he was talking about and came away with bloodstained fingers. "Son of a bitch." Why did these things always have to happen right before a big event? Never failed.

"This is police brutality!" Bryant shouted.

"Shut up. You ran from us. Why'd you do that?"

"Cuz I've got nothing to say to you."

Sam moved carefully to get up, waving off Freddie's offer of help. Searing pain from her hip had her biting back a gasp.

"What happened to your hand?" Freddie asked.

"Nothing. Why?"

"It's bleeding and hanging like it's broken."

"It's not broken."

"Are you sure about that?"

"Nope."

"Sam..."

"Let's get him back to HQ so we can ask our questions."

Bryant resisted Freddie's attempt to walk him toward the corner, where an MPD cruiser awaited. "I want my lawyer! You'll regret treating me this way. I'm still a United States congressman!"

Sam gave him a scathing look. "Tell it to the judge."

SHE LIMPED TOWARD THE SUV, feeling more certain with every step that she'd reinjured her hip and that her wrist might be broken. But she didn't have time to deal with any of that right now.

Vernon greeted her with a first aid kit in hand. He took one look at her and withdrew gauze and ointment. "Take a seat."

She moved carefully, gasping when her backside connected with the leather seat.

"What's the story?" Vernon asked as he dabbed at her face.

Hissing, she recoiled. "What the hell was that? Battery acid?"

"That's exactly what it was. How'd you guess?"

"Most of the time, I appreciate your sarcasm. This is not one of those times."

"Do you need the ER?"

"No."

"Hold up your arm."

"I don't want to."

"Sam."

"Vernon."

"I'm required to notify my supervisor that the first lady has been injured."

"If you do that, I'll never speak to you again."

"Yes, you will."

"I won't."

"Sam."

"Vernon! I have a fitting for my dress for tomorrow night that I can't miss at three thirty. In addition, I've got the entire Federal Bureau of Investigation breathing down my neck to get their sweaty paws on the Forrester case. I've got to make something happen *today*, or we're going to lose control of this thing."

"Might I point out that you have your very own physician on staff at home who could meet us at HQ to tend to your injuries while you tend to your work?"

"Yes, you may point that out to me."

"And might you speak to me again if I were to notify Dr. Flynn that his services are needed by the first lady at her place of employment?"

Sam gave him a side-eyed look to gauge whether he was trying not to laugh. "Are you managing me, by any chance?"

"Would I do that?"

"Yes, I believe you would."

"Shall I reach out to Dr. Flynn?"

"Yes."

"Was that so hard?"

"Learn to quit while you're ahead."

"My wife has been saying that to me for thirty years."

"I'd think you would've learned by now."

"Learned what?" Freddie asked when he joined them.

"How to quit while he's ahead."

"What'd you do, Vernon? Suggest she might need the ER or something?"

"Or something. I'll make that call now and get you back to the office ASAP."

After Vernon stepped back, Freddie said, "What was that about?"

"He's getting Harry to come to HQ to deal with... this." She used her chin to gesture to the injured hand.

"That's a good idea."

"I have to be there for that fitting." She looked up at him. "I know it's so stupid, but he hardly asks me for anything. This is important."

"Yes, it is, and it's not stupid."

"Compared to finding the person who killed Tom, it is."

"Different kinds of important."

"Dr. Flynn is at the ER with Dr. McNamara, but he agreed to meet you since her fiancé is there with her."

"Now I feel like shit because Terry and Lindsey need him more than I do."

Vernon glanced at the hand sitting awkwardly on her lap. "I'm not sure that's true."

Sam hoped her glare spoke for her. "Do *not* tell my husband about this—or tell anyone who'll tell him. He's busy."

"Yes, ma'am."

He waited for her to turn to put her legs in the car—and *holy shit, that hurt*—before he closed the door and got in the driver's side.

"That was an awesome takedown, Sam," Jimmy said when they were on the way to HQ.

"I got lucky when I crashed into him."

"Did you, though?" Freddie asked.

"I kept him from getting away. That's what matters."

Freddie gave her a concerned look. "I really hope it's nothing serious."

As pain radiated from her hip, she was filled with dread that it might be very serious. No way did she have time to deal with that —again.

TERRY FELT like a bear trapped in a cage as he paced the length of that small room at least a thousand times.

Harry took a call. "Yes, I can meet her there in thirty minutes." He turned to Terry. "Sam's been injured on the job. I'm meeting her at HQ."

"Why not here?"

"She says she doesn't have time—and she doesn't want Nick to know about it yet. Call me when you hear from the doctor."

"How much longer do I have to wait to see Lindsey?"

The door opened to Dr. Anderson. "You can come in, Mr. O'Connor."

Terry took off toward the door and nearly knocked the doctor over in his haste.

Harry stayed with him while they went into Lindsey's exam room.

Upon seeing her, Terry was filled with dread. He'd never seen her so pale.

She held out a hand to him.

He went to her and took hold of her cold hand.

"Sorry to scare you."

"I'm fine if you're fine." He glanced toward Anderson, who was typing on a computer terminal. "What're we dealing with, Doc?"

"Lindsey is extremely anemic, which is concerning. We're trying to figure out what's going on."

"Is that why I've been so tired?"

"Definitely."

"Have you been sick at all in the last few months?"

"I had a weird virus a few weeks ago that included a high fever for several days."

"How many days?"

She looked to Terry. "Most of a week."

Terry nodded.

"That's good to know," Anderson said. "It's possible you wiped out your red blood cells fighting that off."

"That can happen?"

"Sure can."

"I like that better than leukemia," Lindsey said.

"I do, too. Let me dig into the blood work a little deeper."

"Can I go home?"

"I want to keep you overnight so we can get to the bottom of what's going on."

That wasn't what she wanted to hear.

Terry wanted her right there with people who knew what they were doing. "You're in the best place to figure out what's we're dealing with, Linds."

Her eyes filled with tears. "We've got the state dinner tomorrow."

"There'll be others."

"Terry's right," Harry said. "Let Dr. Anderson run some tests and get to the bottom of this so we can get you feeling better."

Lindsey nodded and used a tissue Terry gave her to wipe away tears that further rattled Terry's already-shredded nerves. His Lindsey rarely shed a tear. In fact, she teased him about being moved by movies and TV shows that had no effect on her. He said she'd breathed too much formaldehyde fumes at work and had gone numb.

He loved that they had their own language and inside jokes. His relationship with her was like nothing he'd experienced before, a connection so deep, she was truly a part of him.

"Whatever you're thinking, knock it off," she said when they were alone in her room.

Harry had left to see to Sam, and the doctor had promised to return shortly.

"I'm not allowed to think about how much I love you?"

"Oh, that's perfectly permissible."

"I thought it might be."

"Hey."

He looked up at her. "Hey, what?"

"Stop spinning. I'm okay."

"Can't help the spinning."

"Don't let it lead to the dark places, you hear me?"

"I hear you."

"Whatever this is, we'll figure it out and move on."

He couldn't get the word *leukemia* out of his mind. What would they do if she had something like that?

"Terry. *Stop.*"

"Don't worry about me. This isn't about me."

"Of course it is. It's about both of us, but I can't focus on getting well if I'm worried about you. This is such a big week for you—"

"Don't even think about that. I'm not."

"How can you not be?"

He'd been working twelve-hour days for weeks preparing for the Canadian state visit to make sure everything went perfectly for Nick. "It hasn't crossed my mind since I heard you were in an ambulance."

His work phone rang with a call from Nick.

"Take it," Lindsey said.

He released her hand to fish the phone out of his suit coat pocket. "Mr. President."

"How is she, Terry?"

"Feisty," he said with a smile for his beloved.

"That's always a good thing."

"Yes, sir, it is."

"I met with Derek, and he's on board to see things through tomorrow." Derek Kavanaugh was the deputy chief of staff, who mostly focused on their dealings with Congress. "Take the time you need with Lindsey."

"But—"

"No buts. It's done by executive order."

Terry gave a soft laugh. "I appreciate that, and I'm a phone call away if needed."

"We know how to find you. Take care of your family. Thanks to your preparation, everything will be fine tomorrow."

"Thank you, Mr. President."

"Keep us posted on how she's doing and give her our love."

"I will, sir. Thank you again."

"Anything for family. I'll check on you in the morning."

The line went dead.

He smiled at Lindsey. "Well, I guess you've got yourself a full-time nurse."

"No one I'd rather have."

CHAPTER TEN

By the time they arrived back at HQ, Sam was in serious pain, but made an intense effort to hide that from Freddie, Vernon and Jimmy. She had to push through this day, move the Forrester case along and get ready for tomorrow's first lady duties. In her mind, there was no option other than to forge ahead.

Vernon and Jimmy, who normally remained outside while she was working, led the way into HQ, as if they didn't trust that she'd allow Harry to check her before resuming the investigation.

"What're you guys doing?" she asked them.

"Our jobs," Vernon said.

She gritted her teeth as she walked into the morgue entrance, stopping to confer with Byron. "Any word on Lindsey?"

"Nothing yet. Terry is with her, and they promised to update us later. She asked me to get back here because we're so in the weeds with the Stahl case."

"Keep me in the loop if you hear anything."

"I will."

She left the morgue and continued the trek to the pit, which had never seemed farther away than it did now.

"What's going on?" Freddie asked in a low tone that couldn't be overheard.

"Nothing."

"Sam."

She turned her formidable glare on him. "*Nothing.* End it." Thankfully, he backed off as they reached the pit, where Harry leaned against the wall outside her office, checking his phone.

"Hey," she said. "Thanks for coming by. How's Lindsey?"

He did a quick visual assessment and then frowned. "She's doing okay, but you, on the other hand..."

"Hush. Come in."

With her left hand, she fished her keys out of her right front pants pocket, which wasn't as easy to do as it might seem.

"Jesus, Sam."

"Please... If you care about me at all, don't say another word out here."

He followed her into the office and closed the door.

"I'm up against it, Harry. We've got the Feds trying to take over our investigation, the Canadians coming to town, and there is no way I can be out of commission right now. Can you patch me up until I get through tomorrow?"

"I can try." He reached for a medical bag she hadn't noticed. "Where should we start?"

"The face. Vernon put some stuff on it that stung like a bitch. What else does it need?"

Harry moved in for a closer look. "Possibly a few stitches."

"What's our other option?"

Sighing, he pulled something out of his bag of tricks and applied it to her cheek.

She tried not to flinch.

He handed her an ice pack. "You're going to want to use that to keep it from swelling more than it already has."

"Okay."

"What's next?"

"Um, maybe my arm? Not sure what's up with it."

Harry helped her out of her coat and gasped when he saw her swollen wrist and hand. "Sam, for God's sake. Your wrist could be broken."

"No, it isn't."

"I can't treat that here. You need X-rays and an orthopedic doctor and..."

"Can you treat it at home?"

"Yes, but—"

"Then we'll deal with it there after my tour."

"You can't just walk around with a possibly broken wrist all day."

"Yes, I can. I'll be careful."

"This is crazy, even for you."

"I have a murdered U.S. Attorney who was not only a colleague but a friend. I've got the Canadians coming. *I cannot deal with this right now.*"

"You'll need to be very careful with your hand and wrist until you can get it set. If it's broken, the bone can burst through the skin, causing additional injuries."

Sam nearly fainted at the thought of that happening. "I'll be careful."

"Do you have anything here for pain?"

Sam used her chin to point to the Motrin on her desk.

Harry shook out four pills that he handed to her with an open bottle of water that'd been sitting there for days.

Sam took the pills and chased them with the water, praying they worked to take the edge off.

"I want you to acknowledge that you're acting against medical advice."

"So noted. I'll come straight to you when I get home."

After he'd put something on the road rash on the palm of her hand, which hurt like a mother-effer, he reached into the bag and produced an Ace bandage. "You have to wear this."

"What if I don't want to?"

"I'm not giving you the choice."

Sam again had to grit her teeth to keep from screaming as he wrapped the torture device around her injured wrist.

"Come home as soon as possible so you don't compound the injury."

"I will."

"Anything else?"

"That's it."

"Are you sure?"

She never blinked as she looked him in the eye. "Positive."

"Please be careful."

"I will. Thanks for coming."

"Any time."

"Don't tell Nick about this."

"Don't ask me to keep secrets from my boss and friend."

"I'm your friend, too."

"I won't tell him, but you should. Soon. You know how he feels about you keeping stuff from him."

"I'll tell him when I get home. He's got enough on his plate without worrying about me."

She could tell there was more Harry wanted to say, but he only nodded, grabbed his bag and left the room. If it wouldn't have hurt more than she could bear, she would've removed the Ace bandage the second he was gone.

Freddie came to the door, registered that her hand and arm were wrapped in an Ace bandage, but didn't comment. "We've got some new info from the others. They're ready to brief in the conference room."

"I'll be right there."

"Should you maybe go home?"

"Nope." She gestured for him to move and then followed him into the conference room, trying not to cry from the pain radiating from multiple sources. What did it say about her that taking down one measly suspect caused so many injuries? She was getting old. That's what it said.

A quick glance at the wall clock in the conference room showed she had forty-five minutes until her meeting with Marcus in the morgue. How in the hell had another day gotten so completely away from her?

"What are we hearing about Dr. McNamara?" Gonzo asked.

Sam assumed he was being more formal due to the presence of detectives from outside their squad. "Nothing new yet. Dr. Tomlinson has promised to update us when he hears something. Where's the congressman?"

"He's being booked on new charges," Freddie said.

"I want him in an interrogation room as soon as he's through intake."

"I'll see to that," Freddie said.

He walked out of the room.

"What does everyone else have?" Sam asked.

"Are you all right, Lieutenant?" her friend Detective Erica Lucas asked.

"I'm fine." She used her left hand to encourage them to get on with it.

"I did a thorough review of the autopsy report and found nothing more than what we already know," Gonzo said. "Tom Forrester was killed by a single shot to the head while seated in his car on Constitution Avenue."

Sam wanted to growl in frustration at having to review things they already knew. "What did the text messages on his personal phone reveal?"

"Nothing other than a once-a-day call to his wife at nine p.m. three days in a row during the time they were being detained by Bryant's people." Lucas had shoulder-length dark hair, hazel eyes and the kind of cheekbones other women would kill for. "There was a text from his dentist with an appointment reminder and one from Animal Control in Gaithersburg, checking on the Forrester's dog. I called their office to ask if it's routine to check on a dog injured by another dog and was told that they're required to confirm there's no sign of rabies in either animal. Other than texts from some personal friends talking about mundane things like the upcoming fantasy baseball league draft, there wasn't anything else of note over the last week."

"Thank you for your report," Sam said. "Since it was encrypted, I've turned over Tom's work phone to Agent Hill for FBI analysis."

"We spoke with every member of Forrester's team, one-on-one," Harper said with a gesture to include Coheeny.

Harper had dark hair and eyes and was built like someone who spent a lot of time in the gym. Coheeny was blond and had an aura of insolence about him that immediately put Sam on edge. She had no patience for insolence, attitude, chips on shoulders or whatever his deal was.

"We didn't hear anything helpful," Harper said. "His people loved him and are grief-stricken over his death."

"A lot of tears," Coheeny added.

"We pressed them to talk about cases or situations that might've led to murder, but no one could think of anything specific other than the usual criminal stuff they deal with routinely," Harper said. "But Forrester wasn't directly involved in those cases."

Sam processed the information, looking for threads to pull but not finding any.

Freddie returned to the room. "Bryant is in interview two."

"Thank you," Sam said. "Appreciate the updates, everyone. Let's get back to it."

After the others had left the room, Sam looked to Freddie. "Without making a spectacle of it, push me to interview two in this chair."

"Like, roll you over there?"

"Yes."

Sam could tell he had questions, but thankfully, he did as she asked and guided the office chair out of the conference room and down the hall to interview two. Outside the door, she said, "Stop."

Steeling herself, she rose from the chair, gasping as the pain registered.

"Sam."

She ignored him and waited until she had her bearings so she could open the door and barge into the room with as much moxie as she could muster under the circumstances. Seeing that Bryant had angry-looking road rash on his face made her feel a little better about her own injuries.

He gave her a filthy look. "I'm not saying anything to you without my lawyer here."

"That makes things easier. Detective Cruz, will you make the congressman comfortable downstairs?"

"Yes, ma'am."

She made her way to the door.

"Wait."

She gritted her teeth as she turned back. "What?"

"How long will I be down there?"

"Until your lawyer gets here. Detective Cruz will make the call for you."

"I, uh... My lawyer fired me. I need to find a new one."

"Do you have someone in mind?"

"Not really. Mine came with me from Wisconsin... Been together a long time. I, uh, have no idea who to ask."

"Would you like us to notify the public defender's office for you?"

"God, no."

"Mr. Bryant, do you have the resources to hire your own attorney or not?" Sam took great pleasure in the scowl he directed at her when she didn't address him as Congressman Bryant.

"As I've mentioned, my assets were frozen."

"Then I suppose you'll need to reach out to the PD's office since you can't pay for representation."

"How long will that take?"

"They're often pretty backed up. Could take a few days."

"I want a bail hearing."

"That doesn't happen until we have a conversation and an arraignment, and since you're facing new charges after being released on bail the first time, I wouldn't hold your breath on getting out of here any time soon."

With that, she left Freddie to deal with the congressman, who screamed something at her that she ignored.

She lowered herself to the desk chair and scooted back to her office.

As she rounded the corner into the pit, Captain Malone came toward her, stopping short when he saw her in the chair.

"Dare I even ask?"

"Please don't."

"What the hell happened?"

"Bryant ran from us. I stopped him."

"Do you need the ER?"

"Harry was here, and he checked me out."

Malone gave her a skeptical look. "You should go home, Sam."

"I'm not going home. Too much to do here. We're getting nowhere fast on the Forrester investigation."

"I was coming to ask if you'd be willing to brief the media."

"We have less than nothing. I'll take a beating out there. Give me twenty-four hours."

"What did Bryant have to say?"

"He wants a lawyer, but his assets are frozen, so Freddie is calling the PD."

"So he'll be our guest for a day or two."

"Looks that way. I want him held, pending trial. Who knows where he was going when I crashed into him? If we let him out, he'll disappear."

"I agree."

"I'll talk to Faith."

"How're they holding up?"

"Soldiering through, doing the job, but heartbroken."

"What've you decided to do about Cox?"

"I'm not sure yet. I really needed to talk to Bryant about him before I plan my next move."

Gonzo came to the office door.

"What's up?" Sam asked him.

"Rosemary Bryant and her son, Randy, who was supposed to turn himself in today, have gone dark. Their phones are going straight to voice mail."

"Is it possible they're on a plane?" Malone asked.

"They were booked on a flight early this morning, which landed at DCA on time, right around noon. The Patrol officers I sent to meet them said there was no sign of them. Rosemary knew our officers would be meeting them. I checked with the airline and confirmed they weren't on the flight."

"Shit," Sam said. "Should we call in the marshals?"

"I already left a message for Jesse Best," Gonzo said, referring to the agent in charge of the DC office. "I felt like the mom was playing it straight with me, but maybe when push came to shove, she freaked out about her son being charged with murder and ran."

"What about their passports?" Malone asked.

"I've had them flagged."

"Good work, Sarge," Malone said. "Keep us posted on what you hear."

"Will do."

"Why can't anything ever be simple and straightforward?" Sam asked Malone.

"Is that a rhetorical question?"

Sam glanced at her new watch and saw she had six minutes to get to the morgue for her fitting. "Gotta roll."

"Where you off to, Speed Racer?"

"The morgue."

"What goes on there?"

"Final dress fitting for tomorrow night."

His lips quivered as he tried—and failed—to stop the laughter. "For real?"

"Very. Had to be done, and that's the only way the whole place isn't buzzing about it in five minutes."

"Don't let me keep you."

"How do you feel about pushing the chair to the morgue for me?"

"Why is it that you need a ride?"

"No reason."

"Just seems like a fun way to get around?"

"Exactly."

She appreciated that he didn't press the issue. Instead, he got behind the chair and wheeled her out of the pit and down the hallway toward the morgue.

"Any word on Dr. McNamara?" he asked.

"Not yet."

As they approached the morgue, the door to outside opened, and Marcus came in, wearing a purple down coat that covered every part of him but his face. His curly blond hair was wilder than usual thanks to the brisk wind. A young woman stood next to him, holding a garment bag.

"What are you doing in that chair? And what's on your arm?" He leaned in for a closer look. "A bandage? You're wearing a *bandage*? Your face! *What is happening?*"

His warm brown eyes had gone wide with shock and horror.

"Relax, Marcus. All is well."

"That is a bald-faced lie, and speaking of faces... What the hell are we going to do with yours?"

"That way," Sam said.

The captain rolled her into the morgue as Marcus and his assistant followed.

Sam looked up at Malone. "Thanks for the lift. I can take it from here."

"Call me if you need a ride back."

"I will."

CHAPTER ELEVEN

T he captain headed for the door, and Sam turned to Marcus,
who was unzipping the blanket he called a coat.

"So this is where they keep the dead people, huh?"

"Focus, Marcus. I'm on a tight schedule."

"Look me in the eye and tell me exactly what's injured so I can
work around it."

"Face, arm, hip."

He gasped. "The *same* hip?"

"Yes."

"Damn it, Sam. Did you rebreak it?"

"I really hope not."

"What does that mean? Haven't you been to the ER?"

"No time for that." She reached out an arm to the assistant.
"Help me up and move slowly."

The young woman looked terrified as she gave Sam an arm
up. When she cried out in pain, the woman released her hold on
her so quickly that Sam nearly fell over. She grasped the counter
to remain standing.

"I'm so sorry, Mrs. Cappuano," the woman said tearfully.

"Not your fault," Sam said softly.

Any attempt to put weight on her right leg resulted in agony.
She wanted to wail. This couldn't be happening. Not this week.

"Sam," Marcus said. "You need to be in the hospital."

Tears filled her eyes. "I can't. He needs me. Please, Marcus. Just do the fitting and let me get back to work."

Though she could tell her friend had plenty he wanted to say, he bit his tongue and got to work.

The gown was a lovely burgundy velvet creation that'd made her feel sexy and curvy in a good way the first time she'd tried it on. This time, she focused on staying conscious and not screaming in pain as her injured limbs were carefully arranged around the dress.

"Are you sure—"

"Please. Just do what you need to."

She closed her eyes and focused on breathing while they did their thing.

"That should do it," Marcus said a few minutes later. "Let's get it off."

It hurt as much coming off as it had going on, resulting in cold sweat and nausea.

"You have hair and makeup set for tomorrow?" he asked as his assistant put the dress on a hanger.

"I assume Lilia has that covered. Thank you for coming in."

"Gotta say, this is my first fitting in a morgue."

Sam smiled. "First time for everything."

"Are you sure you're all right?"

"I'll be fine. Don't tell anyone."

"We never would, love." He kissed her cheek. "I'll see you tomorrow."

"Thanks, Marcus."

"For you, anything."

Sam lowered herself into the office chair and exhaled a deep breath before indulging in a pity party. Why did these things always have to happen at the worst possible time? Whenever Nick needed her to be at the top of her game, she got banged up and bruised. She reached up to wipe away a tear and gasped when her fingers connected with the cut on her face.

Son of a bitch.

She had no time for pity parties.

Someone had murdered Tom Forrester, and she needed to

find that person, arrest them and hope they spent the rest of their miserable life in prison.

SAM WHEELED herself back to the pit, fortunately not encountering anyone else in the hallway as she used her left foot to propel herself forward. If this hadn't been the worst possible time for an injury, she would've found it funny. However, nothing about this was funny.

"Cruz!"

He popped up from inside his cubicle. "Yes?"

"Any word on a lawyer for Bryant?"

"That's why I'm here," a very young man said as he came into the pit from the other side, eyeing her in the desk chair as she made her way toward him.

"And you are?"

"Tyson Conway, Esquire." He handed her a business card. "I heard the congressman's attorneys fired him and thought I might be able to help."

"His assets are frozen."

"I'm aware."

Sam eyed him skeptically. "What's in it for you?"

"I'm growing my career. A case like this could help."

"Do you have any idea how much it costs to defend a case like this?"

"I do."

"It's your funeral." She turned to Freddie. "Detective Cruz, please bring Bryant up to meet his new attorney."

"Yes, ma'am."

"You can wait for him in interview one, second door on the left down the hall."

"Thank you, and may I say, it's an honor to meet you in person. I've long admired your work."

Sam wasn't in the mood for suck-up lawyers. "Thanks." She pushed the chair into her office and wanted to scream with frustration when it wouldn't fit between the desk and file cabinet, forcing her to get up and move to the other chair. Fuck, that hurt.

Was it time for more pain pills? She glanced at her watch. Not for a few more hours. She'd never make it.

Gonzo came to the door. "You got a second?"

"Yep."

He came in and closed the door. "There're hundreds of messages between Cox and Forrester in Forrester's email." Gonzo put a stack of pages on her desk. "Archie pulled everything between the two of them for the last year. I thought you'd want to see this."

"You thought right."

He took a closer look at her. "Are you okay?"

"I'm fine. I'll go through this while Bryant talks to his new lawyer."

"Who'd he get?"

"A guy named Tyson..." She looked down at the card she'd tossed on the desk. "Conway, Esquire."

Gonzo smiled. "He introduced himself that way?"

"Sure did, and he doesn't care that Bryant's assets are frozen."

"Interesting."

"Whatever it takes to get Bryant in a room to answer our questions. Any word on his ex-wife and son?"

"Nothing yet, but Jesse's team is on it."

"They'll find them."

"I'm so disappointed in the mother, Rosemary. She seemed to understand the stakes. I didn't expect this."

"I'm sorry she let you down, but people suck."

"Yes, they do. Hey, so I might need to take a little time off in the next few weeks. Christina and I have found a more secure apartment complex, and we're going to move when our lease is up at the end of April."

After the home invasion at Shelby and Avery's, perpetrated by people he'd once arrested, Sam had advised her team to seek out more secure residences. She worried about their increased exposure due to her higher profile as first lady.

"Take whatever time you need. I'm glad you found a place."

"It wasn't easy. Everything is so freaking expensive."

A thought occurred to her. "If you haven't already signed the new lease, why don't you just rent Ninth Street from us? We'll give you a good deal."

"What? No way."

"Yes way. It's sitting empty, and we're never there." Except for that dreaded meeting they had scheduled there for later in the week with Nick's mother... "Well, almost never there."

"Are you serious?"

"Let me talk to Nick, but I'm sure he'd agree that having you guys there would be way better than having it sitting empty. The Secret Service ramped up security big-time there when Nick was VP, so it'd be much safer than where you are now."

"Sam... That'd be incredible. Your place is gorgeous."

"What do you pay for rent now?"

"Thirty-eight hundred."

"*A month?*"

Gonzo laughed. "That's the going rate these days."

"Holy shit."

"You've been out of the rental market for a while."

"Apparently. That's shocking to me."

"What's the rent at the White House?"

"Hahaha. We pay for all our own food, not to mention a huge nonfinancial price to live there."

"I wouldn't trade what you guys deal with for free rent. No way."

"No such thing as a free lunch. I'll text Nick and let you know."

"Even if it doesn't work out, thank you for the idea."

"It'll work out."

"You're the best."

"I know!"

He walked out laughing, and she felt good about the idea she'd come up with. She sent a text to Nick outlining her thoughts on Ninth Street and then got to work reviewing the work and personal emails between Cox and Forrester. They'd spoken in a cryptic language, which had probably been intentional. Maybe they'd known their messages would be reviewed someday. She could hear Forrester saying, "Why make it easy on them?"

She learned they'd played tennis, sailed Cox's boat, had dinner with their wives and families, participated in baseball and football fantasy leagues together and had lunch at least once, if not twice, per week. By any measure, Forrester appeared to have been Cox's best friend. So why hadn't Cox told her that when she'd asked about their relationship? Why would he want to hide that fact from her?

Had their friendship soured?

Had Bryant been the cause of that?

After thinking it through for a few minutes, she picked up the phone and called Leslie Forrester.

A man answered the phone.

"This is Lieutenant Holland with the MPD. May I please speak to Leslie Forrester?"

"She's lying down at the moment. Could I have her call you?"

"I'd really like to speak to her now, if possible."

After a long silence, the man said, "Let me see if she's able."

Resigned to waiting, she pressed the speaker button on the phone, put down the receiver and continued to read the message traffic between the two men, becoming more confused with every message that made no sense to her.

A rustling in the background on the call preceded Leslie coming on the line.

"I'm so sorry to bother you again at this difficult time," Sam said.

"It's okay. I want to help if I can."

"I have a question about Tom's relationship with Reginald Cox."

"Reggie is one of Tom's closest friends. They went to college and law school together."

"It's interesting to me that when I met with Cox yesterday, he didn't mention that. He talked about Tom in his role as a U.S. Attorney but said nothing about the outsized role Tom played in Cox's personal life. Do you know why that would be?"

"No, I can't imagine why he would've kept that part out of it.

The two of them are like brothers. Or I guess I should say they *were*. I still can't believe Tom is gone."

"I'm so sorry to have to add to your grief with my questions."

"I understand you're just doing your job."

"Did you notice any strain between Tom and Reggie in recent weeks?"

"Not that I can recall, but like Aurora mentioned yesterday, Tom was unusually stressed in the last few months. I tried to get him to talk about it, but as was often the case with his work, he couldn't say much."

"Did he ever indicate undue pressure on him from Cox or anything like that?"

"Not to me. Conlon might know more about that. Would you like to speak to him? He's here."

Sam was intrigued to realize that Young was still at the Forresters' home and must be the man who'd answered the phone. "I'm due to see him tomorrow." She wanted to be able to see the man's face when she asked her questions. "If you wouldn't mind keeping our conversation between us, I'd appreciate that."

"I won't say anything."

"If you think of anything else that might be relevant, even if it seems like something insignificant, will you please give me a call?"

"Of course. Whatever I can do to help."

"Thank you, Leslie. And again, my heartfelt sympathies to you and your family."

"We appreciate your kindness. Conlon will have the details about the service when you see him."

"Good to know. I'll be there."

"Thank you again for being willing to speak about Tom."

"It's an honor to be asked. I'll see you there, if not before."

Sam ended the call with more questions than she'd had before. What was the deal with Conlon Young?

She used her cell to call Faith.

"Hey, Sam. How's it going?"

"Slow and frustrating."

"I heard Bryant got a lawyer."

"He's with the guy now. Not sure what the deal is with him. Do you know Tyson Conway?"

"Never heard of him."

"Me either, but whatever gets Bryant into a room for an interview works for me."

"Agreed."

"I want to talk to you about Young."

"What about him?"

"What's his story? I just called Leslie, and he answered the phone."

"I'm not surprised. They're tight."

"Where's he from?"

"Minneapolis, but he came here for college and never left. He's worked for Main Justice for twenty years and with Tom the whole time he was the USA."

"I still find it odd that I work with you guys every day and had never heard of him before Tom was killed."

"He works in the background. You wouldn't have encountered him."

"Have you ever picked up a vibe from him?"

"What kind of vibe?"

"The what-you-see-isn't-what-you-get kind."

"Never. He's a super supportive colleague and friend. He's the glue that keeps our office humming on all cylinders. He's the first one to show up when someone has a baby or a death in the family or anything like that. We all love him."

"Hmmm."

"You can't possibly be looking at him for this."

"Not actively. Just trying to figure out the players and the various relationships."

"It's not him, Sam. There's just no way. He'd have taken a bullet to protect Tom."

"I appreciate the insight."

"Promise me you aren't going to let him think you suspect him. That would crush him."

"I'll be mindful of that."

"Is anything popping?"

"Not yet. We're still sifting through a mountain of messages and other data."

"I heard some people here talking."

"About?"

"It's a rumor. There's no way it's true."

"What, Faith?"

"That he was involved with someone outside his marriage. I don't believe that for a second."

"Who said it?"

"I'm not sure exactly."

"Faith, come on. Of course you know who said it."

"It was one of the admins."

"I need a name."

"You won't say it came from me, will you?"

"Never."

Her deep sigh came through loud and clear. "Anita Wentworth. She works with Conlon."

A tingle traveled down Sam's backbone.

She wrote down the woman's name. "I'll be at your office tomorrow to speak to Conlon and Anita. Please don't say anything to her ahead of time."

"I never would."

"Thanks. See you then."

Every case was frustrating in its own way, but the stone walls she kept crashing into with this one were infuriating. It seemed to her they'd been erected intentionally, to keep someone like her out in a situation like this.

Throbbing from her wrist and hip had her reaching for the pain pills. So what if it was too soon for more? Shit, Harry had put the cap back on, and there was no way to open them with only one working hand.

"Cruz!"

He came to the door, looking perturbed.

She held up the bottle. "Open this for me, will you? And without commentary."

Now he looked even more annoyed. He took the bottle from her, shook out two pills and dropped them into the palm of her left hand.

"One more."

He scowled as he added the third pill.

Sam took them with a sip of water while hoping they'd work quickly.

"Why don't you go home?"

"Not yet. I'm taking a short day tomorrow."

"No one cares if you take two short days in a row."

"After taking a whole week off and missing most of the last two cases? I'm not leaving."

"We're not keeping score, Sam."

"You're not, but others are. You know they are."

"No one who matters."

"Perception is reality around here, and it's bad enough I'm being driven around by the Secret Service like a princess. I don't need to give them any more reason to talk shit about me."

"But you're injured after taking down a suspect on the job. Anyone would go home because of that."

"I need to see through this day. I'll go home as soon as we're done."

Avery Hill appeared in her doorway.

Sam waved him in, noting he looked tired but happy. "How's the new baby?"

"Loud."

Sam laughed. "How's Shelby?"

"Exhausted but thrilled." He did a double take when he noticed the bandage on her arm and cut on her face. "What happened to you?"

"Nothing. I'm fine."

Avery glanced at Freddie, who shrugged.

"I, uh, wondered if I might have a word in private?"

"Sure."

Freddie ducked out and closed the office door behind him.

"What's up?"

Avery took a seat in front of her desk. "I'm ethically torn."

"How so?"

"I want to show you a private all-hands message that came through secure channels to all Justice employees."

"Like, everyone?"

"Yes."

"Is that unusual?"

"Sixth one I've ever gotten."

"Who was it from?"

"Cox."

The telltale tingle attacked her backbone. "Can you share it?"

"Absolutely not, but I can show it to you if you swear to never tell anyone it came from me."

"I swear."

Avery handed over his phone.

Sam read the all-hands message from Reginald Cox to every employee at Justice, encouraging them to do everything in their power to assist in the investigation into U.S. Attorney Tom Forrester's murder. "If you know something, say something," Cox had written. "It behooves us all to assist law enforcement in quickly resolving the senseless murder of our colleague. If you have information about USA Forrester's murder, please report it to a supervisor immediately."

Sam read the message twice, becoming more perplexed the second time. "Is he insinuating an inside job?"

"That's how I read it."

"I don't understand. Who does he think would know something?"

"No idea, but the implication was clear to me and my team that he thinks it came from within the department—or he wants people to think that."

"Is it possible he wants someone like you to do exactly what you're doing now by showing that to me and hoping I'll pick up that direction?"

"I thought of that and can't rule it out."

"What is happening?"

"I wish I knew."

"I feel like the AG is fucking with me."

"I understand why you'd feel that way."

"When I interviewed him, he never said a word about how he and Forrester went all the way back to college and had been tight ever since. Leslie Forrester said they were like brothers. He never said he was also close friends with Bryant or that the three of them regularly spent time together."

"That's weird."

"I know, which leads me to wonder if Cox is involved."

"You think the AG might be involved in the death of a USA he was friends with for twenty-five years?"

"I don't know what to think. Why wouldn't Cox tell me everything there is to tell about his friendship with Forrester? If he cares about his friend and getting justice for him, wouldn't he vomit details to assist in the investigation? How would their long friendship count as something he couldn't share with me, especially when that friend is now lying in the morgue?"

"It makes no sense that he'd keep that from you."

"Am I going to have to interview him again? Please say no."

"I wish I could."

"I plan to try to get a minute with him at the state dinner. I figured he can't very well publicly avoid the first lady when she wants to have a word with him."

Avery smiled. "I wish I could be a fly on the wall for that."

"I'm sorry you guys won't be there, but I'm so glad Miss Maisie has safely arrived, and all is well."

"Me, too. Shelby is such a badass. I know I never should've worried about her, but pregnancy risks are so much greater in the forties. It's a relief to have it behind us. She's already scheduled the big V for me."

"Ack, TMI."

He laughed. "Sorry."

"It's fine. I'm so happy for you guys."

"I'm happy for us, too. She's the best."

"Yes, she sure is."

"So, are you pretending not to be injured?"

"Perhaps."

"Are you okay?"

"I will be."

Apparently realizing she wasn't going to talk about it, he said, "Two other things. I looked into all the threats that've been made against USA and the office in the last year and didn't find anything that stood out as particularly worrisome. It was mostly the usual claims of prosecutorial overreach and unfairness. Also, I've put pressure on the lab to get that phone processed. I'll let you know what I hear from them."

"Thank you, Avery."

CHAPTER TWELVE

After Avery left, Freddie came to the door. "Bryant's lawyer says they're ready to talk. They're in interview two."

"Excellent." Sam painfully transferred herself to the rolling office chair and headed for the door.

Freddie jumped to get out of her way. "Easy, Speedy Gonzales."

"That name is trademarked," Gonzo said, grinning as they laughed.

Sam scooted down the hallway to the interview room.

Freddie opened the door and let her go in ahead of him.

Both men gave her an odd look when she rolled the chair into the room.

"We heard you're ready to talk."

"That's correct," Conway said. "My client is willing to answer your questions in the hope that you might let the prosecutor know he was cooperative."

"I'll be sure to call her the second we're done here." Sam hoped they could hear the sarcasm in her tone. That son of a bitch Bryant was the reason she was injured—again. She wasn't doing a goddamned thing to help him. "Detective Cruz, please record this conversation."

Freddie turned on the recording and listed the people in the room as well as the time and date of the interview.

"Why'd you run from us?" Sam asked.

Judging by the way he glanced at the lawyer, Bryant hadn't expected that to be her first question.

"I was scared."

"Of what? You've already been charged with multiple capital felonies."

"I don't know. I freaked out. That's allowed, right?"

"Sure, why not? Where would Rosemary have taken your son?"

He glanced at the lawyer and then at her. "What?"

"She promised us he'd turn himself in today, and they've gone missing. Where would they be?"

"I, uh, I don't know. I'm not in touch with her now that the kids are adults." He ran a trembling hand over his mostly bald head and leaned in to whisper to the lawyer.

Sam eyed the flame of his cheeks and nose, wondering if he was an alcoholic or if he had rosacea. Her ex-husband had suffered from the latter, and it'd made him miserable. Or more miserable, rather.

"Rosemary's family has a cabin up north in Wisconsin. I'm not sure what town it's in."

"You've never been there?"

"Once, years ago. I don't remember where it was."

"Would your daughter know?"

"Yes, I suppose she would."

"How can we get in touch with her?"

"I don't have her number anymore. She stopped taking my calls years ago."

"Didn't that bother you?"

"Of course it did, but Rosemary was with them all the time while I was here. She poisoned them against me. I couldn't fight that, so I stopped trying."

"I would never stop trying to make things right with my kids."

His face twisted into a mean sneer. "Wouldn't we all like to be more like you?"

"I would," Freddie said, earning him a smile from Sam. "We'd be lucky to be more like her."

"Who would have your daughter's number?"

"My sister, Donna." He recited her phone number. "She keeps in touch with the kids."

Sam wrote down the number and handed the paper to Freddie, who left to pass the info on to Jesse Best. "What's your relationship with Reginald Cox?"

"The AG?"

No, the mayor of Phoenix. "Yes."

"I've known him almost as long as I've been in Washington. He was a prominent lawyer before becoming the AG. I met him at a few dinner parties back in the day."

"And you became friends with him?"

He shifted in his seat the way people did when something made them uncomfortable. "Acquaintances."

"Did he play cards at your house every week?"

The question shocked him. "What? No."

"We have witnesses who say he did."

"I mean, like, I knew him, but we weren't buddies or anything."

"Weren't you?"

"No!"

"Did it make you mad when he asked his pal—and yours—Forrester to investigate your campaign finance irregularities?"

Judging by the way Bryant's already red face turned an alarming shade of purple, he'd cared very much about that. "That was a wild-goose chase. There was no *there* there."

"So you say, but according to Forrester's team, he'd found significant concerns that he'd reported directly to Cox." As far as she knew, that wasn't true, but Bryant didn't need to know that.

Freddie returned to the room and took his seat next to her.

"What did he find?" Bryant asked, sputtering. "That's bullshit. I run a clean operation."

Sam didn't believe that for a second, but he probably knew how to make it *look* clean even if it wasn't. "I'm not sure of the details. All I know is that Forrester had reported to Cox that he was finding irregularities."

"I don't believe that for a second."

"Don't shoot the messenger."

Bryant sat back in his chair, fuming. "What's the point of this anyway?"

"I want to know about your friendship with Forrester and Cox."

"Friendship? I wasn't *friends* with Forrester. Not after he started trying to ruin my life!"

"Where'd you go after you were released on bail?"

"Home. I went straight home."

"We have people working on tracking the pings on your cell phone. Are we going to find anyone associated with you anywhere near Constitution Avenue at the time of Forrester's shooting?"

"No, you won't. I wouldn't have had any idea where to find him."

"Even after your thugs took his family hostage?"

The lawyer glanced at him nervously. "What is she talking about, Congressman?"

"Oh, he didn't tell you about how he and his goons took Forrester's family hostage and held them for days at a hotel while telling them that Tom was trying to keep them safe? Did he leave out that part of the story?"

The lawyer recoiled, probably in fear of losing his brand-new law license by associating with this guy. "Is that true?"

"I had nothing to do with that."

Sam laughed at the absurdity. "So the men who worked for you got that idea all on their own?"

"You'd have to ask them."

"We have. They say you told them to detain Forrester's wife and daughters."

"That's a lie."

"We don't think it is."

"What are they getting in return for telling you that?"

"What I want to know is what reason in the universe would they have for detaining Forrester's family other than following orders that came right from you? How would they even know Forrester if they didn't work for you?"

Bryant glared at her, but he seemed to have no answer.

"I'd, um, like a moment to confer with my client, please."

Freddie turned off the recording and rolled Sam out of the room.

"Funny how Bryant never mentioned to his new attorney that he kidnapped Forrester's family and held them hostage days before their husband and father was murdered."

Freddie chuckled. "Ironic."

Since it was inching closer to six, she looked up at him. "Go on home if you want. I can finish this."

He leaned against the cinderblock wall. "I'll stick around until we're done with Bryant."

"How's Elin?"

"She's good. Mostly back to her old self."

"I'm glad to hear that. Miscarriage is a tough thing."

"Sure is. I had no idea how tough until it happened to us."

"You're going to make me an aunt many times over. I feel it in my bones."

"I've learned to trust your bones."

Sam's cell rang with a call from an unavailable number. "Lieutenant Holland."

"This is Attorney General Cox's office calling."

"What can I do for you?" She mouthed the word *Cox* to Freddie.

"General Cox would like to see you."

"When?"

"As soon as possible."

"It'll have to be tomorrow."

"He'd like it to be tonight."

"I'm sorry, that's not possible."

Her reply was met with silence.

She would bet the farm that the AG wasn't used to people saying "not now" to him. "What time and where tomorrow?" Sam asked.

"General Cox would like to see you now."

"I'm not available now."

"I will get back to you."

The call ended abruptly.

"What was that about?"

"The Attorney General wants to see me now, and his lackey seemed astounded to hear I'm not currently available."

Freddie snorted. "No one says no to him."

"Someone just did."

"We could see him tonight. I'm just saying…"

"As soon as we're done with Bryant, I'm going home to get my hip X-rayed to make sure I haven't refractured it."

His eyes popped. "Do you think you did?"

"I can't put any weight on it, so…"

"Sam…"

"Think positively. Hopefully, it's just a setback."

"You shouldn't be here."

"So I've heard. Knock on the door and see what's going on in there. I want out of here."

While Freddie went to check on Bryant and his attorney, Sam texted Harry. *Should be home within the hour.*

I'll be ready.

Thanks, Doc. Does POTUS know about this?

Not from me.

Sam would be shocked if he hadn't heard about it from someone, but the fact he hadn't texted had her hopeful that he maybe didn't know. He had enough to contend with. He didn't need to be worried about her, too.

"They're ready for us," Freddie said.

He rolled her back into the room.

"Gentlemen, my patience tends to run out right around this point every day. Let's move this along, shall we?"

"My client would like to know what sort of concessions he might receive if he provided information that could be useful to your investigation."

"That depends on the information."

"He's unwilling to share the info until he knows what the concessions will be."

"We're not in a position to offer concessions. Those would have to come from the U.S. Attorney's Office, and since we're talking about the murder of their beloved boss, they're not feeling overly generous."

"Then I have nothing further to say to you," Bryant said.

"Detective Cruz, will you please take Mr. Bryant back to lockup?"

"When is my bail hearing?"

"Not sure yet, but you probably ought to get comfortable downstairs."

"I'm still a United States congressman," he reminded her.

"So what?"

"That should count toward something."

"I believe that probably counted toward you getting out on bail in the first place after being linked to a murder, which means that chip has been played—and you blew it. Detective Cruz, after you deliver Mr. Bryant to lockup, please brief Carlucci and Dominguez on what we need from them tonight."

"Yes, ma'am."

With that, she wheeled herself out of the room and back to her office to get her coat so she could get the hell out of there.

"You can't just walk away from me when I'm still talking to you," Bryant called after her.

"Oh, yes, I can."

She texted Vernon to tell him she was on the way out.

A minute later, he appeared at her office door. "Thought you might need a push."

"You get me, Vernon."

He helped her position her coat around her shoulders. "Sadly, I do."

Sam laughed. "Let's roll." She was ready to get home and figure out what the hell was going on with her hip.

ON THE WAY, she took another call from an unavailable number. "Holland."

"General Cox would like to see you at nine thirty tomorrow. Is that possible?"

"Where?"

"At his office."

"I'll be there."

"Thank you."

This call ended the same way the other one had—abruptly.

She texted Freddie to tell him they had a meeting with the AG at nine thirty tomorrow.

Got it, he replied.

Tomorrow was going to be a long-ass day. Thinking about that made her even more tired than she already was.

When they arrived at the White House, Harry met her with a wheelchair.

Vernon put an arm around her and half carried her inside.

"Thank you, Vernon." She used her chin to point to the chair. "Is that necessary?"

"Can you walk the thousand or so steps to the clinic?"

She scowled at Harry and carefully lowered herself to the chair while pulling her coat hood up over her face so there'd be no photos. "Be quick about it."

"Yes, ma'am."

She wanted to tell him not to call her that, but she bit her tongue as he propelled her deeper into the White House, down a ramp and around several corners before arriving at the clinic. No way could she have walked that far. "What're we hearing about Lindsey?"

"Nothing yet. They're waiting on test results."

"Are you worried about her?"

"I'm not sure yet."

"Let me know what you hear."

"I will."

"We're ready for you, Mrs. Cappuano," a nurse said, smiling.

"Thank you. Please keep this private."

"Of course. We won't say a word."

"Everyone here is under an NDA," Harry said as he delivered her to an exam room and handed her a gown.

"Do I really need a gown?"

"Yes. Do you need help changing?"

"I can do it."

"I'll be back in a minute."

Working with a bum hip and arm, she struggled her way out of her clothes and into the gown that tied in the back. Since she couldn't tie it with one hand, she held it together as she sat carefully in the chair. God, it hurt to sit, to stand, to breathe. If her hip was broken again, she didn't know what she would do.

She'd forgotten how painful it'd been to get X-rays the first time she injured her hip. The tech was super gentle, but even still, she was in tears by the time she was delivered back to the exam room, where Harry waited to talk to her.

"Nothing's broken," he said.

"You already know that?"

"Yep."

"So why can't I walk on it?"

"You should be able to in a day or two."

"I have the state dinner tomorrow. I have to be able to walk!"

"I can give you a cortisone shot to get you through the event."

"What does that entail?" she asked warily.

"I stick a needle in your hip and fill it with a steroid that will take the pain away while it heals from this latest trauma."

"I assume the needle to the hip doesn't feel good."

"I'd numb you up beforehand."

"What about my arm?"

"Your wrist is sprained. I can wrap it better, so it's supported while it heals."

Sam decided she could live with an Ace bandage in the state dinner pictures, but she wouldn't be able to manage crutches. "I'll do the shot." The only thing she hated more than flying was needles, but she'd do whatever was necessary to function tomorrow. Nick was counting on her, and she didn't want to let him down.

"I'll get it ready."

CHAPTER THIRTEEN

S am had worked herself into a complete panic when a knock sounded on the door.

Nick poked his head in. "Heard a rumor that my wife was in the clinic. I said, 'How is that possible when my wife notifies me any time she gets hurt on the job?'"

The sight of his handsome face made everything better. "That's true, except for when the Canadian prime minister is coming to town and her focus is on being able to first-lady tomorrow."

"What'd you do to yourself, love?"

"I tackled an errant congressman, sprained my wrist and aggravated my healing hip."

He winced. "And did some damage to my favorite face, too, I see." He ran a gentle finger over her cheek.

"I'd forgotten about that."

"Only you, Samantha."

"I know. I'm such an accident waiting for a place to happen."

He rested against the exam table. "I meant only you would think last about an injury to your face."

"I was a bit preoccupied with fears that I'd rebroken my hip."

"I suppose that would be the headline. I'm so glad it's only aggravated and not broken."

"Harry is giving me a cortisone shot."

"Ouch."

Her eyes went wide. "You think it'll hurt?"

"Uh, I mean... Maybe? A little?"

"You won't feel a thing," Harry said as he came into the room. "I promise."

"That'd be good."

"My Samantha doesn't like needles."

"Does anyone?" Harry asked. "Let's get you back into the X-ray room for this."

"How come?"

"I use imaging to make sure I hit the right spot."

"Okay."

"Can Nick come?"

"Of course. Not sure if you've heard, but he's the boss around here."

"Don't make me laugh when I'm freaked out."

Harry wheeled her into the other room and got her settled on the table as she tried not to scream from the pain.

"Easy, honey." Nick smoothed the hair back from her face.

She wanted so badly to be brave so she wouldn't upset him, but that was easier said than done when needles were involved.

A nurse wheeled a table into the room that contained a variety of things that Sam quickly realized she'd be better off not studying too closely.

She focused instead on Nick's handsome face.

Harry lifted the right side of the gown and painted something onto her skin. "Just some Betadine to clean the area. We're going to start with a shot of lidocaine to numb you up," Harry said. "You'll feel a small pinch and a slight burn as it goes in, but it shouldn't hurt. Okay?"

Nothing about this was okay. "Uh-huh." After a pause, she said, "Have you done this before?"

"Many times when I was a resident."

Sam practically levitated off the table. *"How long ago was that?"*

Harry laughed as he put a hand on her shoulder to keep her still. "Don't worry. It's like riding a bike."

"Oh my God," she muttered. "Get me out of here."

"How long does it take to work?" Nick asked.

"Some people get immediate relief. For others, it takes a day or two."

Sam hoped with all her heart that she was in the former category. She didn't have a day or two to wait for relief. "I'm sorry this happened right before your big day." Her chin quivered as she looked up at Nick.

"Don't give that a thought."

"Right. It's just another Monday around here."

"All I care about is that you're okay. The rest will work itself out."

"Here we go, Sam."

The "small" pinch and "slight" burn took her breath away and brought tears to her eyes.

Nick took her left hand and held on tight. "You're doing great."

"Yeah, cuz that was the easy part."

"You've got this, Sam. I'm going to inject a small bit of dye to make sure we get the exact spot where you need it most."

She felt another needle go in, but that one didn't hurt, thankfully.

"There it is. Right there. Hang tight, here we go."

Oh, holy fucking shit, that hurt!

"Don't move. We're almost done."

"*Please,*" she gasped as tears rolled down her face.

"All done. You did great."

She felt like a big, fat baby as Nick wiped away her tears with a tissue.

Her hands were shaking, and she felt like she might hyperventilate.

"Let's sit her up," Harry said.

He and Nick helped her up.

Harry rested a hand on her shoulder. "Take a deep breath, Sam. It's all over."

That might be true, but she still felt like she was going to be sick.

"Can you stand?" Nick asked.

"I can try."

With one of them on each side of her, she tentatively got down from the exam table, waiting for the predictable blast of pain from her hip that didn't materialize. "Oh, that feels better. Wow. Much better." Other than the dull aches coming from her face and wrist, she felt no pain. "Thank you, Harry. That totally sucked, but it worked."

"I'm glad it worked quickly for you."

"Me, too. I have no time to be injured this week."

"Let's get your wrist wrapped properly and send you home."

Twenty minutes later, Nick walked her slowly to the elevator that would take them to the second-floor residence. Her face stung from whatever Harry had put on it, and her throbbing wrist was immobilized in a bandage. "Sorry about all this. The last thing you needed this week was an injured wife."

"As always, I'm thankful my wife is only injured when we both know it could be much worse."

"I hope I never again have to have a shot to the hip. I almost passed out."

"I almost passed out from watching it."

"I'm going to have nightmares about that for the rest of my life."

He ushered her into the elevator and pushed the button for the second floor. "Nah, you'll forget all about it in a day or two."

"If you say so."

"I say so, and I'm the boss of the whole country."

"Not letting it go to your head or anything, right?"

"Of course not."

They emerged from the elevator to the sound of children laughing as they played chase in the hallway. Scotty was in hot pursuit of the twins, who were doing most of the laughing as they came barreling toward Sam and Nick.

He reached for them so they wouldn't crash into Sam. "I've got them, Scotty. Now what should we do with them?"

"Tickle them until they puke?"

"*No*," the twins said, shrieking.

"Anything but that," Aubrey said.

She hated being tickled, while Alden loved it.

"How about some dinner?" Nick asked, kissing both little faces before he put them down to run off again.

Celia came down from the third floor with Sam's mother, Brenda.

Sam was surprised to see her mother. "Did I forget something?"

Brenda laughed. "No, I was meeting with Celia to get the kids' after-school routine down so I'm ready to cover for her while she's away."

Celia and her sisters were leaving on an Alaskan cruise on Wednesday.

"Ah, okay."

Celia eyed the bandage on her arm. "What happened to you?"

"A little skirmish on the job. No biggie. Can you join us for dinner, Mom?"

"I'd love to, if it's no imposition."

"The lovely staff is always prepared for an extra guest or two. I just need to change, and then I'll meet you all in the dining room."

"I'll go with you," Nick said.

He was probably afraid she might fall over, which wasn't outside the realm of possibility.

Her hip felt disconnected from the rest of her body, which was keeping the pain away but made her feel off-balance and out of whack. Hopefully, she'd figure out getting around before she had to put on heels tomorrow night.

Scotty signaled to her as she walked toward her room with Nick. He waggled his finger to bring her closer so he could whisper in her ear. "The study guide got here today and is already a game changer."

"Glad to hear it."

"Best mom ever," he said as he ran off to find the twins.

His words took her breath away.

"Aw, what've you done now to be the best mom ever?" Nick asked.

"That's between me and him."

"Why does that make me very suspicious?"

"Because you're suspicious by nature. Everything is fine."

"Hmmm."

In their suite, he helped her change into track pants and a clean sweatshirt and found the fleece-lined slippers he'd given her for Christmas. The others were already at the table when they joined them. Nick had changed into sweats and the T-shirt she'd given him for their anniversary.

"Nice shirt, Dad," Scotty said.

"Mom gave it to me for our anniversary."

"Nice one, Mom."

"I thought so, too."

"I'm not sure how I feel about you two being in cahoots," Nick said.

Scotty grinned. "Don't worry about it."

"I'm going to lose sleep over what you're up to. She's not telling you that you can drop out of eighth grade or anything, is she?"

"Not yet."

"Well, that's a relief."

"What does it mean to drop out?" Aubrey asked.

"Never mind, you," Nick said with a smile. "It's not something we do in this family."

"I want to drop out," Alden said.

"I blame you for this," Nick said to Sam.

"What did I do?"

"Mom! What happened to your arm? And your face!"

"Are you just seeing that?" Sam asked Scotty.

"Yes!"

"A little scuffle at work. I won. All is well."

"You always win, and Dad has the T-shirt to prove it."

Everyone laughed.

"Is it like this every night?" Brenda asked, wiping away tears from laughing.

"Most nights," Celia said.

"This family is a mess," Nick said, his eyes dancing with amusement.

Sam smiled at him. "But we're your mess."

"Thank goodness for that."

AFTER DINNER, Sam supervised the twins through baths and bedtime and then went upstairs to check on Shelby and the baby. She was amazed by how she could walk again with no pain, thanks to Harry's magic shot, although thinking about that needle still made her shudder. She knocked softly on the door.

Avery answered. "Hey, come in."

"How're things?"

"Calm at the moment, but that could change at any second."

"I was hoping to say hello to my pal."

"She'd love to see you."

He led her into the bedroom, where Shelby was propped up on pink pillows as the baby slept in her arms.

"You look like a queen," Sam whispered.

"Ha! I smell like a cow."

"I doubt that."

"How's Lindsey?"

"Still waiting to hear."

"That's so scary. I hope everything is okay."

"Me, too. How are you?"

"A little better every day."

Sam leaned in for a closer look at the sleeping baby's face.

"What happened to you?" Shelby asked.

"Scuffle at work."

"Did you win?"

"Duh."

Shelby laughed. "I talked to Lilia earlier. Everything is set for tomorrow."

"You're on maternity leave. Don't worry about it."

"I'm not worried about it with Lilia in charge."

"She's the best."

"Yes, she is."

"And so are you, Shelby Hill. I know you've seen to every detail, and Lilia is following your plans to the letter."

"I do what I can for my people."

"That saying is trademarked."

Shelby grinned. "How's your case going?"

"Nowhere fast, and lots of high-ranking complications."

"I'm sure you'll figure it out."

"Hope so." Sam leaned in to kiss Shelby's cheek. "I like having you right upstairs so I can come visit."

"I like being here, but Avery tells me we're moving out this weekend."

"Boo-hoo."

"I'll miss my roommates and the room service."

"They do have a way of spoiling you around here."

"Indeed. Thank you again for giving us a place to be when we needed it."

"My home is always your home. Sleep tight, Tinker Bell."

"You, too."

When Sam walked out to the living area, Avery stood. "I've made Tom's phone the lab's top priority."

"Thanks, Avery."

"Anything else I can do?"

Sam debated whether she should air it out with the FBI agent who wanted in on her case, but he was her friend first and foremost, so she took a seat.

He returned to his post on the sofa.

"The AG called me today. Or, I should say, his office called."

"What did he want?"

"To see me right away. I told him I couldn't do it today, and we're meeting tomorrow."

"I'll bet he didn't like being told no."

"His lackey didn't like it at all."

Avery gave her a small grin. "Cox is used to getting his own way all the time."

"So I gathered. Why do you think he asked to see me again?"

"I have no idea."

"Maybe he wants to tell me how he and Forrester go way back to college, which he failed to mention the first time around."

"Could be. When are you seeing him?"

"Nine thirty. Can I ask him about the all-hands message without getting you in trouble?"

"You could've heard about that from anyone, so feel free to ask."

"Any other insight you can give me?"

"What's Bryant saying?" Avery asked.

"Nothing useful. He has no idea why anyone would want Forrester dead. He had nothing to do with taking Forrester's family hostage, despite his goons being the ones to hold them and the goons being willing to testify that they were acting on Bryant's orders."

"Were they given deals to testify?"

"Yes."

"Bryant's attorney will call their motivation into question."

"And he knows that, so he's not moved by their willingness to throw him under the bus. The thing is, I know that slimeball is smack in the middle of this, but how do I prove that?"

"Keep working the case and pulling your threads. Something will pop."

"I hope so. Thanks for listening."

"Any time. Did Shelby tell you we're moving out?"

"She did."

"I found an apartment in Georgetown that's perfect. It has full security and an excellent view."

"You're putting the other place on the market?"

"Already did. I've got movers coming to pack up everything for us. I don't want Shelby to ever have to go back there again."

"You're a good man, Avery Hill. Thanks for taking such good care of my friend."

"I appreciate that you can say that when it was my fault she was attacked in her own home."

"That's not true, and you know it."

"I'm having a really hard time living with what could've happened to my family at the hands a scumbag I arrested." He shook his head. "Willy Peckham is the worst of the worst. I wake up in a cold sweat in the middle of the night thinking about the worst-case scenario."

"You're doing all the right things to keep them safe going forward. No one blames you for what those assholes did."

"I blame myself."

"Nothing good will come of that. We both do jobs that other people could never handle, with built-in risks we try not to worry about until we have to. I have to think that at the end of the day, we're doing more right than wrong."

"I guess so, but I sure do wish I had the benefit of hindsight when I was deciding a career path."

"You wouldn't have gone into law enforcement?"

"No fucking way."

"Really?"

"Really. You would have?"

"I can't imagine doing anything else that would interest me the way this does."

"Weirdo."

Sam laughed. "Believe me, I know I am. Always have been. I used to follow my dad around, asking questions about his cases. My favorite day of the week was Saturday, when he'd take me to work with him."

"That's very sweet."

"I'm not sweet."

"If you say so."

"I say so." She got up from the chair, moving carefully as she still expected to be hit with pain whenever she moved, but was pleased to not experience the knife-sharp agony from earlier. Maybe needles were good for something after all.

Avery walked her to the door. "I'll check in tomorrow."

"Thanks for listening."

"Any time."

She walked to the elevator because she didn't want to test her luck with the stairs. That damned shot needed to get her through tomorrow. After that, she'd be able to exhale again. She looked in on the sleeping twins and then went into their suite to find Nick and Scotty on the sofa watching a Caps game while Nick worked on his correspondence.

"How's Shelby?" Nick asked.

He looked ridiculously sexy in those black-framed reading glasses. "Doing well."

"That baby is so cute," Scotty said.

"She sure is. They're moving out this weekend."

"Aw, bummer. I like having them here," Scotty said.

"I do, too, but they need to get back to their own place." Sam sat between them and leaned her head on Nick's shoulder.

"Is that the signal for me to get lost?"

Laughing, she reached out a hand to her son. "Not even kinda. I wanted to talk to Dad about renting Ninth Street to Gonzo and Christina. Since the break-in at Shelby's, they've been looking for something more secure for their family, and I thought of our place with all the Secret Service enhancements."

"I meant to text you back about that earlier but got sidetracked," Nick said. "That's a good idea. It's just sitting empty."

"That's what I said, too. I told him they could pay whatever their rent is now, and he was thrilled."

"Good plan, babe. I like knowing our friends will be safer there and keeping an eye on the place for the next three years."

"Seven," Sam and Scotty said together.

"*Three.*"

"Poor guy," Scotty said. "He has no clue."

"I know, right?"

"I can hear you two."

"Have you heard anything from Terry?"

"No, and I was just about to text him when you came in."

"Do that, will you?"

"Yes, dear." He typed out the text on his phone and then read Terry's response to her. "'Nothing specific yet, but Lindsey is resting comfortably and feeling better.'"

"That's great news." Sam yawned and then made herself get up to prepare for bed before she fell asleep on the sofa. "Get yourself to bed when the game is over."

"Yes, Mother."

"I love all this obedience from you guys."

"Don't get used to it," Scotty called after her. "We feel bad for you because you're injured—again."

"Haha. Love you."

"Love you, too."

Nick followed her into the bathroom. "Do you need help changing?"

"Is that a come-on?"

That grin of his was too sexy for words. "Not this time.

"I think I've got it, but thanks for asking."

He kissed her. "I'll be in as soon as the game is over."

"I'll be there."

"Can't wait."

After he went back out to Scotty, she changed into pajamas, which was harder than she'd expected it to be with her bandaged wrist and hand, and then brushed her teeth. Once she was settled into bed, she called to check in with Carlucci.

"Hey, LT."

"How's it going?"

"Slow and tedious. We're still reviewing reams of texts and emails. I gotta say, though, I keep coming back to this thing with the neighbor."

Sam closed her eyes and rested her head against the pillow. "Tell me more."

"The neighbor, Ralph Sellers, has three Dobermans, one of which got out of his yard and attacked Forrester's dog, Snowflake, while the daughters were walking her. The incident was traumatic for the kids, who had to fight off the much bigger dog to save theirs. Naomi Forrester, the older of the two girls, said the Doberman had Snowflake in its mouth and was shaking her violently."

"Jeez, that sounds terrifying."

"They said it was. Needless to say, Tom and his wife were outraged and reported the incident to Animal Control as well as their neighborhood association, demanding that something be done about vicious dogs in their midst. Sellers has fought them every step of the way, and they've each sued the other, claiming damages."

"What grounds did Sellers have to sue Tom?"

"Emotional distress and harassment."

"So his dog attacks Tom's dog, and he's the one with distress?"

"That's what he said. I read both lawsuits, and Sellers claims his family has lost their ability to enjoy their home due to the aggression of their neighbors."

"Didn't it occur to him that he could rehome his dogs to somewhere other than a residential neighborhood and begin enjoying his home again?"

"He said he'd never rehome them. They're part of his family."

"I think we should have a chat with him tomorrow. Find out where he is during the day and shoot me a message."

"Will do."

"Thanks for the good work."

"You got it."

Sam closed her phone and plugged it into the bedside charger as she thought about how she might approach an interview with the neighbor. First, she'd speak to Leslie Forrester about the dispute. She should also ask Leslie about Tom's potential affair, but she wanted to dig into that further before she mentioned it. If it was just a rumor, there was no sense upsetting Leslie more than she already was.

That was the last thought she had before she was startled awake when Nick got into bed.

"What the hell?"

"Huh?"

"I was thinking about something, and the next thing I know, it's quite a bit later, and you're here."

"I believe it's possible you fell asleep."

"How does it just happen like that? Awake one minute and dead to the world the next?"

"You're asking me? That's never happened in my life."

"I think, and please don't laugh at me..."

"I'll try my best not to, but I can't wait to hear this."

"I might be getting old."

He laughed so hard he had tears in his eyes. "Shut *up*."

"I'm serious! Old people do that. They'll be talking one second and snoring the next. That's what I just basically did. Next, I'll be drooling."

"You're exhausted, Samantha, after a long, difficult day that involved blood and needles. Cut yourself a break."

"Don't forget you promised to still love me when I'm old, which may happen sooner than expected."

He put his arm around her and made her comfortable in his embrace. "I'll love you for as long as I'm drawing breath, and then I'll love you for all of eternity."

"Wow, you're good. Who writes your stuff?"

"All original material. Get some sleep. Tomorrow's a big day around here."

"I'll love you for all eternity, too, even if you're making me have *tea* with the prime minister's wife."

He rocked with silent laughter. "That's good, because I'm kinda counting on that."

She fell asleep smiling.

CHAPTER FOURTEEN

I n the morning, Nick gently reminded Sam one last time that she needed to be ready for her date with Mrs. Hutchinson at three.

"Yes, dear," she said as she kissed him goodbye. "I'll be home in plenty of time."

"I appreciate it."

"You're lucky I love you."

"I'm the luckiest guy in the world because you love me. Be safe out there."

"Always am."

On the ride to HQ, she called Leslie Forrester. "I'm sorry to bother you so early."

"It's okay. I'm not sleeping very well, and I was going to call you today to tell you the funeral is scheduled for next Wednesday at the National Cathedral. Conlon will follow up with the details."

"I'll be there. The reason I called was to talk about your neighbor and the situation with the Dobermans."

"Oh my. You don't think that's related to Tom's death, do you?"

"Not really, but we're investigating all possibilities, up to and including that. I wanted your take on that."

"I wouldn't put anything past him or his crazy-ass wife. They're super entitled and think they should be able to do whatever they want on their property, including raising dogs that attack other pets."

"Had it happened before your dog was attacked?"

"The neighbors on the other side of them say one of those dogs killed their cat. They can't prove it, but they're certain it was them. They're always getting out of the yard. People are afraid to let their kids play outside."

"Where does Animal Control stand on this?"

"To be honest, they've been mostly useless. They come by, cite the owners, and then we never hear from them again."

Sam's first stop at HQ would be to visit the folks at Animal Control. "What's the wife's name?"

"Laurel, and he's Ralph. Tom called him Ralph Kramden." It took a second for Sam to connect the name to the iconic grouch from the old TV show *The Honeymooners*.

"To his face?"

"Yep."

Sam laughed. "That's funny."

"Not sure Ralph thought so." She sighed. "I can't believe I'll never hear Tom call him that again."

"I'm sorry. I can't imagine how awful that must be." And she didn't want to imagine it.

"Thank you. It's just such a shock. Ten days ago, we were laughing at dinner with the Coxes, and Damien Bryant. And now Tom's dead, and Damien has been charged with crimes."

"Wait. You had dinner with them ten days ago?"

"Yes. We got together frequently. Not so much since Damien started dating JoAnn, but before that, it was almost every week."

"Who's JoAnn?"

"She's a nurse he started dating about six months ago."

"Do you know her last name?"

"I don't. I only met her a couple of times."

Sam made a note of the woman's name. "How does Damien fit in with Tom and Reggie?"

"He'd been a good friend of theirs for about twelve years. Tom used to say it never hurt to have friends in Congress, especially if they were on the Judiciary Committee."

"Wouldn't that be a conflict of interest? For a congressman on that committee to be close, personal friends with the AG and a USA? Or for even the AG and a USA to be close?"

"I'm not sure how all that works. Tom used to say Washington is a small town, and everyone is friends with everyone."

"Thank you for this added insight. I really appreciate it."

"I wish there was more I could do."

"I'll let you know if we have other questions. I'll see you Wednesday, if not before."

"Thank you again for all you're doing."

"I'll keep you posted."

Sam closed her phone and took a minute to process the information Leslie had given her. Every time she talked to someone close to Tom, she found out more about the deep ties between him and Reggie Cox, not to mention she had proof that Bryant had lied to her about being close friends with Forrester.

At HQ, she went straight to Animal Control on the second floor and asked to speak to the lieutenant in charge. Everyone in their office stared at her from the second she walked in. She ignored them while she waited for the LT.

A heavyset woman Sam hadn't met before appeared from an office in the back of the space. She had a dour expression and drab brown hair that needed a brush.

"I'm Lieutenant Diane Webster."

"Lieutenant Holland."

"No kidding," she said with a sneer. "What can I do for you?"

What the hell was her problem? "I'm investigating the murder of U.S. Attorney Tom Forrester. It's come to our attention that he was involved in an altercation with one of his neighbors after the neighbor's dog attacked Tom's."

"What about it?"

"I was wondering if you have any contacts at Gaithersburg Animal Control who could get us a copy of the report and any impressions as well as what, if any, follow-up was done about the dog."

"Are you accusing them of something?"

"What? No. I'm asking for information for a case."

"'What, if any, follow-up was done about the dog' sure sounds like an accusation to me."

"Well, it wasn't. I'm asking what was done or not done about the dog. Sometimes, something is done. Other times, it isn't. I'm asking which this was."

"I'll reach out to them."

"Thanks. I'll wait."

"It'll take me a minute, and I was in the middle of something else."

"Something more pressing than the murder of a U.S. Attorney?"

Oh, she didn't like that. "I'll ask for a copy of their report and get it to you." She turned and walked away.

"Was it something I said?" Sam asked the admin.

"She has a beef with you," she whispered. The young woman had light brown skin and pretty dark eyes. Her braids were wrapped in a tall bun.

"Whatever for? I've never seen her before today."

"I've said too much."

"Bring me that file when it's ready. Let's talk."

"Um, okay."

For fuck's sake, Sam thought as she headed downstairs. "How do I manage to piss off people I've never met?"

"What'd you say, Sam?" Freddie asked as he stood in his cubicle.

"Do you know Webster in Animal Control?"

"Not personally."

"Me either, but apparently, she has a beef with me."

"What'd you do?"

"It's probably the fact that I breathe that annoys her."

"Or maybe it's because you're so good at your job, and she wishes she was you."

"I think the breathing thing is more likely. I want to talk to Forrester's neighbors. The ones with the dog."

"Is that why you were tangling with Webster?"

"I wasn't tangling with her. I asked for a copy of the report on the incident with Forrester's dog. Apparently, I was out of line."

Captain Malone came into the pit, looking stressed and aggravated. "The media is going nuts for an update on Forrester."

"I've got dick to tell them."

"You have to tell them something before they stampede the building. I've rarely seen more of them out there."

"I'll take care of it. After that, we're going to see Cox and then to Gaithersburg to talk to Forrester's neighbor."

"What's up with Cox?"

"He asked me to come in."

"Interesting, no?"

"For sure. I'm worried he might be up to his neck in this, which could cause me some trouble at home."

"First sign of it crossing that line, I'll take over anything to do with him. I'd go with you today, but I can't. I've got other fires to put out."

"Got it."

"What's with Forrester's neighbor?"

"A dispute over dogs."

Malone gave her a skeptical look.

"I'm pulling the threads, Cap."

"All right."

"Don't forget I'm leaving early today."

"Ah, yes, the Canadian state dinner. I've got my monkey suit ready to go."

Sam smiled. "See you there, if not before." To Freddie, she said, "Let me do the press briefing, and then we'll get going."

"I'll be ready."

"Have you given everyone assignments for today?"

"I'm waiting on Gonzo to get here. He's running late. We'll have the others focus on emails and texts. We're only about halfway through what Archie gave us."

"Do me a favor and pull warrants for the cell phone data for Ralph and Laurel Sellers."

"Who're they?"

"Forrester's neighbors. He had a beef with them over their dog attacking his that led to lawsuits. It's just a hunch, but I'd like to know where they were when he was killed."

Cameron came over to them, looking upset—or maybe shocked.

"What's wrong?" Sam asked tentatively.

"Avery's been shot."

"What? Where?"

"Coming out of the gym on 22nd."

"Is he..." Sam was afraid to finish that question.

"He was alive but unresponsive when EMS arrived. They took him to GW."

"Does Shelby know?"

"I called Avery's deputy, George Terrell, to find out how that was being handled. He said he was on the way to the White House now to notify her."

Sam wasn't sure whether she should go to the hospital or home to be with Shelby. "I need to go to her."

"No," Malone said.

Sam looked at him as if he'd said something she didn't understand.

"I need you on Forrester. I know Avery's a close friend, but there's nothing you can do for him right now. We'll put people on it and figure out what happened to him."

Lucas and Harper came into the pit.

"Did you hear about Hill?" Lucas asked.

"Just now," Sam said.

"You two get over to GW and see what you can find out," Malone said to her and Harper. "Tell Archie to pull the film from around the gym on 22nd."

"Yes, sir," Lucas said.

She and Harper headed toward the morgue exit.

Sam very much wanted to go with them, but Malone had given her an order. "I, uh, I'll get ready to brief the media on Forrester."

"Take a minute," Malone said.

"H-he just had a baby. They just had a baby..." Her heart ached for both of them, especially after the recent home-invasion trauma.

Sam hadn't been this upset in a while.

"I'll brief the media," Freddie said.

"That's okay."

"I'll do it, Sam. It's good experience for me, and you're in no condition to do it."

"Are you sure?"

"Very."

"Thank you, grasshopper."

"No problem."

"I'll help you get ready," Malone said to Freddie.

After they walked away, Sam's phone rang. Her heart sank when she saw Shelby's name on the screen. "Hey, I was just going to call you."

"Sam! What do you know? Is he... He can't be dead. Please tell me he isn't."

"I heard he was unresponsive but alive when EMS took him to the hospital. Where are you?"

"I'm with George. He's taking me and the baby to GW. Celia offered to keep her for me, but I didn't know how long I'd be gone."

Sam gave Shelby credit for keeping her shit together and thinking about practicalities at such a terrible time.

"I would come there, but—"

"I know you can't. Do what you have to do. That's what Avery would want. I'll keep you posted."

"I'm praying for you all, Tinker Bell."

"Thank you."

Sam put down her phone and dropped her head into her hands. How was Shelby holding it together when her husband had been *shot*, only days after they'd welcomed their new baby?

The secure BlackBerry rang.

She took the call from her husband. "Hi."

"What do you know about Avery?"

"He was unresponsive but alive when EMS transported him."

"Good God. Have you talked to Shelby?"

"Just now. Avery's deputy, George, is transporting her and the baby to GW."

"Are you going there?"

"I can't. We're under tremendous pressure on Forrester... Malone basically told me to stay put."

"Oh shit. You must be so torn. I'm sorry, babe."

"It's okay. He's right. We're getting nowhere fast on Forrester, and I've got a lot of ground to cover today."

"And I'm cutting your day short."

"It's fine."

"I can't stop thinking about Avery and how they just had the baby..."

"I know. It's horrible."

"Could it be related to the home invasion?"

"Not sure how. The people who did that are in custody."

"It was just a thought."

"It's a good thought, and I'll pass it on to the team working that case."

"Hang in there, babe. He's young and strong. I'm sure he'll be fine."

"Look at you... Worried about Avery Hill. Once upon a time, you wanted to kill him yourself."

"Times change. He's a friend. I'm worried."

"Me, too. I'll text you if I hear anything."

"Thanks. Be careful with my love, especially with someone out there shooting your colleagues."

"Will do. See you soon."

"Can't wait."

Gonzo came to the door, looking pissed off. "Motherfucking traffic in this city. Thirty minutes to get across the Memorial Bridge." He took a closer look at her. "What's wrong?"

"Avery was shot this morning, coming out of his gym on 22nd."

"Oh my God. Is he okay?"

"Not sure yet."

"Jeez, and they just had a baby."

"Yeah."

Sam was still standing there, lost in thought, when Freddie and Malone appeared behind Gonzo, who turned to them.

"How'd it go?" Sam asked.

"Brutal," Freddie said.

"He did a great job telling them what we know so far and that we're working the investigation with all available resources, etc."

"Thank you for handling that, Freddie."

"I'd say it was no problem, but I may need hazardous duty pay. Any word on Avery?"

"Nothing new. We need to get going to the meeting with Cox." To Gonzo, she said, "Pick up where Carlucci and Dominguez left off with the paper trail. Get me a thread to pull."

"On it."

"Let's go see what the Attorney General wants with us."

CHAPTER FIFTEEN

S helby told herself that her only goal was to hold it together, no matter what was waiting for her at the hospital. The possibility that Avery could be...

No.

No.

No.

She would not let her mind go there.

With baby Maisie strapped into her car seat next to her in the back of an FBI SUV, Shelby focused on breathing and staying as calm as she possibly could.

"Is there any word?" she asked George when they were stopped in traffic.

"Only that they're working on him."

What would she do if he died? How would she survive without the love of her life after waiting so long to find him? When she glanced at her baby girl and pondered the possibility of her and Noah growing up without the daddy who loved them so...

Stop it, Shelby Faircloth Hill. Just stop that.

George had apparently decided he'd had enough of the traffic and turned on the siren that had cars moving out of their way to let them through.

They pulled up to the Emergency entrance at GW a few minutes later.

George turned to her. "Let me go in and figure out what's going on. I'll be right back for you."

Shelby appreciated him doing what he could to make this horrific situation easier for her. "Thank you."

For the rest of her life, she'd never forget opening the door to their third-floor suite to find one of the White House ushers and George at her door. Her knees had turned liquid when she'd had a second to register George's presence as well as his tormented expression.

"Avery's been shot," he'd said.

Shelby had nearly blacked out from the sudden wave of adrenaline that had overtaken her entire system.

George had reached out to steady her. He'd been steadfast as she'd gathered the baby and what she needed to take with her to the hospital, which was the last place she'd wanted to bring a newborn. But she'd had no breast milk pumped or anything prepared to leave her with someone else.

Celia, having heard the news, had come running to help, offering to keep the baby for her, but Shelby hadn't wanted to have to leave Avery to come home to feed her. So she'd asked Celia to take over from the nanny with Noah that afternoon so she could stay put for as long as she'd need to be at the hospital.

She wasn't sure how she'd thought so clearly, but all that had mattered was getting to Avery, telling him she loved him and that he had to be okay.

Tears filled her eyes, but she fought them off. If she started crying, she might never stop.

George opened the back door to the SUV. "They've got him stabilized and are taking him up to surgery. They said you could see him, but we need to be quick."

Shelby unclipped the baby from the car seat, gathered her into her arms and followed George inside.

They took her directly to a cubicle where it looked as if a war had been fought. The sight of blood had her feeling faint for a second before she forced herself to move to her husband's bedside.

Oh God, he looked awful. Pale and pasty with tubes coming from all over. A massive, blood-soaked bandage covered his right shoulder.

"This is Mrs. Hill," George said to the doctor, who stood on the other side of the bed.

"How... how is he?"

"He suffered a gunshot wound to the upper chest that narrowly missed his aorta. We're taking him to surgery to retrieve the bullet and clean up the damage."

"So he... he's going to be okay?"

"He should make a full recovery, but it'll take some time."

Full recovery were the only words she wanted to hear.

She turned to George and handed over the baby.

He seemed flustered for a second before he accepted the tiny bundle into his arms.

Shelby leaned over the bed rail to kiss her husband's cheek and to brush the hair back from his forehead. "You need to do whatever they tell you to because we love you and need you. Noah and Maisie need their daddy, and I need my love."

"We should go," the doctor said.

Shelby kissed Avery's cool lips and forced herself to pull back, to let him go so the doctors could do whatever was needed to return him to her healthy and whole.

After she stepped back, they whisked him away with urgency that shattered her nerves, even with the optimistic prognosis. She retrieved the baby from George.

"They said the surgery will take about three hours. Do you want to go home to wait?"

She thought about that for a second. "No, I'll stay here so I can be there when he comes out."

A nurse told them where the OR waiting room was.

"I'm going to move the SUV, and then I'll find you there."

"Thank you for everything, George."

"No problem."

Shelby walked to the elevators and found the waiting room.

At the reception desk, she was given a number to watch for updates from the OR on a digital board.

Just as she settled into a chair, the baby woke with a gasp and a hungry cry.

As she took off her coat and worked to situate the baby to breastfeed, Shelby hoped that George remembered to bring the diaper bag she'd left in the back seat in her haste to get to Avery.

What was she doing in an OR waiting room anyway?

Her phone was vibrating in her coat pocket with one text after another from concerned family and friends. She'd texted Avery's parents and her own sisters on the way to the hospital and would update them as soon as she got the baby fed and changed.

Juggling a newborn in a hospital waiting room would make for a very long day, but she wouldn't be anywhere else while her love was in surgery.

"He's going to be just fine," she whispered to the baby, who was covered by the pink cashmere scarf Avery had given her for Christmas. "There's nothing he wouldn't do for us. He'll fight so hard to come home."

Tears slid down her cheeks despite her intense desire to hold it together.

She thought she was seeing things when her sister Ginger came rushing into the room and took the seat next to Shelby.

"I came as fast as I could. How is he?"

"He's in surgery. They said he should make a full recovery, but it was a close call."

Ginger put her arm around Shelby, who leaned into the support.

"Thank you for coming."

"I'm here for as long as you need me."

COX MADE them wait fifteen minutes past nine thirty.

Fuming, Sam was about to leave when a young male assistant, whose voice she recognized from the phone calls, came to get them.

"We're sorry for the delay. General Cox had to deal with an emergency."

Sam wondered if that emergency had anything to do with the shooting of FBI Agent Avery Hill.

They were led into a wood-paneled office with shelves full of books and awards of every imaginable kind.

Cox stood behind a massive desk and gestured for them to have a seat in leather chairs. "I'm so sorry to keep you waiting. One of our federal agents was shot this morning, and needless to say, it's thrown a wrench into the day."

"Agent Hill is a good friend of ours," Sam said.

"Yes, of course. I understand he and his family have been staying with you at the White House."

"Yes." The details of their arrangement were none of his business. "What're you hearing about his condition?"

"He has a gunshot wound to the upper chest and is in surgery now. They're saying he should make a full recovery."

"Well, that's a relief."

"Indeed. So soon after welcoming a baby, too."

"You asked us to come in, General Cox. What can we do for you?"

"After we spoke the other day, it occurred to me that in my shock, I failed to mention my decades-long friendship with Tom Forrester."

"We're aware of it."

He seemed surprised to hear that.

"What I'd like to know is how you could've failed to mention such a relevant detail to us when we met the first time."

His amiable expression instantly hardened. "As I said, I was in shock the first time we met. You'll have to excuse the oversight."

"You've been around a long time."

"Much longer than you have."

And he was petty, too. "Long enough to know what information is important to an investigation, especially one as high-profile as this one. I must be honest when I tell you I was shocked to hear that you and Forrester go all the way back to college. And knowing the stakes of this investigation, why, I wondered, wouldn't you have told us that yourself?"

For a long moment, he simply stared at her, as if he couldn't believe she'd had the audacity to speak to him that way. Apparently, that didn't happen very often.

"I can only blame my lack of clarity on shock. Losing Tom is like losing a member of my immediate family."

"Tell me the truth about his investigation of Bryant. The one that was kept off the books while the two of you continued to socialize with him and his girlfriend, JoAnn."

Again, Cox seemed flabbergasted that she'd have the audacity to ask such a thing. Or maybe it was because she was so well-informed. "I told you before that I can't speak about confidential investigations."

"Even if that investigation might've gotten someone who was like a member of your immediate family murdered?"

"That's not what happened."

"You sound rather certain of that. Do you know what *did* happen?"

"Of course I don't! If I did, I would say so."

"You issued an all-hands email to Justice Department employees."

He looked stunned. "How do you know about a confidential in-house message?"

"How many people work for the DOJ?"

"Uh, around a hundred and fifteen thousand."

"You sent a message to a hundred and fifteen thousand people and expected that to stay confidential?" She looked at Freddie. "I mean, I don't know anything about being the AG, but I know people, and most of them can't keep their mouth shut about anything. I could've heard about that message from any one of them."

"You can be certain I'll launch a full investigation into who leaked that message."

"Knock yourself out. In the meantime, maybe you can tell me why you suspect someone inside the department in Tom's murder."

"I never said that!"

"Your message said that."

"No, it didn't. It said that anyone who knows anything should come forward."

"In other words, 'I suspect someone in this department knows something.'"

"You read it wrong, but it wasn't intended for you, was it?"

Sam's frustration with him was about to boil over. "I feel like we're talking in circles here. Why did you ask us to come in?"

"I wanted to be forthright about my long relationship with Tom and offer the resources of the Justice Department to your investigation."

"Thanks. We're good."

Cox shifted his gaze to Freddie. "I saw your press briefing this morning."

"What about it?" Sam asked.

"It looked to me—and I could be wrong, of course—that you don't know anything more today about what happened to Tom than you did the day he was killed."

Sam wished she could throat-punch the man. "When you're running an intense investigation, do you go before the media and tell them everything you know? You've overseen a criminal investigation before, right? Oh wait, that was a hundred years ago for you. So maybe you don't know. I'd be happy to educate you if that would help you understand."

His expression was thunderous. "This meeting is over."

"Since you may not be clear on how these things work, if you know something about what happened to Tom, it's in your best interest to tell us now. If we find out later that you obstructed our investigation, you'll be charged."

"Get out."

Sam and Freddie got up and left the room. They walked past the young man at the desk outside the AG's office and were headed for the elevators when Sam turned back to speak to the admin. He was of average build with thinning brown hair and eyes that might've been hazel. It was hard to tell, as he wore glasses. "Are you the one who called me to set up this meeting?"

"I am."

"What's your name?"

"Why does that matter?"

"It matters because I say it matters."

He seemed to scoff at that.

"We could take this downtown to my office if it's too difficult for you to answer my question here."

"You can't just arrest people."

She glanced at Freddie. "Can I just arrest people?"

"If the person is hampering a homicide investigation, you absolutely can."

"How am I hampering a homicide investigation?"

"You're failing to answer the most basic of questions. Let's try this one more time... What is your name?"

"Tell her," Cox said from the doorway to his office.

Sam hadn't noticed him there.

"Henry Allston."

"How long have you worked for General Cox?"

Henry glanced at his employer, who gestured for him to tell her.

"Eight years."

"Thank you. I hope that wasn't too difficult for you. Let's go, Detective Cruz."

"That was amazing," Freddie whispered while they waited for the elevator.

"What was?"

"You. In there and then with the assistant. Face-to-face with the AG with no effs to give."

"Did you just kinda swear?"

"Maybe, but damn, Sam. I wish we'd recorded that."

"Don't be too impressed. I just made a powerful enemy of a man who answers to my husband, not to mention he could cause big trouble for us and the department."

They stepped into the elevator. "Why'd you do it?"

Sam pressed the L for Lobby. "Because I wanted to know if he was feeding us a load of bullshit."

"And?"

"He isn't telling us everything he knows. That's for sure."

"Wouldn't it be in his best interest to help figure out who killed one of his USAs as fast as we can?"

"You'd think so, wouldn't you?"

"Did you tell Nick you were meeting with him?"

"He knew, but we didn't talk details. We're keeping it separate."

"I suppose that's for the best. What're you thinking with the assistant?"

"I'm not sure, but him not being willing to share his name put up some red flags."

"I'll take a look at him later today."

"That was going to be my next request."

At security, they reclaimed their weapons and headed outside, where a squad of Secret Service agents kept about thirty reporters from pouncing on them. The minute they saw Sam, they started screaming questions at her.

"Why are you meeting with Cox?"

"Is he implicated in the Forrester murder?"

"What did he tell you?"

"Who shot your friend Hill?"

"Who killed Forrester?"

"Was it the same guy?"

Vernon hustled them into the SUV.

"Other than that mess," Sam said to Vernon, using her chin to gesture to the media, "what's wrong?"

"Nothing. Why?"

"You look extra vigilant."

"A USA was murdered, and an FBI agent was shot. You're meeting with the AG, which has the media going wild. Calls for extra vigilance."

"I guess so."

"Any word on Agent Hill?"

"He's in surgery and expected to survive." Sam thought about her next move and decided she wanted to see Shelby, even if just for a minute. "Let's stop at GW on the way to Gaithersburg." It wasn't technically on the way, but she couldn't stay away when one of her closest friends needed all the support she could get.

"Yes, ma'am."

Sam would've scowled at him for calling her that, but the door closed before she could. He couldn't help himself. While Vernon drove them to the hospital, Sam called Malone.

"How'd it go with Cox?"

"Not great." She filled him in on what'd transpired. "Needless to say, he's not happy with me, but I still feel like he's not telling me everything he knows."

"What's your next move where he's concerned?"

"I don't have one. I doubt he'd willingly speak to me again. We had media outside Justice when we were leaving. One of them asked if the same shooter did Forrester and Hill."

"We'll get to work on the ballistics once we have Avery's bullet."

"Thanks, Cap. That feels like a long shot, but we have to cross the T's. Next stop is to talk to Forrester's neighbor."

"Let me know how that goes."

"Will do." She closed her phone. "I feel guilty about the hospital stop."

"Don't sweat it," Freddie said. "He wouldn't care."

"He told me to stay focused on the case, and he's right. That's what I need to do, especially when I have to leave early today."

"If Avery's shooting turns out to be somehow related to Forrester's, then you're focusing on the case by going to the hospital."

Sam spun in her seat to stare at him.

"What?" he asked.

"It's official."

"What is?"

"I've thoroughly corrupted you."

Vernon and Jimmy laughed.

Freddie scoffed. "Whatever."

"It's true! You just produced a plausible justification for me defying a direct order from the captain. That's impressive."

"A normal boss would say, 'Freddie, don't help me defy the big boss.' Mine gives me props for helping her to skirt a direct order."

"You're damned right she does."

"On another note, can we stop at the cafeteria while we're at GW? I'm starving, and they have the best pizza there."

"Do you think about anything other than food?"

"I think about sex. *A lot.*"

"Cripes, I walked right into that one, didn't I?"

Vernon cracked up. "Y'all are funny."

"I'm funny," Sam said. "He's coming along nicely."

She loved Freddie so, so much. And more than anything, she loved bickering and bantering with him. Her relationship with him was one of her favorite things in life. She was almost certain he felt the same way. Most of the time, anyway.

"So is that a yes to the pizza?"

"We'll see if we can squeeze it in."

"Do you guys want food?" Freddie asked the agents.

"Nah, we're good," Vernon answered for both of them.

At the hospital, Vernon turned to them. "Give me five minutes to clear a path."

"I don't have much more to spare."

"I'll be quick."

"Thank you, Vernon." After he walked away, she glanced at Freddie. "I'm afraid to look at my watch."

"Almost ten thirty."

"Ugh. We've got to get in and out, get to Gaithersburg and then to the meeting with Conlon." It would be tight.

"Since I'm not under Secret Service protection, perhaps I could procure lunch while you wait for Vernon to deliver you to Shelby. To save time, that is."

She rolled her eyes. "Go ahead."

"What do you want?"

"I guess I'll have some of that pizza you raved about because it's all I can think about since you mentioned it. And a bottle of water." She pulled out her wallet and handed him her debit card. "My treat."

"Wow, my lucky day."

"Don't push it. Get going and hurry up."

"I'm hurrying."

CHAPTER SIXTEEN

As Sam watched him jog into the hospital, she envied his ability to move about freely. In all likelihood, she'd never have that luxury again, as she and Nick would have Secret Service protection for the rest of their lives.

That was a daunting thought that she chose not to entertain any further on a day when her first lady duties were already weighing on her. What in the hell would she talk to the prime minister's wife about? She'd rarely experienced true social anxiety until she became first lady and was expected to know what to say to dignitaries in any situation.

Vernon returned and told Jimmy to stay with the SUV while he escorted Sam inside.

Like always, everything stopped when people realized who'd walked into the room.

Sam ignored the stares and kept her focus on getting to Shelby.

When they were in the elevator, she turned to Vernon. "Can I ask you something?"

"Anything."

"What do I talk to the Canadian prime minister's wife about over tea?"

His lips rolled into his mouth as if he was trying not to laugh.

"It's not funny!"

"I'm not laughing."

"You are on the inside."

"You gotta admit the idea of you at a tea is kind of funny."

"I don't even like tea! It tastes like dirty water."

"Maybe refrain from saying that to her."

"I'm serious, Vernon! *What* do I talk to her about?"

"Doesn't she have kids, too?"

"I think so."

"Didn't you get a briefing document about the visit?"

"Lilia gave me something yesterday. I haven't read it yet."

"Sam!"

"What? I've been busy."

"The woman is coming *today*. You might want to take a second to figure that out so you know what to talk to her about."

"That's probably covered in the brief, right?"

"I can't with you."

"Don't tell anyone I'm like this, you hear me?"

"Your many, *many* secrets are safe with me."

The doors opened, and they stepped off the elevator across from the surgical waiting room. Sam spotted Shelby right away, thanks to the fact that she was dressed all in pink, as per usual.

Shelby burst into tears when she saw Sam coming.

They came together in a tight hug. "How is he?"

"Still in surgery. They said it could take three hours."

"They're being thorough. I'm sure he'll be fine."

"I really hope so. The waiting is making me crazy."

Sam would be a raving lunatic and prayed to all the gods in heaven that she was never in that situation. "Hi, Ginger."

Shelby's sister held the sleeping baby. "Hi, Sam. Nice to see you again."

"You, too. Wish it was under better circumstances."

"Same."

Sam returned her attention to Shelby. "I wish I could stay and wait with you, Tinker Bell."

"You've got the Canadians today. I can't believe you're here at all."

"I had to come hug you and tell you I love you and Avery, and I'm sure he'll be back to normal in no time."

"He has to be," Shelby said softly. "He just has to be."

"He will be. He's tough."

"Do you know anything about who did this to him?"

"Not yet, but we've got people on it, as does the FBI."

A doctor wearing scrubs and one of those matching caps came into the waiting room. "Avery Hill's family?"

"Me." Shelby raised her hand. "I'm his family."

"Everything went well, and he's in recovery. You should be able to see him in an hour or two."

"Oh, thank you. Thank you so much."

Sam stepped forward.

The doctor did a double take when he recognized her.

"Needless to say, Metro PD is interested in examining the bullet. Were you able to remove it?"

"Yes. I'll have someone bring it to you."

"If you could do that yourself, I'd appreciate it. Chain of custody is important."

"Understood. I'll be right back."

And with that, Sam had justified her side trip to the hospital.

Sam hugged Shelby again. "I'm so glad he's all right."

"Me, too." Shelby sniffed. "I can't believe how close I came to losing him. Right after he nearly lost me. It's too much."

"You've had a rough couple of weeks, but everyone is okay, and that's all that matters. We're here to help you guys with whatever you need."

"I'm very thankful for everyone who's rallied around us." She wiped away tears. "As long as he's okay, so am I."

The doctor returned a few minutes later with a plastic bag containing the bullet.

"Can you give me your email address? I'll need you to sign the evidence form indicating everyone who had the bullet in their custody." Sam wrote down the address he recited. "Thank you very much."

"No problem. A nurse will find you when he's ready for visitors, Mrs. Hill."

"Thank you again for saving him."

"He got very lucky."

"I'll check in later." Sam hugged Shelby again. "Hang in there."

"I will. Thank you for coming by on such a busy day."

"I needed to see you and to hear he's okay."

Freddie came into the waiting room, carrying two small pizza boxes. "That took forever. How is he?"

"All good. Out of surgery and on his way to a full recovery. Let's get going."

He gave Shelby a one-armed hug. "Glad to hear the good news. Elin said to tell you she's thinking of you guys and congrats on the baby."

"Thank you. Tell her I appreciate it."

Sam took Freddie by the arm to steer him out of the room. "I've got the bullet. Tell Lucas we'll deliver it to the lab. She's working on Avery's shooting."

"I'll text her from the car."

They ate the pizza while Vernon drove them to Gaithersburg.

Sam had to admit the pizza was exceptional for hospital fare. She tried not to think about the extra calories or whether she'd look bloated in her dress later. "I can't believe we have to go to a freaking state dinner tonight."

"Elin has never been more excited. She took the day off to get ready."

"I'll look like dog shit next to her."

"Stop," he said, laughing. "You will not."

"I didn't take the day off to get ready the way I should have."

"You'll be fine."

"What if I'm not? What if I screw this up somehow for him? What if—?"

"Sam, stop. You'll be great. I have no doubt."

"Nor do we," Vernon said.

"I'm glad you guys are confident. This is where I feel comfortable. Out here, tracking down murderers, pissing off the AG, pulling threads. I know who I am here. That's not the case as first lady. I don't know who I am in that role."

"You're Nick's wife," Freddie said, "and that's all he needs you to be. If you're there for him when he needs you, then you're a success as first lady in the opinion of the only person who matters."

Vernon met her gaze in the mirror. "I agree with Detective Cruz."

"Thank you for that. I appreciate the reminder."

"Nick wouldn't want you freaking out about this, would he?"

"It would annoy him if he heard me saying I'm worried about messing up."

"I think it's amazing," Jimmy said.

"What is?" Sam asked.

"That someone like you would ever be worried about what people think or about messing up at the state dinner. Everyone who knows you thinks you're incredible."

Sam was unreasonably touched by the young agent's kind words. "Thank you, Jimmy. That's very sweet of you to say, and for the record, not everyone who knows me thinks I'm incredible."

"We do," Freddie said. "And Nick does. Your kids certainly do. Your sisters, nieces, nephews, many friends..."

"That's more than enough." She released a deep breath, feeling better about how this day might unfold after what they'd said. "Means a lot to me to have your support, guys. It really does."

"We're here any time you need a boost," Vernon said. "And personally, I can't wait to watch you shine tonight."

That was something Skip Holland might've said once upon a time. "You're going to make me weepy. Knock it off."

Vernon chuckled. "Yes, ma'am."

They pulled up to the guardhouse in Forrester's neighborhood a few minutes later.

Vernon spoke to the guard, and they were allowed in.

Sam was glad they hadn't had to argue about it. She had no time for that nonsense today. As they passed Forrester's home, Sam noted a driveway full of cars and was glad to know the family was being well supported in their time of grief.

The Sellers home was bigger than Forrester's, with twice as

many third-floor dormers as well as a huge front porch. The brick façade had been painted white, and wood shutters adorned the windows. Sam preferred that look to the red brick that was so popular in the area.

Vernon followed her and Freddie up the sidewalk to the front door.

As expected, the doorbell was ridiculously over the top.

"*Why?* Just, why?"

Freddie grunted out a laugh.

The sound of dogs barking nearly drowned out the doorbell, but not entirely.

Sam took a step back, intimidated by the dogs, who sounded huge and vicious.

The woman who came to the door appeared to be in her midforties, with graying blonde hair and blue eyes that immediately widened when she recognized Sam. "May I help you?"

Sam and Freddie showed their badges. "Mrs. Sellers, I'm Lieutenant Holland, and this is my partner, Detective Cruz. We'd like to ask you a few questions."

"This isn't really a good time."

"We can do it at our place, if you'd prefer."

Sam took great pleasure in watching her meaning register with the woman.

"I, uh, just give me a minute to secure the dogs."

"That'd be good."

The door closed.

"'We can do it at our place, if you prefer,'" Freddie said with a laugh. "Did you see her face when she realized what you meant?"

"I enjoyed it very much." Sam leaned in to look into the window on the side of the door. "I'm giving her two more minutes to get her ass back here before I start robo-ringing that hideous doorbell."

"Is that a thing? Robo-ringing?"

"It's about to be."

Fortunately, Laurel Sellers returned before her two minutes were up. "Come in." She glanced at Vernon, who followed them inside. He didn't normally do that, but with the heightened state of alert, he was staying closer to Sam than usual. "Who's that?"

"I'm with the Secret Service, ma'am."

"Oh. Okay." She led them into a living room that smelled of lemon polish and potpourri. "What can I do for you?"

"Is your husband here, by any chance?"

"He's working in his office."

"Here?" Carlucci hadn't been able to figure out his work situation the night before.

"Yes."

"Will you please get him?"

"He's in meetings."

"Like I said before, we can do this here, or we can do it downtown. It's up to you."

She gave Sam a foul look before she got up and left the room.

Freddie chuckled. "That line works every time."

"I need to use it more often."

The husband appeared with her a few minutes later. Ralph Sellers carried extra weight that gave him a burly appearance. His salt-and-pepper hair was cut short, and his complexion was ruddy. He wore a Bluetooth phone thing in his ear. "What's this about?"

Sam and Freddie showed their badges, and she introduced them.

While Laurel returned to her seat on the sofa, Ralph stood in the doorway to the room as if he couldn't be bothered to come all the way into the room. "What can we do for you?"

"We're investigating the murder of Tom Forrester."

"What's that got to do with us?"

"You countersued him when he filed a claim to get you to pay for his dog's vet bills after your dog attacked his, right?"

"Yeah, so?"

"I've never been sued by a neighbor, but I have to think there's a lot of anger exchanged before lawsuits are filed."

"He was a self-righteous prick."

"Ralph! Stop."

"What? He thought he was Mr. Law Enforcement at home, too. It was his way or the highway around here. Ask anyone."

"Did he have challenges with the other neighbors?"

"No one liked him. He made sure everyone knew he was a bigwig at Justice."

Sam glanced at Freddie, who seemed as perplexed as she felt. "That doesn't sound like the man we knew."

"Well, that's who he was around here. He liked to be right about everything."

"Did you feel you bore any responsibility for your dog harming his?"

"We apologized for what happened to his dog and offered to contribute to the vet bill, but he wasn't satisfied with that. He wanted us to pay ten grand, which was ridiculous."

"We were told Snowflake required significant surgery."

"So he said, but he refused to provide invoices from the vet. He said it was none of our business and told us to pay ten grand, or he'd sue us. We refused and he sued. We countersued for emotional distress and harm to our reputation."

Sam wondered why Tom wouldn't have provided the invoices and made a note to ask Leslie that.

"If you're thinking I killed him, I didn't," Ralph said.

"Where were you early Sunday morning?"

"Asleep in my bed."

"If we subpoena your phone records, is that what we'll find?"

"That's exactly what you'll find. I was looking forward to beating that smug bastard in court. I had nothing to do with what happened to him, and neither did Laurel. We feel for his wife and daughters, but we're not sad to see the last of him."

Heartless, Sam thought.

"Is there anything else? I need to get back to work."

"That's it for now, but please stay available in case we have follow-up questions."

"You know where to find us."

He turned and walked away.

"Will you please write down your cell phone numbers?" Sam asked Laurel.

She took the pad and pen from Sam and wrote down the numbers. "Ralph didn't like Tom, but I thought he was nice enough. They butted heads from the minute the Forresters moved in next door. I told Ralph he needed to let it go, but he wouldn't listen. I also wanted to pay the ten thousand dollars, because I believe that's what Snowflake's care probably cost. Vets are crazy expensive. But Ralph wouldn't hear of it."

"Thank you for that insight. We appreciate it."

"A few days before Tom died, there was a lot of activity at their house. More than usual. Cars I didn't recognize in and out. That kind of thing."

Sam assumed that had to do with the kidnapping of Leslie and her daughters, as well as their return home, accompanied by federal agents. The news of their kidnapping had not been made public, so Mrs. Sellers wouldn't have known about that.

"That's good to know." Sam handed her a business card. "If you think of anything else, please call me."

"I will." She walked them to the door. "How are Leslie and the girls? I feel so badly for them."

"They're holding up as best they can."

"It's such a terrible shock."

"Yes, it is. Thank you for your time."

"It was nice to meet you, despite the circumstances."

Sam nodded and followed Freddie out the door as Vernon brought up the rear.

"Where to?"

"I want to see Leslie Forrester again before we head for Main Justice for our meeting with Young."

At this rate, they'd just barely get back to town in time for that.

CHAPTER SEVENTEEN

They walked next door to knock on Leslie's door.

A woman Sam didn't recognize came to the door and did the usual double take when she recognized Sam.

She showed her badge. "I'd like to see Leslie Forrester, please."

"Come in." She led them to the same formal living room they'd used the last time they were there.

They waited ten precious minutes before Leslie appeared in the doorway. "Have you found the person who killed my Tom?"

"Not yet, but we're working hard on the case. We just met with Ralph and Laurel Sellers."

Leslie grimaced at the mention of their names as she took a seat across from them. "I'm sure they had nothing but good things to say about us."

"Laurel asked for you and the girls. She said her heart went out to you."

"That's nice of her."

"I wondered why Tom was unwilling to provide receipts from the vet when demanding ten grand from the Sellers."

"He felt it was none of their business."

"But he still expected them to pay without proof of how much it cost?"

Leslie sighed. "I said the same thing, but he was adamant that

Snowflake's medical treatments weren't their business. He was unusually unreasonable when it came to Ralph Sellers."

"How so?"

"The guy infuriated him from the get-go. It was a case of instant dislike."

"And he never said why?"

"I don't think even he knew why he detested Ralph. He just did, and then after their dog attacked Snowflake, Tom was out of his mind with rage."

"Why did Tom ask for ten thousand from the Sellers when the surgery only cost five?"

"He said we deserved something for the pain and agony we'd endured seeing Snowflake through a complicated recovery, not to mention the trauma to the girls, who witnessed the attack."

"Ralph said that Tom liked to act like he was in charge around here. Is that true?"

"Tom stood up for what was right in all aspects of his life."

"Did that annoy the other neighbors?"

"Sometimes. For instance, our homeowners' association prohibits boats on trailers in driveways. Our neighbor across the street used to have his boat in the driveway all the time, saying it was temporary, but then it would be there for weeks. Tom didn't like that, and he told him so."

"How did that go over?"

"The man said his wife had breast cancer, and he had bigger things to worry about than whether his boat was pissing off his neighbor. He shut the door in Tom's face. Tom felt bad about that confrontation. I took a meal over to them a week or so later, and they were very appreciative. Things have been fine with them ever since. And they eventually moved the boat."

"Did he have trouble with anyone else that you know of?"

"The golf pro at the club."

"Do you recall his name?"

"Tristan O'Walsh."

"What was the issue?"

"He moved Tom's tee times without telling him—three times.

After the third time, Tom reported him to management and got the guy fired."

"How long ago did that happen?"

"About eight months ago."

"What came of that?"

"Nothing that I know of."

Sam made a note to figure out what'd become of Tristan O'Walsh and where he'd been on Sunday morning. "Which country club?"

"Woodville."

If she'd had more time, they'd go straight to the club, but that wasn't happening today. Ugh, she hated days when she didn't have time to do everything that needed to be done.

"Can you think of anyone else that would fall into the Ralph Sellers/Tristan O'Walsh category?"

"Not off the top of my head."

"If you do, please call me. It's critical that we have all the information we need to fully investigate Tom's murder."

"I will. I'm sorry I didn't think of the golf pro sooner. That was quite a while ago, though."

"I understand completely. This has been a terrible time for you, and we appreciate all your help."

"Our goals are the same—justice for Tom."

"Indeed they are. We won't take any more of your time."

Sam asked Vernon to use the lights to get her to the U.S. Attorney's Office as fast as possible as the clock ticked down to her departure for the day. She was due for hair and makeup at two o'clock. The very thought of stopping what she was doing for that was unfathomable. But she kept remembering why she was doing it—and who she was doing it for—and that helped to keep her attitude properly aligned.

There was nothing she wouldn't do for Nick. Today was proof of that.

She took advantage of the time in the car to check on Lindsey with a text. *Hope you're feeling better and will be sprung soon. Sorry I haven't been able to check on you in person. Thinking of you!*

Thanks for the message! Aren't you dealing with the Canadians today?

Not until later. How are you?

Better. They've ruled out all the really bad stuff and determined a virus I had before Christmas depleted my red blood cells and led to the current anemia. They think they caught my red blood count on the way back up. They're keeping me for one more day to monitor vitals and then sending me home.

Glad to hear they found the cause and you're on the mend. How's Terry holding up?

He's been amazing.

That's great! I'll check in tomorrow.

Can't wait to see the pictures from tonight. We're SO SAD to miss it.

There'll be others. Focus on getting back to full health. We need our Lindsey!

I'm on it. Xo

Xoxo

Sam filled Freddie in on what Lindsey had told her.

"That can happen?"

"I guess so. Never heard of it before, but I'm glad it's not something more serious."

"Me, too."

She had two hours before she had to head home for tea. That word rankled her. *Tea.* What a stupid word to describe a stupid event. Why did the women have tea while the men had high-level meetings? It made her feel like a fifties-era housewife. Next, she'd be vacuuming in a plaid suit and pearls.

She planned to take up that question with Nick as soon as she got the chance.

In the meantime, she needed to prepare for *tea* with the other guy's wife.

Ugh.

Since she still had some time in the car, she called Lilia.

"Hi there," her chief of staff said. "How're you today?"

"Just ducky."

"Uh-oh, what's wrong?"

"I forgot everything you told me about the prime minister's wife, and now I'm meeting her in a few hours, and I'm unprepared. I was hoping you might have a minute to review the info with me."

"Of course."

"I'm sorry I'm like this."

"Like what?"

"Unprepared despite your efforts to give me what I needed for this."

"You're the busiest person any of us knows, and we're happy to do this however it works for you."

"I don't deserve you."

"Oh stop. Of course you do. I'm so delighted to work with you as you make history."

"You're too kind. Thank you for all you do. I'll never be able to say it enough."

"It's my enormous pleasure. Now, about Mrs. Hutchinson... She's an accountant by trade and the mother of four. Her youngest daughter has cystic fibrosis. She's been very active in that community, advocating for funding, etc. She's also a fierce advocate of early childhood education and vaccinations for childhood diseases."

"Wow, that's a full plate."

"Indeed. By all accounts, she's a lovely person. I think you'll like her."

"Will she like me?"

Lilia, that bitch, laughed. "Yes, Sam, she'll like you. Most people do."

"I'm not sure that's true."

"Well, the people I know adore you, so I assume she will as well."

"Tell me her first name again?"

"Courtney."

"Okay. Got it. Thank you for going over it with me after you already put it in writing weeks ago and gave me a copy—again—yesterday." If the shoe were on the other foot, she'd never be as patient with Lilia as Lilia was with her.

"Whatever you need, whenever you need it."

"You're the best. I'll see you shortly."

"I'll be here. We're ready to help you shine."

"Thank God and all the angels in heaven for you and your team."

Lilia was laughing as they ended the call.

"That woman is a saint," Freddie said without looking up from his phone.

"She sure is. Imagine having to manage me."

"No, thank you."

Sam sputtered with laughter as she smacked his arm. "Be quiet."

"I'm just saying... She's a saint."

"She and Roni and the others in the first lady office are making it possible for me to continue to do this job while they make it look like I'm doing that job, too."

"You *are* doing that job. Just because you're not out doing some event every day doesn't mean you're not an active first lady."

"Others did much more than I ever will."

"And you put murderers in prison."

"When you say it that way..."

"You're doing something no one else has ever done. Your tenure as first lady won't look like others, and that's okay."

"You need to listen to your grasshopper," Vernon said.

"I'm trying to figure out when he got so wise."

"Puleeze. I've always been wise. You just actually listen to me now."

The laughter, the bantering and the reinforcements were just what she'd needed as she walked the tightrope between the competing demands in her complicated life.

They arrived at the U.S. Attorney's Office for the meeting with Young.

Vernon walked them inside, where they navigated security and took the elevator.

A receptionist jumped up when she saw them coming. "Mr. Young is waiting for you." She seemed to take great pleasure in showing them the way.

"Thank you."

The young woman beamed with pleasure that told Sam she was a fan. "You're welcome."

Conlon Young stood when they came into his office. He looked like he hadn't slept in days.

"Thank you for seeing us at such a difficult time," Sam said.

"Of course. I want to do whatever I can to assist in your investigation." He gestured for them to have a seat. "Can I get you anything?"

The pizza had made her thirsty, so she would love some water, but didn't want to take the time. "We're good, thank you."

"How's the investigation going so far?"

"Slowly, but we're making some progress. Naturally, we're focused on Damien Bryant, the campaign finance investigation and the men who took Forrester's family hostage. They say it was on Bryant's order. He denies that, but why else would they have done such a thing? Bryant says he had nothing to do with Forrester's death, but we find that hard to believe. In the meantime, we're also looking at a number of other possibilities, including the dispute with his neighbors, the Sellerses."

Conlon pushed a manila folder across the table to her. "This is everything on the campaign finance investigation. As you'll see, Bryant had recently been made aware that he was the subject of a criminal inquiry."

Sam glanced at Freddie, who seemed as astounded as she was that Young was being so forthcoming with evidence. They rarely got that kind of easy help. "We appreciate the information. Can you elaborate on what we'll find when we review it?"

"Bryant was up to his eyeballs in criminal enterprises."

"How long had Forrester and Cox known that?"

"About a year."

"And yet, they continued to hang out with him like old pals, knowing they were fraternizing with a criminal?"

"They were staying close, hoping he'd slip up and help the investigation."

"You'll have to pardon me if I find it preposterous that the AG and a top USA would hang out with someone they knew was a criminal for more than a year without doing something about it."

"They were building the case."

"Bryant knew Cox had asked Forrester to look into his campaign finance irregularities."

"He didn't know that until recently."

A loud clicking sound rang out in Sam's mind as pieces came together. That was why Bryant had taken Forrester's family—because he'd found out what Forrester had been up to while pretending to be his buddy.

"How did he find out about it?"

"We aren't sure about that."

"If Cox and Forrester were the only ones who knew about it—in addition to you, I presume—who could have told him?"

"It's possible that someone Forrester had spoken to inside of Bryant's campaign as part of the probe tipped off Bryant."

"I bet that made him good and mad."

"Yes, I believe it did."

"And that would explain why Bryant ordered his good friend Tom's wife and daughters taken hostage, so he'd have leverage to put a stop to the investigation that was going to blow the lid off his whole game, an investigation overseen by two of his closest pals. Do I have that right?"

"That's my thought as well."

"What did Tom do when he realized Bryant had his family?"

"As you might imagine, he was extremely upset and concerned."

"Did he fear that Bryant would harm them?"

"He wanted to think not, but he couldn't be certain. All he cared about during the hours they were missing was their safety and getting them home."

"Was he in contact with Bryant while they were missing?"

"Yes. Bryant made sure Tom knew who had them and why, and he outlined what he expected to happen next."

"Which was?"

"For the investigation to be dropped and all documents associated with it destroyed."

"What did Tom and Reggie say to that?"

"They told Bryant that wasn't possible, and that by taking Tom's family hostage, he was ensuring he'd die in prison. Reggie told him to let the Forresters go, and then they would talk about next steps in the investigation, but nothing would happen until Tom's wife and daughters were safe."

"How did Randy Bryant's arrest on murder-for-hire charges play into this?"

"That was a wrench we didn't see coming. Damien Bryant lost his mind when he heard his son had been arrested. He was facing stiff headwinds at home in Wisconsin with a primary challenger for the first time in more than ten years. The polling was looking rough, and having his son arrested was a disaster for him."

"Not to mention if it got out that he'd kidnapped the wife and daughters of a U.S. Attorney..."

"Yes."

"This whole thing sounds insane to me. Are you able to see that from your vantage point?"

"I am."

"What was your advice to Tom while his family was missing?"

"To do whatever Bryant wanted to get them back."

"Did he?"

"He talked to Bryant repeatedly, begged him to let them go and said he'd figure out a way to protect Bryant. But he didn't believe that Tom and Reggie would stand down. He was furious that they'd pretended to be his friends while secretly investigating him."

"How did you feel about Tom's friendship with Bryant?"

"I'd repeatedly advised him that it was dangerous to his career and reputation to be associated with Bryant, especially knowing what we did about his criminal enterprises, but he said he needed a little more time to make the case. Then his family went missing, and we quickly tracked that to Bryant. Tom was frantically trying to secure their release when Bryant's son was arrested, and everything unraveled quickly."

"How so?"

"Bryant became unhinged. He thought Tom and Reggie were behind the arrest of his son."

"Unhinged how?"

"He told them to get his son out of lockup, or he'd start killing Tom's family one by one."

"That was when we got the order to release Randy."

"Yes. I told Tom it was a mistake to play ball with Bryant when we could send in the FBI to arrest him, but Tom was adamant that his family was more important than nailing Bryant. We didn't know where they were or who was with them. He knew his request to Chief Farnsworth would be met with disbelief, but he did it anyway."

"It was a shocking request, especially coming from him."

"Tom was a rule follower all his life, but when his family was in grave danger, he didn't care what he had to do to keep them safe."

"As a wife and mother, I understand that, but why didn't he ask for help in finding his family?"

"Bryant told him if he sent law enforcement after him or them, he'd kill them."

"What happened when Tom received word that his family had been rescued?"

"He cried. He was so undone that he couldn't speak for a few minutes. In all our years together, I'd never known him to cry. I asked him where he was, and he said he'd be in the office shortly. He had something he had to do first."

"Did he say what that was?"

"No, and I asked, but he wouldn't tell me."

"Bryant was still in custody, so he couldn't have been the one to kill him."

"I honestly don't know where Tom went or why he was parked on Constitution Ave."

"I'm going to be blunt with you, Mr. Young. I have no idea what we're dealing with here. The person with the greatest motivation, as far as we can tell, to kill Tom was locked up at the time of his murder. He wasn't released on bond until later that day. Bryant's thugs were locked up as well. Was there anything else Forrester was involved in that could've led to his murder?"

"I mean… Of course we're always dealing with people who'd like to see the prosecutor killed for daring to charge them with crimes, but there's nothing recent that stands out."

"How about over the last few years?"

"I've racked my brain, trying to think of something that would've led to this happening now, and I just can't figure out how it wouldn't be related to Bryant."

"He told us he barely knew Forrester," Freddie said.

"I can't imagine why he'd say that when they've been friends for years," Young replied. "A lot of people know that. It wasn't a secret."

"Was Cox's friendship with Bryant well known, too?"

"Bryant would've met Reggie through Tom. You have to understand… Bryant was fun to hang out with. There was always a lot going on around him. I've played poker at his place with them. It was a good time. Staying close to a congressman on the Judiciary Committee would've been appealing to Reggie—and Tom to a lesser extent."

"I'm still having a hard time picturing the Attorney General and a USA staying cozy with Bryant after figuring out he was a criminal," Sam said.

"As I said, they were hoping he'd slip up and help the case they were building."

"I'm not sure how we'll prove he was involved in what happened to Tom, with him and the men who worked for him locked up at the time of the murder."

"Were all of Bryant's guys locked up?"

Sam glanced at Freddie.

"Not all of them."

"Let's figure out where the rest of them were when Forrester was killed." To Young, she said, "Thank you for your time and the cooperation. It's very much appreciated."

"Whatever I can do to find the person who took Tom from us."

Sam handed him her card with the usual instructions to call if anything else came to mind that might be relevant. "We'll be in touch."

CHAPTER EIGHTEEN

Outside Young's office, Sam stopped at the admin's desk. "Are you Anita?" In her mid- to late-twenties, she had dark hair, pale skin and big brown eyes.

The woman seemed stunned that Sam was talking to her. "Uh, yes, I am."

"Could we have a word in private, please?"

She glanced at Conlon's closed door and then back at them. "I'd need to ask Mr. Young."

"You don't need to ask anyone. You just need to lead us to a room where we can speak privately."

"I need to tell Mr. Young that I'm leaving my desk."

"Tell him you're going to the restroom."

Anita's hands were shaking as she lifted the phone receiver.

Sam rolled her eyes at Freddie, who seemed amused by the woman's reaction to Sam.

"Mean and scary," he whispered.

Sam didn't think she was either of those things, but she did get some interesting reactions from people.

Anita got up from the desk and led them to the smaller of the two conference rooms.

"Close the door."

She did as she was asked and then leaned back against it,

keeping her hand on the door handle as if preparing for a quick escape.

"You worked with Tom Forrester?"

"Y-yes, we all did. We're heartbroken over his death."

"In the course of our investigation, we've heard a rumor."

Her brows furrowed. "What kind of rumor?"

"That Tom was engaged in an extramarital affair. Do you know anything about that?"

She hadn't been expecting that question. Her mouth flopped open in shock.

"Ms. Wentworth? Do you know anything about that?"

"I, uh..." Her eyes filled with tears as her chin wobbled frantically. "I don't know."

"Did you or did you not hear that rumor?"

"I... I heard some people talking."

"What people?"

"You want, like, their names?" Her voice got very high as that sentence went on.

"That'd be good."

"I... I don't know them. I just overheard them talking in the restroom."

"Were you romantically involved with Mr. Forrester?"

The woman crumbled like a house of cards hit by a stiff breeze. "Noooo. I'd never do that." She sobbed as she slid down the door, landing on the floor. "It wasn't me."

"Who was it, Anita?"

Shaking her head, she was sobbing so hard, she couldn't breathe.

"For fuck's sake," Sam muttered to Freddie as she went to help the woman up and into a chair.

The door swung open.

Conlon Young stood in the doorway, visibly displeased. "What's going on here?"

"We're speaking to Ms. Wentworth."

"About what?"

"That's between us and her."

"I'm sorry, Mr. Young. I'm so sorry."

"What're you sorry for, Anita?" Sam asked as her head threatened to explode.

Conlon came into the room, staring at the woman with outrage. "What the hell are you talking about?"

"Tom... Mr. Forrester... He... he was nice to me. I..."

"You what?" Conlon asked.

She withered under the heat of his glare. "I loved him."

"What? Are you *out of your mind*? You *loved* him? He was a married man!"

"I know," she wailed. "I know he was."

"Then what the fuck are you talking about?"

Sam appreciated Conlon taking over this interrogation, since she was out of patience with the entire situation.

"I can't help how I felt about him."

"Surely he never acted on whatever it is you think was going on."

She shook her head. "He didn't."

"But you put the word out around the office that he did, right?" Sam asked.

"I... I didn't mean to..."

Conlon exploded, "How *dare* you besmirch a good man's reputation this way? Go pack up your desk and get the hell out of here."

"No! Mr. Young, please."

"*Get out of my sight!*"

After the woman ran from the room, Conlon turned to them. He was so furious, his hands were shaking. "I'm so sorry you had to witness such an ugly scene. I had no idea about any of that. If I had..." He shook his head in disgust. "How dare she say such things about Tom, who was loyal to Leslie from the minute they met in college?"

"Sorry you had to deal with that on top of everything else," Sam said.

"How did you know to ask her about that?"

"Something we heard in the course of the investigation."

"I'll put out a memo detailing her actions and subsequent dismissal."

"We'll, ah, just be going, then," Sam said, eager to get out of there.

"Holy crap," Freddie said under his breath on the way to the elevator.

"No kidding."

Sam glanced at her watch. "Goddamn it. I've got to go home."

The elevator doors closed for the ride to the lobby. "Don't worry. We've got it from here. I'll talk to the goons about who else might've acted on Bryant's behalf to kill Forrester and go over this file that Young gave us. I'll also track down the golf pro."

"Thank you. I know this entire situation is preposterous."

"What do you mean?"

"I'm the boss, the *commander*, and I'm leaving in the middle of a hot investigation into the death of a colleague to go have *tea* with the Canadian PM's wife. It's madness."

"It's fine, Sam. No one else is stressing about that."

"Tell me the truth."

"Always."

"Am I crazy to try to do both of these things at the same time while pretending I'm a good mother, too?"

"You're a wonderful mother, and you're not crazy to do both. You're an inspiration to so many women and young girls who want to be just like you."

"You're only saying that because you love me. Tell me the *truth*."

"That is the truth, and I'm not just saying it because I love you. I'm saying it because it's what everyone else is saying."

"Not in the department."

"Screw them. Who cares what they say? You never have before, so don't start now."

"That Animal Control lady—"

"Is green with envy because she'll never be a *fraction* of what you are."

"He's right, Sam," Vernon said. "She wants to be you. Don't let her get in your head. She's not worth the brain cells."

"No, she isn't," Freddie said. "Just do your thing. We've got you covered at work when you can't be there."

"And you promise you're not going to start to resent me for all the time I'm not there?"

"Promise. How can I resent you when I get to watch my best friends be the president and first lady? When I get invited to state dinners? Do you have any idea how exciting that is for all of us? My parents are losing it that I'm going to a fancy party at the White House."

"We should've invited them, too. Next time."

"Nah, they'd never come. They'd be too freaked out. It's enough for them to see Elin and me there."

"Thanks for propping up me and all my insecurities today, guys."

"You have no reason to be insecure about anything," Vernon said. "Imagine how nervous Mrs. Hutchinson must be about having tea with you."

"No kidding," Freddie said, laughing. "She's probably having a panic attack."

"I hope not! Jeez. I'm a disaster."

Freddie scoffed. "She doesn't know that."

"You were supposed to say, 'No, you're not.'"

The three of them were laughing when they stepped off the elevator, reclaimed their weapons at security and headed outside where it was drizzly and cold. She was ready for spring to show up any time now.

Sam glanced at Freddie. "Can you get back to HQ?"

"Yep, no worries."

"I'll see you tonight."

"We'll be there with bells on."

She handed the evidence bag containing Avery's bullet to him. "Get this to the lab with 911 urgency and keep me in the loop."

"Will do."

He took off toward the Metro while she got into the back seat of the SUV.

She appreciated what he and Vernon had said and how they provided unwavering support as she stretched in all directions at the same time, trying to cover as many bases at home and at work as she possibly could.

Her phone rang with a call from Gonzo. "Hey, what's up?"

"Animal Control produced the report on the incident with Forrester's dog and the Doberman. It practically tore that little thing apart. The pictures are gruesome."

"Oh God, don't show me."

"I won't."

"That LT from AC is a peach, huh?"

"I didn't get to meet her. One of her people brought me the info."

"Probably the one who wanted to tell me why the LT can't stand me. I've decided I don't care."

"That's the way."

"I'm headed home. Freddie is on the way back to HQ with threads to pull."

"We're on it."

"Sorry to duck out again."

"Don't be. It's all good in the hood."

"It really isn't, but I appreciate you guys more than you'll ever know."

"And we appreciate the invites to the White House. Everyone we know thinks we're the shit because you guys are our friends."

"I do what I can for my people."

"And we do what we can for you. It all comes out in the wash, Sam. Don't sweat it, okay?"

"Trying not to. We need a suspect—and we need it now."

"I'm meeting with Archie in half an hour to look at cell phone pings."

"Sounds good, and by the way, Nick agrees with renting Ninth to you guys. It's all yours if you want it."

"Christina and I talked about it last night, and we'd love to live there. If you're sure."

"We're sure. We're not using it, and it's just what you guys need."

"It's way more than we need, but we're excited just the same."

"We'll arrange to put our stuff in storage so you can have the run of the place."

"Thank you again. You'll never know what this means to us."

"It's our pleasure. Keep me posted on the case?"

"Will do."

Sam closed the phone and put her head back against the seat, trying to decompress from an intense few hours so she could change gears when she got home. She closed her eyes and let the details of the case run through her mind, picking it over from every angle. Why, she wondered, had Cox's admin refused at first to give her his name? What had become of the golf pro Tom had gotten fired? Had Ralph and Laurel Sellers really been at home on Sunday morning? The shooter she'd seen on the video was a much smaller person than Ralph Sellers. Could it have been Laurel? What would she have to gain by killing Forrester?

None of it added up.

How could it not lead right back to Damien Bryant and his criminal enterprise, which was threatened by Forrester's investigation?

And then there was Avery's shooting. What, if anything, did that have to do with Forrester?

She opened her eyes and reached for her phone to call Archie.

"What's up?"

"Is there film of Avery's shooting?"

"Our cameras didn't catch it, but I've asked for the gym's footage. They're sending it over. What are you thinking?"

"Is it related to Tom?"

"That'd be a stretch, no?"

"I suppose, but worth looking into. Freddie is delivering Avery's bullet to the lab."

"We'll let the ballistics analysis tell us whether there's a connection. In the meantime, I still say it's a stretch. I'm headed downstairs to talk cell tower pings with Gonzo."

"He told me. Thanks."

"Have a great time tonight." He'd declined her invite to attend, saying fancy dinners weren't his thing.

"Thanks. I think."

He was laughing when he ended the call.

Vernon drove the SUV through the White House gates, where Sam immediately noticed a tent on the South Lawn, as well as catering trucks and frenetic activity. She'd much rather chase murderers for a living than be responsible for pulling off an event of this magnitude.

Lilia met her inside. She wore a sharp red suit with black heels and looked more like the lady of the manor than Sam ever would. Fortunately, the lord of the manor preferred her, for some weird reason.

"How'd you know I was on the way?"

Lilia gave her a look that basically said "duh" in the classiest way possible.

"Don't tell me. It's your job to know."

"That's right." She led Sam through an elaborate maze of corridors to the in-house salon that was one of the cooler perks of being the first lady.

In a matter of minutes, Davida had washed and conditioned her hair, using the best-smelling products Sam had ever encountered. With no choice in the matter, she closed her eyes and tried to relax her racing mind while Davida worked her magic with the hair dryer. Next up was Ginger with makeup to cover the bruise on her cheek, while Kendra did her nails in a lovely shade of burgundy to match her velvet dress.

Ginger was careful around the wound on her face. "Tell me if it hurts."

"I will."

By the time Ginger was finished, it was impossible to tell that Sam had been injured.

"That's amazing, Ginger. Thank you."

"My pleasure, ma'am."

"You ladies have scrubbed the feral right out of me," Sam said when they were finished. "Thank you so much."

"You're very welcome," Davida said. "Have a wonderful time."

"I will."

"Is Nick in the Oval?" Sam asked Lilia as they left the salon forty minutes after they'd arrived.

"He is."

"Could I have just a minute with him?"

"That's about all we've got, but I'll make it happen. Right this way."

Thankfully, Lilia knew the place inside out and led her to the Oval in a matter of minutes, when it would've taken Sam all day to figure out how to get there from the salon.

When the admin outside Nick's office saw them coming, she stood to greet them. "Good afternoon, Mrs. Cappuano."

Sam could never remember her name and hated that. "Hi there. Is he free?"

"Of course. Right this way."

"I'll wait here," Lilia said. "Be quick."

"Yes, ma'am."

She was shown into the Oval Office, where her gorgeous husband sat behind the Resolute Desk.

He was so focused on what he was doing that he didn't look up until she cleared her throat.

For the rest of her life, she'd never forget the way his entire face lit up with pleasure when he saw her. That, right there, was why she'd cut her workday short to come home to support him.

CHAPTER NINETEEN

S till smiling, Nick got up and came around the desk. "This is a nice surprise."

He'd removed his gray suit coat and rolled up the sleeves of a light blue dress shirt.

"You look beautiful."

"Funny, I was thinking the same thing about you." He put his arms around her. "Why does your hair smell different?"

"I've just come from the salon."

"Ah, I see. I want the usual scent back tomorrow."

"Yes, sir."

"Not that this one is bad. It's just not you." He nuzzled her neck. "What brings you by?"

"I needed this." She tightened her arms around him. "Before things get crazy, I just needed this."

"This is available to you any time you need it."

"I wish that were true. I need it a lot."

"What's up?"

"Just a chaotic day capped off by a state visit. Nothing I can't handle now that I've had five minutes with you."

"In case I forget to tell you later, I so appreciate you being here this afternoon."

"I'm right where I belong, but I need to get going before Lilia has a stroke."

"One more minute."

She held on tightly to the only man in the world who could make her thankful to be his first lady. "Guess what?"

"What?"

"Farnsworth and Malone told me they're not retiring until we're out of office because my dad would've wanted them watching over me while I try to do something no other first lady has ever done."

"Wow. What'd you say to that?"

"I cried."

"Aw, babe. I'm so glad you've got them watching out for you at work. That makes me feel so much better."

"Me, too."

"Tonight, after all the hoopla, let's you and me have a date in the loft."

"Yes, please." She'd be dead on arrival tomorrow, but so be it. "I really gotta go."

"See you in a couple of hours."

"Good luck with the PM."

"Good luck with the PM's wife."

Sam smiled up at him as he kissed her and then reluctantly released him to go change for *tea*.

SHELBY HAD WAITED hours for the chance to see Avery. Thank goodness Ginger had come to help with the baby because she never could've done it on her own while being so consumed by worry. Even after they'd told her Avery would make a full recovery, she wouldn't be able to breathe properly until she saw him for herself.

"What's taking so long?" she asked Ginger. "They said I could see him soon."

"They're taking good care of him. That's what we want. Come sit for a minute. You'll wear yourself out."

Already long past worn out, Shelby sat next to Ginger and took the sleeping baby from her. "How could this have happened? Who would want to shoot Avery?"

"I keep thinking about the people who broke into the house. Could it be related?"

"I don't know how. They're in jail."

"I'm sure the FBI and others are working to figure out what happened. He's one of their own. They'll be all over it."

"I know." Shelby blinked back tears that had threatened for hours. She was trying to be strong for Avery and their children, but it wasn't easy. Her hormones were still out of whack from pregnancy and childbirth, not to mention the lingering trauma from the home invasion. Now she'd nearly lost the love of her life. It was all too much to bear.

A nurse came into the waiting room. "Mrs. Hill?"

Shelby stood quickly and then winced from the aches and pains that remained from the baby's birth. "That's me."

"Would you like to see your husband?"

"Very much so." She handed the baby to Ginger. "Thank you."

"No worries. Take your time."

The nurse gestured for Shelby to come with her. "Right this way."

She had to remind herself to keep breathing as she followed the nurse through the doors to the recovery area. "How is he?"

"He's doing very well."

"That's such a relief."

"All he wants is to see you. And he asked about the baby."

"We just had her a few days ago."

"That's what he said. He said he loves being a daddy."

Shelby swiped at the tears that came despite her fierce desire to be strong for him. "He's a very good daddy."

She was in no way prepared for the sight of him attached to machines with tubes and wires everywhere.

He held out his hand to her. "Come here, sugar."

That voice. That one-in-a-million face. Thank God he hadn't been killed. What in the world would she have done without him?

Shelby took his hand and bent over it when her composure cracked.

"Aw, sweetie, I'm fine."

"Now, you are."

"I'm so sorry to put you through this."

"Don't apologize. It's not your fault. I'm just so, so thankful you're all right."

"Where's my baby girl?"

"Ginger has her in the waiting room. She's very excited to see her daddy."

"I can't wait to see her, too. Come here and give me a kiss."

Shelby wiped away her tears and then leaned over the bed rail to kiss her love.

He wrapped his arm around her. "Everything's fine. I promise."

If he said so, it must be true.

"George is eager to speak to you about what you remember."

"Give me five more minutes of you, and then you can send him in."

COURTNEY HUTCHINSON WAS INDEED LOVELY.

Sam wasn't sure why she was so surprised by that, but as soon as she realized the other woman was more like her than not, she relaxed and tried to enjoy the opportunity to talk to another mom. They'd posed for photographers in the Blue Room and waited for Harold to pour their tea before they relaxed a bit. Sam had made sure to put her bandaged arm behind her guest to hide it from the photographer.

"Tell me everything about your work." Courtney tucked a strand of sleek blonde hair behind her ear. She had the most adorable bob cut that would look ridiculous on Sam, but Courtney pulled it off effortlessly. "It's fascinating to me."

"Oh, well... Um, mostly it's frustrating and upsetting and overwhelming to me. And that's on a good day."

Courtney smiled at her description of the job.

Sam held up her bandaged arm. "As you can see, I recently had a not-so-good day."

"Is it broken?"

"No, just a bad sprain and some road rash, but it was the last thing I needed this week."

"I read about the prosecutor who was murdered. Did you know him?"

Sam nodded. "I knew him well. His office prosecutes our cases. His death is such a tragedy."

"I'm so sorry for the loss of your colleague and friend. Where do you even begin to figure out who did it?"

Sam hadn't expected to discuss her work, but she preferred that topic to many others that could've come up. "We look for motive. Who would've benefited from removing Tom from the equation? That kind of thing."

"I really admire that you're doing both jobs. I can barely handle my official duties as Matthew's wife. I can't imagine an intense full-time job on top of that."

Sam smoothed a hand over the skirt of the most gorgeous wool suit she'd ever owned. The chunky tweed included a variety of colors, including pink, purple and navy. She'd be hard-pressed to describe it except to say she *loved* it and couldn't wait to tell Marcus that. "My goal is to survive every day, to make sure as many balls are kept in the air as possible and that my kids are fed and loved and have what they need. It's a bit of a Tilt-A-Whirl, to be honest."

"I'd say so."

"I could never do any of it without the tremendous team of supporters I have here and at work. They're the ones who really make it happen. But enough about me. Tell me about you and your family."

They talked about kids, the funny things they said, the unique challenges of raising them in the spotlight and Courtney's work on behalf of cystic fibrosis research.

"How's your daughter's health?"

"She's doing very well. They've made amazing advancements in treating CF, and while it requires daily management, she's living a relatively normal life."

"That's wonderful. I'm so glad to hear it." She noticed Courtney hadn't touched her tea. "May I warm up your tea?"

"Honestly?"

"Of course."

"I'd rather have a glass of wine. Would that be possible?"

"This is the White House. Anything is possible here." She smiled at Harold, who was positioned by the door. "We'd like to trade our tea for wine, please."

"Right away, ma'am. What kind of wine do you prefer?"

Sam looked to Courtney.

"Rosé would be wonderful."

"Make it a double, please, Harold."

"Coming right up."

"Since we're being honest…" Sam wasn't sure if she should be, but whatever. She only knew how to be herself, and herself was blunt. "I was kind of dreading this meeting. I feared I wouldn't know what to talk to you about, and I hate tea."

Courtney laughed. "It's like drinking dirty bathwater."

Sam laughed right along with her. "Yes, exactly! I know people love it, but I never have."

"Me either."

"This is my first state visit since Nick became president. I've been so nervous, but you're just a regular person like me."

"You're not a regular person."

"Oh my God. Yes, I am. If you only knew… I worry all the time that my 'regular-ness' will cause embarrassment for Nick."

"I never would've guessed that. Your public persona is a bit intimidating for someone like me coming to meet with you."

"Nothing to be intimidated about with me unless you're a murderer, or you mess with my family. Then I can get a little ugly."

"Can't we all? I've been appalled by some of the things that've been said about your husband since he took office. The shooting at Fort Liberty… Such a tragedy."

"Indeed. It's been hard to take. People saying awful things about him simply because he stepped up when asked by President Nelson to be vice president and then again when the president died so suddenly. A service member killing other personnel because he doesn't support the commander in chief. It's…"

"A lot on top of a lot."

"Yes. It certainly is." Sam appreciated that the other woman understood—probably better than anyone Sam had spoken to since Nick became president.

"Do you have to go there to offer support and condolences?"

"We were told we're not wanted there, which stung a bit."

"I'm sure it does. With all the sacrifices you and your family are making so he can serve his country at the highest level, it's not easy to face the constant criticism."

"No, it sure isn't. It's nice to talk to someone who understands."

"I really do. Matthew came into office with an ambitious agenda that's run up against fierce resistance from all corners. Somedays, you wonder why you bother to try."

"We have to keep trying. That's what Nick says."

"He's right. Of course we have to keep trying, but sometimes it's just exhausting."

"All the time."

Harold returned, bearing a tray with two glasses of wine that he served to them.

"Thank you, Harold," Sam said.

"Yes, thank you."

"May I remove the tea service?"

"Yes, please, but leave the cake. That won't go to waste."

Smiling, he said, "Yes, ma'am."

"Don't you get tired of being called ma'am?" Courtney asked when they were alone again.

"*So* tired of it. I've got my Secret Service agents calling me Sam when it's just us, but that didn't happen overnight."

"This wine is delicious."

"It is. I've always loved rosé the best."

"Me, too." Courtney held up her glass to Sam. "Here's to new friends who get it."

Sam touched her glass to Courtney's. "I'll drink to that."

. . .

THE SECOND GLASS of wine had probably been a mistake, Sam thought, as Lilia accompanied her to the residence to dress for dinner. She was a tiny bit wobbly but elated after a delightful time with Courtney Hutchinson. With hindsight, she'd wasted valuable energy worrying about something that'd turned out much better than fine.

Before they'd parted company, they'd exchanged phone numbers so they could stay in touch after the visit.

Skip Holland used to tell his daughters not to be overly impressed by illustrious people. The putting-their-pants-on-one-leg-at-a-time saying came right from him. She should've taken his advice as she'd prepared to meet with Courtney. Turns out, she'd been every bit as intimidated as Sam had been, which was amusing. She didn't think of herself as particularly intimidating, except when someone was irritating her on the job, so it had come as a surprise that Courtney had been nervous about their meeting, too.

While Lilia waited in the sitting room, Sam went into the bedroom to change and encountered her husband in a tuxedo.

"Holy smokes."

"What?"

"You in that tux. Yum." She went to him and rested her hands flat on his chest. "It's giving me ideas."

"We don't have time for ideas. How'd it go with Courtney Hutchinson?"

"We had a great time."

"Is that right?"

"Yep, and we had *two* glasses of wine."

"Ah, that accounts for the somewhat glassy look in your eyes." He kissed her. "I'm glad you had a good time."

"We really did. She's very nice and normal."

"Unlike you."

Sam laughed and then burped. "Whoops."

"Oh my God, Samantha. Are you tipsy before our first state dinner?"

"Maybe just a little, but it's not my fault. She said tea tastes like dirty bathwater, so we asked for wine instead."

His smile was devastating all the time, but extra devastating when he was dressed to kill. "I'm so glad you enjoyed yourself. Now hurry up and change so we aren't late for a very important date."

"Yes, sir, Mr. President. I may need you to zip me into my dress."

"I much prefer to *unzip* you."

"Save that for later."

"Oh, I will. Don't worry."

She went into her closet and quickly changed into the underwear and dress that Marcus had dropped off earlier. The burgundy velvet dress that left one shoulder bare was one of her favorites of all the amazing things she'd gotten to wear as second and first lady. She added the key necklace and bangle bracelet Nick had given her and then placed her engagement ring on top of the band she wore to work.

As she stepped into a sexy pair of heels, she wished there was something she could do to hide the bandage on her wrist, but that wasn't going to happen. Thank goodness the cortisone shot was working, and her hip didn't hurt at all.

After a deep breath to prepare herself, she stepped out of the closet to find him leaning against the doorframe, arms crossed.

His face lit up with pleasure when he saw her. "Wow." He made a circular motion with his index finger, asking to see the full picture.

Sam gave a careful little spin on her heel. God forbid she should aggravate her hip again.

"Sexiest first lady in history."

"I thought we'd already decided that honor should go to Eleanor Roosevelt."

"None of them has anything on my first lady. She's a knockout."

"Are the kids ready?"

"Celia said they're good to go as soon as we are."

The Littles would be joining them for photos and appetizers before returning to the residence for dinner. Scotty was along for the full ride, at his request.

Sam and Nick stepped into the hallway, where the kids were waiting for them—Scotty and Alden in tuxedoes and Aubrey in a tiny version of Sam's dress.

"Oh my goodness! Look at you guys!"

"You look so pretty, Sam!" Aubrey said.

"So do you! Do you feel fancy?"

"So fancy!"

"You boys are so handsome!"

Scotty put a hand on Alden's shoulder. "Alden wasn't digging the top button, but I convinced him that grown-up guys have to button the top to wear a bow tie."

"You look very grown up, Alden," Sam said.

His blond hair had been slicked down, and he grinned with pleasure at the compliments.

"Let's get this show on the road," Nick said.

"The road to downstairs," Scotty replied.

Nick smiled. "Makes for a quick ride home."

Sam stopped to give Celia a hug. "Thank you so much for all you do for us. We'd never survive this without you."

Celia had declined their invite to attend the gala, preferring to hang out with the kids instead.

"It's my pleasure, honey. You all look gorgeous. Best-looking family in the world."

"Aw, thanks. We clean up pretty well."

"I told the kids' agents I'd be right here waiting for them to come back up. Don't worry about a thing."

"I never do when you're here."

"I love every minute of it. Have the very best time."

"Thank you. Love you."

"Love you, too, sweetheart." Celia hugged her. "He'd be *so, so* proud."

"I hope so."

"I know so. He'd be busting his buttons."

"Thank you for that. I needed it."

She took Nick's hand and walked with him and the kids downstairs to greet their public.

CHAPTER TWENTY

After the White House photographer took family photos, the kids went ahead of them, with Scotty in charge, as Sam and Nick met up with the Hutchinsons outside the East Room.

Nick greeted Courtney and introduced Sam to Matthew Hutchinson.

"It's so nice to meet you," Matthew said. "We're great admirers of you and your work."

"Thank you. That's nice to hear."

Courtney leaned across her husband to speak to Sam. "The second glass of wine might've been a mistake. I had to talk myself out of a nap."

Sam laughed. "Same!"

The Marine Band played "Hail to the Chief" as the two couples entered the reception for members of Congress in the East Room. Even though she'd heard that tune so many times, it never failed to give her chills, especially now that it was being played for her husband. The room had been decorated with U.S. and Canadian flags and other decorations honoring their guests.

Vice President Gretchen Henderson, dressed in an icy light-blue gown, with diamonds hanging from her ears, smiled when they entered the room. She came over to greet them.

"It's nice to see you again," she said to Sam.

Sam tightened her grip on Nick's arm. "You as well."

What was it about her that bugged Sam so much? She'd never been anything other than nice to her, but there was something. She couldn't deny it, but this was not the time to worry about that.

Everything from the flowers to the dinner menu was intended to be a celebration of the two countries and their cultures.

Sam had been to a state dinner once before, but she'd never hosted one, nor had she paid much attention to the details at the first one. Well, besides the detail that had transpired in the Rose Garden when Nick proposed to her. That, she'd never forget. But this... This was a production of magical and epic proportions. The photos of their entrance with the Hutchinsons would be released around the world in a matter of minutes.

Tracy and Mike had come early to help wrangle the kids and were waiting for them in the East Room. Angela had chosen not to attend. She'd said she wasn't ready to socialize after having lost her husband so recently.

Sam hugged her eldest sister. "Thank you for being here."

"Are you kidding me? My friends are green with envy."

"Mine, too," Mike said as he hugged her. "Everyone thinks we're wicked cool to be dining at the White House with celebrities and heads of state."

"Brooke said to tell you to break a leg—not literally, of course —and she and Nate can't wait to come to the next one."

Sam's niece, a junior at the University of Virginia, was dating one of their favorite Secret Service agents. Nate was the lead agent on Eli's detail.

"How's she doing?"

"Great, since the transfer to Princeton came through. She can be with Nate full time next year."

"Ah, young love."

"She'd better not flunk out."

"She won't!"

Sam introduced Tracy and Mike to the Hutchinsons.

Courtney asked Tracy where they lived.

"About six miles from here."

"You're so lucky to have your sister close by!"

"Both my sisters are close," Sam said, "and I'm very thankful for that. My stepmother lives here with us to help with the kids, and my mom helps out, too. It takes a village."

"Yes, it sure does."

Scotty joined them with a hand on the shoulder of each twin. Nick introduced them to the Hutchinsons.

While Scotty and Alden shook hands with the prime minister, Aubrey hid behind them.

"She's a little shy." Sam reached out a hand to the little girl, who came around the boys to grasp Sam's hand.

"Samantha, our guests are arriving. Are you ready?"

Tracy fanned her face. "When he calls you Samantha..."

"I know, right?"

"You guys look amazing. More gorgeous than ever."

Nick kissed Tracy's cheek. "Thanks for the vote of confidence." He extended his arm to Sam. "Shall we, my love?"

Sam kissed Aubrey on the cheek and turned her over to Tracy. "I'll see you in a bit, sweetie." To Nick, she said, "Let's do it."

"So much I could say to that," he whispered as they walked to their assigned positions for the receiving line that would send guests into the tent for dinner.

Their guests were a Who's Who of political, media and entertainment, including the surprise appearance by her favorite singer, Jon Bon Jovi, and his wife.

Sam hugged him. "My husband has been keeping secrets again!"

"We love to surprise you," Jon said. "Thank you for having us. It's such a thrill to be here."

"The thrill is all ours," Sam said.

"She means it's all *hers*," Nick replied.

Sam couldn't deny that, so she didn't try, even as she flushed with embarrassment to have her fierce crush outed by her husband. "Are you singing for us later?"

"You know it."

"I can't wait."

Sam's squad and others from the department arrived together, minus Dominguez and Carlucci, who were holding down the fort on the Forrester investigation. They'd be on the guest list for the next big event.

"You guys look gorgeous," Sam said.

Deputy Chief Jeannie McBride, whose pregnancy was beginning to show, hugged her. "Was about to say the same to you. Stunning."

"Aw, thanks. It took a whole team of people to make it happen."

"I have no doubt."

Sam laughed, appreciating her friend keeping things real. Next, she hugged Elin Cruz. "Been thinking of you, friend. How're you doing?"

"Better every day, and hopeful for the next time."

"That's the way to be. As I told Freddie, I feel in my bones that you two are going to make me an auntie several times over."

Elin pulled back and gave her a warm smile. "I hope so."

Sam adjusted Freddie's bow tie, which didn't need fixing. "My little grasshopper has grown up to be a damned handsome man."

He flashed an irreverent grin. "I know, right? Thanks for this. We'll never forget it."

"Thanks for being here. Means everything to have my besties here."

Gonzo, Christina, Captain Malone and his wife, Val, Chief Farnsworth and his wife, Marti, Jeannie's husband, Michael Wilkinson, Matt O'Brien and Cameron Green hugged her and raved about the event and how pretty she looked.

"Save us a minute if you have one," Gonzo said. "We've got some developments."

"I'll find a minute."

Derek Kavanaugh and Roni Connolly arrived, hand in hand. Seeing them together after both had been widowed filled Sam with joy.

"You're glowing, Mama," Sam said to the pregnant Roni. She was expecting her late husband Patrick's child in June.

"If you say so."

"I say so, and I'm the boss of you."

Roni laughed as she hugged Sam.

"Thank you for all you did to fill in for Terry," Nick said to Derek.

"I never want to have to deal with a state dinner again."

"So noted," Nick said, grinning.

"Give me four hundred thirty-five temperamental Congress members over one caterer."

Sam, Nick and Roni laughed at the face he made.

"What're you hearing about Avery?" Derek asked.

"He was out of surgery and expected to make a full recovery the last time I heard from Shelby," Sam said.

"Thank goodness," Roni said. "I texted Shelby earlier, but I haven't heard back. I'm sure she's got a million texts from concerned friends."

"For sure," Sam said. "She's got her hands full with a new baby and now with Avery laid up. I know she'll appreciate you checking in."

"I'm thinking of her."

Sam rested a hand on the younger woman's arm. "I'm sure it was hard for you to hear what'd happened to Avery." Her husband, Patrick, had been killed by a stray bullet while on his way to lunch.

"Yes, for sure. Brought it all back."

"Call me tomorrow if you need to talk."

"Said the busiest person on the planet."

"I always have time for my friends."

"Thank you. That means a lot."

"We'd better move to the tent to make sure everything is good to go," Derek said, "and once it is, I'm having a very big drink."

Sam and Nick laughed as they sent them on their way, and then they greeted Lilia and her fiancé, Harry.

"You two look stunning," Lilia said.

"All thanks to you and the White House team," Sam replied.

"We had a gorgeous first lady to work with."

"You're looking pretty gorgeous yourself." Lilia wore a red gown that clung to her curves.

"I couldn't agree more." Harry put his arm around his love. "She's a showstopper."

Lilia giggled. "Hush. This isn't my show."

"It's more your show than it is mine," Sam said.

Harry and Lilia were still laughing as they walked away to find their table.

The crush of people, each face more famous than the last, was dazzling and overwhelming, each of the illustrious people wanting a moment with her and Nick.

Supreme Court justices, senators and congresspeople... Including Damien Bryant.

He offered her an insincere smile. "Mrs. Cappuano."

"What are you doing out of lockup?"

"A little thing called bail."

She couldn't believe he'd been released—again—after he'd run from them. "What're you doing here?"

He feigned insult. "I was invited."

"I assume that was before you were charged with multiple felonies."

"Timing is everything, is it not?"

"I'll have you removed."

"Go for it. In the meantime, I'll enjoy the White House hospitality. Have a nice evening."

"What was that about?" Nick asked.

"Bryant shouldn't be here."

Nick made eye contact with Brant and tipped his head to request a word with his lead agent.

"Yes, sir?"

"Congressman Bryant's invitation should've been rescinded after he was charged with crimes. Will you see to removing him?"

Brant frowned. "Right away, sir."

Nick placed a hand on Sam's lower back. "All set."

"Power is sexy on you."

"Stop."

"Seriously hot." Sam never got tired of how flustered he became when she commented on his hotness.

As they greeted more guests, Sam watched the Secret Service escort Bryant from the event, not making any effort to be discreet about it.

After catching the filthy look he directed her way as he was marched toward the exit, she waggled her fingers at him.

"What the hell was Bryant doing here?" Gonzo asked when she was able to break away from the formalities to have a word with her team.

"I believe he slipped through the Shelby-had-a-baby, Terry-is-home-with-Lindsey cracks in the fortress."

"It was kind of fun watching him be tossed out on his ass," Gonzo said.

"For me as well. What's the latest?"

"First of all, the Davies hearing was postponed to tomorrow after the judge had an asthma attack." They'd learned that Stahl had framed Eric Davies on rape charges after he complained about Stahl after a traffic stop years earlier. Davies had been in prison for sixteen years because of fabricated charges.

"Oh jeez. That poor guy has to spend another night in jail."

"I know. That's what we were saying earlier. Second, we can't find any sign that O'Walsh, the golf pro, ever existed. We think it's possible he was working under an assumed name."

"Great. Now what?"

"We're tracking down some coworkers who knew him to see what they can tell us. More to come on that. I tracked down the rest of Bryant's now-former employees and discovered they'd all returned to Wisconsin the minute they heard he was arrested. One of them told me that they'd been disgusted by him for a while, but when they heard he ordered their friend and colleague Zach killed and to make it look like Zach was Bryant's son, that was it for them. We've confirmed that most of them were gone that same night."

"Thanks for closing that loop. At least we know now there wasn't some other member of his team on the loose who might've killed Tom."

"We also looked into Cox's assistant, Henry Allston, and there's not much to be found online."

"By not much..."

"Hardly anything. No school info, no job history, not much of anything other than being part of a winning Little League baseball team when he was a kid."

Sam scanned the huge tent and found Cox at one of the VIP tables in the front. He was laughing at something the man next to him had said.

"I'll have a talk with the AG and see what he can tell me about his assistant."

"Here?" Freddie asked.

"It's not like he's going to invite me back to his place after our last conversation."

"True. Sam ripped him a new one," Freddie told Gonzo.

"It needed to be done. He's an arrogant asshole."

Cox looked up, caught her watching him and frowned.

"No time like the present."

As she walked to Cox's table, she took great satisfaction in watching him realize she was coming to speak to him. He became less animated the closer she got. "A word, General Cox?"

He forced a smile. "Of course."

They walked to a corner of the massive tent that glittered with strands of lights and gleaming crystal.

"Is this necessary?" he asked with a scowl.

"If it wasn't, do you think I would've left my husband's side to come speak to you?"

"What do you want?"

"Tell me about your assistant."

He hadn't expected that. "What about him?"

"Who is he? Where does he come from?"

"Why in the world do you care about him?"

"Because I've chosen to."

She stared at him without blinking until he finally realized she wouldn't back down.

"This isn't the time or the place."

"I decide when, and I decide where. I couldn't care less about your lofty title or anything other than getting justice for my friend Tom Forrester."

He didn't like her referring to Tom as *her* friend.

"Do you know what it means to be a true friend, General Cox?

It means when your true friend is murdered, you do whatever you can to find the person who did it and make them pay, starting with answering questions from the lead detective on the case. I know it's been decades since you tried a criminal case, but you should know by now how this works."

"*Enough.*"

"Who is Henry Allston, and why was he so weird about giving me his name earlier?"

"He's my nephew. I raised him. My first wife and I did, I should say."

"And you've disclosed that your assistant is actually a family member?"

He shifted his weight from one foot to the other. "Not formally."

"Why not?"

"It doesn't matter."

"Aren't you in charge of enforcing rules and regulations? Wouldn't it be awkward for you if it came to light that your assistant is actually your nephew and you failed to disclose that through proper channels? Did the two of you lie on his background check?"

"Are you threatening me?"

"Not at all. I'm merely pointing out that your lack of candor in this investigation is beginning to get tedious. We're supposed to be on the same side, and yet, it took multiple conversations for you to come clean about your longtime relationship with Tom. Now it seems you're trying to hide your personal connection to your assistant. You know what I often observe about people who lack candor?" When he only stared at her with a stone-faced expression, she said, "They tend to have something to hide."

"I have nothing to hide."

"I don't believe you, and I'm going to shake your closet until all the skeletons fall out."

His expression turned into a nasty sneer. "It's true what people say about you."

"Is it? I love to hear that. Let me tell you something else. I'm going to rip your life apart—and your nephew's—and I'm going to enjoy it, you smug son of a bitch."

"Everything all right over here?" Nick asked as he joined them.

Cox's entire demeanor immediately became more amiable in Nick's presence. Interesting. "Of course, Mr. President. I'm just having a friendly chat with your wife."

"It didn't look friendly from a distance, which is why I came over to see what's going on."

Cox smiled at him. "Nothing at all, sir. As you might imagine, tensions are running high for all of us in law enforcement after the murder of a USA and the shooting of a high-ranking FBI agent."

"Yes, they sure are," Sam said with a meaningful look for Cox. "And you'd think that people with information about those crimes—especially those who know better—would be forthcoming, but alas, they're not."

If looks could kill, Sam would be so dead.

Judging by the thunderous expression on Nick's face, Sam's not-so-subtle message had registered with him, too.

"It would displease me, General Cox, if you were to obstruct my wife's investigation in any way or attempt to pull rank on her or the MPD as they seek justice for Tom Forrester."

The not so thinly veiled threat had Cox going pale.

Mr. President would be getting the good sex later.

Sam curled her hand around Nick's arm. "I've had enough of this conversation. Let's go talk to our friends."

"Lead the way, my love."

As they walked away from Cox, Sam whispered, "You're going to get luckier than you ever have in your life later."

"Is that right?" he asked with a chuckle.

"That guy is an insufferable boob, and you just made him shit his pants."

"Judging by the stink, you'd already done that before I showed up."

"Oh, I love you. So, so, so much."

"Why didn't you tell me he was giving you grief?"

"Because I'm handling it."

"Am I going to have a problem with my AG?"

"I'm not sure yet."

"Do what you must, and don't worry about me. I'll handle whatever comes up."

"You're the best husband I ever had."

Grunting out a laugh, he said, "The bar was set pretty low."

"And you've soared so far over it, you're in outer space."

CHAPTER TWENTY-ONE

When Sam rejoined her squad, she leaned in to talk to Freddie and Gonzo. "Allston is his nephew."

"Curiouser and curiouser," Gonzo said.

"And apparently, that relationship hasn't been publicly disclosed."

"We'll dig into Allston in the morning."

"Pass it on to Carlucci to get started tonight. Where there's smoke..."

"We'll find the fire."

Tracy brought the twins over to say good night to Sam and Nick, who hugged and kissed them both.

"We'll see you in the morning," Nick said.

"Be good for Celia," Sam added.

"We always are," Aubrey said.

"We love you," Sam said.

"Love you, too!"

With their detail in tow, Tracy took the twins upstairs to Celia, who'd see them through dinner and bedtime.

Nick stood to toast the Canadian prime minister and his wife. "Mr. Prime Minister, Mrs. Hutchinson, it's our honor to host you at the White House and celebrate all things Canadian tonight. I can't wait to try the poutine. I've heard it's amazing. The partnership between our two countries is one that's stood the test of time and more challenges than we can possibly name in just a few minutes. Our alliance has been steadfast through two world wars and numerous other crises. Our support for each other never wavers. Matthew, Samantha and I are delighted to welcome you and Courtney to the White House and to offer our friendship in the years to come. Please raise your glasses to our guests of honor."

As their guests applauded, Matthew Hutchinson stood. "Thank you, Mr. President and Mrs. Cappuano, for the warm welcome you've shown Courtney and me. We've very much enjoyed the time we've spent together and look forward to working with you both to advance the interests of our North American partnership. We also invite you to visit us at your earliest convenience. Cheers."

During dinner, they were entertained by solo performances from some of the country's most talented musicians on violin, trumpet and vocals. Sam couldn't believe she was in the same room with them, let alone the hostess of an event like this.

If only her dad could be there with them, she thought, it would've been perfect. He'd be blown away by it all. She hoped that somehow he knew and was proud to see his daughter and son-in-law living in the White House and hosting world leaders along with a Who's Who of famous guests.

Sam wasn't sure what she thought of the poutine, which was french fries with salty, softened cheese curds and gravy, but everyone else at their table of family and friends loved it.

Courtney leaned in to whisper to Sam, "Poutine is a Québécois, or Quebec French, slang term for 'mess.'"

Sam laughed at the apt description.

"Frankly," Courtney added, "I prefer my fries with vinegar."

"Me, too!"

The menu consisted of one exquisite course after another of some of the most delicious food she'd ever had. She had to refer to the printed menu to identify a few things, but most of it was familiar to her.

Dessert was coconut cake with strawberries, followed by more champagne and Canadian chocolate in the shape of maple leaves.

"I'm stuffed," Tracy declared.

"That was amazing," Mike said.

"I had nothing to do with it," Sam said, "but I'm glad you enjoyed it."

"And here we thought you planned and prepared the whole meal," Scotty said.

The others lost it laughing.

"Very funny. If I'd been in charge, it would've been pizza and french fries for everyone." She reached for Nick's hand under the table. "Somehow, our amazing White House team pulls off a daily miracle, especially on days like this."

"I understand our hosts recently celebrated their second wedding anniversary," Jon Bon Jovi said from the stage. "I was honored to perform at their wedding, and if they'd come to the dance floor, I've got a throwback to that day ready for them."

Nick stood and offered Sam his hand. "Shall we, my love?"

"Yes, we shall, Mr. President."

Tracy fanned her face. "Swoon."

Nick led the way to the dance floor as everyone in the massive tent applauded.

After recently having had tomatoes thrown at them by protesters, it was nice to be surrounded by a friendly crowd.

Sam would never get used to being the center of attention, so she chose to focus on her gorgeous husband and the opportunity to dance with him to music by her favorite singer.

The opening notes of "Make a Memory" reminded her of a few special moments, including the night he'd come home to find her reading *Congress for Dummies* because she wanted to understand his job as a senator. She'd had the song on blast that night. It also made her think of their glorious wedding day and all the amazing days since then.

"You and me, kid," he whispered in her ear. "Forever and ever."

His sweet words gave her goose bumps. For him she juggled

two full-time jobs while trying to be a halfway decent mother. He was worth all the stress and aggravation.

"Best part of my day, hands down," he said.

"Same, love."

Being held by him, even with hundreds of people watching, was the best thing ever.

Jon invited the Hutchinsons to join them on the dance floor for the second half of the song.

"Am I drooling?" Courtney asked Sam as she gazed at Jon.

"Hands off. He's mine."

"She's not kidding," Nick said.

They laughed as they swayed to the final notes of "Make a Memory."

Then Jon played an up-tempo set that got everyone dancing.

She and Nick posed for photos with most of their guests. Fortunately, he knew just about everyone and handled most of the small talk for both of them. She was beginning to run out of steam after the long, busy day and was beginning to crave her bed—and some time alone with him.

They'd sent Scotty up to bed after dinner since it was a school night.

Nick, being Nick, tuned in to her exhaustion and orchestrated a smooth escape that included a few minutes with the Hutchinsons before they headed for the door without drawing much attention from guests who were now dancing to music from a jazz band.

"What time will the party go to?"

"Probably after two."

"Jeez. Thank God we don't have to stay until then."

"I could see you were starting to wilt."

"Long day."

"Yes, it was."

He guided her up the stairs to the residence, where they looked in on sleeping kids and a dog before heading into their suite.

"I'm ready to kick off these heels and get comfy."

"Before you do..." He came up behind her and ran his hands

over her hips as he kissed the back of her neck. "You looked so incredibly beautiful tonight."

"Aw, thanks. I loved this dress the first time Marcus showed me the drawing of it."

"Please pass along my appreciation for his fine work."

"I'll do that." They stood with his arms around her from behind and his chin on her shoulder for a long moment. "It all seemed to go well, right?"

"It was exceptional in every way. The White House staff and our teams pulled off a stunner, and I'll tell them so tomorrow."

"They'll appreciate hearing that from you."

"It's hard to believe what goes on here every day, most of which you and I have nothing to do with, but they know exactly what's required and how to pull it off without breaking a sweat."

"Thank goodness for all the great people who make it happen."

He kissed her neck and sent a shiver through her. "And thank goodness for my first lady, who had to cut a busy workday short to come home for tea and frivolity when she certainly has more important things to do."

She stepped forward so she could turn to face him, curling her arms around his neck. "There is nothing in this world that's more important to me than you and our family and whatever you guys need from me."

"Figuring out who killed Tom and getting justice for him is more important than a silly state dinner."

"No, it really isn't. As much as I want justice for him—and we'll get it, eventually—today was all about you and whatever you needed."

"I'm very thankful for you every day, but especially on days like this when you have to put aside your own important work to support me."

"I was very happy to support you. I love you. There's nothing I wouldn't do for you, which I hope I've proven by allowing myself to be referred to as your first lady."

His smile lit up his face and her world. "That term could use an update."

"Do you think?"

He found the tab to the zipper of her dress and tugged it down. "Are you still up for some loft time?" Waggling his brows, he added, "You mentioned something about the good sex, not that any sex isn't good sex."

She smiled. "I've been looking forward to it all night."

Sam's cell phone rang on the bedside table, where she'd plugged it in earlier. She groaned. "I have to take that."

Nick went to retrieve the phone and handed it to her.

Sam took the call from Carlucci. "Hey, what's up?"

"I'm sorry to bother you when you're having such a big night there."

"It's fine. We're back in the residence."

"Ah, okay. Hope it all went well."

"It did."

"I'm calling because Gonzo passed me the info about Henry Allston being Cox's nephew and how he was raised by Cox and his first wife. I looked into him, and it's the strangest thing. There's no info about him online at all. No high school or college graduations, no social media, no nothing. I think I should request a warrant for his phone data, but I wanted to clear that with you before I did it."

"Go ahead. I'm getting a buzz that something's up there."

"Me, too. Gonzo said the guy is in his thirties?"

"Maybe early thirties."

"And no presence at all online? That's bizarre."

"Yep."

"I'll text you with any developments."

"Thanks, Dani."

Sam brought the phone with her into the bathroom, where she found Nick stripped down to boxers and standing at the sink to brush his teeth. "Thank goodness the rest of the world can't see you like that, or there'd be a line at the door for a turn with the POTUS."

"As if the POTUS would have anything to do with that nonsense. He's a one-girl kind of guy."

"She must be one very lucky girl."

"She's about to be if she'll hurry it up."

"She's hurrying!"

Sam went into her closet, removed the dress and everything underneath it before changing into a nightgown and robe that she tied tightly around her waist. In the bathroom, she removed her makeup, washed her face and brushed her teeth.

She found Nick in the sitting room, also wearing a robe.

"Ready?"

Sam grabbed the monitor for the twins from Nick's bedside. "Yep."

Hand in hand, they went upstairs to the third floor and ducked into the room where he'd re-created their loft from their Ninth Street home that'd been inspired by their trips to Bora Bora.

He lit the candles while she sat on the edge of the double lounger.

"It's been too long since we came up here. The days go flying by."

Nick sat next to her. "They sure do. I've never been so aware of how fast the time goes by than I have since we've been here."

"I guess it's a good thing that it's going by fast."

"It's a very good thing. I'm looking forward to being a private citizen again."

"You'll never be that again. Neither of us will be."

"Well, it'll be much more private than it is now."

He put his arm around her and leaned his head against hers. "Today was a good day for the Cappuano administration. The pictures will be blasted around the world, which will help with the illegitimacy bullshit."

"That's all it is, you know. Bullshit."

"I do know that, but the shooting at Fort Liberty hurt. That a military member could shoot his fellow service members because of me..."

"It was because of *him*, not you. Tell me you know that."

"I do, but enough about that. This time is for us."

She gave him a side-eyed look. "Whatever shall we do?"

Smiling, he kissed her as they reclined on the lounger, arms and legs intertwined as the kiss quickly became urgent.

"Vacation feels like a very long time ago, doesn't it?" he asked as he kissed her neck and pulled at the tie to her robe.

"Ages and ages ago."

Since it was late and they were both tired, he helped her up and out of the robe and nightgown.

He shrugged off his robe and removed his briefs and came to her, fully erect and ready.

Sam held out her arms to him as he made himself at home on top of her. "Absolute best part of my whole day."

"Mine, too."

"Although dancing with you and seeing the kids all dressed up was pretty great, too."

"Sure was. They're so cute."

"It was fun to watch Scotty work the room."

"He's a politician in training."

Nick groaned. "Not if I can help it."

"Oh stop. He wants to *be* you when he grows up."

"Enough of that and more of this." He kissed her as his hand found her breast, his thumb skating over her nipple.

That sent shivers all the way through her.

"I've missed you since we left the beach," he said.

"Me, too. I've wished we were back there a million times since we left."

"That many, huh?"

Sam curled her hand around his erection. "Possibly two million."

He gasped when she stroked him. "Samantha..."

"Yes?"

"This is going to end quickly if you keep that up."

"We can't let that happen." She gave his chest a push and moved carefully to straddle him, taking him by surprise.

"Nice move."

She was relieved to have pulled it off without hurting her hip. "You liked that?"

"I like all your moves. What else have you got?"

"How about this?" She sank down on him, going slowly while enjoying the way his gorgeous hazel eyes heated with desire.

No one else had ever made her feel the way he did, which gave her the confidence to take the lead, to focus on his pleasure rather than her own.

"Sexiest wife in the history of sexy wives."

"Nah."

"Hands down. No competition."

She smiled as she pivoted her hips, drawing a deep groan from him.

His fingers dug into the flesh of her hips. "Let's turn over so you can come, too."

"I'm fine just like this."

"Sam…"

"Shhh, just enjoy it. What you said to Cox might go down as the single sexiest moment in your entire sexy life."

"You liked that, huh?"

"I liked it a lot. You scared the shit out of him. It was epic."

"Anything for you, love."

"Right back atcha." She wanted to give something to him, something only she could give him—a few minutes in which he wasn't thinking of anything other than pleasure.

His gaze stayed focused on her every move, as if he didn't want to miss anything. She hoped he'd think of this the next time the weight of his responsibilities became too heavy once again.

Her own worries felt far away as she drove him up and over the top.

He brought her down to rest on top of him. "It's not fair that only one of us got the big finish."

"I got everything I wanted and then some."

"Not sure what I did to get so lucky to have the best wife ever."

"You loved me like no one else ever has. That's all you had to do."

He caressed her back as he held her close. "That's the easiest thing I've ever done."

CHAPTER TWENTY-TWO

They were back downstairs, asleep in bed, when a whimper on the baby monitor woke Sam from a sound sleep around two a.m. She stayed still to listen as the whimpering continued. She got up, put on her robe and went to check on the twins. It was rare for either of them to wake during the night.

Aubrey sat up in bed, weeping.

Sam scooped her up and carried her out of the room so she wouldn't disturb Alden, who was asleep on the other side of the bed they shared.

She carried the little girl into her sitting room, where a night-light put out a warm glow. "It's okay, sweetheart. I'm here."

The little one's sobs shook her body and broke Sam's heart.

"Do you want to talk about it?"

Aubrey shook her head.

Sam had learned that the best thing she could do at times like this was to be there and to take her lead from them as they grieved the loss of their devoted parents. The grief struck less often these days than it had at first, but it was always with them. Her heart ached for the child, who'd lost so much in a senseless act of violence. While Sam was forever thankful to have Aubrey and Alden in their lives, she would give anything to take away their pain.

"You want a drink of water?"

"Y-yes, please."

Sam brought her with her when she got up to get the water and some of the animal crackers Aubrey loved.

She took a tentative sip of the water and a bite of a cracker as Sam ran a hand over her golden curls. "Do you feel any better, love?"

Aubrey nodded. "I had a dream about Mommy."

"Oh, sweetie."

"I was sad when I woke up."

"I'm sure you were."

"I miss her."

"I know you do. I'm so sorry you're hurting."

Aubrey rested her head against Sam's chest as she nibbled on her animal crackers. Sam couldn't imagine enduring a loss like hers and Alden's at their tender age. They were far too young to understand any of it, but hopefully they knew how loved they were in their new life.

She must've dozed at some point because she woke quite a bit later with Aubrey asleep in her arms, which were tingling with pins and needles. Moving carefully, she got up to carry Aubrey into their bed, to keep her close if she woke again during the night.

"What's up?" Nick whispered as she got into bed, putting Aubrey between them.

"A dream about Mommy."

"Oh no. Is she okay?"

"She will be."

"How about you?"

"Sad for her."

"Get some rest. I'll get up with her if she wakes up again."

Sam reached across the sleeping child to hold his hand as she closed her eyes and tried to sleep.

The blast of her alarm was a rude awakening at six o'clock.

She was so not ready to be awake as she reached for her phone to see if there was anything new from Carlucci.

Dug all night and didn't find anything, not so much as a credit card or a credit score. I also couldn't find an address for him. Was going to request the warrant for his phone, but was unable to get the number, carrier or anything else that would help. The guy is truly off the grid. I dug a little deeper on Cox and learned he had a messy divorce from the first wife. His current wife, Bianca, winters in Palm Beach and is the toast of the polo set there. Her dad raises champion polo ponies, and her brother is one of the best polo players in the world. She and Cox have been married for twenty years, second marriage for both, never had children. If he visits her in Palm Beach, I can't find any record of it. He's not in any of the society photos that I sent to your email.

Thanks for being thorough. Will pick it up today.

Sam copied Dani's text and forwarded it to Gonzo and Freddie. *Possible threads from Carlucci.*

Aubrey never stirred when Sam got out of bed and stretched muscles sore from hours in heels and probably from dancing, too. It'd been a while since she'd gotten her groove on and would pay for that today. Thankfully, the cortisone shot was holding, and her hip didn't hurt at all. In the bathroom, she unbandaged her hand and ran her sore palm under cool water, wincing at the sting. After a shower, she applied the antibiotic ointment Harry had given her and put on a new bandage. Her wrist was still stiff but felt a tiny bit better than it had yesterday.

She felt like she was trudging through quicksand or something equally dense as she made coffee and tried to act like she was awake.

Nick came into the kitchen as she poured coffee into a travel mug. "How are you?"

"Tired."

He put an arm around her. "You took one for the team overnight."

"I was glad to do that. I always want to be there for them when they need me."

"I'll make sure she's okay before school."

"Celia is leaving this afternoon, and my mom is coming to stay, so if there's any issue, let my mom know."

"I will. Don't worry. She'll be fine."

He kissed her goodbye and sent her on her way with a protein bar and her travel mug of coffee. "Be safe out there. I love my wife more than life."

"I'm always careful. Got a lot to live for. Have a good day leading the free world."

She was heading for the stairs when Scotty came out of his room, looking grumpy and out of sorts, like he did every morning. Skippy followed, full of her usual morning energy. If Scotty didn't love that dog so much, he'd be annoyed by her. Rather, he was amused.

"Why did I have to get a morning-person dog?"

Sam kissed his forehead. "She's keeping you on a good schedule."

He and Skippy walked her down the stairs as they headed outside for Skippy to pee.

"Have a good day. Love you."

"Love you, too."

As she zipped up her own coat, Sam knew she should've told him to put a coat and shoes on, but that was pointless. Tracy had told her that teenagers often disdained coats and shoes, and it was a battle not worth fighting in the grand scheme of things that came with kids that age.

Vernon was waiting for her and opened the back door to the heated SUV.

"Morning."

She got in the back seat, thankful for the heat and the ride to work. "Morning."

"Has Cinderella's coach turned into a pumpkin this morning?"

Sam chuckled. "Something like that. Too much partying, not enough sleep makes Cinderella cranky."

"You and the president were stunning last night. We were so proud."

"Aw, thank you. That's nice to hear. It seemed to go well."

"Very well." Jimmy handed the *Washington Star* to her. "You got rave reviews."

"Did we?"

"Yep."

Sam scanned the headlines and photos from the state dinner. "We clean up pretty well."

"Very well," Vernon said. "The whole world is buzzing about the elegant first couple."

"How'd the tea go?" Jimmy asked.

"It was actually fun. She asked for wine because she doesn't like tea either."

"That's great," Jimmy said. "I love it."

"Any word on Agent Hill?" Vernon asked.

"I haven't talked to Shelby yet today. Let me text her."

Shelby replied a few minutes later. *He had a good night, and thankfully so did we. Mama got some sleep so she can take care of everyone else. Heard you guys were a huge hit last night, not that there was ever any doubt.*

Glad to hear all is well. We were a huge hit thanks to you and the incredible team that supports us. We were dazzled by it all.

It was a pleasure to put it all together. So much fun. I still can't believe I work for the first lady and the president. Pinch me!

I'd rather hug you when I see you later.

That'll work! So proud of my friends.

I'm so thankful to hear Avery is doing well.

God, me, too. Let me know what you hear about the investigation.

Will do.

"Avery had a good night and so did Shelby. She got some sleep."

"That always helps."

She dashed off a text to Celia, wishing her a great time on her cruise to Alaska with her sisters.

Celia responded a minute later. *Thank you! I'll miss you all.*

We'll miss you, too. Love you.

Love you, too!

Next she sent messages to Terry, Derek, Shelby, Lilia and Gideon Lawson, the chief usher, complimenting them in a job well done with the state dinner. *Nick and I were blown away by every detail. Please pass along our thanks and appreciation to everyone who had a hand in pulling off such a wonderful evening.*

Sam's phone rang with a call from Gonzo. "Hey, I'm almost there."

"We got ballistics back. Same gun did Tom and Avery."

Sam sat back in her seat as the implication hit her square in the chest. The investigation had just taken a whole new turn.

"EVERYONE IN THE CONFERENCE ROOM." Sam unlocked her office and dropped her coat onto one of the chairs. Grabbing the travel mug of coffee, her notebook and a pen, she followed her team into the room and closed the door.

Before she could say a word, Captain Malone came in with Chief Farnsworth.

"Good morning, gentlemen," Sam said.

"Morning."

They took seats at the table.

Sam turned to Gonzo. "Talk to us."

"Ballistics determined the bullet that killed Tom and the one that was retrieved from Avery are from the same gun. There was a telltale mark in the same place on each bullet. It was determined they came from a nine-millimeter Glock."

"What does this mean for the investigation?" Freddie asked.

"It changes the whole picture," Sam said, "and forces us to ask who'd want to kill both Tom and Avery."

"It also forces us to ask who might be next," Malone said.

"That, too."

"As much as I hate to say it, we're going to need some help on this from the Feds," Sam said.

"Agreed," Farnsworth said. "I was about to say the same thing. We need them to tell us what cases Tom and Avery worked on together. We need to know what judges and other personnel were involved so we can warn them."

"If they weren't already locked up, I'd be looking hard at the couple who did the home invasion at Avery and Shelby's," Sam said.

"Might be worth having a conversation with them," Cameron said.

"Where are they?"

Freddie went to the computer terminal. "Jessup. As a repeat offender and parole violator, he was denied bail. The wife, a first-time offender, was apparently unable to come up with the bail. I'll request she be brought over from the women's prison."

Sam didn't feel like trekking to Jessup, but if that's what it took, so be it. "Freddie and I will start there. The rest of you get with Avery's deputy, George Terrell, and Faith Miller to sync up on cases they had in common. I want everyone else involved in those cases put on notice as soon as possible that the two shootings are connected."

"What are we doing about the follow-up we started on Tom's case?" Gonzo asked. "Carlucci briefed me on the problem with getting the warrant for Henry Allston's phone. Before she left this morning, Dani called the AG's office and asked Allston for his cell number, saying it was for the file. He gave it to her, and she requested the warrant. It came through ten minutes ago."

Sam thought about that for a second. "Go ahead with requesting his cell phone data." She updated the others on her conversation with Cox the night before. "Something is off with him. I want to know what it is. I also want to know where that golf pro has gone."

"I'll put Lucas and Coheeny on that," Gonzo said. "Harper is in court today for one of his ongoing cases."

The mention of court reminded Sam of the hearing Thursday in Spencer's case. She needed to check in with Angela about whether she planned to attend. Either way, Sam would be there.

"Before you disperse, I want to give you an update on the situation at Stahl's house," Farnsworth said. "As of this morning, we've recovered fourteen bodies from the yard and four from inside a cell that'd been sealed off with a concrete wall. Haggerty's team believes it's possible those victims were still alive when they were imprisoned in that room."

Sam felt sick at the thought of what they must've endured before death claimed them.

"What about the storage unit?" Gonzo asked.

"We've hit a dead end," O'Brien said. "When the new owner

took over the facility, Stahl was in arrears on payment for the unit for several months. When he was unable to locate Stahl—because he was in prison—the new owner had the unit cleaned out. That happened months ago. Whatever was in there is long gone."

"Damn it," Gonzo said.

"My thoughts exactly," O'Brien said. "We looked into what it would take to try to track down the contents at the landfill. I made a few calls and learned that there'd be a mountain of shit on top of it by now, and it would be nearly impossible to find anything."

"Thank you for being thorough, Detective," Malone said.

"I just wish I had better news."

While they talked about the storage unit, Sam couldn't stop thinking about the tomb Stahl had erected in his house of horrors. She felt cold all over as she recalled being wrapped in razor wire and threatened with fire at his hands.

"Sam."

Freddie's voice broke through the daze she'd slipped into as past trauma resurfaced.

"Yes?"

"Are you all right?"

"Uh-huh." She took a deep breath and realized her hands were shaking.

"Get her some water," Malone said.

Freddie rushed out of the room.

Malone sat next to her.

"I'm fine."

"You're not, and that's understandable."

"We shouldn't have shared those details when you were in the room," Farnsworth said regretfully.

"I don't want to be given special treatment. You know that."

Malone leaned in. "In this case, you should have *all* the special treatment."

"We'll keep the details away from you going forward," Farnsworth said.

"That's not necessary."

The chief gave her a meaningful look. "It wasn't a suggestion."

"Yes, sir."

"If it makes you feel any better, I'm sick over it, too." The chief shook his head in disbelief. "It's reached the point where I have to share details with family members and the public. How do I go out there and tell people what one of our former colleagues has done? Eighteen people. So far..."

"It's unfathomable that he was doing this while pretending to be a law enforcement officer."

"The job gave him cover," Malone said.

"Yes, I guess it did." She shuddered. "The thought of him sealing off those people in a tomb while they were still alive..."

"It's the stuff of nightmares," the chief said bluntly. "As is the hearing we have this afternoon to vacate the charges against Eric Davies, who Stahl framed on rape charges."

"Sixteen years in prison," Malone said, "all because Davies complained about the way Stahl treated him during a traffic stop when Stahl was in Patrol."

"What's the blowback going to look like on all this?" Sam asked.

"We're working with Public Affairs to craft a statement that adequately reflects our shock and revulsion at learning a colleague we trusted could've betrayed us all this way."

"That's a good angle to put on it," Sam said.

Freddie returned with a cold bottle of water.

"Thank you," she said with a grateful smile.

"Are you okay?"

"I am. Don't worry." She took a few sips of the water, made sure she had her emotions in check and then stood. "Let's get to Jessup. I don't want another day to get away from me." To Gonzo, she said, "I'll call with an update."

"We'll get with George and Faith in the meantime."

"Sounds good."

"One other thing for you before you go... The golf pro. We ran him through NCIC, and it turns out his real name is Tristan

Walsh—he'd added the O to get the job at the country club. As Tristan *Walsh*, he's wanted in multiple jurisdictions in the area on charges ranging from B&E to larceny."

"Wow."

"I've updated those departments on the info we've found on him, and they're picking it up from there."

"Excellent work, Gonzo. Thank you."

She and Freddie left HQ a few minutes later with Vernon driving them to GW so she could see Avery.

"Are you sure you're okay?"

She wanted to tell him to quit asking her, but she'd never do that. He loved her and was concerned. "It was a lot to hear what they'd found at the house, but I'm okay."

"I'm trying to imagine how anyone gets to the point in their life where they decide to do something like that to other human beings."

"I think he probably came out that way. It's baked into the DNA with people like him."

"I guess but imagine actually doing that and then going on with your life as if you hadn't condemned people to the most unimaginable death."

She shuddered. "I can't."

"I'm sorry. I'll drop it."

"It's okay. I get the desire to understand it, even though we never will."

"No, we won't." He looked over at her. "You should check in with Trulo on this."

"Yeah, I will."

It'd been a lot lately. More than usual. Between Nick's ascension to the presidency, Spencer's shocking death, her fractured hip, the revelation of Stahl's murder spree, her nemesis Detective Ramsey smashing his car into her Secret Service SUV, the home invasion at Shelby and Avery's, the shooting at Fort Liberty, Tom's murder, Avery's shooting, the relentless pace at work and home, it was all she could do to keep her head above water sometimes.

She fired off a text to the department's psychiatrist, Dr. Trulo. *Got time for an old friend this week?*

He wrote back ten minutes later. *Always.*

I'm in the field but will check in when I'm back at the house.

I'll be here all day.

Thanks, Doc.

"I'll see him later," she told Freddie.

"Good."

"Don't worry about me, okay? It was a shock, but I'm over it."

"Are you? How does anyone ever get over what he did to you, let alone the rest of what we know now?"

"I have to get over it, or I can't function on the job or at home. I can't dwell on the bad stuff. I just can't. I hardly ever think of it anymore, until something happens that brings it up again."

"You shouldn't be anywhere near this new investigation with him."

"The chief said the same thing—and added it wasn't a suggestion."

"That's just as well. You know that, right?"

"I do. A few years ago, I would've objected to being sidelined. But now? I have a family to think about, multiple jobs to do, and I have to protect myself from things that'll make it impossible to get shit done."

"I'm glad you're thinking that way."

She put her hand on his arm. "I'm fine. I swear. Let's get our heads back in the game, okay?"

"Sure thing."

"I appreciate you."

"Same. I hate to see that guy hurting you any more than he already has."

"Hopefully, after all this, we'll have seen the end of him." Even as she said that, she feared they might never see the end of Stahl.

"We'll lock him away and toss the key."

Sam gave his arm a squeeze and then released him, determined to take the time it took to get to Jessup to get her head straight and be ready to face off with the scumbags who'd threatened Shelby and Noah.

Thinking about the terror of that day made her so furious that she was able to push aside everything else to focus on justice for people she cared about.

CHAPTER TWENTY-THREE

"Refresh my memory on these reprobates," Sam said as they got closer to the Maryland state prison.

Freddie consulted notes on his phone. "Willy and Justice Peckham were the ringleaders of a massive gun trafficking organization. They also specialized in defrauding the federal government. If there was a way to scam money from Medicaid or other aid programs, they found it and exploited it. They got away with it for a long time, until a federal task force, led by Avery, took them down years ago.

"Justice died in prison, and Willy married a much younger woman named Amber while he was in prison. Willy was sentenced to fifteen years, served twelve and was recently paroled. From what we can tell, Amber picked up Willy when he got out, and they went straight to Avery's home, looking for revenge."

"Avery referred to it as the Farmington investigation. Why was it called that?"

Freddie poked around on his phone for a minute. "It was named for the person who first brought the fraud to the attention of federal officials."

"Ah, I see. You just gotta wonder what motivates people. Willy Peckham and his family were guilty as sin, they knew that, and yet, when they were caught, it wasn't their fault. Oh no, it was the

FBI agent who led the investigation that shut down their sugar shack. It was all his fault."

"I know, right?" Freddie said. "And when Willy is paroled after years in prison, rather than go home, humbled by the experience, he decides to go after the guy who put them there, hold his pregnant wife and his son hostage, and end up right back in jail less than forty-eight hours after he got out. We're not talking about the sharpest tools in the shed here."

"Avery said the whole family is the epitome of the word 'scumbag.' What else do we know about them?"

"Their criminal enterprise was run out of Corbin, Kentucky, a town of about eight thousand off Interstate 75, located halfway between Knoxville, Tennessee, and Lexington, Kentucky. There's a higher-than-average crime rate in the town, and it has a history of racial unrest dating back to the early twentieth century."

"You said they oversaw a criminal enterprise. What became of the other players in this so-called enterprise?"

"Let me check." He did some more scrolling and reading. "Twenty other people were indicted along with the Peckhams. Most of them did at least ten years before being paroled. Willy's first wife, Justice, died of cancer in prison. She was the mother of his children, all but one of whom also did time on this case."

"We're going to need a list of who they are and where they are now."

"Should I ask Gonzo to look into that?"

"Yes, please. Last question... Who prosecuted the case?"

"Due to the Peckham family's deep roots in the area, DOJ prosecutors requested a change of venue from the Eastern District of Kentucky. It was granted, and the trial was moved to DC. Tom Forrester was the lead prosecutor, and Avery Hill was the star witness."

"Holy shit," Sam said. "There's the connection."

"I don't understand the timing. Their lieutenants have been on the loose for years after being paroled. Why'd they wait until now?"

"Maybe Willy wanted to seek his revenge personally."

"Possibly," Freddie conceded. "Nothing about this case or the last one makes sense. Bryant takes Forrester's family hostage after learning he and Cox are secretly investigating him while pretending to be his buddies, and that's not related to Forrester's murder?"

"It doesn't seem to be."

"How can it *not* be?" he asked.

"Ballistics don't lie."

"No, they don't, but I still feel like we're missing something big here."

"If we are, we'll figure it out, like we always do. All my Spidey senses are saying Cox is up to no good."

"I agree."

"I'd very much like to figure that out, if for no other reason than to save my husband from a humiliating issue with his AG."

"That's as good a reason as any."

"I should walk away from that part of the investigation, but how do I do that when my radar is picking up a hit?"

"You can't. We have to see it through."

"I worry about making another powerful enemy for myself and Nick."

"The AG is only powerful as long as he holds that office. If there's something dirty going on, Nick will fire him, and he'll lose all his power."

"That's true." The thought of Nick firing the AG because of her investigation certainly wasn't ideal. But there was no way she could walk away from the feeling of something amiss and hope that didn't blow up in her husband's face. "Did I tell you we're meeting with Nick's mother on Friday at Ninth Street?"

Freddie spun around in his seat. "You're doing *what*?"

"You heard me."

"Sam... Seriously?"

"She requested the meeting to 'make amends,' and Nick decided he wants to hear what she has to say."

"No way."

"Way."

"Did you try to stop it?"

"It's not up to me. She's his mother. If he wants to see her, what can I do besides go with him and get in the middle of it if she pulls the usual shit? Apparently, the lawyer that got her out of jail has convinced her she needs to make things right with her son."

"What's his angle?"

"I'm not sure."

"Are you going to find out before Friday?"

"I suppose I should look into that."

"I'll do it. What's his name?"

"Collins Worthy from Cleveland, and P.S., I don't deserve you."

"Yes, you do."

"No, I really don't. I'm surrounded by people who'd do anything for me, and you're at the top of that list. I just hope you know…"

He gave her a fierce look. "I know." After he sat back in his seat, he looked over at her. "I hope it's okay to say I can't believe he's actually going to meet with her."

"It's okay. I can't believe it either. She's got this weird hold over him. It's like he becomes a little boy again when she resurfaces, and he's full of hope that things might be different. It never is, of course, but he can't seem to give up the hope."

"I hate that for him."

"I do, too, but I've learned to follow his lead where she's concerned. He was so upset that I didn't tell him I'd asked Avery to look into her before she got arrested. I never want to be the cause of that again."

"You weren't the cause of that. She was."

"But it never would've smacked him in the face if I hadn't asked Avery to investigate when I was in a fit of rage over her shenanigans and then forgot to mention that to him."

"It might've blown up anyway. At least this way, he had some notice that it was going down."

"I guess, but it was unsettling to see him that upset over something I'd done. I didn't like that. So my new policy is to follow his lead with her and let him call the shots."

"I suppose that's wise, but if I had a vote, I wouldn't want him anywhere near her."

"You and me both, pal."

"So Collins Worthy is a well-regarded defense attorney in Cleveland with a reputation for being a shark on behalf of his clients. I'm scrolling, looking for anything negative about him, but not finding it other than the usual criticism levied at defense attorneys who work for criminals."

"Thanks for looking him up for me."

"What do you think the odds are that she's decided to clean up her life?" he asked.

"Slim."

"Yeah, probably."

Upon arriving at Jessup, Sam, Freddie and Vernon went through the usual routine of surrendering their weapons and proceeding through security. They were shown to a room to wait for the Peckhams.

Sam felt unusually anxious for some reason, which was strange. She often interacted with hardened criminals and was never particularly unsettled around them. It was probably because of the way Avery had spoken about Willy and the trauma they'd inflicted on Shelby during the home invasion that had Sam's nerves on edge. Sam would never forgive them for what they'd put her sweet friend through by threatening her life, Noah's life and that of her unborn child. It was almost too much to bear.

When they came in, Willy more than lived up to his reputation.

Both wore orange jumpsuits. He had stringy hair and a haggard face, as if he'd lived a hundred lifetimes and done them all the hard way. Amber was much younger, pretty and seemed terrified. Their hands and feet were chained, and the deputy made no move to unlock them once they were in the room.

Vernon usually stood outside the door when she was in an interrogation room. This time, he came in.

"They told us the first lady was here," Willy said in a twangy accent. "Couldn't believe it till I saw it with my own eyes. As I live and breathe. Whatever can my humble spouse and I do for you on this fine day?"

"I'm Lieutenant Holland, and this is my partner, Detective Cruz. We'd like to record this conversation."

"Go for it. We got nothing to hide."

Sam rather doubted that. "We'd like to talk to you about Agent Avery Hill and U.S. Attorney Tom Forrester."

Willy's expression turned to stone at the mention of their names. "Those sons a bitches ruined our lives."

"By tying you to a vast conspiracy to defraud the federal government as well as gun trafficking and drug dealing?"

He shrugged. "That's their story."

"Their so-called story was enough to convince twelve jurors to convict you and your associates on multiple charges."

"Don't mean it was true."

"Okay, whatever. So you get out of jail and go right to Avery Hill's home, hoping for what, exactly?"

"I wanted to have a talk with him. Met his wife. She's a pretty little thing." When he smiled, he revealed rotting teeth that made Sam's stomach turn. Her heart ached imagining her sweet Shelby being threatened by the likes of him.

"Shut your mouth about his wife."

Freddie's hand on hers under the table reminded her not to lose her cool.

"Heard she was a friend of yours."

Sam wished she was allowed to punch that smarmy smile off his face.

"Let me tell you how this is going to go. We're looking at you and your associates hard for the murder of Tom Forrester and the attempted murder of Avery Hill."

"Knock yourselves out. We had nothing to do with it."

"Guess what? We don't believe you. If you know who did this, and you come clean with us, it could help to reduce your sentences."

Amber perked up for the first time. "By how much?"

"Shut your mouth, woman."

"I want to know what they're offering. I've got kids I want to see grow up."

He gave her a murderous look that had her shrinking into herself.

Sam glanced at the deputy. "Would you mind removing Mr. Peckham from the room?"

"You're not talking to her without me."

"Is that what you think?" Sam asked with a laugh.

The deputy hauled Willy to his feet and marched him out of the room.

"If you know what's good for ya, woman, you'll keep yer fucking mouth shut!"

The door slammed shut behind him.

Sam looked to Amber, who was quivering.

"I, uh, I shouldn't say anything. Willy will be mad."

"You mentioned your children. How old are they?"

"Six and four. They're from another relationship."

"You must miss them."

"Very much so."

"Where are they?"

"Back home in Kentucky. I was with them every day until Willy got released. He told me to pick him up. I thought we were going right home, but that's not what happened. I didn't want to bother that pregnant lady or her son. Willy made me do it."

"Do you know anything about the murder of Tom Forrester or the attempted murder of Avery Hill?"

She looked down at the table. "What would be in it for me if I knew stuff?"

"That depends on what you're able to give us."

"If I tell you, Willy will have me killed in jail."

"We'd have you put into protective custody."

"He'd find a way. He don't do snitches."

"Let me make a call and see what can be done." Sam got up to leave the room to call Captain Malone. "I'm with Amber Peckham, who did the home invasion at Shelby and Avery's with her husband, Willy. I think she has info on the shootings of Tom and Avery, but she's afraid to talk because her husband threatened her to keep her mouth shut. She said he'd find a way to kill her even if she was in protective custody. What can we do?"

"Let me get with Faith and see what she thinks. I'll call you right back."

While she waited, Sam texted Shelby to see how Avery was doing.

Much better. They transferred him out of ICU. Hopefully home by the end of the week.

That's great news. I'm so glad to hear it. How are you?

I'm fine as long as he is. Will be glad to get him home. Will probably delay our move-out, however.

Don't worry about that. Stay as long as you need to. We like having you guys upstairs.

So thankful for you all.

Love you.

You too!

She took a call from Malone. "What'd she say?"

"She'll have Amber transferred back to our place."

"When?"

"Right away."

"Should we bring her back?"

"Not sure the Secret Service would go for that."

"True, and I don't want to get my agents into trouble."

"Stand by. I'll text you with the plan."

"Will do."

He texted six minutes later. *FBI can pick her up on your go-ahead and transport her to our house. You would wait there until they arrive. They'd come in hot, so it won't be long.*

Got it. Let me see if she's on board. This could be our big break.

Hope so!

A deputy let Sam back into the room to update the others about the plan to transport Amber to MPD headquarters.

Amber's gaze darted nervously around the room. "So what does this mean?"

"We'll get you out of jail and away from Willy's reach so you can tell us what you know. If you cooperate fully with our investigation, the Assistant U.S. Attorney may be inclined to cut you a break. But that only happens if you're truthful with us and if you give us information that helps locate the person or people who killed Forrester and shot Hill. Do you understand?"

Amber was trembling so hard, Sam wondered how she remained seated.

"Amber? Do you have information relevant to this investigation, and are you willing to share it with us to potentially reduce your sentence?"

"I... I'm afraid of people other than Willy, and I'm worried about my kids. They... They're with my mother."

"We'd do everything in our power to keep you and your family safe, but you'd be required to testify in court to whatever information you provide."

She rocked in her chair, as if she'd been plugged into an electrical outlet.

Sam wanted to scream at her to move it along, that she had a million other things to get to and couldn't wait all day for her to decide. But she bit her tongue, hoping Amber would agree to cooperate and point them in the direction of the shooter.

With so much riding on the information she could potentially provide, Sam gave her another full minute before she spoke up again. "I'm sorry to put a time limit on this, but we've got a lot of ground to cover today. Are you in?"

"You're sure they won't be able to kill me or my kids?"

"We can never guarantee that. All we can do is tell you we'll do everything we can to keep you safe. One thing I'll add is that you've already been in with us, on your own, for forty-five minutes. At this point, Willy would assume you're telling us everything you know."

Her already pasty expression became more so when that detail registered with her. "I'm in. I'll cooperate. Get me out of here."

"I'll order your ride."

CHAPTER TWENTY-FOUR

When she and Freddie were back in the Secret Service SUV, following the FBI vehicle south on the Baltimore-Washington Parkway, Sam decided she wanted to see Avery.

"Let's go to GW first," she said to Vernon.

"Will do."

She saw him glance at Jimmy. "Do you have to report all our movements to the higher-ups?"

"Yes, ma'am. In case we ever need backup, they'll know where to find us."

"Ah, I see. Not sure why I didn't notice that before."

Vernon smiled at her in the mirror. "Your job is to relax and enjoy the ride while leaving the details to us."

"I'll let you know when I start to relax and enjoy the ride."

"We need to ramp up the beverage service, Jimmy."

"A little vodka might do the trick."

"So noted."

"I'm kidding." To Freddie, she said, "They know I'm kidding, right?"

"I sure hope so. She's a wicked lightweight."

"Shut up! That's not true!"

"Yes, it is."

"Not."

"Yes."

"Children…"

"God, he reminds me of my dad when he does that."

"Me, too."

"You couldn't pay me a nicer compliment."

"I was really wishing he was there to see us hosting a state dinner last night. He'd have been losing it."

"He was there," Vernon said. "He's always right there."

"You really think so?"

"I'm sure of it. I didn't know him, but I feel like I do from your stories about him. That's why I'm so sure he wouldn't want to miss a minute of your time at the White House."

"Well, I hope he's not watching *all* of it."

After a heartbeat of silence, the other three laughed.

Freddie scrubbed at his ears. "I want to unhear the last thirty seconds."

"What? I'm just saying that if the ghosts are watching, I hope they're being selective in their viewing. Are there parental controls or something we could employ?"

"You're too funny, Sam," Jimmy said as he wiped his eyes.

"Don't encourage her." Freddie's tone dripped with disdain. "That's how she got this way."

"This is the most fun I've ever had at work," Jimmy said. "I tell my wife every night how funny y'all are."

"I hope you tell her I'm funnier than he is," Sam said as Freddie rolled his eyes at her.

"You're at your funniest when you're with him," Jimmy said.

Freddie sent her a smug smile.

"He's my favorite victim."

"If that ain't the truth."

"I've made you into the man you are today."

"Sometimes I think she honestly believes the nonsense she spews."

"All fact. Make yourself useful and get me some info on the people who were convicted along with the Peckhams."

"Yes, dear."

A thought occurred to her as they got closer to where they would peel off from the FBI vehicle to head to the hospital. "Do I need to be worried about the Feds taking her somewhere other than our place?"

"Crap," Freddie said. "I hadn't thought of that."

"Ask for a Patrol escort from the District line," Sam said.

Freddie got on the phone.

"Tell them to direct the car only to our place. Nowhere else."

He nodded and passed along her request to the Patrol commander.

"They're on it."

"If the Feds kidnap her, they're gonna be sorry they ever met me."

Sam texted Shelby to get Avery's room number.

Is it okay if I stop by for a minute on official business?

He says he's fine and to come on down.

Sam was deeply relieved to know Avery was doing well and sounding like himself through Shelby. "It's amazing how things happen, isn't it?"

"Which things are you referring to?"

"How Avery, who was once the biggest pain in my ass, has turned into such a treasured friend and colleague."

"That is amazing when you think about how he used to go weak in the knees over you."

Sam cringed. "He did not."

"Yes, he did. He was crazy about you. I thought Nick was going to have him killed."

"That was another lifetime ago."

"Like two years?"

"Shut up! We got past that, and now…"

"Now you love him like a brother, and it was devastating to hear he'd been shot."

"Yeah, that. All I could think of was Shelby losing him days after having the baby they both wanted so much."

"Thank goodness that didn't happen."

"For sure."

At the hospital, Vernon escorted them inside to the fifth floor. They were met by FBI agents who asked for ID, even though they recognized Sam.

"He's in five thirty-five, Lieutenant."

"Thank you."

Another agent was positioned outside Avery's door.

They showed her their IDs, and she let them into the room. As annoying as the delays were, Sam was glad her friends were being well protected with his shooter still on the loose.

Shelby and baby Maisie were keeping Avery company. He looked pale, but otherwise much better than Sam had expected. He had a huge bandage over his right shoulder, and that arm was in a sling.

"Come in," he said when he saw Sam and Freddie.

"Thanks for seeing us."

"No problem."

Sam gave Shelby a one-armed hug as she glanced at the baby and melted. "My goodness, Tinker Bell, but that baby is gorgeous."

"Isn't she dreamy?"

"The dreamiest."

Sam forced herself to tear her gaze away from the baby and focus on why she'd come. "I need to talk to you about the Peckhams."

Both Shelby and Avery tensed at the mention of that name.

"I'm going to find a quiet corner to feed the baby." Shelby grabbed the diaper bag, kissed Avery and headed for the door.

"Sorry to upset her."

"She wants to know who shot me as much as you do."

"I know. I met them earlier at Jessup." Sam shuddered. "I can't imagine Shelby being confronted by that guy and fearing for her life and Noah's."

"Right? He's the worst of the worst. You're looking at him for me and Tom?"

"Your bullet matches Tom's. You were both involved in their case. He and his new wife broke into your home, threatened your wife and son. We're taking a hard look."

"They were locked up again when both of us were shot."

"The rest of their crew wasn't. Our theory is once they heard that Willy had failed to get to you, one of their people tried to finish the job."

"Jesus," he whispered. "When I first heard about Tom, I was sure it would lead right back to Damien Bryant."

"Me, too, and that's where we were focused until ballistics told us your bullet and Tom's came from the same gun." Sam refilled his cup of water, handed it to him and took a seat next to the bed. "We've had Amber Peckham transported to HQ and are offering her some leniency in exchange for telling us what she knows. We got her out of jail because she feared Willy would have her killed for talking to us."

"She's right to be afraid of him. The DV history with his first wife, Justice, goes back years. Police were regulars at their house."

"Why wasn't he ever put away for that?"

"She always refused to testify."

"Ah, I see, and I guess I understand why. I'd be afraid of him if I was married to him."

Avery grimaced. "Every time I think about it, my whole body goes hot with rage at the thought of that son of a bitch being anywhere near my precious family."

She took out her notebook and pen. "Talk to me about who they are and what they did. I want the details of the investigation from your point of view."

Avery took a sip of water and then handed the cup to Sam to put on the table. He rested his head against the pillows piled behind him. "It was early in my career, like the second year with the Bureau. They asked me to go undercover for up to six months. I moved to Corbin, got a job pumping gas, was a regular at the local hangouts and eventually infiltrated the Peckhams through one of their guys. Lonnie Marsden, one of Willy Peckham's many first cousins, sat next to me at a bar one night, bought me a beer and got to talking, the way guys do. 'Where you from?' 'What'd you do for fun?' 'What teams do you like?' That kind of stuff. He invited me to a cookout at the Peckham's 'farm,' which was really a run-down collection of buildings that housed their extended family."

"I'm trying to picture you assimilating with these people."

"I grew my hair out, didn't shave, let my hands get dirty—and stay dirty—at the station."

"Are there pictures of dirty Avery?"

"Focus, Sam."

She laughed. "Sorry, but I'd love to see those pics."

"You might find them in the file."

"Can George get that for me?"

"Yeah, I'll ask him to send it to you." He reached for his phone and winced.

Sam got it for him.

"Thanks." He sent the text to his deputy. "He said he'll take care of it right away."

"Appreciate the cooperation."

"If it was them, I want them taken down as much as you do."

"Tell me about what happened after you became friends with Lonnie and the Peckhams."

"We started hanging out on the weekends. They'd have bonfires and shooting contests, and one of the cousins had a boat we'd take out on the lake to go fishing. I got the sense for that first month or so that they were trying to get a read on me and whether I could be trusted.

"All I knew going in was that they all had lengthy records, going back to when they were juveniles, and it was suspected they were into bigger things. The HHS inspector general had identified irregular Medicaid activities in Whitney, Knox and Laurel Counties. Corbin touches all three, and the Peckham family ties ran deep in that area."

"What did these irregular activities entail?"

"Excessive billing for routine services, hospital bills that were five times what they should've been, people who'd been dead for years, including Willy's parents, receiving medical care that was billed to the government. They threatened local doctors, forcing them to participate or their families would be harmed. They got away with it for years until President Harrigan came into office, vowing to crack down on fraud, waste and abuse. His HHS secretary and IG were the ones who uncovered the operation in Corbin. The doctors were our star witnesses."

"If they're gunning for the people who put them away, those doctors' lives are in danger."

He made a call and put it on speaker. "George, I'm with Sam at the hospital, and she just made a good point. The doctors who testified against the Peckhams need to be warned they might be killing, or trying to kill, people involved with putting them away."

"I'll alert our office in London, Kentucky, and get some agents out to talk to them right away."

"Tell them it's an emergency," Sam said.

"Will do."

Avery pressed a button to end the call.

"Who else do we need to be worried about protecting?"

"I'll have George work on that from our end."

"Who would they send to do their dirty work with you and Tom?"

"Probably their son Harlan."

"Freddie, can you call up the video from Tom's shooting?"

He went to work on his phone and then brought it to the bedside so Avery could see it.

"Could this be him?"

"He's the right height and size. Willy used to bust his balls about being such a small guy. It made Harlan ruthless. He worked out like a demon and could kill a man with one hand around his neck."

"Did you see him do that?"

"Twice."

"Jesus. Why isn't he locked up?"

"He got off on a technicality when the rest of their crew went to prison."

"What kind of technicality?"

"He was able to prove he was never read his Miranda rights when he was arrested."

"For real?"

"Yep. One of the local agents was his best friend from high school and torched his career with the Bureau by 'failing' to do the most basic part of his job."

"Was he in on the scheme?"

"We were never able to prove that, but he buckled to threats from Harlan and screwed over the rest of our team by letting that fucking rat skate free."

"Has the FBI monitored Harlan since then?"

"I mean, I'd like to say yes, but we're stretched thin everywhere. I wouldn't be surprised if more pressing priorities have pushed him to the back burner."

"So he's running free and doing God knows what."

"Possibly."

"What do you think about a deal for Amber?"

"I wouldn't be opposed, especially if she can give us Willy and Harlan. From what I know about Willy, she probably felt she had no choice but to marry him and do his bidding."

"How does a wedding even happen when he's in jail?"

"Prisoners have rights, you know." He rolled his eyes. "They got married about a year ago. I'm sure she didn't know what he had planned when she picked him up when he got released. I'll bet he threatened her to make her go along with the plan to come after me."

"Did you ever see his first wife, Justice, commit other crimes?"

"Never. The rest of them? Yes, and most of them were charged with the stuff I saw, but she was only charged as a participant in the Medicaid scheme."

"What I don't get is why they'd seek revenge the minute he got out."

"They're always angriest at the people they feel betrayed them, and that was me. I'll never forget the way he looked at me when he found out I was a Fed. Like he wanted to murder me in the most painful way possible. He nearly succeeded when he had my family…"

Sam reached out a hand to him. "I know it's hard not to let your mind go there, but they're safe and well, and you'll be back on your feet again in no time. Everything's okay."

"As long as Harlan Peckham is running loose and following his father's orders, none of us are safe."

. . .

SAM AND FREDDIE rode back to HQ in silence, each of them absorbed in their own thoughts as they processed what Avery had told them.

"I have a question," Freddie said when they were about six blocks from HQ.

"I'm listening."

"What're we doing about Cox, his nephew and your Spidey sense that he's up to no good?"

"While we hunt down Harlan Peckham, we're going to continue to work on figuring that out."

"Good, because something's up there. The nephew put out a vibe that I've been mulling over since we first met him."

"Same. I haven't stopped thinking about what a little weasel he was about giving us his name. You and I both know that when someone won't give us the most basic of info, it's because they're hiding something."

"I want to know what."

"Me, too. Let's keep working that part of this case on the down-low while we look for Harlan Peckham and whatever else Amber gives us."

"Sounds good."

As they walked into the pit, Captain Malone was coming in from the other side.

"We've got a person of interest in the shootings of Tom Forrester and Avery Hill," Sam said.

"Fill me in."

Sam gestured for him to lead the way into the conference room.

Freddie went to the computer and called up the info they had on Harlan Peckham and projected his image and rap sheet onto the screen at the front of the room.

"Harlan Peckham, age thirty-eight, is the son of Willy and his first wife, Justice Peckham. Willy and his second wife, Amber, are the ones who broke into Avery's home. Avery was undercover with Willy's family years ago and put together the case against them for massive Medicaid fraud, among other crimes, including gun trafficking. He was sentenced to fifteen years in prison. The first wife died of cancer in prison. Willy did twelve years, married Amber in prison about a year ago and was released the day before the invasion at Shelby and Avery's home. Other members of their gang did six to eight years in prison and were on the loose at the time of the shootings. According to Avery, Willy and Justice's son Harlan matches the physical description of Tom's shooter. He managed to get off on a technicality and never did time."

Just as Sam was about to suggest they call in the marshals to assist in locating Harlan, Jesse Best appeared. At six and a half feet tall, he took up most of the doorway.

"Brought you something you've been looking for."

Sam got up and went to the door.

Jesse stepped back to let her out.

"Gonzo," she called.

He stood and smiled when he saw Jesse. "You found them?"

"Yep. They're being processed as we speak."

"Where were they?"

"Hiding out, if you want to call it that, at the mother's family cabin in northern Wisconsin. The daughter told us where to look, but not before we had to remind her she could be charged for aiding fugitives."

"Great work, Jesse," Sam said.

"I'll take care of welcoming Rosemary and Randy to DC," Gonzo said as he headed out of the pit toward the main lobby area.

Sam turned back to Jesse. "I was just about to call you. We could use your help with another matter."

"What's up?"

"Step into our office." She followed him into the conference room, where Harlan Peckham's face was still on the screen.

"That's Harlan Peckham," Sam said, "son of Willy and the late Justice Peckham, who headed up a Medicaid scam and gun operation in Kentucky."

"I remember that case," Jesse said. "The son went missing for a time after the parents were arrested, and we tracked him into the hills of Kentucky. Took us about two weeks to smoke him out.

He's got survival training. After all that, he got off because of a dirty FBI agent. If he goes under, he'll be hard to find. What'd he do?"

"We like him for the shootings of Tom Forrester and Avery Hill."

Jesse released a low whistle. "That's a heck of an escalation from Medicaid fraud, gun dealing and petty crime."

"Our theory is that the Peckhams blame them for wrecking their cushy scam and sending them to prison. They're looking for retribution."

"Not sure I'm buying that they'd go to the trouble of revenge when they could get back to doing what they do best, which is running scams."

"Did you hear about Willy and his new young wife showing up at Avery's home and taking his pregnant wife and son hostage?"

Shock registered on his face. "I've been in the field for weeks and hadn't heard about that. Wow. I guess that proves me wrong. Just when you think people can't get any stupider than Willy Peckham already is, he goes and tops himself. Hill's wife and son are all right?"

"They were badly shaken but not hurt."

"Thank goodness for that."

"Yes, definitely. She's my close friend. We're about to issue a BOLO alert for Harlan Peckham in the District and surrounding areas. Detective Cruz will notify the airports, train and bus stations as well as the Metro to be on the lookout for him locally."

"Shoot me everything you've got on the cases, and I'll put some people on it."

"Thank you for the help."

"That's what we do. Take care."

He was gone as quickly as he'd appeared.

"I'd love to know that guy's story," Sam said. "He's such an enigma."

"He sure as hell gets the job done," Malone said.

"Yes, he does."

"I'll take care of issuing the alerts for Harlan Peckham and sending the case info to Jesse."

"I'm going to read the reports on the original investigation."

"I don't know about you, but I want to see those pictures of Hillbilly Avery."

Sam laughed. "Me, too. Let me know when Amber is processed and in a room. She and I are going to have a chat."

"Will do."

CHAPTER TWENTY-FIVE

Gonzo walked into the processing area, where Rosemary and Randy Bryant were being fingerprinted, photographed and booked. Rosemary would be charged with aiding a fugitive from justice and Randy with the first-degree murder-for-hire of Rachel Fortier.

Randy gave him a filthy look that said a great deal about his level of contrition. *Go ahead,* Gonzo wanted to say, *blame me for this if that helps you to sleep at night.*

Rosemary, who was in her late forties or early fifties, wept as the officer set up her mug shot. She had short, curly brown hair and a round face. She looked as if she hadn't slept in days. Running from the law must be exhausting.

"I'm Detective Sergeant Gonzales."

She gasped when she heard his name and broke down into sobs. "I'm sorry. I'm so sorry."

He looked at Randy, who had his head down as he was led through the motions of being booked for a crime that would send him to prison for the rest of his life.

Gonzo wondered if he knew that yet. He probably did, and that's why he'd convinced his mother to run.

"Wh-what's going to happen to us?"

"You'll be arraigned at some point. Have you called an attorney?"

"I don't have one. I don't know anyone here."

"Do you have the resources to pay for someone, or shall I ask them to reach out to the public defender's office for you?"

"I could pay."

"We have a list of local defense attorneys that you'll be given when you're through processing. You'll be allowed to call three of them. Once you have someone representing you, your arraignment will be scheduled."

"I'm sorry, Sergeant." Her chin quivered as tears slid down her cheeks. "I panicked at the thought of Randy going to jail. I should've kept my promise to you and brought him here."

"Yes, you should have."

"He's my only son, my whole heart. Do you know what that's like?"

"I do. I have a son, and if he'd committed murder-for-hire, I'd have done as I was advised and delivered him to the authorities. I'm sorry you're in trouble. I really am, but you had every opportunity to do the right thing."

"I bought the plane tickets to come here. We were getting ready to go to the airport, and then... I just couldn't do it. I had to try to save him. I panicked, and I was wrong to do that."

"If you tell the judge that, you might get off without prison time or a lesser sentence."

She blanched as if it hadn't occurred to her that she could do time. "*Prison?*"

"Yes, Rosemary. People who help others run from the law go to prison."

Deep, gulping sobs shook her.

The processing officer gave Gonzo a frustrated look.

He stepped back so she could finish. "Good luck to you, Rosemary."

"Th-thank you for being kind to me."

"Sure."

"I'm... I'm sorry I disappointed you."

"It's okay. Happens a lot in my line of work."

She wiped the tears from her face. "Keep a close eye on your boy. You can do everything right..."

"Take care, Rosemary."

Gonzo returned to the pit, weighed down by Rosemary's grief. He couldn't imagine what it would be like to raise a child into his twenties only to have him charged with murder-for-hire while away at college. That's not something any of the parenting manuals warned you about.

"All set with the Bryants?" Sam asked.

"Yeah."

"What's wrong?"

"Nothing, why?"

"You looked upset when you came into the pit."

"Something Rosemary said... About how you don't raise a kid to adulthood thinking you might someday have to worry about him being arrested in a murder-for-hire plot."

"Ain't that the truth? But don't forget that Randy's upbringing was disrupted by a nasty divorce and protracted custody battle—not that that causes a kid to become a criminal—and his arrogant, self-involved father is up to his eyeballs in crime."

"All that's true, but it's a reminder that you can try to do everything right—"

"Your son will never be a murderer, Gonzo."

"Listen to her," Freddie said when he joined them. "She's always reminding me that we're skewed by the crap we see every day on the job, and she's right."

"Yes, she is," Sam said with a smile for her partner. "She's always right."

Freddie groaned. "You just had to add that."

"I did. Let's go talk to Amber Peckham and see what she can tell us about her husband's retribution tour and where her stepson might be."

Faith Miller came into the pit with a thick folder tucked under her arm. "I brought you the Peckham case file."

"Are there pictures of Hillbilly Avery in there?"

"There might be."

"I'm gonna save that for dessert after we nail this son of bitch."

"You really think it was one of the Peckhams?"

"All I know is the same Glock did Tom and Avery, and in light of the Peckhams' recent invasion at Avery's home, we're taking a hard look at Willy's son."

Faith looked skeptical. "How can it not be related to Bryant?"

"I'm not sure yet that it isn't, but this is where we are."

"I hate that Tom was possibly murdered for no good reason other than some sort of twisted game of revenge." Her always professional veneer was showing some cracks. "And if it was Harlan..."

Sam felt for her. "Let's see what Amber has to say and go from there, okay?"

"Yeah, sorry. I don't mean to let it get to me."

"Of course it gets to you. Tom was your friend and colleague, and it's a reminder that there're a lot of people out there with grudges toward those of us who enforce the law."

"It's easy to forget that sometimes, as we go about our business and do the job."

"Yes, it is, until it strikes close to home like this."

Faith nodded. "Thank you for the support. It means the world always, but especially right now."

"You got it."

"I'll be in observation."

Sam and Freddie walked with her toward interview one, parting company in the hallway. They went into the room where Amber sat alone at the table, her shoulders curled in and her demeanor fearful. Sam couldn't believe she actually felt a little bit sorry for the woman. Amber's certainty that Willy would have her killed if she talked to them all but confirmed that he'd threatened her.

While that didn't excuse her from what she'd done to Shelby and Noah, Sam had empathy for her, nonetheless. If she'd been in fear of her own life or her children's lives, she would've done whatever Willy told her to.

"Wh-what's going to happen?"

"We're going to talk. Detective Cruz will record our conversation, if that's all right with you."

She eyed the recording device on the table with trepidation. "He'll find a way to kill me."

"He won't find out, and even if he does, he can't get near you in our custody."

She laughed harshly. "Is that what you think? You have no idea what he's capable of."

"Why don't you tell us about it?"

"Where do I start?"

"The beginning is the best place. How did you meet Willy?"

"I've known him all my life. I went to school with his daughter from first grade on. I was in eighth grade when he started paying "special" attention to me, and that was that. You didn't say no to Willy Peckham, the meanest man in the county."

"He paid you special attention even though he was married?"

"He and Justice hated each other. She wouldn't have dared said a word to him about it."

"Your parents had nothing to say about it?"

"They were afraid of him and his people. Everyone was. They were known for being meaner than rattlesnakes and willing to do whatever it took to get what they wanted. He wanted me. My parents wouldn't have dared to get in the way of that, even if it broke their hearts to see me caught up in the madness that surrounded the Peckham family."

"Tell me about the madness."

"Oh Lord, it was always something. Willy has six brothers, and between them, they had about thirty kids. One of 'em was always in trouble for something. Drunk driving, cooking and dealing meth, stealing, raping, shooting. You name it, they did it. Local law enforcement turned a blind eye to most of it cuz no one wanted to be in their crosshairs. It was easier to look away. I heard a local sheriff say once that he needed to keep his own family safe, so he ignored them. Everyone ignored them."

Amber wiped tears off her face. "He made me have sex with him starting when I was fourteen and controlled every aspect of my life, from the time he first decided I belonged to him."

Even though Sam would never forgive her for what she and

her husband had put Shelby through, her heart went out to the woman as she took notes.

"While he and most of his family was in jail, I got a break of sorts. They seemed to forget about me. I had two babies with another man, which infuriated Willy. But he said he'd forgive me if I continued to write to him and married him. He said it was in the best interest of my kids that I do what I was told, even though I didn't want to marry him. When they got released from jail, his brothers made my life a living hell, showing up at all times of the night and day to make sure I knew I still belonged to Willy. I was so afraid of them." She wiped away more tears.

"When Willy was released, his brothers drove me to meet him, and after he took me to a hotel to 'catch up,' he insisted we go straight to that agent's house to get revenge for what he did to Willy's family. He told me if I didn't do everything he said that he'd kill me and then go home and kill my babies."

Sam believed every word Amber said and was horrified by her story. "I'm sorry for how you were treated by Willy and his family."

Amber waved a dismissive hand. "It was the least of what happened to me at that man's hands. He's a monster." She looked over at Sam with weary eyes. "I did what I could to make sure he didn't hurt that pregnant lady or her little boy while pretending to go along with him so he wouldn't kill me."

"That woman is my close friend, and her child is like a nephew to me."

"I told him we shouldn't go there, but he was determined to make Hill pay for what he did to us."

"Do you know how Willy first met Agent Hill."

"Willy's cousin Lonnie brought him around. The Marsdens were as wicked as the Peckhams, if that's even possible. Lonnie was tight with all the Peckhams, and they trusted him and his kin. So when Lonnie vouched for Jimmy Hill, as he was called, they were satisfied. They made him part of the family, took him hunting and fishing and invited him to their parties. Over time, Willy started to include him in some of the business stuff. He said

Jimmy was smart and savvy. Willy liked him a lot, which was amazing because he didn't like anyone except his own people."

"How did he find out Jimmy was actually a federal agent named Avery Hill?"

"After twenty-two of them was arrested, including two of his three sons, one of his daughters, three of Willy's brothers and six nephews. Willy said he was going to have Hill disemboweled the first chance he got."

Sam cringed as she realized Avery was lucky he'd "only" been shot.

"He would've done it, too, if Hill had been home that night. Willy would've made his pretty wife watch when he gutted him like a pig."

Thank God Avery had been in Cleveland, dealing with the case against Nick's mother when the Peckhams broke into his home.

"What can you tell me about Willy's son Harlan?"

She seemed surprised by the question. "What about him?"

"I understand he managed to elude prosecution."

"Yes, he was never read his rights, so they dismissed the case against him."

"He must've been pretty upset when his parents, siblings, uncles and cousins were locked up."

"Hardly. He loved it. He was finally free of his father and could run his own operation, making use of the Peckham name to get things done. He was very busy while they were gone."

"What else was he busy doing?"

"Mostly drugs. He's a major meth dealer and has ventured into fentanyl, from what I'm told. I haven't seen him in a while, thankfully. I was always terrified of him."

Sam's skin crawled at the mention of the poisonous substance that had killed Spencer. "What else can you tell me about Harlan?"

"Harlan is as mean as his father. He's spent his whole life trying to get his father's approval. He's small for a man, and Willy was relentless about that, always after him for being a runt.

Harlan turned himself into a machine so no one could ever screw with him, but even that didn't impress his father. Nothing did."

"Would killing the U.S. Attorney who put them in prison and trying to kill the FBI agent who built the case impress his father?"

The question brought Amber up short. "Are you saying he did that?"

"I'm asking if him doing that would impress his father."

"I think it would. Willy hates the two of them—and the judge who presided over what Willy calls his sham of a trial. He blames them for everything."

Sam glanced at Freddie, who would know she was telling him to make sure the judge was protected. Even as she had that thought, another one occurred to her. Perhaps they could use the judge to lure Harlan out of hiding.

Freddie got up and left the room.

"Where do you think Harlan is?"

"I'd be the last one to know where to find him. Other than making sure I was terrified of him, he's hardly ever said a word to me."

"Who would know where he is?"

"Maybe his brothers, Dusty and Bubba. The three of them are tight."

"Where are they?"

"Probably back in Kentucky. They rarely leave home since they were released."

"Do you know Harlan's phone number?"

"He doesn't have a phone. He never has."

Sam couldn't recall the last time she'd met someone who'd never had a cell phone. "How does he communicate?"

"I honestly don't know. If he uses phones, it's probably them throwaway kinds. He believes the government is using phones to keep tabs on people. That's why he won't have one."

"What about Dusty and Bubba? Do they have phones?"

"I'm not sure. They tend to do whatever Harlan tells them to. They're bigger than him, but he's meaner."

Lovely, Sam thought.

"Wh-what's going to happen to me?" Amber asked. "I've told you what I know, like I said I would."

"Let me talk to the Assistant U.S. Attorney and see what we can do." Sam started for the door and then turned back. "Are you hungry?"

She shrugged as if she'd been hungry all her life. "I could eat something."

"Any preferences?"

"Could I have some pizza?"

"You sure can. What do you like on it?"

"Just cheese, please."

"How about a drink?"

"Is there Coke?"

"I can get you one."

"Thank you for your kindness."

"No problem."

Sam met Faith in the hallway.

Faith shook her head. "What a horrifying story."

"I don't think I've ever met a better candidate for witness protection or something like that."

"She could walk away with her kids and never look back if someone helped her. I'll see what I can do for her."

"Even though she didn't really give us anything we can use in court?"

"You never know what she might be able to do for us in the future. It'd be in our best interest to keep her safe—if for no other reason than she hasn't been safe a day in her life since Willy Peckham set his sights on her when she was still a girl."

Freddie came down the hallway. "Judge Corrinne Sawyer presided over the Peckham trial in the U.S. District Court here in DC. She now sits on the DC Court of Appeals. I spoke to the admin in her office, explained I had an urgent security briefing for the judge, and she had Sawyer call me. I filled her in on what we know so far. She's requesting added security for her home and office."

"Good work. Would you please see about a cheese pizza and a

Coke for Amber? There's cash in the top left-hand drawer in my office."

"Sure."

"Thanks. Also, will you please issue the BOLO for Harlan Peckham?" Sam asked, referring to a "be on the lookout" alert. "I want everyone looking for him, especially Patrol in the Northwest quadrant. Make sure they know he's armed and considered extremely dangerous."

"Will do."

CHAPTER TWENTY-SIX

Aftter he walked away, Sam turned to Faith. "What would you think of me using Sawyer as bait to draw out Harlan Peckham?"

Faith's brows lifted in surprise. "You want to use a federal appeals court judge to lure a killer?"

"You got a better idea? You heard what she said. Harlan Peckham doesn't own a phone, so we're not going to find him that way. Jesse Best told us he's had survival training and can stay hidden for as long as it takes. He could be anywhere, lying in wait for a chance at her so he might finally have his father's respect. I mean, if he kills, or tries to kill, the three people who his father believes were the most responsible for ruining their family, then maybe his daddy will finally respect him."

"I hear you, and I see the motivation, but wouldn't he be more interested in killing Avery, who built the case, than the prosecutor and judge?"

"Willy would view them as equally responsible." Sam's backbone tingled. "He'd probably feel it was enough to badly wound Avery, especially since he'd already put a massive scare into him by breaking into his home and holding his pregnant wife and son hostage."

While Sam liked the idea more with every passing second,

Faith still seemed skeptical. "How would you use the judge to lure him out?"

"I haven't got that fully worked out yet, and of course I'd have to gauge her willingness, but I think it could work. If Harlan shows up carrying the nine-millimeter Glock that was used to kill Tom and shoot Avery, we'd have him nailed."

"I agree, but I'm still not feeling the connection to the Peckhams. I like Damien Bryant for this much more."

"We worked that from every angle, but I never got a buzz this strong."

"A buzz?"

"You're going to think I'm weird."

"Too late. I already do."

"Haha, but when I'm on to something, really on to it, I get this tingle along my backbone. I've learned to trust the tingle. I've got a huge buzz with Harlan Peckham's name on it."

"I'm not sure how I'd get something like this approved without an acting USA in place yet. We'd have to go to Cox."

"He'd never approve it if I'm involved."

"Approve what?"

Sam hopped to at the sound of the chief's voice. "An idea I had, sir, that could lead to us capturing the man who killed Tom Forrester and shot Avery Hill."

"What's the idea?"

"To make a long story short, I believe it's possible both instances were part of a three-part revenge tour to take out the people who busted a family crime ring in Kentucky years ago. Avery was undercover with the family early in his career. The case was transferred to the jurisdiction of the U.S. Attorney in DC with Tom prosecuting. Judge Corrinne Sawyer, who now sits on the circuit court of appeals, was the presiding district court judge. My idea would be to use Sawyer as bait to lure our suspect."

When her words registered with him, he tipped his head as if trying to hear her correctly. "Did you just say you want to use a federal appeals court judge to bait a murderer?"

"Um, yes, but it sounded better when I said it than when you did."

The chief huffed out a laugh. "I'm sure it did. Think of something else."

"Hear me out... The guy we're looking for has no phone, no local address, no ties to anyone here, and he has survival training. We're never going to find him unless we do something to smoke him out."

"You're asking me to approve putting a federal judge in mortal danger, Lieutenant."

"I'm trying to find the man who killed Tom and tried to kill Avery."

"I understand the goal and the urgency, but I'm not liking the plan to use Sawyer. There has to be another way."

"I think this is the fastest way to him."

"Unless," Faith said, "we use his stepmother to lure him."

"What do you mean?" Sam asked.

"She told us his father's approval means everything to him, right? What if we put the word out that Amber has a message for him from his father and use her to get to him?"

"That won't work because he could easily find out that she's in our custody. He'd be immediately suspicious of anything involving her."

"You're right."

Sam bit back the retort she would've given Freddie—*I usually am.* "I like the idea of using Sawyer. According to Amber, Willy Peckham blamed Avery, Tom and the judge for all their problems and was determined to get revenge when he got out of prison. He took Avery's family hostage. Amber said if Avery had been at home that night, Willy would've gutted Avery like a pig and made his pretty wife watch."

Chief Farnsworth swallowed audibly.

"He killed Tom Forrester, shot Avery and will be coming for Sawyer next. If we don't stop him, he'll try to finish the job with Avery as soon as he gets the chance." She looked to Faith. "Who supervises federal judges?"

Faith used her phone to get the correct info. "The Federal Judicial Center, which is governed by a board of directors that includes the chief justice, director of the Administrative Office and seven judges chosen by the Judicial Conference. The FJC does orientation for new federal judges and provides continuing education for judges and court personnel. They also make recommendations to improve the operations of federal courts."

"I had no idea how any of that worked," Sam said.

"Me either," the chief said. "The federal government is like an onion. Layers on top of layers on top of layers."

"Indeed," Faith said. "In order for us to be involved in this in any way, I need the AG's approval."

"In that case, how do you feel about us leaving you out of it until we have Harlan in custody?"

"I feel very good about that."

They glanced at the chief, knowing it would be his call as to whether they went forward with Sam's plan.

"I'd want to hear from the judge that she's on board and willing to be part of this."

"She's my next stop."

"Talk to her and let me know what she says. If she approves, then we'll put together an airtight plan with no room for error."

That had Sam swallowing hard, knowing from experience there was no such thing as a fully foolproof plan. Her experience undercover with the Johnson family had led to a dead child in a crack house. She'd never seen the kid in the house prior to the night they raided the place and had carried the grim lessons learned in that case with her ever since.

Freddie returned with Amber's pizza and Coke. "George Terrell is here asking to see you."

"Go see what he wants and keep me in the loop on the judge," the chief said.

"Yes, sir." She walked toward her office, where Terrell was seated in one of her visitor chairs. "Hey, how's Avery?"

"Still doing well, thankfully." He handed her a large, thick envelope. "The dump of Tom's work phone with some redactions to protect ongoing cases. Please keep this under lock and key."

"Thank you, and I will. Any smoking guns?"

"I'm not sure. There was a lot of back-and-forth with Cox, which is somewhat unusual in the course of regular business.

While the AG heads the Justice Department, he's not regularly in contact with the USAs."

Sam sat behind her desk. "He and Tom were longtime friends."

"Yes, I'm aware, but their correspondence wasn't related to being friends or about work."

"Okay, I'll bite. What was it about?"

"I'm not sure. It was cryptic, like they were talking in code or something."

"I'll take a look."

"Are you investigating Cox?"

"I might be. Something is off with him. I can't figure out what it is, but these messages might shed some light."

George released a low whistle. "Like that won't be nuclear or anything."

"I know, but he's been weird with me several times now and so has his nephew-slash-assistant."

"Wait, Allston is his *nephew*?"

"Yeah, do you know him?"

"I know of him. People can't stand the way he acts like a firewall to Cox. You can't get to the AG without going through him, and he's a pain in the ass about granting access."

"As I've learned. You didn't know he's Cox's nephew?"

"First I've heard of that."

"The stink around Cox gets more fragrant with everything I find out about him."

"You can't honestly think the U.S. Attorney General is involved in something criminal."

"You say that like it'd be the first time in history."

"True, but it's still unbelievable."

"I don't know anything yet, but I'm picking up the scent of something rotten. My goal right now is to find Tom's killer and Avery's shooter as soon as possible, and then I'll figure out what stinks at Justice."

"Let me know if we can help, on the deepest down-low, of course."

Sam smiled. "Of course." An FBI agent wouldn't want to be

caught investigating the AG, which Sam certainly understood. "Thanks for delivering the phone dump."

"No problem."

George had no sooner left than Dr. Trulo appeared in her doorway.

Sam waved him in.

He closed the door behind him. "I thought you might come by, but I figured you got busy."

"You figured right." His presence was a reminder of the horrors she'd heard earlier and how she'd reacted to them. "It's been a day, but what day around here isn't?"

"Truth." He took a seat and crossed his legs, his pose casual, but his eyes sharply focused on her. "I take it you heard the latest from the Stahl investigation."

Sam had done her best to stuff that into the back of her mind so she could function. At his mention, it came roaring back to the forefront. "I did."

"It's a lot for everyone to process, but I imagine it's even more so for you."

She shrugged, hating being singled out on the job for any reason. "It's a horror no matter how you cut it."

"You and me... We'll never understand what could possibly motivate someone like him."

"I don't want to understand what motivates him."

"What can I do for you today?"

"I'm okay. It was a shock at first, but I'm coping. We've got a hot lead in the Forrester case. It helps to keep busy."

"You and your husband looked marvelous last night. I was so proud."

"Aw, thanks. We clean up pretty well."

"Indeed, you do, my friend. I won't take any more of your time. I wanted to remind you I'm here. I'm always here. If you need me..."

"I know where to find you. Thank you, Doc. Your friendship means a lot to me."

"Likewise."

After he left, Sam tried to get her head back into her work, but the latest horrors surrounding Stahl were hard to push aside. She reached for the painkillers she kept in her top drawer and took a couple to ward off the headache she felt coming on.

There was no time today or any day for an emotional setback tied to that monster. She'd worked hard to come back from the nightmare he'd perpetrated on her, and she wouldn't let him get the better of her again.

She called for Cameron Green.

He came into the office. "What's up?"

Sam handed him the file George had brought. "Data from Tom's work phone, compliments of the FBI, which we're to keep airtight. I'm most interested in his dealings with AG Cox and Congressman Bryant."

"I'll get on it right away."

"How are things?" Sam had learned to check in with her team, especially after something like what Cam and Gigi had recently endured, with Gigi forced to kill his ex-girlfriend to save herself.

"Better."

"How's Gigi holding up?"

"She's taking it a day at a time. Even though she knew it was her life or Jaycee's, she's struggling with having taken a life."

"If she wasn't, she wouldn't be the person we know and love."

"That's what I tell her every day. We ran away for a couple of nights last weekend. It helped."

"Glad to hear that. Let me know if there's anything I can do for either of you."

"I will, thanks. Last night was an incredible experience. None of us will ever forget it."

"Thanks for coming. It meant a lot to us to be surrounded by friends."

"My entire family is green with envy."

Sam laughed. "No pun intended."

"That's right. I'll let you know what comes of the phone data."

"Thanks, Cam. Tell Freddie to come in, will you?"

"Sure thing."

Her partner appeared at the door a minute later. "You summoned?"

"Will you please figure out where we might find Judge Sawyer?"

"Yep."

He returned a few minutes later. "She's in her office at E Street Northwest. I spoke to her clerk, and she said it's fine to come by."

"Let's go."

LINDSEY STRETCHED out on the sofa in her favorite room in the townhome she shared with Terry. Afternoon sun streamed in through the windows she kept uncovered to take full advantage of the natural light. The cheery blooms on her orchids that lined the windowsills filled her with delight. Raising orchids had become a hobby after Terry bought her one for her birthday last year, and now she was obsessed with understanding the complicated, moody plants.

Terry came in with a tray that he placed on her lap. He'd made her tea and toast with the strawberry jam she loved. Next to that was a bowl of berries and a medicine cup with her afternoon pills.

"This looks delicious. Thank you."

"Can I get you anything else?" As he took a seat on the coffee table, she noticed his handsome face was still pinched from the strain of the last few days.

Lindsey held out a hand to him. "I'm all right. I promise." The doctors prescribed rest and relaxation until she felt back to normal.

He kissed the back of her hand. "That's all that matters to me. You know that, right?"

"I do, and I'm sorry I scared you."

"You don't have to apologize to me."

"Yes, I do. I feel bad that I put you through such an ordeal, especially during such a big week at work."

"As long as you're feeling better, I'm fine."

"Are you?" She studied him, looking for cracks in the veneer.

"I've been doing meetings twice a day online and talking to my sponsor several times a day."

"I'm proud of you."

He snorted. "Why?"

"Because you recognized the makings of a crisis and acted accordingly. Not that long ago, you might've made different choices that would've led to trouble."

"I have every good reason to stay clean and sober these days. I have the woman of my dreams, the job of my dreams, the life of my dreams. I'd never do anything to mess up any of it, especially with the woman of my dreams."

Lindsey smiled. How could she not? "We're so lucky. So, so lucky."

"Yes, we are."

His work phone rang. "Gotta take that. Enjoy your snack."

"You can go to work if you're needed there."

"Maybe tomorrow." He kissed her cheek and got up to take the call. "Hey, Derek, what's up?"

While he talked to the deputy chief of staff, Lindsey sipped her tea and took bites of toast. Her phone buzzed with a text from Sam.

How you feeling, Doc? Miss you around the house.

Much better. Can't wait to get back to business.

Eh, take it easy and enjoy the time away. You deserve a break.

Heard the latest about the monster. How you holding up?

I'm ok. It's not about me.

Sure, it is. Call me if you need to talk.

Thank you, but I'm fine. On to something with Forrester, pulling the threads, doing what I do.

You looked stunning last night. Both of you.

Thanks. It was a team effort. Will check on you later.

I'll be here.

Hey, so... We don't do sappy around here, but you should know... I love you, and I'm so glad you're ok.

Lindsey's eyes immediately flooded with tears. *Love you right back, my friend.*

There was nothing like a health crisis to make a girl feel loved and supported by those closest to her.

Terry returned to the sunroom, phone in hand. "Derek said everything was perfect last night, which is a huge relief."

"It was perfect because you and the rest of the White House team saw to every detail weeks ago."

"Still nice to hear we pulled it off."

"I'm sorry you had to miss it."

"I'm not. I'd rather be home in sweats with you than in a monkey suit at the White House any day."

"Liar."

"I'm not lying. You know I'd rather be here with you than anywhere else."

"I do, but it was still a bummer to miss a fun night with our best friends."

"Speaking of our best friends, Derek told me he and Roni went public at the state dinner. They arrived holding hands."

"Ah, I love that for both of them." She knew Derek and Roni had been spending time together but hadn't made any official announcements. "When's her baby due?"

"June. He said they plan to help raise each other's children."

"That's wonderful. They deserve all the happiness in the world after what they've been through."

"Yes, they do, and so do we." He kissed the back of her left hand. "I can't wait to put another ring on this gorgeous hand."

Their wedding was scheduled for July at his parents' farm in Leesburg. "I can't wait either."

CHAPTER TWENTY-SEVEN

"Talk to me about Judge Sawyer," Sam said to Freddie as Vernon drove them to E Street.

He clicked around on his phone. "She graduated from Stanford—undergrad and law school. She came up through the ranks as a local prosecutor in Marin County, California, followed by ten years with the state Attorney General before she was tapped to be a federal district court judge. She was elevated to the DC Court of Appeals two years ago."

"What an impressive career."

"No kidding."

"Her husband is a trauma surgeon, and they have six children, ages thirteen to twenty-five."

"Wow. Now I'm even more impressed."

"She's got nothing on you."

"Shut *up* already."

Vernon and Jimmy chuckled.

At the courthouse, they surrendered their weapons and went through security before being shown to the judge's chambers, where a deputy stood watch outside the door.

Though he recognized them, he studied their badges carefully. Then he knocked on the door and opened it for them.

Judge Sawyer rose to greet them. She was tall, with brown

skin, long curly hair and a warm smile. She shook hands with Sam. "What a pleasure it is to meet you. I've admired your career for years, long before the latest developments."

Sam liked her immediately. "'Latest developments.' That's one way to put it."

The judge laughed and gestured for them to take seats at the small conference table.

"This is my partner, Detective Cruz."

"He's almost as famous as you are."

That earned her a big grin from Freddie.

"Don't tell him that. He's incorrigible."

Freddie scowled at her.

"It's so difficult to raise kids these days, isn't it?" Sam asked.

"Incredibly challenging."

"I can hear you," Freddie said.

The two women shared a laugh.

"As wonderful as it is to meet you in person," Sawyer said, "I know this isn't a social call."

"No, it isn't. You've been made aware of our direction on the Forrester murder and Hill shooting investigation?"

"I have, and it's appalling. I remember the Peckham case. I've rarely encountered people who were more devoid of basic human decency, and that's saying something with the people I meet in this job."

"That's a very good description of them. 'Devoid of basic human decency.'" It applied to Stahl as well, Sam realized. "Your security has been increased here and at home?"

"It has, and I appreciated the heads-up. I just can't believe retribution would be their first priority after being released from years in prison."

"We believe their son Harlan could be responsible for Tom's murder and Avery's shooting."

"He's the one who got off on a technicality, right?"

"Yes, that's him."

She frowned. "Such a travesty. He was as guilty as the rest of them."

"From what Agent Hill and his stepmother told us, he was forever trying to get his father's approval. Apparently, he was the smallest of their sons, and his father teased him mercilessly about being the runt of the litter. So he turned himself into the most lethal and meanest of them all, and now it seems he's taking care of his father's list of grievances."

"What an accomplishment."

"I like you," Sam said, smiling.

"She doesn't like anyone."

"Hush, Freddie. Don't tell all my secrets on the first meeting."

The judge laughed. "I feel you. I hate people, too."

"We see the worst of them in our line of work."

"Yes, we do, and the older I get, the more I crave peace, quiet and time with my loved ones. Anything else is so far down the list of priorities, it's like it doesn't exist."

"I think we might be sisters from another mister."

"I would love to be your sister from another mister. My friends will *die* when I tell them I met you."

"No way."

"Way."

"She has no idea how cool she is," Freddie said.

"I'm going to mute him."

"You two are entertaining."

"We've been told that a time or two."

"I can see why."

"So, listen, Your Honor…"

"Call me Cori. I think we're going to be friends."

"I'd like that, Cori. But you may not want to be friends with me after you hear what I've come to ask you."

"Lay it on me."

Sam liked everything about her, which was such a rare thing that it took her by surprise. "Harlan Peckham is a professional criminal, described by his stepmother as ruthless and violent. He has no cell phone, has never had one, and knows how to stay out of sight until he sees his chance to come for you."

Cori swallowed hard. "Are you trying to ensure I won't sleep tonight?"

"Not at all, and I'm sorry to have to scare you, but this guy is legit."

"So what do you want to ask me?"

"How would you feel about being the center of an operation to draw him out of hiding?"

"Are you asking me to be the bait in this operation of yours?"

"'Bait' is not the word I'd use..."

"What word would you use?"

"The incentive?"

"The bait."

"Okay, yes. You'd be the bait."

Cori seemed to mull over the idea. "How would it work?"

"I don't have the details yet. First, I wanted to know if you'd be willing to work with us on this. Harlan has shown himself to be a patient man. Probably on his father's orders, he waited years for the opportunity to make the people who he thinks ruined his family pay for what they did. We believe he waited until his father failed to get to Avery Hill through the invasion at his home, and then he took over where Willy left off. In just a few days, he managed to kill Tom and seriously injure Agent Hill. There's no doubt in our minds that he's coming for you next. Our goal is to grab him before anyone else gets hurt."

"How would you ensure my safety? I have children... I'm not looking to do anything foolish that would leave them without their mother."

"I understand, and while we'd do everything possible to keep you safe, there're no guarantees that we'd succeed."

Cori crossed her hands and kept her gaze trained on the table. "I haven't been able to think about anything else since I heard the Peckhams were suspects in the Forrester and Hill cases. Before my clerk could tell me the full story, I knew what she was going to say. That I'm in danger because I presided over the case and ordered the longest possible sentences for each of them. Even as I sent them away for years, I knew it wouldn't matter. As soon as they were released, they'd be up to their old games again. I even told Tom that I feared what they'd learn in prison would make them more effective the second time around.

"They're the kind of people who blame everyone else for their problems, who lack any form of self-reflection or contrition. I looked into what Harlan has been up to while his family was in prison. He's has been allowed to run free for years, presiding over their enterprises while his father and siblings were locked up. From what my sources report, he's become even more ruthless than he was before, if that's possible." She shifted her gaze up to look at them. "I want this guy off the streets and locked up for the rest of his miserable life. I'll do whatever I can to help make that happen."

"We appreciate your assistance."

"As one woman to another in a field dominated by men, I believe in you. I trust you to do this right."

Sam was honored by her trust, but intimidated, too. Absolutely nothing could go wrong. They spent the next thirty minutes going through Sawyer's weekly schedule.

Freddie wrote down the addresses of Sawyer's home, her children's schools, her favorite coffee shop, gym and church.

When they had what they needed, Sam stood. "I'll be back in touch as soon as I've had the chance to formulate a plan with our team. We'll most likely be working with the FBI on this."

Sawyer got up to walk them out. "I'll be ready whenever you are."

"Thank you, Cori."

She hugged Sam. "It was such an honor to meet you."

"Likewise."

"Wow," Freddie said when they were in the elevator. "Never seen you take such an instant liking to someone before."

"She was awesome. I loved her."

"I could tell."

"My dad used to say that people either get it or they don't. She gets it, and I appreciate that in a person, especially when I'm asking her to be the bait in a plan to lure a ruthless killer."

"I'm worried about how we'll keep her safe."

"I am, too, but we'll take that up with the team we'll assemble to get this done and make her safety our top priority. Text George and tell him what we're planning and that we need their help."

Freddie sent the text. "He said to let him know what they can do."

"Tell him to meet us at HQ at eight in the morning, and we'll get to work on forming a plan."

"Done." He looked up from his phone. "Eric Davies was ordered released from prison, and he's holding a press conference on the courthouse stairs."

"Can we watch it?"

Freddie tapped on the screen and held the phone so she could see.

"I want to thank my legal team for never giving up on me. From the very beginning, they believed me when I told them I'd never met Tiffany Jones, let alone raped her. Leonard Stahl framed me after I complained about his behavior during a traffic stop years ago. He set me up to take a mighty fall, and I've paid for that with sixteen years in prison.

"My new life begins today. I plan to use every minute I have left focused on bringing truth to power, to identifying dirty cops and getting them off the streets and out of our communities. That's my mission now, and that mission begins today with a wrongful-imprisonment lawsuit against the Metro PD and the District of Columbia, which is being filed as we speak. I'm going to make them pay for what they allowed him to do to me and others."

"That's just great," Sam said. "Not that he doesn't deserve all the money in the world for what Stahl did to him. It just sucks that the rest of us will get dragged through the mud as a result of Stahl's sins."

Her phone rang with a call from Darren Tabor.

"What's up, Darren?"

"Have you seen the Davies presser?"

"Just now. Yes."

"Do you have a comment about the lawsuit or his new mission in life?"

"Anything on that will need to come from the chief, as I'm sure you know by now."

"You can't give me a little something?"

"No, Darren, I can't."

"I'm hearing rumors about what's being found at Stahl's house. Confirm or deny?"

"Later." She slapped her phone closed. "He said he's hearing rumors about what's being found at Stahl's house."

"The rest of that story will blow up at any second, right as Davies files the lawsuit that he'll win."

Sam's phone rang again. This time, it was Captain Malone. "Hey, Cap. What's up?"

"I assume you heard about Davies."

"I did."

"His is the second lawsuit filed against us today."

"Who was first?"

"Ramsey, asserting the wrongful death of his son by everyone involved in the park that day, including you."

"Awesome."

"Tell me you've got some good news for me."

"I'm fairly confident I know who killed Tom and shot Avery, and I've got a plan coming together to smoke him out that involves using a federal judge as bait."

"I asked for *good* news."

"That is good news."

"Is the judge on board?"

"She is. I've just come from seeing her, and she's willing to participate if it means getting this guy thrown in jail for the rest of his life."

"We'll need to run this by the chief."

"He's aware that I was speaking to her. I'll update him when I get back to the house. I'm putting together a meeting at eight in the morning to bring all the players together to make this happen. Can you be there?"

"Yep. Who else are you asking?"

"I want my squad, Lucas and Archie to start, and I've invited George Terrell and his team as well."

"Sounds good. I'll be there."

Sam closed her phone. "Ramsey filed suit over his son's shooting." Shane Ramsey had been shot by an MPD sharpshooter in Rock Creek Park after he took a woman hostage. In addition, he'd been tied to several rapes and murders.

"That won't go anywhere. Despite what his father might believe, if Shane hadn't been killed, he would've spent the rest of his life in prison. We had him nailed every which way. I doubt that lawsuit will make it past the preliminary stages."

"I doubt Ramsey cares about winning. He wants to make us look bad by piling onto what's happening with Stahl and Davies and the rest of it." Prior to learning that Stahl was a serial killer, they'd uncovered irregularities in most of his earlier cases. He'd failed to do even the most rudimentary investigations.

"Yeah, that's probably true. Remember what your dad used to say."

"Which pearls of wisdom are you referring to?"

"No matter what's happening at the moment, it'll pass, and something else will come along that'll take everyone's attention off the thing that has us so worried."

"He was right, most of the time. But I don't think this thing with Stahl will blow over quickly or easily."

"Probably not."

"What else is going on in the outside world?" she asked.

"Are you sure I can't interest you in a smartphone of your very own?"

"Why do I need that when I have you and yours?"

"God, I walked right into that one."

"She does have a point, Detective," Vernon said.

"Don't tell her that."

Sam gave him a smug smile. "I love being right."

"See what you did, Vernon?"

"I see, and I'm sorry."

"You were racking up the points, Vernon," Sam said. "Don't ruin it now."

When they arrived back in the pit, Malone and Farnsworth were waiting.

Sam gestured for them to lead the way to the conference room.

"I understand you've spoken to Judge Sawyer."

"We have, and she's agreed to participate."

"How do you see this going down?"

"If Harlan Peckham has been watching her, he's begun to know her routine. He'd know when she leaves the house, when she leaves the office, when she goes to one of her kids' games or when she goes to church or whatever else she does. I suggest we zero in on one of those events and make her a sitting duck who'd be surrounded by every form of protection we can provide, including sharpshooters on every nearby roof. I'm thinking church could be our best bet, with the other churchgoers being plainclothes officers who'd surround her coming and going."

"What do we do with the rest of the congregation?"

"I haven't gotten that far yet. Maybe we ask them to exit through another door while Cori and the officers leave through the main door?"

"I'd want to see the layout of the church you plan to use and to figure out whether it's conducive to something like this. We'd have to involve the pastor and the judge's security as well."

"I'll figure out the details and have a better plan in place by tomorrow morning."

"I want Emergency Response brought in on this," Farnsworth said. "Leave nothing to chance."

"Yes, sir. The FBI will be assisting as well."

"If a federal judge is killed in an operation we organized, it'll be the end of all of us in this business."

Sam swallowed. "Yes, sir."

"Don't let that happen."

After he left the room, Malone said, "He's not exaggerating. If you don't think you can make this happen smoothly and with no harm coming to the judge, don't do it. We'll find another way to get this guy."

"I don't know how we'll ever find him. By now, he probably knows we have his stepmother in custody, which means he realizes we're taking a hard look at his family and at him. This is a guy who knows how to get gone. If we don't find a way to draw him out, we'll never find him."

"I tend to agree, which is the only reason I'm going along with this."

"I understand the stakes, Cap. We'll run through all the contingencies and game it out every which way. We'll be ready."

"What's your next move?"

"I'm going to church."

CHAPTER TWENTY-EIGHT

"Mr. President, Mr. Kavanaugh would like a minute."

"Send him in, please."

Nick stood and walked around the desk to greet his deputy chief of staff and longtime friend. It was such a comfort to him to have people like Derek, Terry, Christina and Harry with him on this journey.

"What's up?"

They sat on sofas facing each other.

"With Terry out, I wanted to check in to see if you need anything other than all the usual madness of nonstop meetings, briefings and other fun stuff."

Nick laughed. "It's nonstop fun around here. I have been thinking about Fort Liberty and the aftermath of the shooting. What are we hearing from General Stern about the situation there?"

"I'll check in with Secretary Jennings and ask for an update."

"It doesn't feel right to me that we didn't visit after the shooting."

"I understand and will see what can be done."

"Thank you. Now, about this upcoming travel schedule..."

"It's a beast."

Nick was leaving the following week on a West Coast fundraising trip in support of the upcoming midterm elections.

He'd be in six cities in three days, with stops to meet with labor leaders in Detroit and Chicago on the return trip. He was already dreading four days away from home.

Had he told Sam about the trip? He couldn't recall. That needed to be taken care of as soon as possible. What did it say about him that the thought of being away from his wife for a few days made him as depressed as he'd been in a while? Since assuming the presidency in late November, he'd stayed close to home in an effort to show the American people he was doing the job.

"You have time blocked on the schedule for Friday afternoon. Will you need staff support for that?"

Nick grunted out a laugh. "No. I'm afraid to tell you where I'm going."

"Uh... Not sure what to say to that..."

"Sam and I are meeting with my mother and her attorney at Ninth Street."

Derek's expression went flat with shock. "You're doing *what*?"

"You heard me correctly. She requested a meeting, and I agreed to see her."

"*Why?*"

Nick wasn't surprised by Derek's reaction. His longtime friend had witnessed the pain and suffering Nicoletta had inflicted upon her only child over the years. "Apparently, she wishes to make amends."

Derek stared at him without blinking.

"I know what you're thinking..."

"Do you?" He cleared his throat. "I apologize, Mr. President."

Nick frowned at the formality. "Keep it real with me, Derek. I know what you're thinking, and I've thought the same things myself, but I want to hear what she has to say."

His friend finally blinked and looked away.

"Say what you want to say."

Derek hesitated before he finally spoke up. "I hate how she treats you and how her behavior affects you. I hate how she's never given so much as half a shit about you unless there was something you could do for her. I hate how she's let you down your entire life and how you still hope she might someday change. She's not going to change. She's a grifter and a user and an *asshole*." He stopped himself and seemed embarrassed by his outburst. "Sorry. That was probably too much."

"You're fine, and you're right. About all of it. Of course you are, and I know all that. And yet..." Nick shrugged, feeling mortified by how he'd never outgrown his need for her love and attention.

"She's still your mother."

"Yeah."

Derek sighed. "I'm sorry I was so blunt."

"It's fine. I always want to hear what you have to say."

"It's hard for those of us who care about you to see her hurt you over and over again."

"I know, and it's hard to be hurt, but something about this time feels different."

Derek eyed him skeptically.

"And yes, I can hear myself, and part of me doesn't believe it either. It's possible her time in jail humbled her, and this lawyer guy seems very invested in her."

"What's his motivation?"

"Not sure, but he's encouraged her to try to make amends with me."

"Why? Is he trying to get to you?"

"I don't think so."

"Nick... Mr. President... Let me look into him and make sure he's legit."

"If you think that's necessary."

"I absolutely do."

"Fine, go ahead. His name is Collins Worthy from Cleveland. Let me know what you find out."

"I will."

"Don't look at me like you're worried I won't like you anymore because you spoke your mind to me. You know how much I value that, especially now."

"I do, but I also know you love your mother, even if she doesn't deserve it."

"She's but one small annoyance in an otherwise blessed life.

Ever since I've had a family, people of my own who love me unconditionally, she doesn't get to me the way she used to. Don't worry about me, okay?"

"I'll try not to."

"I want to hear more about you and Roni. Tell me everything. Well, the PG parts."

"It's all PG so far, which is fine. She only lost her husband about six months ago, and neither of us was looking for anything..." He shrugged and gave a sheepish smile. "At first, I thought she was stalking me."

"For real?"

"Yeah, and she kinda was. Apparently, I look a bit like her late husband from behind, and she started following me. After everything with Vic, I'm extra paranoid and confronted her at the coffee shop we both like. That's when she told me I look like her late husband from behind and that being a widow has made her weird, which I certainly understood. I ran into her at a meeting of a widow group I've belonged to for a while now, and then she showed up here as Sam's communications director. After all of that, how could we not be friends, you know?"

"I love that for both of you. Sam does, too."

"It's been... well, kind of amazing, actually. Maeve is crazy about her, and Roni is so great with her. It's all quite effortless, even if it's probably way too soon for her. But it's not like we were out there looking for this. It just kind of happened."

"That's the way it should be. No one deserves happiness more than you two do."

"I'm feeling truly optimistic for the first time since Vic died."

"I love to hear that."

"Life is so very strange sometimes."

"And wonderful, too."

"Yeah, for sure. It's nice to have some of the wonderful after a whole lot of awful."

"I hope you know how much we all admire you for the way you've survived the unimaginable."

"What choice did I have? Maeve needed me, and I had to step up for her."

"You and I both know if you'd told your parents that you couldn't handle it, they would've been there."

"That never occurred to me, although I wouldn't have survived without their help."

"I can't wait to dance at your wedding."

Derek laughed. "Don't get too far ahead of me. Roni has me strictly in the friend zone until at least October, which will be the one-year anniversary of her husband's death. In the meantime, I'm supporting her through her pregnancy and becoming more captivated by the day."

"She's not going to suddenly balk when she decides it's all too soon, is she?"

"I don't think so. We've talked a lot about it, and she seems pretty committed. That's one of the things I love best about her. We talk about everything. Nothing is off the table. She's made me realize how little I gave to Vic."

"That's not true. You gave her everything."

"No, I really didn't. I thought I did, but with hindsight, I see that I held back a lot because I was too focused on work and not present enough with her."

"I don't believe that."

"It's true. I've had a lot of time for self-reflection since I lost her the way I did, and it makes me sad to realize how disconnected I was in so many ways."

"I think you've always done the best you could."

"Roni has helped me to see that I can do way better. I like who I am with her." He stood. "I'll let you get back to work. Thanks for listening."

"I'm glad we got a chance to catch up." Nick stood to give his friend a quick hug. "I'm so, so happy for you and Roni."

"Thanks. I'll let you know what I hear from Jennings and look into Worthy."

"Keep that on the deepest possible down-low."

"Will do."

After Derek left, Nick returned to the Resolute Desk and sat in his chair, marveling at what his friend had told him about his romance with Roni. There'd been a time after Derek's wife,

Victoria, was murdered—and later found to have been doing the bidding of one of President Nelson's rivals—when Nick and their other friends had feared Derek might never recover from the shock and betrayal. A letter from Vic, provided by her attorney, had professed her profound love for Derek, which had helped to soothe some of the hurt. But it had been a long, difficult journey for Derek and his daughter, Maeve. Nick was delighted to hear Derek speaking so effusively about Roni and their relationship.

He spun around to look at the family photos Sam had put on the credenza behind the desk. He picked up the one of all of them from Christmas and smiled at the gorgeous family they'd created for themselves. As long as he had them, whatever his mother had in store for him would be nothing he couldn't handle.

Or so he hoped.

SAM WENT into her office to call Judge Sawyer.

"She's due in court in five minutes," her clerk said.

"I only need one minute."

"Please hold."

Sam listened to the annoying music that played as her mind raced with a million details that would need to be seen to ahead of this plan coming to fruition.

"Hi there. Sorry to keep you waiting."

"No problem. Tell me more about your church."

"We go to Citizens Community in Northwest. It's a lovely nondenominational service focused on better understanding Scripture."

"What's the address?"

"It's on 16th. I'm not sure of the street number."

"I can find that. What time is the Sunday service?"

"Ten o'clock."

"Do you go every week?"

"Every week that we can. Sometimes a kid's game will interfere, but we usually divide and conquer, with one of us taking some of the kids to church while the other parent goes to the game. I always choose church if I can. My husband prefers the games."

"And the pastor's name?"

"The Reverend Eleanor Simpson."

"Do I have your permission to reach out to her to set something up for this Sunday?"

"How will you protect the regular attendees?"

"We'll plan for that and everything else."

"Okay."

"I understand your trepidation, and I promise you we're working it from every possible angle to ensure the safety of everyone involved."

"I spoke to my husband about this, and he's concerned, naturally."

"My greatest concern is Harlan Peckham getting to you before we can set this up."

"The sheriff deputies are taking my security and that of my family very seriously."

"As they should. Please be careful, Cori. Every minute of every day."

"I'm scared, Sam."

"I know, and I'm sorry to put you through this."

"You're not putting me through it. You're trying to end this madness."

"I hope it'll be over by Sunday. In the meantime, we've put out a departmentwide alert for all officers to be on the lookout for Harlan Peckham, and it's possible someone will spot him before Sunday and spare us from having to go through with this plan."

"That'd be good."

"I'll keep you posted."

"Thanks for all you're doing. I appreciate it."

"Don't thank me yet. I won't be happy until this scumbag is handcuffed and on his way to life in prison."

Sam was leaving her office when six people wearing civilian clothes came into the pit with Deputy Chief Jeannie McBride. Sam's heart nearly burst with pride every time she saw the former detective in the same uniform Sam's father had once worn.

Jeannie smiled when she saw Sam in the doorway to her office. "Sam Holland, our lieutenant in charge of the Homicide division, needs no introduction."

The people on the tour went bug-eyed when they realized they'd come face-to-face with the first lady. As they started to reach for their phones, Jeannie sternly said, "No photos, no videos."

Sam recognized one of the men in the group but couldn't immediately recall his name. She remembered him as the bartender she'd met while investigating her brother-in-law's death from fentanyl poisoning. He'd told her how he'd been on the job in Baltimore. "I know you."

"Tim Child. We met at Zénitude."

Sam shook his hand. "Right! I did a reference for you."

"And I got the job because of it. Thank you."

"Welcome aboard."

"Thanks."

"Let's continue on straight ahead," Jeannie said.

One young woman stopped to speak to Sam. She was petite with dark hair and eyes. "If I may... I just want to say... I so admire your career. I hope I can be just like you someday."

It was all Sam could do not to laugh in her face, but she was so sincere that Sam wouldn't dare. "You can probably do better than being like me."

"I don't think so. Thank you for the inspiration you've provided that brought me to a career in law enforcement."

"Best of luck to you. Be safe."

"Thank you. You, too."

Gonzo stood in his cubicle, pretending to wipe away tears. "I wanna be *just* like you."

"Shut *up*," Sam said, laughing.

"That was so sweet."

"If only she knew what a red-hot mess she's aspiring to be."

"What'd you do now?" Freddie asked as he came into the pit.

Gonzo filled him in. "Some new recruits were coming

through on a tour, and one of them was gushing to the LT about how she wants to be just like her."

Freddie's eyebrows lifted to his hairline.

"Whatever you're gonna say, stuff it. We need to go to church."

"Do you have a fever?" Freddie asked.

While Gonzo laughed, Sam said, "No, we're going to speak to the pastor about setting a trap for Harlan Peckham."

"Oh good, because I thought hell had finally frozen over."

"Nope. Hell is safe for another day. Let's go." As they headed for the morgue exit, Sam said, "Do you want to take your own car so you can go home after this?"

"Nah, I'll ride with you and hop on the Metro after."

"Are you getting spoiled by my chauffeured ride?"

"Maybe?"

"Don't do that. I can't have you going soft on me."

"Soft... Whatever. Ask Elin if I'm soft."

Sam spun around, in a state of total shock. "Did you just make a penis joke?"

"*What?* No! I meant in general! What the hell is wrong with you?"

Sam lost it laughing. She laughed so hard she saw stars.

Freddie pushed her out the door ahead of him.

Vernon jumped out of the SUV when he saw them coming. "What's so funny?"

"She's ridiculous."

"I thought he..." She couldn't even say it without losing her shit all over again. Even seat-belted into the SUV, she continued to laugh so hard, it was a wonder she didn't wet her pants.

"I need to know what's so funny," Vernon said.

"She said she doesn't want me going soft, and I said, 'Soft, ha! Ask Elin if I'm soft,' and she thought I meant—"

"Say no more. I've got the picture."

That set Sam off all over again.

"She's like a twelve-year-old who just heard her first D joke."

"He can't even say it."

"Because I'm an adult with decorum, unlike someone I could name."

"This might be the funniest thing that's ever happened in my entire life."

His disdainful expression was frosting on the funny cake.

She wiped away tears and made a Herculean effort to pull herself together. There was work to be done and a delicate plan to put together. She had no time for tomfoolery.

"Are you done now?"

"I think so."

Sam took a deep breath and released it slowly, hoping to reset herself to focus on more important things than whether her once-innocent partner had turned into a heathen on her watch.

"Can someone tell me where we're headed?" Vernon asked.

Freddie gave him the address of the church that Sam had written down.

She took a call from Captain Malone. "Hey, Cap. What's up?"

"Park Police in Rock Creek spotted someone matching Harlan Peckham's description this morning, but he managed to elude them. They found a campsite they believe might belong to him. I'm sending Crime Scene there now, but I thought you might want to take a look, too."

"You thought right. We'll head there now."

"I texted a pin to Cruz with the location, and we've dispatched multiple units to assist the Park Police in the search for Peckham."

"Okay."

"Be careful, Sam. If he's feeling cornered, you'd be a really nice prize."

"I hear you."

CHAPTER TWENTY-NINE

S am slapped the phone closed. "We need to go to Rock Creek Park. Police there have uncovered a campsite that might belong to Peckham." To Freddie, she said, "Malone texted you a pin for the campsite."

"Where is he?" Vernon asked.

"They spotted him, but he got away."

"I can't let you go in there knowing there's an armed and dangerous felon on the loose."

"Vernon... We have a deal."

"This might be a bridge too far, my friend. How do I let you go in there, knowing there's an armed and extremely dangerous man in the park?"

"That's my job, and you agreed to let me do my job."

"I could lose mine for letting you do this."

"Don't say that! Come on. The place will be crawling with cops. Besides, he's probably long gone from there by now."

"I don't like it."

"So noted, and I'm sorry to stretch the boundaries of what's acceptable for you under normal circumstances, but nothing about my job is normal by Secret Service standards."

"No, really?"

She loved his sarcasm. Absolutely loved it.

"We're blazing a whole new trail, you and me."

"Oh, joy."

Freddie used his phone to direct them to the campsite as Sam watched from the next seat.

"That's pretty cool how you can do that," she said.

"That's why they call it a *smart*phone, dummy."

"You're full of beans today, young Freddie."

"Whatever that means."

They arrived at the campsite, which was overrun by Park and Metro PD officers. She hoped they hadn't compromised what could be a crime scene.

She got out of the car and greeted a young Park Police officer, showing him her badge. "Lieutenant Holland, MPD. Do you mind if I take a look?"

"I, uh, um... Sure, ma'am. Go right ahead."

"The correct answer would be, 'Not until we secure what could be a crime scene.'"

"But you... You're..."

"For fuck's sake. I don't care who I am. Protect that scene."

"Y-yes, ma'am." The officer scurried off, shouting orders at other officers who were getting too close to the ragtag tent and other items that looked like they'd been abandoned.

Lieutenant Haggerty joined her. "I see you're making friends and spreading joy."

"My mission in life. What the hell is wrong with people?"

"Am I expected to answer that question?"

"It was rhetorical."

He gestured to the tent. "Who is this guy?"

"We're looking at him for the Forrester and Hill shootings. We believe he's got his eye on a federal judge next. Time is of the essence."

"We're on it."

"Harlan Peckham's prints are in the system, so I need to know ASAP if this is him."

"Will do. It's nice to get a break from working at Stahl's."

"How're you and your team holding up?"

"Toughest scene we've ever worked. It's taking a toll on all of us."

"You're talking to Trulo?"

"Daily, and I've got my team seeing him, too."

"Good."

"It's just hard to fathom this kind of depravity from a guy we worked with, saw every day... All that time, he was hiding behind the badge as he became one of the most prolific serial killers we've ever seen. People will be studying this case forever."

Sam felt the impact of his words in the deepest part of her soul. She understood Stahl's depravity better than most, and even knowing what she already did about him, these new revelations were unbearable.

"The damage to the department will reverberate for years, too," Haggerty added.

"Yeah."

"I was thinking... I know you hate seeking publicity of any kind, but you're in a unique position to put a human face to this, to make people understand how much it hurts those of us who work hard every day to keep our community safe." He shrugged. "Just a thought."

"It's a good thought, and I'll take it under advisement."

"Better get to it with this." He gestured toward the campsite. "Another day, another monster."

He called to his team to follow him to process the scene.

As she took a walk around the perimeter of the campsite, Sam couldn't stop thinking about what he'd said. *Another day, another monster.*

If that didn't sum up her life, she wasn't sure what ever would.

With the scene under the control of Haggerty and his team, Sam returned to the SUV.

Vernon and Jimmy had stayed close to her the entire time she was out of the vehicle. As she was accompanied by highly trained police officers everywhere she went, usually one of the agents stayed back, so it said a lot about their level of discomfort that they'd both come with her.

Vernon was visibly relieved as he held the back door for her.

"Let's go to church, gentlemen."

. . .

THEY WERE TOLD they'd find Eleanor Simpson in a small office located in the back of an open, airy sanctuary that didn't resemble any church Sam had ever attended. It had a contemporary vibe, with white walls and wood accents.

"Nice place."

"I've heard great things about this church," Freddie said. "They do a ton of work in the community."

Sam liked knowing there were places like this where people could come together to worship and then spread the good word to people in need.

Eleanor was petite, with blonde curls, blue eyes and a friendly, welcoming smile. "Are my eyes deceiving me? Is the first lady at my door?"

She said that with such disbelief that Sam couldn't help but smile as she showed her badge. "I'm undercover at the moment as Lieutenant Holland, Metro PD. I wondered if I might have a moment of your time."

"Please, come in."

"This is my partner, Detective Cruz."

"Of course I know of him, too."

Judging by his goofy grin, the comment pleased Freddie tremendously.

"Don't tell him that. I'm trying to raise him with humility."

While Freddie scowled, Eleanor laughed.

"It's such a tough job to raise them humble."

"You know it."

"I understand you investigate homicides. I'm not sure what I can do for you."

"We're investigating the murder of U.S. Attorney Tom Forrester and the attempted murder of FBI Agent Avery Hill."

"I read about both of those shootings." Her light seemed to dim somewhat as she said that. "Gun violence is such a scourge on our society."

"It is indeed."

"What does your case have to do with me?"

"We believe the person who shot Tom and Avery is coming

next for Judge Corrinne Sawyer, who presided over the trial of his family."

"Oh no. Not Cori! She's the loveliest person."

"Yes, she is. She's agreed to allow us to basically use her as bait to lure this guy out of hiding."

"That sounds dangerous."

"Our goal is to get him before he can get to her."

"What does that have to do with me and the church?"

"We'd like to stage the operation around her attendance at this Sunday's service."

"Oh, I don't know... I couldn't possibly endanger my congregation that way. More than two hundred people attend the ten o'clock service on Sunday."

"We have a plan for that. As the service is ending, you'd ask the congregation to exit through the back door, while Corrinne will exit out the front, accompanied by plainclothes officers acting as fellow churchgoers. We'd have people stationed all around the building to ensure a smooth departure for the rest of the congregation while we take care of business out front."

Eleanor bit on her thumbnail. "Why do you have to use my church for this? Isn't there another option?"

"When we first conceived of this idea, we knew it needed to happen somewhere that Cori goes regularly and predictably. We needed a place that has a wide perimeter to allow us to provide as much security as possible. The church checks all our boxes."

"If it wasn't for the rest of the congregation being in the dark, I wouldn't have a problem with it."

Sam glanced at Freddie, looking for his input.

"We could tell them," Freddie said. "It's not like they know the guy we're after."

"How can we ensure they'll keep a lid on it, though?" Sam asked him.

Eleanor thought about that for a second before she replied, "If we explain it to them in the starkest possible terms, that people's lives are at stake, and if they choose to stay away, we respect that, but we'd ask them not to tell anyone what's going on."

"Do you trust them to keep it quiet? If one person tells someone, and it gets out on social media or wherever, it's a bust."

"We could work together to craft a message to the congregation that would make the stakes very clear."

"Does that mean you're willing to work with us on this?"

"I won't lie to you... I'm scared of something terrible happening at our doorstep. But if it would get this guy before he can harm Cori, well, then I'm willing to do whatever I can to help."

"I promise you we'll do everything we can to ensure no one is harmed."

Eleanor nodded, but her trepidation was obvious and understandable.

Even the best of intentions couldn't prevent tragedy. The plan was risky, and everyone involved needed to know that.

"If you write down your contact info, we'll be in touch about the message to your congregation and other details."

Eleanor took the notebook from Sam and wrote down the requested info.

"We might have a problem," Freddie said as he looked up from his phone.

"What problem?"

He showed her a social media message questioning why the first lady was visiting Citizens Community Church.

"Shit."

How she yearned for the days when she ran around anonymously with no one giving a flying fuck where she was or what she was doing.

"What do we do?"

"Spin it as a first lady thing," Freddie said. "A quick stop to reach out to community leaders about an initiative you're heading up."

"Great idea."

"Let's take a photo of you with Eleanor and have your White House office post it."

"He's good at this," Eleanor said.

"Yes, he sure is."

They posed for the photo that Freddie took.

"Thank you again for this, Eleanor. We sincerely appreciate what you're doing to help us."

"I just hope it works."

"Me, too."

BACK IN THE SUV, Sam called Roni Connolly, her director of communications at the White House.

"Hi, Sam, what's up?"

"I need a favor."

"What can I do?"

Sam explained the situation with the church and the operation involving the federal judge. "We were still there when Freddie noticed someone on social media asking why I was there. He took a picture of me with the pastor, Eleanor Simpson, and we were hoping you could post it under my first lady accounts with a caption about me reaching out to community leaders, to throw people off the scent of something going on there."

"Have him send it to me. I'll post it right away."

"Please let Lilia know, too, so she's aware."

"Of course."

"Thank you, Roni."

"No problem."

Sam slapped her phone closed. "Can you text her the photo?"

"What's her cell number?"

Sam opened her phone and poked around. "How do I find it?"

"For God's sake. Give it to me."

She handed over the phone with a big grin. "My hero."

"It's a wonder you can function in this world."

"Even though you're insulting me, I want to say that was quick thinking back there with the first lady thing."

"Who knew that you being the first lady would actually come in handy?"

"It's because I'm the ding-dang first lady that we had a problem in the first place."

"When you put it that way..."

"God, I miss being anonymous. I yearn for the ease of that life."

"But you don't yearn for life before Nick."

"Not one bit. The tradeoff is definitely worth it. He's worth it."

"He sure is."

Sam looked over at him. "I hope you know I mean that. There're times when the enormous changes in our lives are truly overwhelming. Days like yesterday when we're hosting a freaking state dinner, of all things... And to be raising three incredible kids and guiding another into young adulthood. But I'm always thankful to be married to him and to be on this incredible journey with him and our kids."

"I know that, Sam. We all do."

"I hope he does, too."

"He does. For sure."

"Hey, do me a favor, will you? Get with Archie to put together a summary of the Peckham case for the meeting in the morning so we can quickly bring everyone up to speed on who these people are and who we're looking for."

"Yep. I'll text him right now and get on it when we're back at the house."

"Thank you."

The secure BlackBerry she used to communicate with Nick buzzed with a text from the man himself. *Can you talk?*

Sam put through a call to him.

"Hey, babe. Sorry to bother you when you're busy."

"Please bother me."

"Are you having a day?"

"Every day is a day around here. How about you?"

"Same. I just had a call from Cox."

"Let me guess. He wants you to rein in your wife."

"Something like that. He's extremely upset about your team requesting a warrant for his nephew's phone. What's up with that?"

Sam thought for a long moment about what she ought to say.

"Sam?"

"I believe this is something we shouldn't talk about. For both our sakes."

"Do I have a problem there?"

"Possibly. That's all I'm willing to say right now."

"I understand."

"Do you? Really?"

"Of course I do. We both have jobs to do, and you don't need me or anyone who works for me interfering with your work. I told him I expected him to cooperate fully with the investigation into the murder of one of our U.S. Attorneys and to be forthright in all his dealings with you and the MPD."

"You said that?"

"Yes, I said that."

Sam fanned her face, not that he could see that. "I'm extremely turned on right now."

"Oh my hell," Freddie said loud enough for Nick to hear.

They laughed.

"Poor Freddie," Nick said. "He'll never recover from working with you or being friends with us."

"I know. We ought to start a therapy fund for him."

"Yes, you really should," Freddie said.

"Anyway, back to important stuff. Thank you for your support. You shall be richly rewarded later."

"Is that right? Do tell."

"Not now, Mr. President. The children are listening."

Freddie groaned and put his hands over his ears.

"Got to go. Thanks for the call and for reminding your arrogant AG who he works for."

"Oh, he knows. Believe me, and I'm quite sure he doesn't like it, which will need to be dealt with at some point."

"Power looks sexy on you."

"Freddie is going to leave you."

"Nah, he's stuck with me, and he knows it. I'll see you soon."

"Can't wait. Love you."

"Love you, too."

Sam ended the call and put the BlackBerry in her pocket. "Phew. I need a cold shower."

"Make it stop."

"He told Cox to cooperate with us, to remember his place and not to hassle the first lady."

"Wow, that is sexy."

"Told you."

"I guess they found out about the warrant for Henry's cell data."

"Yep."

Sam's cell rang with a private number. While a normal person could ignore calls like that, she never did. "Lieutenant Holland."

"Reginald Cox."

Sam mouthed the word *Cox* to Freddie. That thought nearly had her laughing again.

"What can I do for you?"

"I understand your team has requested a warrant for my assistant's phone data."

"Your assistant who's also your nephew, but no one is supposed to know that? Yes, we did."

"*Why?*"

"Because I'd like to know what he was doing when Tom Forrester was killed." Cox didn't need to know they had another suspect.

"*What?* Are you insane? You're looking at my assistant as a person of interest in a *murder* investigation?"

"Did I say that?"

"Why else would you want his phone data?"

"To rule him out as a suspect? Have you ever done anything like this before, General Cox?"

"Don't be snide with me."

"It was an honest question. You've given me reason to wonder if you know how these things work."

"I'm going to tell you this in the plainest possible language— leave Henry alone."

"Or else what?"

"That's all I'm going to say."

The line went dead.

"Um, I think the Attorney General of the United States just threatened me."

"No way," Freddie said, eyes gone wide.

"What did he say?" Vernon asked.

Sam repeated the conversation back to them.

"That needs to be immediately reported to your superiors and mine," Vernon said.

"I'll agree to report it to my superiors, but let's not bring yours into it."

"I have no choice, Sam. You've been threatened. I have to report that."

She wished she hadn't said anything. The AG had been spouting off, flexing his muscles, whatever you want to call it. She didn't believe he would dare to harm her. He'd be a fool to come anywhere near her.

When they returned to HQ, Sam went through the conversation with Cox again for Malone and then a second time when he asked her to tell it to the chief.

"I can't believe he'd have the stones to threaten you," Farnsworth said.

"He's used to being able to push people around. He doesn't like being pushed back."

"Still, that's no reason for him to threaten a police officer."

"What do we even do about it? It's not like we can report him to his higher-ups. His boss is my husband, and the last thing either of us needs is to be caught in the middle of something like this."

The BlackBerry rang.

"Speak of the devil."

CHAPTER THIRTY

S am took the call from Nick. "Hi, honey. How's your day going?" She grimaced at the chief as she forced the cheery tone with her husband.

"Is it true that Cox threatened you?"

"How do you already know that?"

"Answer the question, Samantha."

"He said something that some might consider a threat."

"Tell me exactly what he said."

Sam told the story yet again. "Henry is his nephew and admin, and he's probably just being protective of him."

"I'll take care of it."

"Please don't do anything."

"Sam, he *threatened* you. Who in the fuck does he think he is?"

"I understand you're upset but think about it. How stupid would he have to be to come anywhere near me?"

"I don't want to find out if he's that stupid."

Her gaze took in the captain and chief. "If we overreact to this, we may miss our chance to figure out why he's so intent on keeping us from investigating Henry Allston. I want to see that through. If you remove Cox, Allston goes with him, and who knows if we'll ever find him? I'd rather keep them both at Justice, sweating out whatever they're trying to hide. We'll find it."

"How am I supposed to hear that one of my cabinet secretaries has *threatened* my wife and do nothing about it?"

"Your wife is fine. She's surrounded by world-class security and top-notch police officers. Let me do the job. You can deal with him after, okay?" He was silent long enough that Sam began to wonder if he was still there. "Nick?"

"I'm here."

She walked away from the others. "Talk to me."

"You know how I feel about you being in danger. To think that one of my people is putting you there is intolerable."

"I know, and I'm sorry you're upset, but I honestly believe he was flexing his muscles more than anything. Don't worry, okay?"

He huffed out a laugh. "What? Me worry?"

"Vernon and Jimmy won't let anything happen."

"They're the only reason I can sleep at night."

"The *only* reason? Clearly, I need to do a better job of wearing you out."

"You're doing just fine, babe. Be safe and get home to me soon."

"I will. Love you."

"Love you, too."

"What'd he say?" Freddie asked when she returned to the conference room to deal with the other men in her life.

"He wants to hang the AG out to dry, but I convinced him to stand down. Before we quit for the day, I want to see Bryant. I have an itch, right here..." She scratched the back of her neck. "We're missing something in this Cox-Forrester-Bryant Bermuda Triangle, and I want to know what it is."

"I'll ask him to come in for a chat."

"You think he'll come?"

"I'll tell him it's in his best interest to cooperate with us."

"What're we doing about the AG?" Malone asked.

"Nothing for the moment. He was looking for a big reaction, and I don't want to give him that satisfaction. Instead, I'm digging deeper into what he's so eager to keep hidden from me and the rest of the world. And once I figure out what that is, I'm going to nail him."

. . .

DAMIEN BRYANT HAD LOST some of his swagger since Sam last saw him at the state dinner. His complexion had taken on a waxy appearance, and he had huge bags under his eyes. When Sam walked into the room, he scowled.

"What now?"

"Is that any way to greet an old friend?"

"Old friend. Right. You're out to ruin me."

"Not hardly. We wouldn't even know each other if you hadn't been breaking the law for quite some time now."

"You can't prove anything. I came in when you called. What do you want now?"

"Who's Henry Allston?"

Bryant's expression went blank as he blinked and swallowed. "I don't know him."

"Come on. Your entire demeanor changed when I mentioned his name. Who is he?"

"He works for Cox."

"I already know that. Who is he to you?"

"No one. I know him through his boss. That's it."

"Damien, I'm going to be honest with you. I don't believe you. In fact, I believe you know Henry Allston very, very well, and you know exactly what he and Cox are up to."

"What's in it for me to rat out the AG and his stooge?"

"Depends on what you tell us."

Bryant shook his head. "I want the incentive package first."

Sam glared at him for a hot second before she got up and left the room to call Faith. "Bryant has info about Cox and his shady assistant, Henry Allston. He's looking for a deal."

"Do you think he's got the goods?"

"I'm not sure. How about you come over and listen to what he has to say with the goal of getting him to roll on Cox?"

"I'll be there in ten."

While Sam waited for her, she called her sister Angela. "Hey, how's it going?"

"It's been a tough day. Ella has an ear infection, and Jack is extra sad today. I've got the worst heartburn I've ever had, and the baby is having a party in there. Other than that..."

"I'm sorry, Ang. I wish there was something I could do to help."

"You've got your own hands full. I'll get through it. Everything is harder without him."

Sam's heart ached for her sister. "I wish I knew what to say."

"I appreciate you checking on me—and connecting me to Roni. She's been an amazing source of support."

"I'm so glad to hear that. She's the best."

"She is. One of these days, I might even check out her Wild Widows."

"I hope you do. She says they're awesome."

"I talked to her friend Iris, who was also left with three little kids when her husband died. That helped. At least I know I'm not actually insane, despite how I might feel at times."

"You're doing great. Spence would be so proud of you."

"I guess."

"He would be. We all are."

"Thanks." She sniffed. "I'd give anything for this to not have happened."

"Me, too. Everyone who loves you and your kids would give anything to have him back."

"I got your message about the hearing tomorrow. I want to go, but I'm just not sure I'm up to it."

"I'll be there, so don't feel pressured to come."

"Can I let you know in the morning?"

"Of course. Either way is fine. It's going to be a long road, so you need to pace yourself. This is just the preliminary hearing."

"I want to be there for him. These people sold him poison. I want them to see the lives they've ruined."

"You'll have plenty of chances for that before this case is fully adjudicated."

"Thanks for all the support. I don't know what I'd do without you and Trace, Mom and Celia... Everyone has been so amazing."

"We love you and the kids. We'll always be right here for you."

"That means everything to me. Ella's waking up from her nap, and it's time for more medicine. I'll text you in the morning, okay?"

"Sounds good. Love you."

"Love you, too."

Sam closed the phone and took a couple of deep breaths to get her emotions in check so she could focus on what she needed to do so she could get out of there. Her new watch read five thirty.

As she left her office, Faith came into the pit.

"Interview one," Sam told her.

She followed Faith down the hallway.

When they entered the room, Bryant perked up.

"I believe you know Assistant U.S. Attorney Faith Miller."

"I've had the pleasure."

"Lieutenant Holland tells me you're interested in a deal."

"If I give you Cox and Allston on a silver platter, what's in it for me?"

"That depends on whether the info you give us is something we can use to prosecute them and is contingent upon your willingness to testify."

He hadn't expected that last part. "Testify? Cox will have me killed before that can ever happen."

"We have ways of keeping you safe."

"Sure you do, and he's aware of every one of them."

"It's up to you." Faith crossed her arms. "Either you're in or you're not."

"I'd rather be dead than spend the rest of my life in prison, so I guess I'm in."

Faith sat next to Sam at the table. "I'm listening."

"Cox is heavily into gambling. Has been for decades. The first wife left him when he ran them into bankruptcy. The second wife has no idea he's burning through her money as well as his own."

"How did this not come up during his confirmation hearings?"

"It's very well hidden."

"Hidden how?"

"It's all done through Allston."

"Oh my God," Sam said. "I knew there was something."

"Reggie took Henry out of an abusive home. His sister's ex-husband was beating the shit out of both of them. She refused to leave the guy. Reggie rescued Henry and took him in. He and the first wife raised him as their own. There's nothing Henry won't do for Reggie."

"What does Reggie gamble on?"

"Everything. Sports, horse racing, fights."

"How did you find out about it?" Faith asked.

His gaze shifted between them as he seemed to weigh how much he should say. "I run some gambling rackets. Interested people tend to find you when you're in the business. He was in heavy to me over the last seven years. Right now, he owes me about one-point-five."

"*Million?*"

"Yeah."

Faith stared at him in disbelief. "The Attorney General of the United States has a *one-point-five-million-dollar gambling debt*?"

"That's just to me. Who knows what else there is?"

Faith sat back in her seat. "This leaves him open to blackmail."

"I'm aware, and so is he."

"How did Tom Forrester play into this?"

"As they go way back, Tom was aware of Reggie's past problems with gambling, but he didn't know it was ongoing until Henry Allston's name popped up during his investigation into me. That led him right back to Cox and the gambling."

"Is that what the three of you were fighting about shortly before Tom was killed?"

He nodded. "Reggie was after Tom to forget all about that part of the investigation, but Tom, being Tom, wasn't having it."

"Did Reggie have Tom killed?" Sam asked, even though she still believed the Peckhams had been responsible for Tom's murder.

"No! God no. Reggie loved Tom like a brother."

"And his brother was about to blow the lid off his dirty secret."

"Tom said he wouldn't tell anyone, but only if Reggie got serious help."

"How would he do that as the current Attorney General?"

"That was a sticking point. Reggie swore he'd resign and get help as soon as the investigation into the former joint chiefs was completed."

"That could take months," Faith said.

"Which was understood. Reggie felt it was important that he personally oversee that situation."

"Why?" Sam asked. "Couldn't that have been handed off to a deputy AG?"

"Tom said the same thing, but Reggie insisted on seeing to it personally."

Again, Sam's gut was telling her there had to be more to the story. "So Tom was willing to wait, possibly months, to reveal what his investigation into your campaign finance irregularities had uncovered?"

"No, he was going to handle the two things separately."

"Was Reggie's debt covered by campaign money?"

Sam could tell that question made him uncomfortable as his gaze darted toward Faith.

"Are you giving me immunity or not?" he asked.

"I'm concerned about your credibility problem."

"Everything I've told you is true."

"And you'll testify to that?"

"If you protect me and keep me alive long enough to do that."

"Do you honestly believe the sitting AG would have you killed for revealing his gambling issue?" Sam asked, incredulous.

"I think people have killed for much less of a reason than that. Being the AG has been the pinnacle of Cox's life. He loves the attention, the fawning, the respect, the access to power. I do think he'd kill me or anyone who might threaten to reveal him for what he really is—a broke, broken addict who lies to his own wife to cover his trail of financial ruin. Tom was pushing him hard to resign before this came to light."

"Do you think there's a connection between Cox and what the

joint chiefs did?" Faith asked. "Is he sticking around to prosecute or protect them?"

Bryant appeared to give the question careful thought. "I'm not sure. To be honest, it hadn't occurred to me that there might be a connection, but now that you say that, I wouldn't rule it out."

Jesus, Sam thought. *What have we stumbled upon?*

She glanced at Faith, who seemed similarly shocked.

"What else?" Faith asked.

"I don't understand."

"What else do you know that we didn't ask about?"

The two women stared him down until he blinked.

"I heard some talk about the president's military attaché, the one the joint chiefs suspect alerted the president to what was happening with them."

Sam tried desperately to figure out who he was talking about.

"Lieutenant Commander Juan Rodriguez," Bryant said.

She recalled the handsome, dark-haired officer who was frequently in Nick's company as one of the keepers of the so-called nuclear football, which was actually a briefcase containing the nuclear launch codes.

"What about him?" Sam asked.

"They blame him for ruining their plan and leaving their careers and reputations in ruins."

Sam got up and left the room, pulling the secure BlackBerry from her back pocket as she walked quickly toward her office.

The voice-mail message Nick had recorded picked up with instructions to press number sixty-nine for assistance and him laughing as he told her he'd call her back as soon as he could.

She ended that call and put through another to Terry on her regular phone.

"Hey, Sam."

"Terry, I need you to call me on the BlackBerry immediately."

"Will do."

As she slapped the phone closed, she appreciated that he didn't ask any questions. This conversation needed to be had on a secure line.

When the BlackBerry rang, she answered it. "Terry... I'm

hearing rumblings that Lieutenant Commander Rodriguez is suspected of tipping off Nick about the joint chiefs. I tried to call Nick, but he didn't pick up. Rodriguez's life could be in danger."

"I'm on it. Thanks for the info."

She wanted to ask about Lindsey, but she didn't want to delay him acting on behalf of Rodriguez.

Malone came to the door of her office. "What's up?"

"I just received information I needed to pass on to someone who could do something about it."

"What did you hear?"

She waved him in and waited for him to close the door before she updated him on what they'd learned from Bryant.

"Holy. Shit."

"I alerted Terry O'Connor about the possible threat to Rodriguez. I figured he'd know what to do."

"He'll bring in the Secret Service and Rodriguez's chain of command. They'll take care of him."

"Nick has spoken so fondly of Rodriguez. He'll be devastated if anything ever happened to him." She remembered him telling her about the info Juan had brought to him and how upsetting it had been to realize the military leaders had been plotting to overthrow his administration.

"You've done what you can there. Next question is what's the plan with this info you uncovered about Cox?"

"I have no idea. This is way above my pay grade, and it's riddled with conflict of interest for me. I was going to bring it to you guys to figure out next steps. What do you do when you find out the country's top LEO is seriously compromised?"

"You report it to his boss and have him removed from office immediately."

"Really?"

"Really."

"Who'll do that?"

"The chief will make that call. Do you feel the information is credible?"

"I do. Even though Bryant is angling for immunity, I feel like he's being straight with us."

"And he understands he may need to testify if charges are brought against Cox?"

"He does."

"He'll need protection."

"Faith is aware of that and said she'd arrange it."

"Are you comfortable with him getting full immunity?"

"Not entirely. He ordered the murder of one of his own guys in an effort to make us believe his son was dead so he could get him off the hook on the murder-for-hire charges. We know that much for certain, and I don't like the idea of him getting away with ordering the killing of Zachery Calder. But... We won't nail Cox without Bryant's testimony, and to get that, we have to give him something."

"Bryant's crimes are more significant than Cox's."

"Maybe so, but the AG is ripe for blackmail, which could imperil the entire country."

"Do you like Cox for the Forrester murder?"

"I would've liked him and his shady assistant-slash-nephew for it if the same gun hadn't been used in Avery's shooting. To my knowledge, Cox has had nothing to do with Avery Hill, other than being his boss's boss."

"We're moving forward with the plan to use the judge to lure Harlan Peckham out of hiding?"

"We are. There's a meeting at zero eight hundred on that."

"Give me the White House chief of staff's phone number. We'll take the Cox matter from here."

Sam found Terry's number on her phone and wrote it down. She tore the page from her notebook and handed it to him.

"This is the end of your involvement in the Cox investigation. Do I make myself clear?"

"Crystal."

"Good work."

"Thanks. I think."

Malone grimaced as he stood to leave. "Only you, Holland. Only you."

CHAPTER THIRTY-ONE

S am had a knot in her stomach as she rode home in the back
of the Secret Service SUV. Today had been a lot. Not that
every day wasn't a lot, but finding out that your president
husband's AG was seriously compromised and then having to
figure out how to handle that stick of dynamite hardly counted as
a regular day at the office.

Not to mention setting up an operation that would use a
federal judge as bait to catch a killer.

"What time are we leaving in the morning?" Vernon asked.

"Six forty-five."

"Sounds good."

"Does it, though?"

He chuckled. "We can sleep in when we're retired."

Sam met his gaze in the mirror. "You're not retiring any time
soon, are you?"

"Not for at least three more years. Maybe longer."

Her heart swelled with affection for him. "That's good to
know."

She saw the smile in his eyes. He cared as much about her as
she did about him, which was funny, really. She'd been prepared
to hate having a detail. What a nice surprise it had been to love
spending her days with him and Jimmy, and how odd it was to

feel that Vernon had arrived right when she needed someone to fill some of the tremendous void left by Skip Holland's passing.

It was almost as if her dad had sent Vernon to watch over her for him.

She liked to think that was possible.

"Thanks for everything, guys."

"Pleasure to work with you," Vernon said.

"Is it, though?"

They parted laughing as Sam went inside, greeted by Harold.

"Evening, ma'am."

"Evening, Harold. Is the president upstairs?"

"No, ma'am. He's still in the Oval."

Sam was surprised to hear that. He liked to escape as early as possible to spend time with the kids before dinner. "Thanks. I'll find him there."

"I can take your coat and get it upstairs for you."

"That's very kind of you. Thank you."

"My pleasure, ma'am."

Sam glanced longingly at the stairs to home before she headed toward the West Wing to find her husband.

Julie, one of the admins, was seated at her desk outside the office.

"Hi, Julie. Is he available?"

"He's in a meeting. Let me check."

This was the first time Sam hadn't been waved right in.

Julie made the call and hadn't put the phone back in the cradle when Nick came to the door.

Sam went to him, noting he looked stressed. "What's up?"

"We can't locate Juan."

Her heart sank. "Oh no."

"I'm beside myself."

"What can I do?"

"I... I don't know. We're doing everything we can."

"How long has it been since anyone heard from him?"

"He was on his two-day break, so it was the end of the day on Monday when I last saw him. No one has heard from him since he left here that day."

"Have you notified the MPD?"

"Terry did when the chief called earlier about Cox."

"What's the latest there?"

"I'm meeting with Cox in the morning and plan to request his resignation, which is the last freaking thing I need to be dealing with right now. All I can think about is Juan risking everything to make me aware that Nelson's joint chiefs were conspiring to get rid of me. And now he's missing, or worse."

"I wish there was something I could say or do..."

He gave her a quick hug. "Seeing you helps. I'm going to be here awhile."

"Do you want me to stay?"

"You know I do, but you should go relieve your mom with the kids and spend some time with them."

"If you want me to come down, just call me. I'll be right here."

"Thanks. Love you."

"Love you, too. I'm so sorry about this."

His grim expression said everything. "Me, too."

Sam left him to get back to the people waiting for him in the office and went upstairs to the residence. She found her mom, Brenda, at the table with the kids in the family dining room.

"Sam! Ms. Brenda said we could have chicken tenders tonight!"

Alden's excitement almost made her forget all the stress and worries of the day. "How did she find out that's your favorite?"

"I told her! And she said that's what we should have for dinner!"

Sam loved seeing the twins happy and excited and full of joy. She kissed the top of his blond head and then Aubrey's before taking a seat next to Scotty.

"Thanks for this, Mom."

Brenda smiled. "I had the best time this afternoon. Thank you for letting me cover for Celia."

"We appreciate it."

"What's wrong?" Scotty asked between bites of chicken tenders and tater tots.

Sam was glad to see he also had a salad on his plate. "Just a very, very crazy day."

"More so than usual?"

"Yeah, it was."

"We need a different word for those days. Like, nuclear crazy."

"I don't think we can throw the word 'nuclear' around under this roof."

Her son's deep guffaw touched her heart. She loved to make him laugh.

"You're probably right about that. How about ballistic crazy?"

"That's a good one. Today was definitely ballistic crazy."

"Where's Dad?" Scotty knew that Nick never missed dinner with the family if he could help it.

"Dealing with his own ballistic craziness. Have you seen Shelby and Avery?"

"I was up there earlier to see the kids," Scotty said.

"How's Avery?"

"Sore, but glad to be home."

"I'll run up and see them after dinner."

"Are you hungry?"

"I'll wait and eat with Dad."

She supervised dessert, homework, baths and bedtime for the twins and looked in on Scotty, who was finishing his homework. As usual, he was watching a Caps game while Skippy snoozed next to him on the bed. "How was your day?"

"Another day in eighth grade paradise."

"How's it going with *Beowulf*?"

"Much better now that I actually understand it. I'm nominating you for mother of the year for getting me that guide."

Just when she thought he couldn't top the things he'd said to her in the past... "I do what I can for my people."

"I'll never understand the purpose of reading something centuries old when we've got enough problems to contend with in this century."

"I feel like I had this very conversation with my parents once upon a time, and I have to say, I was right and so are you. There's a lot of stuff that doesn't get taught in school that would be far more useful than algebra and *Beowulf*."

"We need to get Dad to make a law."

"I'm sure he'll get right on that. In the meantime, work hard and do your best. That's all anyone can ever ask of you."

"I wish it came naturally to me the way it does for Dad."

"He's a unicorn that way. The rest of us have to bust our rumps for good grades. The hard work makes the good grades worth it. I remember the first time I got all A's on a report card in college. I thought it was a misprint."

"Wow, that's awesome. You must've been so excited."

"I was shocked. I didn't think I was capable. After that, I started to feel like anything was possible."

"That's really cool."

"It took me a long time to hit my stride in school, thanks to the undiagnosed dyslexia that caused me no end of heartache. But things started to change when I decided to really apply myself. It was never easy because of the dyslexia, but I surprised myself and everyone else. That felt pretty damned good."

"I should try harder. I want you guys to be proud of me."

"Oh my goodness, Scotty. We're *so* proud of you. No two parents have ever been prouder of their son than we are of you. Neither of us has any doubt that you're going to do great things with your life, and we'll always be proud of you. No matter what."

"It'll be pretty hard to top you two."

"You don't have to top anyone. Just do you. That's more than enough."

"If you could keep those study guides coming, it'll be easier to make you proud."

She laughed and leaned in to kiss his cheek. "Don't stay up too late."

"I won't."

"Love you."

"Love you, too."

The conversation with him had made her whole day, she thought as she ran upstairs to the third floor to knock on the door to Shelby and Avery's suite.

Shelby answered with baby Maisie in her arms. She looked exhausted. "Come in."

"I'm coming to check on all of you. I was glad to hear Avery is home."

"So was Noah. He's in with him now, taking care of Daddy."

"Aw. Is it okay if I peek in on them?"

"Of course. Go right ahead."

Sam poked her head into the bedroom, where Noah was "reading" to Avery in bed.

"Sam! Dada is home!"

"I see that, buddy. I'm so glad."

Avery gave her a wan smile. His face was still pinched with pain, but thank goodness he was home and on the road to recovery.

"How're you feeling?"

"Sore as heck, but glad to be out of the hospital and home with my loves. Noah is taking very good care of me."

"I get you ice." The little boy scooted off the bed, picked up the plastic cup from the table and toddled out of the room.

"He hasn't left my side since I got home."

"Poor guy."

"It's been a lot for him in just a couple of days."

"For all of you. We're all so thankful you're all right."

"What's the latest on the investigation?"

"We're going to use Judge Sawyer to lure out Harlan Peckham."

"And she went for that?"

"She wants him caught as much as we do. With two-thirds of the key players having already been shot, she's not looking to be next."

"Are they watching her closely?"

"She and her family are surrounded by security, which is another reason she's eager to be done with this."

"What's the plan?"

"We're going to stage her coming out of church on Sunday, surrounded by 'congregants,' who'll be our people. We're working with your people and our Emergency Response Team."

"How will it work?"

Sam talked through the gist of her plan with him, covering every angle from when Corrinne arrived at the church through to when she came out, surrounded by people who'd appear to be friends and acquaintances, but who'd actually be cops.

"Where will her family be?"

"She said she and her husband frequently 'divide and conquer' on the weekends, based on the kids' activities. So we're going to have them not be there that day."

"And the rest of the congregation?"

"At the request of the pastor, they'll be notified of what's going on and asked to depart out the back, if they choose to come to church at all that day. They're also being asked to tell no one about what we're doing."

Avery winced. "I don't like that."

"I didn't either, but our thought is that no one at the church knows Harlan Peckham, and he runs around without a phone, so there's really no way for him to find out about it even if it leaks."

"I guess that's true. What if he doesn't show? What then?"

"A campsite was found today in Rock Creek Park that may be his. If so, we're thinking he's now without shelter or access to food and other supplies. By Sunday, I figure he'll be wanting to get this done so he can get out of here. If he doesn't show, we'll cross that bridge when we come to it."

"This guy is dangerous, Sam. Make sure everyone knows he's capable of killing with his bare hands. I've seen him do it."

Sam could see he was getting tired. "I'll pass that along."

"He also wears his hair in a braid down his back. I've never seen him any other way but with the braid. He must've tucked it into his hat when he shot Tom."

Sam made a note. "That's a good detail. Thanks."

"I'll let you know if I think of anything else that might help."

"You know how to find me."

"I'm still hoping to get us out of here soon."

"Don't worry about that. Stay here and let the staff pamper you and Shelby for a while longer."

"They're spoiling us rotten."

"That's what they do best. The real world will be out there waiting for you soon enough."

"I suppose that's true."

"Plus, we like having you guys here."

"We like being here. Noah loves having the kids downstairs. And the pool is pretty cool, too."

"Relax and heal. Don't worry about anything other than loving on your wife and kids."

"That's my favorite thing to do. I still can't believe we have *kids*, as in *plural*."

"Couldn't be happier for you all. I'll check in tomorrow."

"Watch yourself out there with this guy on the loose. You'd be one hell of a prize for him."

He was the second one to say that, which made her feel anxious. "Don't worry about me. Take care of you."

"Will do."

Sam followed voices to the room Noah was using. Noah, holding his sleeping baby sister, was snuggled into bed with Shelby while she read a story. "Where's your phone, Tinker Bell?"

"In the living room."

Sam went to get it and entered Noah's birthday, which she knew was the code Shelby used for everything. Sam relied on her rudimentary knowledge of iPhones to find the camera and returned to take photos of Shelby and her babies.

"Thank you for that," Shelby said with a weary smile.

"I used an iPhone for you."

"The sacrifices you make."

"I know, right?"

Shelby giggled. "Thanks for making me laugh, too. It's been a minute."

"I do what I can for my people. I'll check in tomorrow. Let me know if you need anything."

"With all of us back under the same roof, even if it's your roof, I have what I need."

"My roof is yours. Always."

"Love you."

"Love you, too." She blew a kiss to the little boy. "Night, Noah and Maisie."

"Night, Sam. Maisie says night, too."

Could he be any cuter?

"Sleep tight, you guys."

CHAPTER THIRTY-TWO

Sam left Shelby and Avery's suite and went down the stairs just as Nick was coming up from the main floor, looking exhausted and devastated. She held out her arms to him, and he walked right into her embrace. "Anything new?"

"No."

Sam held him for a long time. She would've stood there all night if that's what he needed. "Are you hungry?"

"Not really."

"You still need to eat something."

"I'm not sure I could. This situation is making me sick. That he risked everything to warn me, and now..."

"Maybe he's hiding out until it blows over."

"I don't think he'd do that. The military tends to frown on members going AWOL."

Sam led him into their suite and into the bathroom, where she removed his tie, helped him out of the suit coat and began to unbutton his shirt.

"I spoke with his mother just now. She's out of her mind with worry. His father died when he was four. She raised him on her own." His tone was devoid of all the usual animation. "She's so proud of him working in the White House. She owns a hair salon in Philly. Juan grew up sweeping the floors and washing the towels." His voice broke as his head landed on her shoulder. "I know something terrible has happened."

"I'm so sorry, Nick. I wish I knew what to say."

"There's nothing to be said, but God help whoever is responsible for this."

Sam hadn't seen him this undone in a while. Her heart ached for him. After he changed into sweats and his favorite Harvard T-shirt, he dropped onto the sofa.

She poured him a glass of the bourbon Graham O'Connor had given him for Christmas and curled up next to him, resting her head on his shoulder.

They stayed there until the official phone rang almost half an hour later.

Nick got up to answer it.

He listened more than he spoke and then thanked the person. "Anything new?"

"The FBI and NCIS investigators have gained access to Juan's apartment and are processing the scene."

"It sounds like you've got the best people working on it."

Her phone buzzed with a text from Tracy. *Still planning to attend the hearing tomorrow?*

Yes.

Any word on whether Ang is coming?

I don't think so. I told her I'd take this one, and she should pace herself.

Good call. I'll see you there.

"Everything okay?" Nick asked.

"That was Tracy about the hearing in Spencer's case tomorrow."

"I should be there with you."

"Like I told Angela, it's gonna be a long haul. We need to pace ourselves, and you need to stay focused on things here."

"I wish I could be there for every minute of it."

"I know, and that means a lot to all of us. Do you think you could eat a little something?"

"Nah, I'm okay. I had a late lunch, and I'm just not hungry."

"How about some rest?"

"Not likely tonight, but I'll try."

They brushed their teeth and settled into bed a few minutes later.

"Want me to rub your back?" she asked.

"That's okay. You've got a sprained wrist."

"I've got another hand that's fully functional. Come on. That always relaxes you."

"Sure, if you want to."

"Be right back." She went to the bathroom to fetch the massage oil. "Turn over."

He turned so he was facedown, arms around the pillow.

Sam straddled his back and used her uninjured hand to work the coconut-scented oil into muscles so tight they felt like concrete.

"Feels good. Thanks."

"My pleasure."

"I keep meaning to remind you I'm traveling next week."

Sam's hand went still. "For how long?"

"Four days."

"Oh." She was already bereft at the thought of four days without him, as silly as that seemed. "Okay."

"I'm already dreading it."

"Me, too."

"Sorry."

"Don't be. You have to get out there and do the job. We knew your travel would pick up eventually."

"I hate being away from you guys."

Sam hated it, too. "I know."

"Close your eyes and focus on breathing. Just breathe."

He did as directed, and after a while, he seemed to relax ever so slightly.

She kept it up until her hand and back were aching.

His breathing had deepened.

Sam moved carefully to get up to wash her hands. When she got in bed, he turned on his side and put his arm around her, drawing her in close to him.

"Thanks."

She squeezed his hand. "Love you."

"You, too. So much."

While his breathing settled into a steady rhythm that she hoped was sleep, she lay awake with her thoughts spinning from one miserable thing to another. From the concrete prison discovered at Stahl's to the plan to use Cori Sawyer as bait to Tom's murderer, to Nick leaving for four whole days, to Avery's shooting and where Juan Rodriguez might be.

She dreamed that she was trapped inside the concrete prison, with no food or water or any way out. The fear, hopelessness and outrage were palpable. She'd had to watch the monster build the wall around her, one block at a time, realizing he was condemning her to a slow, miserable, painful death. Her body ached, as she hadn't had food or water in days, and the cold floor only added to the misery.

Soon, she'd run out of air, and then what? She didn't think anything could be worse than the razor wire and fire, but Stahl had managed to find a way to top his own depravity. This was worse. She thought of Nick, Scotty, Alden, Aubrey, Eli, her sisters, nieces, nephews... The only solace was that her dad would be there to greet her when she arrived in heaven, and that gave her something to look forward to as her strength ebbed.

She yearned for Nick, for one more minute with him, for the chance to breathe in the familiar scent of home while gazing into his gorgeous hazel eyes, the eyes that had never looked at her with anything other than love, admiration and full acceptance of who and what she was. He never asked her to be anything other than herself, which was such a gift.

He was such a gift.

A sob ripped from her chest.

Nick.

"Babe, wake up. Sam..."

His voice punctured the thin veil between sleep and wakefulness. She opened her eyes, expecting to see a concrete prison. Blinking, she saw the bedroom wall where she'd put a framed photo of their family from Christmas.

"Samantha."

Relief flooded her entire system. *Only a dream. Only a dream.*

She turned to him and buried her face in his chest as tears leaked from tightly closed eyes.

"What is it, love?"

"Weird dream. Sorry to disturb you."

"You want to talk about it?"

"Absolutely not." She wouldn't tell him about the concrete room. He had enough horrors to worry about without her adding more. She snuggled in deeper. "This is all I need."

"I've got plenty of this."

As she wallowed in his comfort, she tried to rid her mind of the images from inside the concrete prison, but that would be much easier said than done.

Sam was "off" from the second she rolled out of bed, through getting the twins up and dressed, to overseeing breakfast for all three kids and leaving them with kisses and hugs and wishes for a good day.

Since she'd be going to court, she'd worn gray dress pants, a white cowl-necked sweater and a navy blazer.

Nick walked her to the stairs. "Are you sure you're okay?"

"Just tired."

"You were restless all night."

"I'm sorry."

He kissed her forehead. "Don't be. I wasn't going to sleep much anyway." He'd already told her there was no news this morning about Juan. "I know you don't like to add to my burdens, especially at a time like this, but I always want to know what keeps you awake at night."

"And I appreciate that, but I can't remember most of it."

"I guess that's for the best."

"For sure." She went up on tiptoes to kiss him. "Keep me posted on Juan."

"I will and let me know how the hearing goes."

She nodded. "Will do. Love you."

"You, too. Be careful out there. My wife is my whole world."

"What a lucky girl she is." She stole one more kiss before heading down the stairs to meet Vernon and Jimmy. "Morning."

"Morning."

When they were on the way to HQ, Vernon asked, "Are you still planning to attend the court hearing this morning?"

"Yes."

"Okay."

Sam looked out the window and watched the city go by in a kaleidoscope so familiar the images were baked into her DNA. This was her town, her home, her place in the world. If she could stay focused on her family, the job and all the good in her life, she might eventually be able to forget the feeling of being trapped and left to die inside a concrete prison.

Her hands were trembling ever so slightly as memories from the dream popped in and out of her consciousness.

Stahl would enjoy knowing that he'd caused her new distress. He would enjoy that very much. She wouldn't give him that satisfaction.

Her phone buzzed with a text from Haggerty. *Prints found at the campsite are a match for Harlan Peckham.*

Excellent. Thank you.

That confirmation gave more credence to her plan to use Cori to lure him out. When she arrived at HQ, Farnsworth was waiting to speak to her outside her office. He held a file folder in his left hand.

She unlocked the door and invited him inside.

He closed the door behind him. "I need a favor."

"Anything for you."

"You might want to think about that before you agree."

"*Anything* for you."

He smiled and took a seat, tucking the file folder under his arm. "I need you to do a full briefing on all the things, including the Forrester case, the latest from Stahl's house, the Davies release and lawsuit, the Ramsey lawsuit. All of it. When I go out there, I come off defensive. I need you to go out there and show the devastation we all feel over these things. You're good at bringing the emotion. I just want to punch them all."

"So do I."

"You're better at not showing it." He looked pained. "I know it's a lot to ask, and I hate to take advantage of your platform this way, but—"

"My platform, such as it is, should be used to my benefit once in a while. In fact, Lieutenant Haggerty suggested I do this very thing."

"Did he?"

"Yeah, he said it might go down better and get added attention coming from me."

"I agree with him."

"I'll need some time to get up to speed."

"I had Public Affairs prepare some talking points." He handed over the file. "This is the company line but use your judgment. Transparency is the word of the day."

Sam opened the file and took note that two of the bodies found at Stahl's had now been positively identified: Tiffany Jones, who'd been used to entrap Davies, and Brittany Carter. Sam's heart ached when she recalled meeting with Carter's parents in Delaware. "Have the families been notified?"

"They have as of last night."

"I met the Carters. They've been through such a terrible ordeal. All these families have."

"I think you should say that."

"I'll do my best."

"You always do. I appreciate this."

"No problem."

"Sure it is, but I appreciate it all the same. Are you going to court this morning?"

She nodded. "I'll do the briefing after the eight o'clock meeting with the team I've assembled for the Sawyer operation."

"That plan gives me major anxiety."

"Me, too, but I think we can make it work."

"I really hope so. I'll let you get to the meeting. Okay if I sit in?"

"It's your house, sir."

"It's our house, Lieutenant."

"Please come. You're always welcome."

Sam collected her files and notebook and headed with him to the conference room to meet with the team that would help her bring Operation Nail Harlan Peckham to fruition.

Captain Michelle Ruiz from Emergency Response stepped forward to shake hands with Sam. "Good to see you, Lieutenant." She was about five seven, with a curvy figure and curly dark hair.

"You as well." Their paths had crossed occasionally over the years, but Sam had never worked closely with her. Ruiz had a reputation for being a hard-ass who went through officers faster than some people changed their underwear. People didn't like working for her. Sam would give her the benefit of the doubt until she had reason to do otherwise. "Thanks for being part of this."

"You got it."

In addition to Ruiz, Farnsworth, Malone, Archie and Sam's squad, Lieutenant Dawkins from Patrol and ten Patrol officers were in attendance. She recognized some of them, including Watts, Keeney and Youncy.

"Thank you all for being here."

George Terrell rushed through the door, looking frazzled. "Sorry I'm late."

"No problem. Thanks for coming in. Detective Cruz and Lieutenant Archelotta have prepared a brief on the Peckham family, headed by Willy Peckham, and managed while his father and the rest of their family were locked up by Willy's son Harlan, who escaped prosecution the first time around due to a sympathetic FBI agent 'forgetting' to read him his Miranda rights. Detective Cruz, you want to take it from there?"

"Sure." Freddie stood and pointed to the screen, where photos of the Peckhams were displayed. He went through the undercover operation led by Agent Hill, who appeared on the screen in all his hillbilly glory, causing Sam to bite back a laugh. She would have some fun with that photo after this was over. Oh, yes, she would.

"Forrester was murdered while sitting in his car on Constitution Avenue. Hill was shot leaving his gym on 22nd Street.

He's now recovering at home. Ballistics tied the bullets in both shootings to the same nine-millimeter Glock. At that point, we began looking at cases that Hill and Forrester worked on together. We quickly focused on the Willy Peckham, who is back in jail after recently breaking into Hill's home. Hill was not home at the time. Thankfully, they were neutralized before Hill's wife or son could be harmed. Willy's wife, Amber, who was with him during the home invasion, told us that Willy planned to 'gut Hill like a pig' in front of his wife and son.

"The case was prosecuted by Tom Forrester, and the trial was overseen by then-District Court Judge Corrinne Sawyer after the Peckhams requested a change of venue out of Kentucky. Sawyer is now an appellate court judge. Lieutenant, do you want to pick it up from here?"

A photo of Harlan came up on the screen.

Sam stood. "Harlan Peckham is notorious for never having owned a cell phone, so tracking him that way isn't an option. We began to think about ways we might lure him out of hiding. A campsite was located yesterday that has been tied to Peckham by fingerprints, but he was able to elude capture. Our plan is to surround Judge Sawyer at her church with our people in the hope of getting Harlan to show himself. We believe he's invested significant time, possibly over weeks and even months, learning the routines of his targets. He'll know that Sawyer attends services almost every week, often alone while her husband takes their children to various activities. He'll want to be done with this mission and on his way home to Kentucky as soon as possible."

"I have a question," Green said. "If he's taken the time to learn the routines, how did he know Forrester would be parked on Constitution?"

"Due to his family being taken captive by Bryant, Forrester wasn't on his usual schedule. I believe it's possible that Harlan was following him. Somehow he knew that Forrester would be there and took advantage of the opportunity. That's my guess, anyway."

"How'd the kidnapping of Forrester's family play into this thing with the Peckhams?" George asked.

"That was an entirely separate matter."

George gave her a skeptical look. "Which happened at the exact same time?"

"Yes. Forrester was investigating Bryant for campaign finance irregularities. In the course of that investigation, he uncovered evidence of numerous other crimes. Bryant had recently learned of the investigation. We believe Bryant took Forrester's family to send the message to back off. That's being treated as an entirely separate matter."

"Interesting."

You have no idea, Sam wanted to say, but the info about Cox was still confidential. For now, anyway. It was only a matter of time before Cox would become the latest mess of leftovers from the Nelson administration that Nick had to clean up.

"Now for assignments." Sam went through each member of the team and what she needed from them on Sunday. The Patrol officers would be in the church when Cori arrived and accompany her outside, playing the parts of friends and acquaintances catching up outside after the service ended.

"What about vests?" Youncy asked.

Sam glanced to Malone to take that one.

"As much as I hate to say it, I don't think we can risk Peckham noticing all the congregants are bulky in the chest area. It would be a giveaway."

That was what Sam would've said, too. "I'd like Cori to wear one under her coat, though."

"Agreed," Farnsworth said.

They went through every detail of the plan, positioning of officers, sharpshooters and federal agents.

"What do you need from us?" Captain Ruiz asked.

"I need your team to provide communication support nearby and to be ready to intervene should the need arise."

"We usually take a more active role."

"That's the role we need you to take this time."

Ruiz didn't like that answer.

Sam didn't care.

"Any other questions, comments, thoughts?" When there

were none, she said, "Thank you all for your participation. We'll convene here at zero seven hundred on Sunday to go through the plan one more time before we head out."

The others filed out of the room, leaving Sam with Cruz, Gonzo, Malone, Farnsworth and Archie.

"Is this plan insane?" she asked them.

"Maybe a little, but I think it's the fastest way to draw this guy out and end this thing," Farnsworth said.

"Have I overlooked anything?"

"Not that I can think of," Malone said.

Sam accepted that the sick feeling in her stomach would stay with her until they got through Sunday. In the meantime, she had a press briefing to handle and a hearing to get to. "After I do the briefing, I'm going to court for the hearing in Spencer's case."

"Do you want me to come?" Freddie asked.

"That's okay, but thanks for offering. Tracy will be there."

"And me," Gonzo said with a small smile.

"And you." He'd served as the lead detective on Spencer's case so there could be no conflicts of interest tied to Sam and her relationship to one of the victims.

"I'll give you a lift, if you'd like," Sam said.

"I won't say no to that."

"It's a date. I'll meet you back here after I do the briefing."

CHAPTER THIRTY-THREE

S am went into her office and texted Vernon to tell him she was headed outside to brief the press.

Give us five to put people in place.

That's all I've got.

She used the time to review the materials once more before taking the folder with her to meet the reporters gathered outside the main doors.

They perked up when they saw her, probably sensing something big because she rarely met with them alone.

Vernon moved up to the front of the gathering to stand behind her, while Jimmy watched from behind the reporters. There were probably other agents in the crowd, but she focused on the task at hand.

"Good morning. I'm here to update you on several ongoing investigations and other situations, after which I'll take a few questions. To make the best use of our time together, a standard reminder that I won't comment on anything having to do with my husband, the White House or other related topics.

"Yesterday, the MPD was served notice of legal action by two parties. The first, Eric Davies, was released from prison this week after serving sixteen years on aggravated rape charges based on evidence that was later determined to have been fabricated by former Lieutenant Leonard Stahl. As part of the case made against Davies, a woman named Tiffany Jones accused Mr. Davies of rape and testified against him. This week, the body of Ms. Jones was found buried in the backyard at Stahl's family home. Seventeen other bodies have been found on the property. Of them, Brittany Carter, who'd long been missing, has also been identified. The families of both women have been notified.

"The MPD medical examiner, in collaboration with the FBI lab, is working to identify the remains of others found at Stahl's home. Needless to say, this has been a grueling and heartbreaking investigation for everyone involved, particularly for our Crime Scene Unit, admirably led by Lieutenant Max Haggerty. He and his team have been working around the clock to fully process the scene at the Stahl home and to bring closure to families who've waited far too long to learn what happened to their loved ones.

"On a personal note, my history with Stahl is well known, and even having experienced what I did at his hands, I cannot fathom the depravity that led to what we're finding at his home. My heart aches for every one of his victims and their families. That each of us at the MPD worked alongside this man who pretended to uphold the law while violating it at every turn is something we're all struggling with.

"I'm sure many of you gathered here and those watching at home will wonder how a department full of seasoned law enforcement officers could've worked adjacent to an alleged serial killer and not known what he was doing while pretending to be one of us. I can assure you that if any of us had had the first inkling as to the true nature of his character, we would've done everything in our power to neutralize him before anyone else could be harmed. We take comfort in knowing he'll spend the rest of his life in prison, where he belongs."

"Lieutenant, will additional charges be filed against him now that these crimes have come to light?"

"We will fully prosecute him for every crime he's ever committed, and we will take great pleasure in seeing him convicted and given additional life sentences." She paused for a beat to change gears. "The other lawsuit was filed by Special

Victims Unit Detective Ramsey, who's currently on administrative leave after ramming a Secret Service SUV and endangering the lives of three people, including two federal agents. He's facing several felony charges as a result of that incident.

"His lawsuit alleges MPD misconduct in the death of his son, Shane Ramsey, who was shot and killed by one of our sharpshooters after Shane Ramsey took a woman hostage in Rock Creek Park. The testimony of every officer present will support the fact that Shane Ramsey had no intention of letting that woman leave alive, and by taking him, we saved her. We believe the lawsuit has no merit and will quickly be dismissed.

"We've identified a person of interest in the murder of U.S. Attorney Tom Forrester and in the attempted murder of FBI Special Agent-in-Charge Avery Hill, who's recovering from a gunshot wound at home. Ballistics analysis has indicated both men were shot by the same gun, and we're actively pursuing our suspect. I hope to have more information for you on that investigation shortly. That's all I have for now. I'll take a few questions."

"Do you plan to attend the hearing in your brother-in-law's case today?"

"Yes, I'll be there."

"Lieutenant, I'm sure you can understand the public's difficulty in understanding how such a prolific criminal could've hidden within the ranks of the MPD for so many years. What do you say to those people?"

"We believe Stahl was able to get away with what he did because he was an insider, who understood how the system worked. That gave him advantages most people wouldn't have in hiding his crimes. When I tell you we're heartbroken that this happened on our watch, I mean it. Having withstood his depravity personally, I ache for the others who were subjected to it. I wish I could've prevented what happened to them, and I know others here feel the same way. Our goal now is to do everything we can to get justice for his victims and their families and to ensure that every corner he ever cut while pretending to do the job is rectified to the best of our ability. That's a very high priority for everyone in this department."

"This week, you've presided over an intense investigation into the murder of a U.S. Attorney while cohosting a state visit. How is it possible to do both those things at the same time?"

Sam smiled at the blonde TV reporter, who'd been fair to her in the past. "That's a good question, Audra. And it gives me the chance to do a huge shoutout to the people I work with here and at my White House office, who make it possible for me to do both things simultaneously while also raising a family. I'm blessed to have the support of incredible teams in both jobs, without whom I couldn't do any of it."

"With the department facing so many challenges, is it fair to split your attention between two high-profile roles?"

The question came from an older reporter from the *Reporter*, a DC gossip rag.

"Fair to whom? I put forth my full effort in everything I do every day. That's all any of us can do. That's it for now. Thanks, everyone."

They were still shouting questions at her as she walked inside and breathed a sigh of relief. As often as she'd done that, it still never became routine to her, especially with the department dealing with so many controversies all at once. Hopefully, they'd nab Tom Forrester's killer on Sunday and notch a big win that they badly needed.

If things went bad there...

No, that couldn't happen.

It just couldn't.

AFTER HIS MORNING SECURITY BRIEFING, which had revealed several new areas of pressing concern at home and around the world, Nick waited impatiently for his ten o'clock appointment to arrive. There'd been no news about the search for Juan overnight, other than to note that the FBI and U.S. Marshals had been brought in to aid NCIS in the investigation. Nick had been around these things long enough to know that every hour that passed without word from the young naval officer made it more likely he wouldn't be found alive.

Nick was heartbroken over that possibility.

Juan had risked everything to warn him about a brewing military coup and had possibly paid for that loyalty with his life.

How would Nick live with that?

He was saved from having to contemplate that dreadful reality by the arrival of Attorney General Cox.

"Show him in, Julie."

Nick got up from the Resolute Desk and went to meet Cox at the sofas. Normally, he offered refreshments to his guests. However, this wasn't a social call or even a regular meeting.

"Thanks for coming in."

"Of course, Mr. President."

Did the man look nervous, or was that wishful thinking on Nick's part? Since Cox had threatened Sam, Nick hoped he was shitting his pants with nerves.

"I wanted to talk to you about the gambling addiction that's been uncovered as part of the investigation into USA Forrester's murder."

Cox clearly hadn't been expecting that.

"I, uh... I'm dealing with that as a private matter."

"Normally, I'd give a cabinet member the opportunity to resign, but that's not going to happen in this case. Your behavior has made you vulnerable to blackmail by foreign and domestic bad actors. As a result of that, we're doing things a bit differently this time."

The man had gone pale. "Sir?"

"As we speak, the White House Press Office is releasing a statement containing all the dirty details of what you've been up to while enjoying the status that comes with being the United States Attorney General. Your office at Justice is being cleaned out, and your personal effects will be delivered to your home. Your access to official government networks has been cut off. In addition, the nephew who's played the role of your assistant while helping to hide your addiction is being told his services are no longer required by the federal government." Nick stood and buttoned his suit coat. "Put your government phone on the table."

Cox glared at him but did as directed.

"You'll be met at home by federal agents, who'll take possession of your computers and any other equipment or documents that belong to us. Is there any part of this you don't understand?"

"No," Cox said through gritted teeth.

"I think you know the way out. Don't let the door hit you."

"Mr. President... if I may..."

"*You may not.* In addition to making our country less safe through your despicable actions, you *threatened* my wife. What did you think would happen next? Get out."

When Cox remained seated, seeming frozen with shock, Nick went to the door and signaled to Brant and the members of Cox's detail to escort him from the Oval Office.

After they left with the now-former AG, Terry came in. "How'd it go?"

"Like clockwork except for the part where he was too shocked to leave, and the Secret Service had to remove him."

"Director Ambrose has instructed his Secret Service detail to drop him off at home, at which point his protection ends."

"You've spoken to the deputy AG about becoming the acting?"

"I have, and she's ready."

Trevor Donnelly, the communications director, came to the door.

Nick waved him in.

"Christina made the statement in the briefing room, and the word is out that Cox has been fired for cause. It's safe to say this'll be the lead story on every network and in every publication as they try to uncover the reason for his firing."

"That doesn't need to come from us," Nick said.

"It'll come out soon enough," Terry said.

AT THE COURTHOUSE, Vernon and Jimmy escorted Sam through the media scrum gathered outside and through security with a minimum of fuss. Having them around was extremely helpful at times like this when she wanted to get in and out without making a scene.

Of course she drew unwanted attention everywhere she went, but the agents were good at creating a path for her through a crowd.

Vernon had told her that other agents were already positioned inside and around the perimeter.

It still struck her as bizarre that she required that kind of security, but whatever it took to stay safe and return home to her loved ones.

Their family had had enough traumatic loss after Skip's somewhat sudden death in October, followed shortly after by Spencer's shocking, tragic death while they were at Camp David during the holiday break.

Today, they were there to begin the process of getting justice for him and the others who'd been killed by laced fentanyl, which had been sold on the street to people desperate for relief. In Spencer's case, he'd injured his back playing football with friends and had been prescribed OxyContin. He'd become reliant upon it, had gone to rehab several times and had resorted to buying it on the street after his doctors cut him off.

Tracy and Mike were outside the courtroom when they arrived.

Sam and Gonzo hugged them.

"What're we doing here?" Mike asked tearfully.

"I know," Sam said. "It's surreal."

She greeted the family members of the other victims, including Brad Albright, whose young wife had sought relief for a persistent knee injury. Sam introduced Brad to Tracy and Mike.

Brad, who was dressed in a navy suit and matching tie, looked better than he had the last time she saw him on the day his wife died. His blond hair was combed, he'd shaved, and his eyes had lost some of the shock and early devastation. But the sadness was still very present.

"His wife, Mary Alice, was poisoned as well," Sam told her sister and brother-in-law.

"I'm so sorry," Tracy said.

"I'm sorry for your loss, too."

"Do you have children?" Tracy asked.

He nodded. "Two. They're six and three."

Tracy shook her head. "So many people hurt."

Sam bit back a gasp of surprise when Angela walked up to them. As Sam hugged her sister, she was alarmed by how frail she felt in her arms.

"I needed to come."

"Of course you did." Sam introduced her to Brad. "He lost his wife, Mary Alice."

Brad shook hands with Angela. "I wish I could say it was nice to meet you."

"Same."

Sam introduced Angela to the other families.

They greeted Angela warmly, which pleased Sam. Angela needed all the support she could get during this difficult time.

Spencer's brother, Jed, and his parents arrived, hugging Angela, Sam, Tracy and Mike.

They went inside and found seats a few minutes before court would be called to order.

Angela sat between her sisters, holding their hands as Sal Vincent was brought in, wearing an orange jumpsuit. His hands and feet were chained as he sat next to his attorneys.

"Is that him?" Angela's asked.

"Yes, he's the main guy."

"I thought he'd be older."

DEA Agent Kevin Kavanaugh, Derek's brother, came in and took a seat. He nodded to Sam.

She gave him the barest acknowledgment. If he'd had his way, she and her team would've been cut out of the Vincent bust, even though they were the ones who'd found him when the DEA had failed to do that for years.

Lieutenant Cooper from Narcotics entered the room, sneaking in a coffee and a brown bag that probably contained his breakfast. The man was revolting.

Over the next hour, the judge heard from Gonzo, Kavanaugh,

Cooper and Leslie Lawton, the wife of rival drug dealer Riggs Lawton. Leslie had been given immunity and federal protection in exchange for her testimony against Vincent and the other members of his organization who faced charges. She testified about how Vincent had stooped to selling laced product to try to run the Lawtons out of business. To hear Leslie tell it, she and her late husband, Riggs, had been trying to help those who'd become addicted to opioids.

Reliving the frantic, gut-wrenching week that'd followed Spencer's sudden death was brutal for Sam. She could only imagine how Angela must've felt.

In the end, the judge ruled there was ample evidence to support the prosecution of the case and set a trial date for late September. She banged her gavel to end the proceeding.

For a long moment afterward, Angela stared straight ahead, as if processing everything she'd heard.

"Are you okay, Ang?"

"I think? I mean... It's still so unbelievable. That people died because one dealer wanted to push another one out of business."

"It's sheer madness," Tracy said in her usual blunt fashion.

Angela looked at Sam, her eyes brimming with tears. "Even though you didn't testify here, I know you're the one who led the charge in finding these people and making them pay. The kids and I will always be thankful for everything you did. You saved other lives. There's no question about that."

"I'd give anything to have Spencer back."

"The initiatives Nick is pursuing in his memory will help a lot of people and keep his legacy alive. That means a lot."

"The media will want me to say something outside. Is that all right with you?"

"Of course."

"Spencer's family won't mind?"

"Not at all. They want the same thing I do—for his life and death to help others, and you're our best spokesperson for making that happen."

Sam was too choked up to speak, so she nodded.

Their group walked out together and stood behind Sam as

she spoke for all of them. "Today, we took a big step forward in getting justice for our beloved husband, father, son, brother and brother-in-law and many others who were lost due to what we believe was a deadly scheme perpetrated by Sal Vincent and others. This'll be a long road, but we'll be here for every second of it, until every person responsible for these murders is sentenced to prison."

She stepped away from the microphone and hugged her family members before sending them on their way.

Tracy and Mike would walk Angela to her car, and Tracy promised to check in with their sister later.

Sam sent them both a text when she was back in the SUV. *Let's have a WH sleepover next weekend. I think we could all use the time together. What say you?*

Tracy replied first. *We're in!*

God yes, Angela said. *The kids will be so excited.*

Excellent. Celia will be back by then, too. She wouldn't want to miss it.

Perfect, Tracy said.

Having the plan for quality time with her sisters and their families made Sam feel better. She hoped it did the same for them. Sometimes it was hard to believe the way life went marching forward after losing their dad and then Spencer. Skip, who used to remind them that their closest friends in the world were the people in their own home, would tell them to stick together and soldier on, so that's what they would do. As long as they had one another, they would find the way forward.

CHAPTER THIRTY-FOUR

S am spent the next two days picking apart every detail of the plan for Sunday, looking for gaps that might invite disaster but not finding any. The plan was airtight and ready for execution.

She spent two hours in the conference room with Vernon, Jimmy and four other Secret Service agents who'd be brought in to supplement her detail on Sunday.

"The main thing I need is for you to be out of sight," Sam told them. "If Peckham senses Secret Service, he'll know he's walking into a trap."

"No one will know we're there," Vernon assured her.

Cox's firing had bumped every other story out of the headlines, even the search for Tom Forrester's killer.

Terry had heard through the grapevine that Cox's wife, upon hearing the news of her husband's firing, had transferred all their available assets to a new account in her name only and had filed for divorce.

His downfall—and that of his weasel nephew Allston—gave Sam tremendous satisfaction.

With every day that passed without any word about Juan, Nick became more despondent over the fate of the man who'd been such a loyal aide. On the advice of the agencies searching for him, they'd managed to keep his disappearance out of the media, but word would get out soon enough.

Before she left work on Friday, she checked in personally with every member of the team to make sure they were set to meet at HQ at zero seven hundred on Sunday morning, that they understood the clothing requirements as well as their roles in the operation.

Officer Neveah Charles, the newest member of Sam's squad, would be with Cori throughout. She would meet Cori at her home at nine fifteen on Sunday morning, and then ride to church with her, sit with her and accompany her outside after.

Sam asked Neveah to come into the office as her last order of business for the day on Friday before going to Ninth Street for the dreaded meeting with Nick's mother. She couldn't think about that yet.

"You wanted to see me, LT?" Charles asked from the doorway.

She had flawless brown skin, expressive dark eyes and long hair that she wore in a tidy bun. She'd impressed the hell out of Sam with her attention to detail when planning Skip's police funeral, and Sam was thrilled to now have Neveah on her team.

"Why didn't you choose modeling rather than something stupid like police work?"

Neveah laughed as she came in and shut the door.

"If I looked like you, I'd be modeling rather than dodging bullets."

"Thank you. I think. My family would much prefer I'd chosen something safer." She'd recently shared how she'd witnessed her mother's murder and how that had made her want to be a police officer.

"I'll bet."

"But what fun would that be?"

"That's why I like you so much. You think this job is fun. You're weird like me."

"That might be the best compliment I've ever received."

"I thought we'd talked about the sucking up."

"I wasn't sucking up. I meant it."

Sam rolled her eyes. "I suppose I ought to enjoy you while

you're sweet and innocent. Cruz was like that until he spent years working with me. Now he's ruined."

"I look forward to being ruined by you."

"Let's talk about Sunday. How're you feeling about your assignment?"

"I feel good about it. I spoke to Judge Sawyer earlier, and I'm set to walk down the sidewalk to her home at nine fifteen, as if I'm a neighbor going to church with her."

"Did she tell you to call her Cori?"

"She did."

"You should do that when you're with her."

"I will."

"This could be dangerous."

"I'm aware."

"This is one of those times when I hate my raised profile, because I'd want to do this myself. It's difficult to ask something of one of my teammates that I can't do myself."

"I understand, and I want to do this. We'll be surrounded by top-rate security the whole time. I trust them."

"I do, too, or I'd never let you do this. That said, if anything happens to you, I'll be mad at you forever."

Charles laughed. "I'd spend all of eternity trying to get back in your good graces."

"I know, which is why you can't let anything happen."

"I won't. I promise."

Since she couldn't ask for anything more than that, she nodded. "Be safe."

"You, too."

After Charles left, Cruz came to the door. "I'm going to punch out until Sunday."

"Have a good weekend."

"Are you okay about this thing with Nick's mother?"

"I'll be glad when it's done."

"Let me know how it goes?"

"I will." She could tell he was hesitant to leave. "We'll be fine. Don't worry."

"Make sure she doesn't hurt my best friends, you hear me?"

"I do, and I will."

"Okay, then. Text me later."

Sam nodded and sent him off with a smile. It was so sweet of him to worry about them, but Nicoletta had given everyone in their lives ample reason for worry with the way she'd treated Nick his entire life. The thought of having to sit down and make nice with that woman was revolting to Sam.

But she would do it because Nick wanted to hear what his mother had to say.

The BlackBerry buzzed with a text. *Still on for 5?*

I'll be there.

Thanks for this. I owe you big.

SO BIG.

HAHAHA. I'll make it up to you.

Yes, you will, and I'll look forward to that.

Me, too.

Reminder: If she's a dick to you, we're leaving.

Yes, dear.

He hadn't slept for shit the night before, tossing and turning over his worries about Juan and in anticipation of this appointment. Sam deeply resented her mother-in-law for that and so many other things. No matter what happened today, Sam would never stop resenting her for all the pain she'd caused Nick in the past. Some things couldn't be forgiven, even if he chose to do so. Sam never would.

Resigned to having to get through this dreaded meeting, she texted Vernon to tell him she was on the way out, gathered her belongings and headed for the morgue exit. As she went past the glass doors to the morgue, a flash of red ponytail caught her eye.

Sam stepped through the automatic doors. "What the heck are you doing here, Doc?"

Lindsey turned to her, still looking paler than usual, but not as much as she had a few days ago. "I'm feeling way better, and I came in to help with the paperwork on the Stahl case. Byron and the others need all the help they can get."

"Are you sure it's not too soon?"

"I'm sure. I saw Gonzo earlier, and he updated me on the Forrester case. You feeling okay about the plan?"

"I'll feel much better about it when it's successfully executed."

"I'm sure."

"It's hard for me to put my people at risk while I sit in the comfort of the comms truck."

"If the suspect saw you, the jig would be up."

"I hate that, too."

"It is what it is, but I get why it's hard for you."

"At times like this, I wonder if I should hang it up here."

"What? No way!"

"What kind of commander sends her troops into battle while she's safely out of the line of fire?"

"The best kind of commander. Any one of them would rather work with you despite the limitations than anyone else. If you don't believe me, ask them."

"Anyway, didn't mean to make this about me. But while we're on the subject of me, don't do that passing-out thing again, you hear me? Scared the shit out of me."

Lindsey smiled. "I hear you, and I'll try not to. Terry said much the same thing."

"He's been doing okay?"

"He's been amazing. He waited on me hand and foot for days and never left my side. He's doubled up on AA meetings, which helps at stressful times."

"Glad to hear it. I've, uh, got to go meet Nick at Ninth Street for a meeting with his mother."

Lindsey's shock registered in every corner of her expressive face. "No."

"Unfortunately, yes."

"Wow."

"Right?"

"I'll expect a full report."

"I hope it's a brief report."

"Go with God."

Sam laughed. "I will, thanks. Good to see you back where you belong, my friend."

"Good to be here."

After leaving the morgue, she pushed open the door and stepped into a brisk early April breeze.

Vernon stood by the SUV, waiting for her.

"Sorry for the delay. I stopped to say hi to Dr. McNamara."

"Glad to hear she's back."

"It was nice to see her."

"Are we still headed to Ninth Street?"

"Yes, please."

Sam sat back with her head against the seat, trying to calm her mind and prepare to give whatever Nick needed at this meeting from hell. Most of all, she reminded herself she couldn't whip out her rusty steak knife and stab the woman through the heart, no matter how much she deserved it or how much Sam wanted to.

"Everything okay?" Vernon asked.

"It will be after this thing at Ninth."

"I heard at our briefing earlier why you're going, and I was surprised."

"The things we do for those we love."

"Indeed."

"And yes, I tried to talk him out of it, but hope springs eternal for him where she's concerned."

"Strange how that works, huh?"

"Very. If I had my way…"

"Don't do anything that'll cause more paperwork for all of us."

Sam laughed. "That's another thing my dad would've said, and I needed that right now. So thanks."

"I do what I can for the people."

"That is trademarked!"

His smile lit up his eyes as he looked at her in the mirror.

Sam was filled with emotion as they took the familiar streets to home. She'd lived in the Capitol Hill neighborhood for her entire life until they moved to the White House. As they turned onto Ninth Street, the line of Secret Service vehicles already parked on the street indicated that Nick had arrived first.

Her heart gave a happy leap at knowing she'd see him in a minute or two. That happy leap almost canceled out her anxiety about what might transpire with his mother.

Vernon held the door for her.

"Thank you for everything."

"My pleasure."

Sam smiled and squeezed his arm before leaving him to head into the place where they'd become a family. She glanced to her right, at the house three doors down that had been her dad's home. The house was dark now, but the ramps in front of both homes were a reminder of what'd been lost. They should probably have them removed at some point, but that wasn't something she wanted to think about today.

Brant opened the door to admit her.

"Evening, Brant."

"Evening, Mrs. Cappuano."

Nick came out of the kitchen, holding a glass containing amber-colored liquid. "We left the good bourbon Graham gave me last year."

"Thankfully, bourbon keeps."

"Indeed, because I needed a drink before this. You?"

Sam followed him into the kitchen, which sealed them off from the room full of agents. "I wouldn't say no to that. What else is there?"

"I saw some vodka and gin." He put his drink on the counter and turned to her. "But first things first." With his hands framing her face, he kissed her. "Hi."

"Hi there." She hated how exhausted he looked and hoped he'd feel better when this nasty detail had been seen to. That might be too much to hope for, however, with Juan still missing.

"Thanks for coming."

"No problem."

He laughed. "Don't lie to my face."

"I love your face. That's why I'm here."

He ran his hands over her, as if looking for something. "No rusty steak knives?"

"What do you take me for?"

"I take you for my fierce, fabulous, sexy wife who'd happily stab my mother through the heart to protect me."

"I'd go for the eye. It would upset her more to be ugly than dead."

He tossed his head back and laughed as hard as he had in a while. "My God, I love you."

Sam wrapped her arms around him and held on tight. "I love you more, and you have the T-shirt to prove it."

"I'd never be able to do any of this shit without you. I hope you know that."

"I do, and likewise, my love. This makes all things possible."

"Yes, it does."

"Promise me we'll get up and leave if this is all about the usual bullshit."

"Give me a signal."

"If I squeeze your hand three times, we're out."

"That means I get to hold your hand the whole time."

"Duh."

"Derek did some digging on Collins, but couldn't find anything that might tell us what this meeting is about."

"Freddie did, too, with the same result."

"I hate going into something like this blind."

"You're not blind. You know exactly who and what you're dealing with when it comes to her."

"True." He kissed her again and leaned his forehead on hers. "I know you think I'm crazy for taking this meeting—"

She kissed him. "I get it. I don't like it. But I get it. Now, about that drink..."

"Coming right up."

He poured her a vodka and soda that was heavy on the vodka and light on the small bottle of soda water he found in the cabinet. "I'm sorry to say this bar has no fresh fruit to top off your cocktail."

"That's okay." She took a sip of the drink and felt the alcohol warm her from the inside. "It's so weird to be here."

"I know. We've been gone just long enough that it doesn't feel as much like home anymore."

"Remember when we said the White House would never be home?"

"Funny how that happens, huh?"

"It's the people with us who make it home."

"I saw the kids after school. I told them we'd be home for dinner."

"Something to look forward to."

A soft knock on the door sounded. "Mr. President, your guests have arrived," Brant said.

Nick pulled back from her. "Here we go. You ready?"

"Ready as I'll ever be."

"Let's get this over with." He took her hand and led her out of the kitchen, both with drinks in hand.

Nicoletta stood next to a tall, distinguished man with silver hair and a tanned face. He wore a sharp suit and reminded Sam of the actor Robert Wagner.

Her mother-in-law looked stunning, as usual, which was just another reason to dislike her. Nick had told her that she loved being compared to Sophia Loren. Whatever.

The agents, who'd already vetted the guests, made themselves scarce.

"Th-this is Collins Worthy. Collins, my son, Nick, and his wife, Sam."

Collins smiled as he extended his hand to Nick. "Mr. President, it's an honor to meet you."

"My name is Nick here."

Sam wished she could give him a high five for shutting down the Mr. President bullshit from the get-go.

"Of course." He shook hands with Sam. "Pleasure to meet you as well."

Nick gestured to the sofas. "Have a seat."

Nicoletta and Collins sat on the sofa that faced the one Sam and Nick settled on.

Sam liked that Nick didn't offer them anything. After all, this wasn't a social call.

"You asked for this meeting," Nick said. "What can we do for you?"

CHAPTER THIRTY-FIVE

His hand had gotten very warm, which was the only reaction Nick showed to seeing his mother for the first time in a while, but only Sam would know that. He appeared outwardly cool, collected and unaffected.

Hey, that rhymes, she thought, forcing herself to suppress a giggle that would be highly inappropriate under the circumstances.

Collins glanced at Nicoletta and gave her an encouraging smile that had Sam wondering about the true nature of their relationship.

"Thank you for seeing me," Nicoletta said.

Nick gave a slight nod.

Sam was so proud of him for not making this easy on her.

"I... I asked for this meeting because I wanted the chance to speak to you, to apologize for my past behavior and... Well, I'd like for us to have some sort of relationship."

All eyes were on Nick, who had no reaction for a full minute.

"What, exactly, are you apologizing for?"

Sam was stunned that Nicoletta seemed genuinely remorseful, but she remained skeptical. A tiger like her didn't just change her stripes after a few days in lockup.

"I, uh, haven't been the mother you deserved. I've been selfish and self-absorbed, and I've disappointed you too many times to count. I deeply regret my actions, and I wish to have the opportunity to do better in the future. I'd like to know you..." She seemed to force herself to include Sam. "Both of you and your children."

"Why?" Sam asked.

In a flash that lasted less than a second, Sam saw how the woman really felt about her.

Nicoletta quickly caught herself and forced a smile, but not fast enough.

"It doesn't matter why," Nick said. "I saw the way you just looked at my wife, even though you tried to hide it. That tells me none of this is genuine. It's more of your games."

"It's not! I swear I mean every word I've said. I... I know she hates me."

Nick frowned. "*She* has a name."

"I know that *Sam* hates me."

"With good reason," Nick said. "She's had a front-row seat to how you've treated me. She sat with me when I listened in shock to your TV interview full of lies about me, when you acted like we were the best of friends rather than strangers who've never had any relationship. She was there when you showed up uninvited to our wedding, knowing it would upset me to have you there but not caring in the least about me on the biggest day of my life, which was nothing new. Sam truly loves me, so yes, she hates the way you treat me. Can you blame her?"

Sam wanted to stand up and cheer for her man. Since she couldn't do that, she gave his hand one big squeeze.

Nicoletta looked down at her hands, which were folded on her lap. "No, I don't blame her. I deserve it."

"You haven't said what caused this sudden moment of self-reflection."

"If I may..." Collins said. "Nicoletta's recent troubles have resulted in her wanting to make some changes in her life, beginning with fixing her strained relationship with you."

"And what role have you played in that?" Sam asked.

"I'm a widower with three grown children who are my closest friends. Two of them work for my firm, and the other has given me two precious grandchildren. In the weeks since we first met, Nicoletta has gotten to witness my warm relationships with my children, and they have her longing for the same with you."

"I don't believe she has it in her," Nick said bluntly.

"I... I want to try," Nicoletta said softly. "I want that so badly."

"Do you know what I've wanted so badly for thirty-eight years? A mother like my friends had. I wanted someone I could count on to be there for me when I needed her, to come to my school events, my hockey games and my graduations, and to act like she gave a shit about me. You've never once done that. Rather, you've done everything you could to hurt me, including taking money for interviews where you spread your bullshit about me at a time when everyone else who cares about me was rallying around me. So you'll have to excuse me if I'm not buying this act of contrition. I'm the president of the United States of America, and frankly, Mother, I don't need your bullshit in my life."

"I know you're the president! I'm so proud. I couldn't be prouder if I tried."

"But now you're suddenly interested in a relationship with me?" He shook his head. "You want what you've always wanted—attention—and you think if you're reunited with me, there'll be happy visits to your grandchildren at the White House and the chance to tell everyone you know that you slept in the Lincoln Bedroom." He leaned in, looking as fierce as Sam had ever seen him. "Let me be crystal clear with you. That is *never* going to happen. Do you think I'd subject my precious children to the same treatment I received when you get bored with this new version of yourself and revert to your old ways?"

"That won't happen," she said on a soft sob.

"Yes, it will, and when it does, my family won't be anywhere near it. I appreciate the apology and that you genuinely believe you've changed, but I'm not buying what you're selling. I'm sorry, but this meeting is over."

He released Sam's hand to walk to the front door, where he summoned an agent with a single knock. "Our guests are leaving, Eric."

"Yes, sir, Mr. President."

He returned to Sam and put his arm around her.

"So that's it?" Nicoletta asked, looking devastated as tears rolled down her face. "Just no?"

"That's it," he said. "Just no."

Nicoletta gave Sam a look that would've killed her if looks alone could do the job. "This is because of *you*. You told him what to say."

"I didn't have to tell him anything."

Collins put an arm around Nicoletta. "Let's go, Nicoletta. You've said what you came to say."

"But he was supposed to be happy to hear it!"

"I'm sorry to disappoint you." Nick glanced at Eric, who'd see them out. "You can show them out, Eric."

Sam held her breath, halfway expecting Nicoletta to do something dramatic that might get her thrown back in jail, but she let Collins help her into her coat and guide her out of the house.

The second the door closed behind them, Sam threw her arms around her husband. "I've never been prouder of you—or more turned on by you—than I am right now."

He laughed and held her tightly. "I gotta say, it felt pretty damned good to give her a taste of her own medicine."

"You were on *fire*."

He took a deep breath and released it. "I'm so glad that's over and done with."

"I thought you were going to give her a shot."

"I was, but you know what changed my mind?"

Sam pulled back to look up at him. "What?"

"The way she looked at you. It was one second of complete disgust, but that was all I needed to know she hasn't changed one bit if she still thinks you're the problem."

"I caught that, too."

"Anyone who looks at my wife that way can go straight to hell."

Sam shivered. "So sexy." She took his hand and led him to the stairs.

"Where're you taking me?"

"Since you sent her straight to hell, I'm taking you straight to bed."

"If you insist."

"I do. I absolutely insist."

NICK FOLLOWED her up the stairs, relieved to have the meeting with his mother out of the way. He'd been dreading it for days, fearing how he might collapse like a house of cards in her presence, the way he would have at almost any other point in his life.

But being loved by his Samantha, their children and an extended group of family and friends had given him strength he hadn't had before he had a family of his own. He didn't need Nicoletta anymore, and realizing that was so freeing.

As he let Sam tug him along to their bedroom, he was once again so thankful for her and everything she'd brought to his life.

He kicked the door closed behind him. "We're supposed to be home for dinner."

She pushed his suit coat off his shoulders. "We will be. It only took you twenty minutes to show her the door. They'd allocated an hour in the schedule, so we've got forty free minutes."

"We can get a lot done in forty minutes."

"You know it." She pulled off his tie and unbuttoned his dress shirt before going to work on his cuff links.

"Don't lose them. I have to go home looking presentable."

"I won't lose them."

With her uninjured hand, she tugged at his belt and had him down to his boxer briefs in a matter of seconds. Not bad for one good hand.

"Let me catch up."

"Hurry."

He removed her sweater and bra and then her pants while she kicked off the shoe boots that had made her two inches taller than usual. With his arms around her, he brought her in tight against him, her breasts flat against his chest.

As he kissed her neck and made her sigh, he said, "It's because of you, you know."

"What is?"

"That I was able to send her packing. I don't need her anymore because I have you and our kids and our family and so many people who care about me. But it's mostly because of you, because I know that no matter what, I'll always have you and this."

"Yes, you will, and we love you more than anything in this world."

"I'd never had that before you. I mean, Graham and Laine... They were the best, and they did what they could to fill the void, but they weren't really mine. They were on loan to me through John."

"They love you."

"And I love them, but it's different having my own people. I didn't know that until I had you, my very own person to love who loved me right back. That's what made all the difference."

"You've shown me how much is possible, things I never dreamed for myself."

"Same, babe." He guided her onto the bed and came down on top of her, gazing into her gorgeous blue eyes. "I believe I promised you a reward for sitting through that encounter."

"Yes, you did."

After placing her arms over her head, he set out to kiss every inch of soft skin he could reach, which drove her wild.

He liked her this way, uninhibited, untroubled—for the moment, anyway—with her attention undivided and focused exclusively on him. How lucky was he to have a woman like her love him the way she did?

The luckiest, and he set out to show her that with his lips, tongue and teeth, until she was all but begging him to give her more.

Not until she'd given him what he wanted, which was at least one orgasm.

He propped her right leg on his shoulder and gave her his

tongue and fingers, the combination always working quickly to take her right over the edge.

This time was no different.

She gasped and thrashed and let loose with whispered words of love that went straight to his heart.

"Nick... Please."

He was happy to give her anything she wanted, pushing into her in one deep thrust that had her biting her lip to keep from screaming. They were always aware of their agents nearby, which was a drag at times like this.

Her fingers dug into his back as her legs encircled his waist.

This was the best thing in life. She and their kids were the best thing in his life.

She looked up at him with big blue eyes. "You took over my seduction."

"I'm seduced the minute you walk into the room."

"So easy."

He smiled as he kissed her. "Where you're concerned."

"I like you that way."

"I like you all the ways."

"Nice how that works out, huh?"

"Mmmm, so nice. Don't stop."

"I won't. Don't worry."

NICOLETTA WAS DEVASTATED AND INFURIATED. If only that bitch hadn't been there, she might've had a chance at persuading her son to give her another chance.

She hated that woman's guts and couldn't imagine what her gorgeous son saw in her.

Her heart ached over how close she'd come to having him back in her life.

Collins kept an arm around her in the car on the way back to the Four Seasons, where he'd booked an opulent suite for their stay in DC.

She'd held out a secret hope that they might relocate to the White House after the meeting, but that's not what'd happened.

And it was all *her* fault.

"I'm sorry you had to witness that. My daughter-in-law has it in for me."

"She only asked a one-word question, so I didn't notice her having it in for you."

"You don't know her like I do."

His deep sigh sent a shiver of fear down her spine. What if he was so disgusted by what he'd just seen that he cut ties with her? What would she do then? Other than one last small nest egg stashed in the Caymans, she had no resources left and no way to make a living after her recent incarceration.

Over the last couple of weeks, she'd begun to rely on Collins to fix things for her. Would he still be willing to do that after witnessing such ugliness with her son and his wife? It'd been a mistake to let him come with her. She knew that now.

Her son had changed. In the past, he would've lapped up whatever attention she tossed his way, but the power had clearly gone to his head if he thought he could talk to his mother the way he had. Who did he think he was, anyway?

Back at the hotel, they walked to the elevators in silence that further unnerved her. What was Collins thinking? Was he done with her now that she'd failed to ingratiate herself with her son, the president? Since he'd taken such an intense interest in her, she'd wondered if it was really about access to power. Without that, would he still care about what happened to her?

She didn't know, which made her feel panicky.

Inside their deluxe rooms, he removed his suit coat and tie and rolled up the sleeves of his dress shirt. He was the most devastatingly handsome man she'd ever met and held the distinction of being the only man she'd ever truly been attracted to.

So far, he'd been a perfect gentleman with her, going so far as to book a suite with two bedrooms. Nicoletta wished he would stop being so polite.

He poured drinks and brought them to the sofa where she'd settled.

"Thank you," she said, taking the wine glass from him. "What're you thinking?"

"I'm sorry things didn't work out as you'd hoped."

Nicoletta gave a harsh chuckle. "I never stood a chance with that woman in the room."

"It wasn't her fault, Nicoletta."

"She's poisoned him against me."

"No, my dear, you did that all on your own."

She stared at him with shock and distress. "I thought you were on my side."

"I was. I mean, I am. But I need you to understand that what just happened with your son and his wife was because of *you*, not her or him or anyone else but you."

Nicoletta looked away from him, feeling ashamed, furious and scared. What would she do if he walked away from her, too? "Fine. It's all my fault. Is that what you want to hear?"

"It's a good start toward making real changes."

"I have made real changes."

"Not yet, but you still can if you really want to."

"I do! I told you that."

"And I want to believe you, but at the first word out of your daughter-in-law's mouth, you reverted to your old ways and ruined your chances with your son."

"I didn't mean to do that. She gets to me."

"Because she *sees* you for what you really are, which is why you resent her."

"Wow, so now you're taking her side?" Why did she even care what he thought, anyway? She hadn't known him a month ago.

"I'm on your side. I want you to get what you want, to have a relationship with your son and grandchildren, but there's no way that's happening without her involvement. I thought you understood that."

"I do!"

"It didn't seem that way to me—or them."

"So what are you saying?"

"If you want to make this work, if you really want it, you have to fix things with *her* before you'll ever get a chance to fix things with him."

"And then pigs flew in hell."

"You'll never know if you don't try."

"What is in this for you? Why are you pushing me so hard on this?"

"Because you told me you want your son in your life. I'm telling you how to make that happen."

"She hates my guts. She'll never have anything to do with me."

"All you can do is try, Nicoletta. Show her you mean it when you say you want to be different. If you can win her over, you'll have him back in your life. And his children."

She didn't have the strength to argue, so she told him what he seemed to want to hear. "You're right. Thank you for coming and for everything you did to support me."

"I was happy to do that."

"I understand if you've seen enough at this point."

"Seen enough of what?"

"Who I really am, what my life has been like."

"Did you think that would make me not want to be with you?"

"Yeah, kind of. I mean, it's not a very pretty picture."

He gazed at her longingly before tucking a strand of her hair behind her ear. "I've seen you—the good, the bad, the ugly—and for some reason, I still want you in my life, in my bed, in my heart."

Oh Lord, the man was going to make her swoon!

"Why?"

"God only knows, my darling, but I can't help but want you with every fiber of my being."

Nicoletta leaned in, drawn to him like she'd never been to anyone, ever.

He met her halfway, his lips connecting with hers, sending a shock through her system. "Is there any chance you might want me, too?"

"*Yes*, I want you." Despite the insane attraction, she still feared his motives. "But I need to know something, and you have to tell me the truth."

"Of course."

"Are you with me because my son is the president?"

His expression reflected pure shock. "No, Nicoletta. That's not why I'm with you."

"I'm afraid it doesn't make any sense to me after what you just witnessed, that you'd still want me..."

"I can't help but want you. From the first second I laid eyes on you, I knew you were going to change everything for me."

"I was in an orange jumpsuit with no makeup."

"Orange never looked so good to me."

"You're crazy," she said, laughing.

"About you." He linked their fingers. "I know today was terribly disappointing for you, but I hope you know you have me and my family and the chance for a whole new life, if that's what you want."

"It is, but only because that new life would be with you."

"Perhaps if your son and his wife see you living your best life, they might one day want to be part of it."

"Perhaps."

He stood and gave her hand a gentle tug to bring her to her feet. "What do you say we get busy living that best life?"

"Right now?" she asked with a coy smile.

"Right this very second."

CHAPTER THIRTY-SIX

"Did we break our own record?" Sam asked Nick when they were in The Beast on the way back to the White House.

"I think we might've. Twice in forty minutes is impressive, even for us."

Sam had forgone a seat belt so she could snuggle up to him. "Which of the agents is most likely to write a tell-all book about the horniest first couple in history?"

His low grumble of laughter made her smile. "I'd put my money on Brant. It's always the quiet ones."

"Nah, he'd never do that to you."

Nick's secure BlackBerry rang with a call. "Gotta take this."

Sam sat up so he could retrieve the phone from his pocket. "It's Terry. Hey, what's up?"

Nick put his arm around her, bringing her back to rest on him where she could hear the other half of the conversation.

"I heard you were on the way back. How'd it go?"

"It was fine. She wanted to make amends. I said, 'No, thanks.'"

"Good for you."

"Felt good. Anything new on Juan?"

"I just had a briefing with the FBI, the U.S. Marshals and NCIS. They're chasing a number of leads, but so far nothing has panned out."

Nick sighed. "I was so hoping for good news."

"I know. Me, too. I'll keep you posted."

"Anything new with Cox?"

"Not that I've heard, but we're keeping ears to the ground."

"Thanks, Terry. Talk to you later."

"I'm sorry, Nick," Sam said. "I know it's so upsetting to not have any progress in the search for Juan."

"I swear to God, if one of the ex-joint chiefs did him in, I might kill them with my own hands."

"No, you won't, but you'll want to."

"He's not going to be found alive, is he?"

Sam hesitated between telling him the truth and telling him what he wanted to hear.

"It's okay. I can handle it."

"Probably not at this point. If someone was holding him, they would've made demands by now."

"Yeah," he said on a deep breath. "I suppose so."

"What'd Terry say about Cox? I couldn't hear that part."

"That they're keeping their eyes and ears open. I don't expect him to go quietly."

"He might. His deepest shame has been revealed to all the world, and he's lost everything in a matter of hours."

"He'll blame us for that, even though he did it to himself."

"Just like Ruskin," Sam said of Nelson's now-disgraced secretary of State. "He can say what he wants, but the truth is on our side."

"I'm worried about what else I don't know about Nelson's remaining people. This is two now who've disappointed me profoundly."

"You can't lump the others in with them. Everyone should be presumed innocent until they show you otherwise."

"Are those more of Skip Holland's words of wisdom?"

"You know it. He used to tell us to give people the benefit of the doubt until they gave you a reason not to trust them."

"It's good advice."

"That said, if you get a gut feeling about any of them, you should trust that instinct."

"I wish I had your instincts about people."

"Mine are calibrated by up-close-and-personal interactions with criminals."

"Which is why you know one when you see one."

"Most of the time."

As they approached the gates to the White House, Sam's phone chimed with a text from Freddie. *Wondering how it went.*

All good. Will update you when I see you, but basically Nick told her to F off.

YES!

Tell me how you really feel!

Just did. He's ok?

Yeah, he is.

That's good. Glad to hear it. See you Sunday AM.

See you then and thanks for checking in.

"That was Freddie making sure you're okay after seeing what's-her-name."

"Nice of him to ask."

"A lot of people were upset about us seeing her."

"I know."

"They'll be proud of how you handled it like Freddie was."

"That's nice to hear."

"It's true. We all know how tough this has been on you, and to see you take control of the situation was amazing."

"I'm glad you thought so."

"You sound a little flat. Are you having regrets?"

"Nope. I'm thinking about Juan."

Since there was nothing she could say to that, she simply took hold of his hand and held on until they were inside and handing their coats to Harold.

"Thank you, Harold."

"My pleasure, Mr. President."

Nick took her hand again for the walk upstairs to the residence. "Follow the noise."

Sam laughed, already feeling lighter now that they were home with their kids. "I was about to say the same thing."

They went up to the third-floor conservatory, where the twins and Scotty were playing Twister, overseen by Sam's mom.

Alden saw them first, let out a scream and collapsed the other two when he rolled out from under them.

Aubrey landed on top of Scotty, giggling as he let out a loud *oof*.

She got up and ran to greet them.

Nick scooped up the twins and kissed their faces as they shrieked with delight.

Scotty came to hug Sam. "They're bonkers tonight."

"Who made them that way?" Brenda asked, giving Scotty a pat on the head.

Scotty flashed a sheepish grin. "I may or may not have riled them up."

"Then you can deal with them at bedtime," Nick said.

"No way. My job is after-school entertainment. Bedtime is all you, Pops."

Sam, who was pleasantly surprised by how nice it felt to come home to her mother after a long day, kept an arm around Scotty. "He's going to be our lawyer."

"I have no doubt."

"Don't talk about me, ladies. I can hear you."

"Who's ready for dinner?" Nick asked.

A loud chorus of "me" had him sending them downstairs to wash up.

"Can you join us, Brenda?" Nick asked. "Sometimes Celia begs off in favor of peace and quiet in her suite after an afternoon on duty."

Brenda laughed. "I don't blame her, but I'd love to if you're sure you don't mind."

"We'd love to have you," Sam said.

"How'd it go just now?" Brenda asked.

"Really well. Nick told her to get lost. It was hot as you-know-what."

Nick sputtered. "Samantha! That's your mother."

"She can handle it."

"I love when he calls you Samantha. No one gets away with that."

"I know, right? Hot AF."

"I'm outta here." Nick spun around and went downstairs, leaving them laughing.

"He's all right?"

"Remarkably so."

"That's good. I've heard from your sisters how it goes when he sees her."

"You should've heard that from me. I'm sorry you didn't. And I want you to know that when I came home to you just now, I liked it. Felt like old times."

Brenda hugged her. "For me, too. Thank you for asking me to fill in for Celia."

"You should come help her when she gets back. There's plenty of chaos to go around."

"I'd love that."

"Then we'll make it happen."

SUNDAY DAWNED cool and cloudy with rain in the forecast for the afternoon. Sam hoped it held off until they'd pulled off a successful mission and had Peckham in custody. It was still dark when she stepped outside to go to work at six fifteen.

Vernon had insisted on coming in to drive her, accompanied by Agent Quigley, the one who was so young he still had acne. Jimmy was away for the weekend with his wife, attending his nephew's second birthday party in Harrisburg, Pennsylvania.

Sam and Vernon would be riding in the Emergency Response truck while Quigley followed in the SUV.

"You told him to park a few blocks away, right?" Sam asked Vernon as he held the car door for her at HQ.

"He knows exactly where to leave the vehicle and where he needs to be while this is going down. We'll have eyes on you, but you won't see us."

"Thank you, Vernon. I know this is a stretch for you guys, but I won't be anywhere near the front lines."

"And for that, I'm thankful. Best of luck with everything today."

"Appreciate it. We need all the luck we can get."

"I have no doubt you've planned this down to the last second, and it'll execute as flawlessly as it was planned."

"You're good for my ego."

"I do what I can—"

"Trademarked!"

She left him laughing as she went into the building, passing the morgue, which was dark at that hour. The ME staff would be in later, as they'd been working seven days a week to identify the bodies coming from Stahl's house of horrors.

By seven ten, the full team had gathered in the conference room, most of them with coffee and breakfast in hand.

Sam wouldn't be able to eat anything until this was done.

They went through the entire plan, point by point, one last time.

Standing at the head of the conference table, she scanned the room. "Questions?"

Seeing none, she glanced at Ruiz. "Let's get everyone wired and ready to roll."

"Yes, ma'am," Ruiz said in a condescending tone.

Sam ignored her. She had no time for manufactured drama when people's lives were at stake. "Thank you, everyone."

Malone followed Sam into her office and closed the door.

"What's the deal with Ruiz?" Sam asked. "Does she really have time to be passive-aggressive today?"

"Captains don't like taking orders from lieutenants."

"That wasn't an order for her. It was an order for everyone else."

"I know that."

"It's disappointing when other women on the job act like that. Like we don't have enough to deal with fending off the misogyny?"

"I hear you." He sat in front of the desk and took a sip from a tall coffee. "Are you still feeling good about the plan?"

"Hell no. I've never felt good about it, but I haven't heard a better idea."

"There hasn't been a single sighting of Peckham since his

campsite was found, even with our people and multiple other agencies searching for him."

"He knows how to stay off the radar."

A knock sounded at the door.

"Enter."

The chief stuck his head in. "Safe to come into the hornet's nest?"

"The queen hornet is perturbed."

Farnsworth came in and shut the door. "Over what now?"

"Captain Ruiz doesn't do teamwork when she's not the one calling the shots."

"Ah, I see. Well, you're in charge of this operation, so hopefully she's giving you what you need."

"Yes, and she's *thrilled* about it."

"Are we all systems go?"

"Yes, sir."

"Then I'll leave you to it and hope for the best possible outcome."

"You and me both."

At eight thirty, Sam was the last one to be wired in the conference room, with an earpiece that would allow her to monitor the activity of the entire team.

"Thank you," she said to Ruiz.

"You're welcome."

Sam and Vernon followed Ruiz to the Emergency Response vehicle parked outside the main entrance. It looked like a cross between a bus and an oversized fire truck, emblazoned with the MPD logo, which gave her pause.

"This can't be anywhere near the church," she said.

Ruiz glanced back over her shoulder. "No kidding."

"What's your problem?"

"I have no problems."

"You could've fooled me."

"I know you're used to being the boss of everything, but in this truck, you're under my command."

Sam laughed, which resulted in a nasty scowl from the other woman. "Whatever you say, Captain."

"That's right, Lieutenant. Whatever I say."

She glanced at Vernon, caught him trying not to laugh and rolled her eyes. "Glad we got that worked out before people's lives were in danger. Phew, what a relief."

Ruiz gave her a filthy look and went to the other end of the vehicle.

"What the hell?" Sam asked Vernon as they took seats on one of the benches behind the row of computer terminals where members of Ruiz's team were positioned.

"She hates you cuz she ain't you."

One of the guys sitting behind a computer turned to them. "That's the truth. She wishes she had your swagger."

Sam never knew what to say to that. "All I care about is making sure this goes off without a hitch. The rest is just a distraction."

"Agreed."

The officer's one-word reply confirmed what she'd heard about the people on Ruiz's team not liking her any more than Sam did.

"Why do people have to be so extra?" she asked Vernon quietly so she wouldn't be overheard.

"Is that a rhetorical question?"

"I guess so."

On the drive toward the church neighborhood, Sam received a text from Detective Charles that she was on her way to Sawyer's home to meet up before church.

Sam's entire system went haywire with out-of-control nerves.

This was a terrible idea.

She should call it off before someone was killed. Perhaps more than one person.

What had she been thinking to suggest they use a federal judge to lure a killer? "We shouldn't do this," she whispered to Vernon as a feeling of panic overtook her.

"It's too late to turn back now, Sam. Take a deep breath."

More than anything, she wanted to go back in time a few days and stop this before it ever got started. Cori should've told her no, no way would she be used as bait to catch a murdering scumbag.

Sam tucked trembling hands between her legs while focusing on breathing.

"When I'm out there in the middle of it, I never get nervous like this."

"Because you can help to control the outcome out there. In here, you're a bystander."

"I'm watching people I command and care about put their lives on the line while I'm safely ensconced. That doesn't feel right to me."

"It's how it has to be."

"Yeah, I know." That didn't help her to feel less guilty about asking her team to take risks that she couldn't take right along with them.

Sam's earpiece crackled to life. "Sawyer and Charles leaving for church with Sawyer driving her Lincoln Navigator."

"Here we go."

CHAPTER THIRTY-SEVEN

T he mission went off flawlessly, with every member of the team playing their role with perfection. From the time Cori and Neveah arrived at church, through the service, to the aftermath outside, where they'd hoped Peckham would make his appearance, every detail went off as planned.

Except for the fact that Harlan Peckham never showed up.

While Sam was thrilled that everyone was safe, she was crushed that the plan hadn't worked as she'd hoped.

With Sawyer and Charles safely back at the Sawyer home, Sam and Vernon got out of the Emergency Response vehicle and into the SUV driven by Quigley for the return to HQ.

As Sam stared out the window, watching the city go by, she was filled with despair. All that time and effort expended for nothing.

What now?

There were so many other opportunities for Peckham to take out Judge Sawyer in the course of an average week, but nothing as easy as this would've been. She'd been ripe for the picking, so why hadn't he come?

Sam had been so certain he would.

They were stopped at a red light when a figure on the street caught her attention. From behind, the man's build matched the photos she'd seen of Peckham as he walked briskly in the opposite direction of the church.

Then she noticed the braid down his back and realized it was him.

Had he been there and picked up the scent of cops?

Without taking so much as a second to think about it, Sam opened the back door and bolted from the vehicle, charging toward the man while dodging several people on the sidewalk until she was right behind him.

And then she jumped, taking him down in a crash to the pavement that would've taken skin off both elbows if she hadn't been wearing a coat. Thankfully, she didn't reinjure her hip or wrist in the takedown, but her elbows would be sore.

"What the fuck?" he cried, bucking against her tight hold.

She had him cuffed and relieved of a nine-millimeter Glock that'd been hidden in the waistband of his pants in the time it took Vernon to catch up to her.

The agent glared at her, clearly furious. "*What the hell, Sam?*"

She smiled up at him, thrilled and relieved. "Sorry about that."

"Honest to God," he said with a huff of aggravation. "You're going to be the living, breathing death of me."

"Believe it or not, I've heard that before." She pressed the mic on her radio. "This is Lieutenant Holland. I've got Harlan Peckham in custody on Connecticut Avenue."

"Only you, Holland," Malone replied. "Only you."

EPILOGUE

After notifying Leslie Forrester, Avery Hill and Cori Sawyer of Peckham's arrest, Sam stood before the lectern an hour later to face the media and announce the arrest. Only Vernon and Jimmy had accompanied her outside. Farnsworth and Malone had told her to make the statement on her own since it was her arrest.

"We've arrested Harlan Peckham of Corbin, Kentucky, for the murder of U.S. Attorney Tom Forrester and the shooting of FBI Special Agent-in-Charge Avery Hill. Peckham came to our attention after we learned the bullets recovered from Forrester and Hill came from the same weapon, which was identified as a nine-millimeter Glock. The only case Hill and Forrester had in common was the investigation and eventual prosecution of Willy Peckham, which also included the prosecution of twenty-one members of his extended family. Upon being released from prison a few weeks ago, Willy Peckham and his new wife, Amber, showed up at the home of Agent Hill, intending to kill him. Agent Hill wasn't home at the time, but the Peckhams held Hill's wife and son hostage for about two hours before they were rescued and the Peckhams arrested on new charges."

"How do you know they intended to kill him?" a reporter asked.

"Amber Peckham told us Willy intended to 'gut Agent Hill like a pig in front of his pretty wife and son.'"

"*Damn,*" the reporter said.

"We believe that Amber went along with the plan because Willy threatened her and her children. After Willy's plans for Hill were foiled, we believe his son Harlan picked up where his father left off on the retribution tour by stalking and killing Forrester, who prosecuted the case, and shooting Hill, who'd infiltrated their family in an undercover investigation that spanned a full year almost fifteen years ago. Thanks to Agent Hill's excellent work, twenty-two members of the Peckham family were indicted and convicted on gun charges, fraud and other crimes in a Medicaid scheme that cost the federal government tens of millions of dollars.

"We believed Peckham's third target was Appellate Court Judge Corrinne Sawyer, who sentenced the Peckhams to the longest possible prison sentences allowed by law. Earlier this week, a campsite belonging to Harlan Peckham was located in Rock Creek Park. Despite the efforts of multiple law enforcement agencies, we'd been unable to locate him. Today, we executed a multiagency operation intended to draw out Peckham at one of Judge Sawyer's regular weekly engagements. Much to our dismay, Peckham failed to show. I was on my way back to HQ to regroup with my team when I spotted him walking briskly on Connecticut Avenue. I was able to take him by surprise from behind and quickly neutralize him. A nine-millimeter Glock, the weapon used to kill Forrester and injure Hill, was found tucked into the waistband of his pants."

"Did you use a federal judge as bait to lure a killer?" Darren Tabor asked.

"Since we believed that Peckham intended to kill her, she was more than willing to help us locate him before that could happen."

"So yes, the judge was bait?"

"That's your word, not ours."

"How did you know it was Peckham if you only saw him from behind?"

"His body had been described to me in detail by Agent Hill, who came to know him well while undercover with the family. Harlan was described as five foot, seven inches at most and very muscular. I was also told he often wears his hair in a braid down his back. When I saw a man matching his description walking away from where Sawyer had just been, I went after him."

"Should you have waited for backup?"

"If I had, he would've slipped away again. I'd like to thank Judge Corrinne Sawyer for her courage and everyone from our department as well as the FBI who came together today in a joint effort to catch a killer. I don't care how it happened. I only care that he's off the streets and no longer stalking a federal judge with plans to kill her for doing her job. I only care that the man who killed my friend and colleague Tom Forrester and tried to kill my friend and colleague Avery Hill for doing their jobs has been apprehended. An official release with additional details will be issued shortly. Thank you."

They were still calling out questions to her when she went back inside, where Farnsworth and Malone watched the briefing on the lobby TV.

"Well done, as always, Lieutenant," Farnsworth said.

He beamed with proud-uncle energy.

"Just another day at the office."

Freddie came over to them, a grim expression on his face. "Juan Rodriguez's body has been found in a clothing-donation bin on New York Ave."

~

Want to know more about Derek and Roni's romance? Read their Wild Widow story, *Someone Like You*, right now! Order a copy from my store at *shop.marieforce.com* or any online retailer.

Oops, I did it again! Sorry about leaving it there. LOL! Hopefully, my little gasp moments at the end of the First Family books make you eager for the next installment. Believe it or not, the teasers help to clarify my mission for the next book and make it easier to get started. Watch for more info on the next First Family book later this year.

To chat about STATE OF SUSPENSE, join the reader group at facebook.com/groups/stateofsuspense. Make sure you're also a member of the Fatal/First Family Series Group at facebook.com/groups/fatalseries.

Thank you so much to everyone who supports me behind the scenes, including Julie Cupp, Lisa Cafferty, Jean Mello, Nikki Haley and Ashley Lopez, as well as my crack editors, Linda Ingmanson and Joyce Lamb. Many thanks to my primary beta readers, Anne Woodall, Kara Conrad and Tracey Suppo, as well as the Fatal/First Family beta readers: Kelly, Jennifer, Gina, Sarah, Jennifer, Karina, Irene, Kelley, Vicki, Amy, Marti and Juliane.

As always, a huge thank-you to Captain Russell Hayes, Newport Police Department (retired), for always reviewing these books for technical accuracy. I'm so appreciative of Russ's friendship and many contributions over the years!

To the readers who eagerly anticipate every new Sam and Nick story, thank you so much for your support. It's been FOURTEEN years since FATAL AFFAIR arrived. Twenty-three books later, thanks to my amazing readers, there's no end in sight for the first couple. MUCH more to come!

xoxo

Marie

ALSO BY MARIE FORCE

Romantic Suspense Novels Available from Marie Force

The First Family Series

Book 1: State of Affairs

Book 2: State of Grace

Book 3: State of the Union

Book 4: State of Shock

Book 5: State of Denial

Book 6: State of Bliss

Book 7: State of Suspense

Read Sam and Nick's earlier stories in the Fatal Series!

The Fatal Series

One Night With You, *A Fatal Series Prequel Novella*

Book 1: Fatal Affair

Book 2: Fatal Justice

Book 3: Fatal Consequences

Book 3.5: Fatal Destiny, *the Wedding Novella*

Book 4: Fatal Flaw

Book 5: Fatal Deception

Book 6: Fatal Mistake

Book 7: Fatal Jeopardy

Book 8: Fatal Scandal

Book 9: Fatal Frenzy

Book 10: Fatal Identity

Book 11: Fatal Threat

Book 12: Fatal Chaos

Book 13: Fatal Invasion

Book 14: Fatal Reckoning

Book 15: Fatal Accusation

Book 16: Fatal Fraud

Contemporary Romances Available from Marie Force

The Wild Widows Series—a Fatal Series Spin-Off

Book 1: Someone Like You

Book 2: Someone to Hold

Book 3: Someone to Love

Book 4: Someone to Watch Over Me (Coming 2024)

The Gansett Island Series

Book 1: Maid for Love *(Mac & Maddie)*

Book 2: Fool for Love *(Joe & Janey)*

Book 3: Ready for Love *(Luke & Sydney)*

Book 4: Falling for Love *(Grant & Stephanie)*

Book 5: Hoping for Love *(Evan & Grace)*

Book 6: Season for Love *(Owen & Laura)*

Book 7: Longing for Love *(Blaine & Tiffany)*

Book 8: Waiting for Love *(Adam & Abby)*

Book 9: Time for Love *(David & Daisy)*

Book 10: Meant for Love *(Jenny & Alex)*

Book 10.5: Chance for Love, *A Gansett Island Novella (Jared & Lizzie)*

Book 11: Gansett After Dark *(Owen & Laura)*

Book 12: Kisses After Dark *(Shane & Katie)*

(Continuation of Green Mountain)

Book 1: Every Little Thing *(Grayson & Emma)*

Book 2: Can't Buy Me Love *(Mary & Patrick)*

Book 3: Here Comes the Sun *(Wade & Mia)*

Book 4: Till There Was You *(Lucas & Dani)*

Book 5: All My Loving *(Landon & Amanda)*

Book 6: Let It Be *(Lincoln & Molly)*

Book 7: Come Together *(Noah & Brianna)*

Book 8: Here, There & Everywhere *(Izzy & Cabot)*

Book 9: The Long and Winding Road *(Max & Lexi)*

The Quantum Series

Book 1: Virtuous *(Flynn & Natalie)*

Book 2: Valorous *(Flynn & Natalie)*

Book 3: Victorious *(Flynn & Natalie)*

Book 4: Rapturous *(Addie & Hayden)*

Book 5: Ravenous *(Jasper & Ellie)*

Book 6: Delirious *(Kristian & Aileen)*

Book 7: Outrageous *(Emmett & Leah)*

Book 8: Famous *(Marlowe & Sebastian)*

The Miami Nights Series

Book 1: How Much I Feel *(Carmen & Jason)*

Book 2: How Much I Care *(Maria & Austin)*

Book 3: How Much I Love *(Dee's story)*

Nochebuena, A Miami Nights Novella

Book 4: How Much I Want *(Nico & Sofia)*

Book 5: How Much I Need *(Milo and Gianna)*

The Treading Water Series

Single Titles

In the Air Tonight (September 2024)

Five Years Gone

One Year Home

Sex Machine

Sex God

Georgia on My Mind

True North

The Fall

The Wreck

Love at First Flight

Everyone Loves a Hero

Line of Scrimmage

Historical Romance Available from Marie Force

The Gilded Series

Book 1: Duchess by Deception

Book 2: Deceived by Desire

ABOUT THE AUTHOR

Marie Force is the #1 *Wall Street Journal* bestselling author of more than 100 contemporary romance, romantic suspense and erotic romance novels. Her series include Fatal, First Family, Gansett Island, Butler Vermont, Quantum, Treading Water, Miami Nights and Wild Widows.

Her books have sold more than 13 million copies worldwide, have been translated into more than a dozen languages and have appeared on the *New York Times* bestseller list more than 30 times. She is also a *USA Today* bestseller, as well as a Spiegel bestseller in Germany.

Her goals in life are simple—to spend as much time as she can with her "kids" who are now adults, to keep writing books for as long as she possibly can and to never be on a flight that makes the news.

Join Marie's mailing list on her website at *marieforce.com* for news about new books and upcoming appearances in your area. Follow her on Facebook at *www.Facebook.com/MarieForceAuthor*, Instagram at *www.instagram.com/marieforceauthor/* and TikTok at *https://www.tiktok.com/@marieforceauthor?*. Contact Marie at *marie@marieforce.com*.

Printed in the USA
CPSIA information can be obtained
at www.ICGtesting.com
CBHW031531260424
7598CB00005B/36

9 781958 035559